ONCE IN, NEVER OUT

ONCE IN NEVER OUT

Dan Mahoney

≈ ST. MARTIN'S PRESS / NEW YORK

FOR

Police Officer Bobby Walsh, NYPD
Killed in the line of duty on January 12, 1981

Police hero and good friend, still missed

Book Design by Gretchen Achilles

Library of Congress Cataloging-in-Publication Data

Mahoney, Dan.
    Once in, never out / by Dan Mahoney. — 1st ed.
      p. cm.
    ISBN 0-312-18228-7
    I. Title.
    PS3563.A36405   1998
    813'.54—dc21   97-40422
                                         CIP

FIRST EDITION: FEBRUARY 1998

10 9 8 7 6 5 4 3 2 1

PROLOGUE

SATURDAY, FEBRUARY 28TH—ROCKALL, NORTH ATLANTIC

Just standing on the bridge of HMS *Courageous* at dawn was usually enough to put Commodore Sir John Wellingsly in a good mood and fill his breast with pride. The *Courageous* was a magnificent light cruiser—sleek, fast, and modern, the peer of any ship in any navy in the world.

But today was different. As Sir John surveyed the nautical traffic around the miserable pinpoint of rock rising from the depths of the North Atlantic, he knew that he was about to lose an embarrassing naval engagement to Iceland, a country that didn't even have a navy. The Icelanders would win because they had done what the British cabinet and its experts from the Admiralty had not thought possible—they had sailed their small, fast, coastal fishing boats to Rockall, crossing at least 230 miles of the most treacherous expanse of the North Atlantic.

A thousand years before, Icelandic Vikings had crossed the North Atlantic in forty-foot open boats and had ravaged the British coast for fun and profit. For the people who had colonized Greenland in the tenth century and traveled to North America four hundred years before the birth of Columbus, the trip to Rockall in a modern forty-foot fishing boat was child's play, nothing more than a delightful sea excursion.

Now the small boats of the Icelandic coastal fishing fleet were there in front of Sir John, clearly visible from the bridge as they prepared for action against the strung nets of the large British fishing trawlers he had been assigned to protect. It was the maneuverability of the small boats, not the speed and the firepower of the *Courageous*, that would decide the day. Sir John knew how it would go because, as a young lieutenant, he had served on the frigate HMS *Manchester* during the last Cod War in 1975.

Then, as now, fishing was Iceland's primary industry. The waters around Iceland, where the warm Gulf Stream meets the cold Arctic Current, were the richest fishing grounds in the world, with catches of cod, haddock, salmon, redfish, shrimp, scallops, Norway lobster, and herring constituting three-quarters of the country's export income. However, in the early seventies there had been a worldwide technological revolution in commercial fishing, with the fleets of the maritime nations employing bottom scanners and sonar to locate the schools and then haul them in using improved lightweight nylon nets.

In Iceland, the catches had plummeted and the country had been thrown into crisis. The Icelanders had claimed that the stocks of marine life off their shores were being depleted due to zealous overfishing by foreign fishing fleets, mostly British. The Icelandic government had reacted by unilaterally claiming authority over their coastal waters for a distance two hundred miles from their shores, the first country to do so. The robust crews of Iceland's small, economically threatened fishing boats had responded with vigor, cutting the very expensive nets of every British trawler found operating within the new limit.

The British fishermen had protested to the British government and the British government had protested to the Icelandic government, but the Norsemen hadn't been prepared to listen. Armed with complaints of net-cutting and righteous indignation, the British ambassador to Iceland had camped out at Government House in Reykjavík. He had been politely ignored until he threatened action by the Royal Navy. The Icelanders had considered the threat to be an undiplomatic breach of protocol and reacted by expelling the ambassador and breaking off diplomatic relations with the United Kingdom, thereby setting the stage for the fourth Cod War in twenty years between the two nations.

Backed into a corner, the British government had sent in the Royal Navy, as promised. It had been a laughable show, with members of the world press covering the incident outnumbering the "combatants" on both sides. The imposing presence of the British fleet off their shores hadn't slowed the Icelandic fishermen in the slightest. The fishermen simply placed their wives and children on the decks of their boats as they went about their merry net-cutting mission under the guns of the British fleet.

The Royal Navy had reacted by sending a warning shot across the bow of any Icelandic fishing boat approaching the strung nets of a British trawler, an action which sent the Icelanders into convulsions of laughter on the decks of their boats as they threw their life jackets overboard for the benefit of the reporters above. Then they had driven in behind the British trawlers and cut the nets anyway, usually giving the honors to the youngest person on board capable of handling the clippers.

The British admirals had been able to do little more than watch and smile benignly for the cameras overhead. Their smiles had become even more forced when the feisty captains of the Icelandic fishing boats, their day's work done, had given the Royal Navy a treat just to show that there were no hard feelings. The admirals were forced to look down over their guns at the Icelanders, standing with their families on the decks of their fishing boats as they regaled the British sailors with a chorus of gospel hymns in the ancient Icelandic language, giving thanks to God for transforming the British navy into, in effect, the much-improved Icelandic Coast Guard.

Beaten and chastened, the British government had seen no way out but to declare their own two-hundred-mile fishing limit around the British Isles, prompting a similar reciprocal action by every maritime nation in the world.

Owing to Iceland's stand, the two-hundred-mile fishing limit quickly became
a respected canon of international law.

By four o'clock, Commodore Sir John Wellingsly was experiencing an un-
wanted bout of déjà vu as he stared down at the singing families of Icelanders in their fishing boats off his starboard bow. It had been a long day
and a complete disaster. Six miles behind the *Courageous* was Rockall, so
tiny that it wasn't even visible from the bridge. Visible instead were many
Icelandic boats, five British trawlers steaming in circles as they tried to
retrieve their nets from the bottom, and four news helicopters overhead
nearly colliding with each other in their efforts to capture the scene.

Sir John allowed himself a moment of reflection as he pondered the
imminent end of his long and otherwise distinguished military career. In
the good old Cold War days he had steamed by Rockall many times while
searching for Soviet submarines operating in the North Atlantic, but he had
never bothered asking himself who owned the half-acre island. If anything,
he had considered Rockall as nothing more than a hindrance to navigation
because it had always been surrounded by large fishing trawlers from nations
around the world, including Iceland.

"I wonder which idiot in Whitehall decided Rockall was part of the
British Isles?" Sir John asked no one in particular, so softly that he didn't
realize that he had given voice to his thoughts until he saw the helmsman
staring at him.

"Sir?" the helmsman responded.

"Nothing. As you were," Sir John ordered, embarrassed at his out-of-
character slip and hoping that the helmsman hadn't heard.

But the helmsman had heard. The entire crew had been embarrassed
by the events of the day and he couldn't hold his tongue. "Begging your
pardon, sir, but I hear that the idiot who put us in this mess was the foreign
secretary. I hear it was Sir Ian Smythe-Douglass himself."

ONE

It was a small bedroom, spartanly furnished. Despite the night chill, there was no wind and the apartment's windows were open. A light was on in the hallway and the bedroom door was open. Lying in bed, sleeping naked with their arms wrapped around each other, the couple could be mistaken for middle-aged Nordic gods.

In a country where people grow tall, Thor Eríkson was taller than most, so tall that his feet hung over the end of the bed. He appeared to be trim and fit rather than muscle-bound and his face looked more rugged than handsome. His hair was short and blond, but graying at the temples.

Frieda Helgadottír looked like she belonged with this man, always. She was the muscle-bound one, wide-shouldered and also tall, although at least a head shorter than Thor. Except for her full, well-rounded breasts, she had the body of a very fit teenage tomboy. Her hair was long and also blonde, but there was nothing rugged about her face. There was not one feature that detracted from her appearance, except maybe for the age lines just beginning to appear at the corners of her eyes. She was pretty without being beautiful and she smiled as she slept.

The bedside phone rang at 2:30 A.M., waking both Thor and Frieda. Thor turned on the light, got out of bed, and stretched as he watched the phone, willing it to stop ringing. It didn't, so he took a pad and pencil from the nightstand.

"Don't answer it," Frieda implored as he put his hand on the phone. "You're on vacation."

He was used to doing what Frieda wanted, but this time he couldn't. "There's been a murder."

"A murder? How do you know?"

"I just do." The phone stopped ringing. No matter, Thor thought. The chief will call again.

"Thor, please come back to bed," Frieda pleaded.

"Sorry, I can't. I'm going to get ready. When the phone rings, answer it and get the information."

Frieda accepted Thor's decision without further comment. No matter what she said, Thor would always do his job because that was the way he was. Although she rarely thought about it, it was one of the many things she loved about Thor and she was intensely proud of him.

He went into the bathroom, closing the door behind him. She heard him turn on the shower and knew he wouldn't be long. Thor showered in the same way he did everything, quickly and efficiently. She got up, closed the windows so that he wouldn't be chilled when he came out, then sat down on the bed with the pad and pen in her hand, waiting and thinking.

Thor's job had many drawbacks, but Frieda enjoyed being married to Iceland's only homicide detective. She especially liked the fact that he was famous and well-respected, so famous that she herself was recognized wherever she went. True, there had been only four murders in the twelve years since Thor had been promoted to detective, but he had solved them all.

Murders weren't the part of Thor's job that Frieda minded. They occurred so infrequently in Iceland that in one period of eight years not a single murder had been committed in the entire country.

It was the training that bothered her. Thor was frequently abroad, leaving her alone while he attended this seminar or that national police academy. He trained constantly for his job, and when he wasn't traveling, he was studying textbooks on the subject of murder.

Or he was playing handball, Iceland's national sport and another thing she loved about Thor. He excelled at everything he tried, excelled so well that in 1980 and again in 1982 he had been recognized as the national champion. That didn't hurt his fame, either, and also added to her stature.

The phone rang again.

I hope this one is in Reykjavík, she thought as she picked up the receiver. If not, Thor would be leaving her to work his case in another of Iceland's far-flung coastal communities. "Hello?"

"Hello, Frieda. It's Janus. Is Thor there?"

"Yes, but he's in the shower," she told the chief. "Has there been a murder?"

"Unfortunately, there's been two. The British foreign secretary and his wife have been killed at the Saga Hotel."

Two murders? That's never happened before, Frieda thought. Worse, important people like the British foreign secretary and his wife. "How?"

"They were killed by bombs."

Bombs? In Iceland? Something else that's never happened before. Many other questions popped into her mind, but she kept them to herself. "I'll tell Thor. Don't worry, Janus. He'll be there soon."

"No, have him wait there. It's very complicated and very delicate, so Erík is on his way over to talk to Thor."

"Erík? The minister of fisheries is coming here now?"

"Sorry, Frieda. I hope it's not too inconvenient, but he insisted."

It certainly was inconvenient, but Frieda didn't say a word. When she didn't answer, Janus added, "Relax, Frieda. It's not as if Vigdís was coming over."

That didn't help Frieda's state of mind at all. Although Vigdís Finnbogadottír had been president since 1980 and enjoyed some status as the world's first elected female head of state, her post was largely ceremonial. Frieda knew that the real power in Iceland lay with the minister of fisheries, and it was Erík who was coming. "When will he get here?" she asked.

"He just left. I'd say about fifteen minutes, if he takes his time."

"Fifteen minutes? Good God! Good-bye, Janus." Frieda hung up the phone and ran into the bathroom, panic-stricken as she screamed the news to Thor.

By the time the doorbell rang, Frieda was dressed and ready, with her hair combed, her makeup on, and coffee perking. Thor went to the door and Frieda was surprised to hear him greet the minister of fisheries as casually as if he were a neighbor dropping by to borrow a cup of sugar. When Thor brought him into the living room she got another surprise.

Although she had seen Erík on TV many times, he was not what she expected. He had always appeared to be very much the man in charge, radiating confidence with facts and figures at his fingertips, ready for any question. This Erík was different; he appeared haggard and worried.

Nonetheless, he still had manners. "So good to finally meet you, Frieda. I know Thor's on vacation and I'm terribly sorry to bother you at this hour, but we're in something of a national emergency," he said as he shook her hand. Then Erík handed her the bag he was carrying. "Sorry, but that's all I could come up with at this hour. Croissants from the Saga's bakery."

"Very nice of you, Erík. Coffee?"

"That would be wonderful."

Frieda went into the kitchen and Erík settled into the couch. Thor sat in the armchair opposite him.

"I guess you're wondering why I'm here," Erík said.

"I am. I'm also wondering if this visit means that I'm working for you," Thor replied.

"No, you're not. I'm not going to get involved in your investigation. However, you'll need to know some things that only I can tell you right now, things that aren't for public dissemination at the moment."

"Why come here instead of waiting for me at the hotel? You hiding from the press?"

"Let's say I'm avoiding the press. The foreign secretary's visit was a secret I didn't let them in on."

"Why? Diplomatic confidentiality?"

"Yes. They'll want to know what the foreign secretary was doing here and what we talked about. And, of course, they'll want to know the reason for the secrecy."

"Something to do with Rockall?" Thor guessed.

"Yes."

"Then you'll have to talk to them, sooner or later. Even before this bombing, Rockall was already big news."

"I realize that, and I'll tell them everything, eventually. Unfortunately, because of the agreement I reached with the foreign secretary, I can't do it now."

"Why?"

"Because news of the agreement has to come from London," Eric said.

"Then I guess the British were the losers in your negotiations?"

"Basically, yes. To save face, it was to have been announced in London tomorrow afternoon by Smythe-Douglass. I don't know when they'll do it now, but it still falls to me to keep our end of the bargain."

"Will the Brits still go along with this deal?"

"Their ambassador here, Roger Chatwick, took part in the discussions and he's assured me that it will still be implemented."

"Can you tell me the reason for all the secrecy?" Thor asked.

"It was Smythe-Douglass's idea. According to him, the Irish government is going to claim Rockall as Irish territory and he felt that would complicate our dispute."

"Why would the Irish do that? They don't have much of a fishing fleet."

"Just to piss the Brits off, I guess. Smythe-Douglass did some research and was afraid the Irish might have a valid claim. Rockall is closer to Ireland than it is to either Iceland or Great Britain, and the medieval Irish monks were a seafaring lot. Since they were the first ones to arrive in Iceland, he felt it was possible they had also discovered Rockall."

"But they have no documentation of such a visit, do they?" Thor asked.

"Not as far as he knew, but he was afraid the World Court might side with them."

"I see. So he sneaks in here to take care of things with us before taking on the Irish."

"I'm sure that's what he had in mind, but that's not the way it worked out. If Rockall must be owned by any nation, it should be us. I was able to convince him of that and we arrived at an accommodation over ownership."

"Do you think the IRA planted the bomb?"

"Nobody's claimed credit for it, yet, but Irish national interests are involved. I'm assuming it's their work, but I don't see how it's possible."

"Because of the secrecy of the visit?" Thor asked.

"Yes, that and the fact that it was so hastily arranged. The IRA simply wouldn't have had the time to formulate a plan and then get a bomb into the Saga."

"Exactly who knew the foreign secretary was in town?"

"Chatwick's trying to find out who knew on their end, but here the list is very small. Should I give you the scenario?"

"Please."

"Chatwick went to see Vigdís yesterday morning to arrange the meeting. Since it was Sunday, she didn't even tell her secretary about it. She knew what he wanted to talk about, so she called me and said that she'd bring them over to my place after dinner with her. I told no one about it, and that's just the way it worked out."

"Not exactly, or they'd still be alive. Were they noticed by anyone at the airport?"

"Chatwick says no, says they didn't attract any attention at all. They were traveling on diplomatic passports, so immigration and customs were no problem for them. They were out of the airport in five minutes."

"And what then? Straight to Vigdís's house?"

"No, that's where it got complicated. Chatwick had reserved the presidential suite for them and they went to the hotel first to change before dinner. Got there about four, stayed less than an hour, and were at Vigdís's house by five. After dinner they came to my house."

"Vigdís, too?"

"No, just the Brits. Got there at seven and left at ten-forty-five. They got back to the hotel at eleven and Chatwick stayed there until midnight. The bombs went off at seven minutes after one."

"Bombs?"

"Yeah, two of them. Thorough bastards, whoever did this. Put one in the master bedroom and another in the servant's room."

"And they went off at exactly the same time?"

"Yep. Got the foreign secretary in the servant's room and his wife in the master bedroom."

"The British foreign secretary was sleeping in the servant's room?" Thor asked.

"Yeah, but let's keep that off the record as long as we can. I asked their ambassador about it and all he said was that they didn't appear to be getting on exceptionally well last night."

"What was your take on them?" Thor asked.

"They seemed fine to me. A very cordial couple. Penelope Smythe-Douglass was apparently a woman of some breeding and it seemed that we *all* enjoyed her company."

Frieda came in carrying the coffee and the heated croissants on a tray. Conversation stopped while Frieda added the cream and sugar for Erík and Thor. "Am I interrupting?" she asked.

"Of course not," Thor said. "Have a seat."

Frieda looked pleased as she settled next to Erík on the sofa. She kept her eyes on Thor as she sipped her coffee, waiting for the conversation to resume. He knew Frieda's curiosity and was sure she had been listening from the kitchen, but she managed to appear very nonchalant.

"Did Chatwick drive them from place to place?" Thor asked.

"Yes, in his own car."

"Make any other stops?"

"He says no."

"Did we provide any security?"

"Yes. I called Janus at nine and asked him to provide a man at the Saga, basically just to keep the press away in case they found out about the visit."

"Who did he send?"

"You know a constable named Haarold Sigmarsson?"

"Yes, a very good choice. One of our sharpest and toughest. Did Janus send Brandy to check out the room?"

"Brandy?"

"Our bomb dog. She's trained to sniff out most types of explosives."

"No, he didn't. I asked him about the bomb dog and he said there hadn't been enough time. Her handler went to Akureyi yesterday for the weekend and she's with him."

"That's too bad," Thor commented. "We have the first bombing in our history and our only bomb-sniffing dog is two hundred and thirty kilometers away."

"Bad luck," Erík agreed.

"What time did Haarold get to the hotel?"

"Ten o'clock. He met them all in the hotel lobby when they arrived, then stood guard outside the room. Handled himself very well when the bombs went off."

"Was he injured?" Frieda asked, concerned. She knew both Haarold and his wife and was one of the few people who liked the taciturn and easily irritated constable.

"No. It wasn't much of a blast because the folks at the front desk didn't even hear it. He got soaked, but he wasn't injured."

"The sprinkler system?" Thor asked.

"Yes. Haarold heard the blast, but he didn't have the code key to get into the suite. So he put a few shots into the lock and then kicked the door in. The lights were blown out in the master bedroom and the sprinkler system was dousing the place, but he used his flashlight and saw the wife's body on the bed. She was dead, so he looked around. Found the foreign secretary in the servant's room."

"Burn damage to the bodies?"

"I don't know. Haarold wouldn't let anybody into the suite except Janus. Not the medical examiner, not the British ambassador, not even me. The fire alarm had gone off, but Haarold wouldn't even let in the firemen. Said he didn't want us destroying the crime scene."

"I guess Janus backed him up."

"Yes, and that was that. Without the medical examiner, those bodies aren't even officially dead yet."

"Who turned the sprinklers off?" Thor asked.

"Nobody. They're pretty sophisticated and they went off by themselves while Haarold was still inside."

Thor silently sipped his coffee for a few minutes as he contemplated the disaster he had just been assigned. Haarold was the one bright spot in the affair and his presence outside the room meant a few things. One was that the bombs had been placed before Haarold's assignment to the post because the astute and singularly unfriendly constable would never fall for any kind of ruse and would let no unauthorized person into the presidential suite. Because of Haarold, he knew he would be dealing with as pure a crime scene as possible under the circumstances, unmuddled by the firemen.

Still, Thor recognized that there was quite a task in front of him. He had known that Iceland would eventually fall victim to the terrorist madness gripping the rest of the world and he had tried to train himself through reading, seminars, and courses. Besides being the homicide investigator, he was also recognized as the nation's best crime scene technician and its only bomb expert. But he had never handled a bombing and he would be under intense scrutiny. "Is the press at the Saga now?"

"A few reporters were arriving as I left, but they didn't see me."

"Who else is there?"

"Janus and the British ambassador."

"Who's going to giving the press a statement?"

"I'm going to be making myself unavailable until the British make their announcement, so it'll be you or Janus."

So the police are elected to be the liars, Thor thought. We're to emphasize the investigation and dummy-up when reporters ask us the reasons for the British visit. Not a good position for us. "I don't like it," Thor said.

"But you'll do it?"

"I can't speak for Janus, but I'll do it if I have to. Reluctantly do it."

It was what Erík wanted to hear. "Good," he said and stood up. The visit was over, but Frieda's curiosity wasn't satisfied. "How did you manage to convince the British that Rockall is ours?"

Thor was surprised to see that Erík appeared pleased by the inquiry.

"Simple. Geography and history," Erík said proudly. "Unlike England and Ireland, both Iceland and Rockall were formed by volcanic activity. From a geographic standpoint, Rockall can't possibly be considered part of the British Isles and shouldn't belong to either Ireland or the United Kingdom. Then there's a story in one of the sagas. Rockall was discovered by an Icelander named Sigmar in 1001. His ship was wrecked on a small, rocky island in the North Atlantic. From the description in the saga, it had to be

Rockall. He and some of his men survived the shipwreck and were rescued a few days later. He eventually died in Iceland, so he's officially one of ours."

Sort of a tenuous claim to Rockall, but better than the claims of either the United Kingdom or Ireland to the island, Thor thought. "Where is this saga kept?"

"That's the best part. It's in the Norwegian National Museum in Oslo, a neutral country not party to the dispute. After I showed Smythe-Douglass an English translation of the saga, I made him an offer and he went for it."

"Joint fishing rights?" Frieda guessed.

"Something like that. Rockall is our territory, but the fishing rights are to be jointly shared by Iceland and Great Britain for ten years. We set the limits on the catch and the British are entitled to fish half the limit. We also agreed that our joint sovereignty over the island is to be enforced by the Royal Navy for the next ten years."

"Meaning they'll exclude fishing fleets from everywhere else?" Thor asked.

"Exactly. What do you think?"

"Good deal. Looks like the British Navy becomes our coast guard again."

TWO

Because of the number of fire engines, ambulances, police cars, and news vans in the Saga Hotel's parking lot, Thor had to park in the rear. The firemen were blocking the entrance to the hotel as they loaded their equipment and hoses back onto their trucks, so Thor sat in his car, waiting and thinking.

In his younger days, the police department had taken advantage of Thor's size and appearance; he had been assigned many times to guard foreign diplomats during their visits to Iceland. Since the Saga Hotel was considered by most to be the nation's best, he had spent many hours standing guard outside the presidential suite, just as Haarold had done. He knew all of the security precautions implemented by the hotel to safeguard the important guests who used the presidential suite, so he mentally reviewed them.

The presidential suite was Room 730, located on the top floor of the hotel. Whenever a foreign diplomat was a guest in the suite, elevator access to the seventh floor was restricted; a security key had to be inserted into the elevator car's control panel or the elevator wouldn't stop on seven. To further restrict access to the seventh floor, the stairwell doors could only be opened from the hallway.

Then there were the two motion-activated security cameras, each hidden behind small, curved, one-way mirrors mounted at ceiling corners at opposite ends of the seventh floor hallway. These cameras were monitored from the front desk and the images were preserved on videotape.

Unauthorized access to the suite itself was also extremely difficult. The Saga used computer-coded access cards, not keys, and every time a guest checked out the access code was changed. Better yet, every time an access card was used to enter any room in the Saga, the hotel's computer logged the date and time of entry.

Extensive safeguards, Thor thought, but all of them had been overcome or bypassed by whomever had planted the bomb. But who knew the foreign secretary was at the Saga and who, armed with that knowledge, had the motive, expertise, and opportunity to place the bombs? Thor could reach only one conclusion. Since the foreign secretary's visit was almost a spur-of-the-moment affair, the bomber had to be an Icelander.

Although everything he knew at the moment pointed to that conclusion, it was still difficult for Thor to believe. Iceland prided itself on being a peaceful, nonviolent nation, a country without an army that hadn't gone to war since the Viking days. The idea that an Icelander could have been responsible for the bomb seemed so preposterous to him that he put it out of his mind for the moment.

After the firemen finished loading their trucks and left, Thor unloaded his crime scene kits from the trunk of his car and lugged the two suitcases of equipment to the hotel's entrance.

Reporters were waiting for him. He knew them all and greeted some of them by name; before they could ask him a single question, he told them that he was sure they knew more than he did.

"Thor, will you be giving us a statement later?" one of them asked.

"Sure, unless for some reason I'm instructed not to."

"Did you know the British foreign secretary was in the country?" said another.

"No. Did you?"

"No, no one told us about it either."

One of the reporters held the door open and Thor carried his equipment into the lobby and straight to the elevator bank. A young uniformed constable was waiting with the elevator security key. Thor prided himself on knowing almost all of the three hundred Reykjavík cops by name and most of the cops in the rest of the country at least by face, but he had to search his mind for a moment. "Hello, Leifur. How's it going upstairs?"

"Don't know, Thor. Haven't been allowed up there. Whatever's happening, apparently it's secret stuff and nobody's talking." Leifur pressed the call button and the elevator doors instantly opened. The constable followed Thor into the elevator, inserted the key into the control panel, and pressed 7 before resuming his post outside.

Janus Arnonson was waiting for Thor in the seventh floor hallway. Janus had been a cop for forty-two years and the police chief of Reykjavík for seven. Tall and broad with a long, wide nose and a mane of thick, white hair, Janus looked like a polar bear, an almost mythic creature in the Icelandic sagas. Since Janus had been around long enough to become something of a myth himself, "polar bear" was what the people of Iceland called him. He didn't mind and had even taken to wearing white suits.

One look at Janus told Thor that something extraordinary had happened. Janus was in full uniform, a rare event, and he had a pistol in a holster on his belt, an even rarer event since police officers in Iceland usually didn't carry firearms unless they were guarding foreign dignitaries. But the look on his face was one Thor had never seen during their long friendship. Like Erík, Janus looked haggard and worried.

Thor put his suitcases down and extended his hand, but the chief grabbed Thor in a hug. "So glad you're here," he said, which was something Thor had never heard before from Janus.

As soon as the chief released him, Thor looked up and down the hallway and was relieved to see only Haarold, still standing guard down the hall outside the presidential suite.

Icelanders are not known for spontaneous shows of affection and the chief's hug was definitely out of character—the national character and his own. Fortunately, Icelanders *are* known for being tight-lipped, and Haarold was just so. He would never say a word and no reporter would ever learn from him just how worried Janus was.

"I guess it's bad," Thor observed.

"It's horrible, exactly the kind of thing that could ruin our national reputation."

"You think it was an Icelander?"

"Unless there's a serious leak on the Brits' end, there's nothing else to think. I can't believe I'm saying this, but someone connected to the hotel must be involved."

Another hard one to believe, Thor thought, although he himself had reached the same preposterous conclusion. "Have you spoken to Jónas yet?"

"Yes, he's here. He handled the arrangements for the foreign secretary and swears there was no leak on his end."

"How can he be sure?"

"I don't see how he can be, but you know Jónas."

Thor did know Jónas, the Saga Hotel's general manager, a man famous in diplomatic circles for being discreet and ensuring that his staff measured up to his high standards of discretion. But the staff was the obvious first place to look. "Where is the ambassador?"

"I have him on ice in there," Janus said, pointing to the door of Room 728. "He's constantly on the phone to London and sweating up a storm. I'm anticipating a request from him, but I think he's having a hard time putting it into words."

"You think he wants to offer us some help from their security services?"

"Yeah, I think that's what he's been instructed to do, but he doesn't know how to make the offer without making us feel like a bunch of yokels when it comes to bombings."

"Let's take a look, but can I tell you something?"

"We *are* a bunch of yokels when it comes to bombings?"

"Exactly. Between the IRA, the Palestinians, the Iranians, and Lord knows who else, the British have loads of experience in this type of thing and we have none. Between us, I'd welcome any assistance they care to offer."

Thor had expected a fight from the chief, but Janus looked relieved. "I was hoping you'd see it that way," he said. "I'll run it by Vigdís first, but it sounds like a good idea."

That settled, Thor was ready to get to work. He picked up one suitcase, Janus the other, and they walked down the hall to Haarold. The constable was still wet and dripping water onto the carpet at his feet, but he showed no signs of discomfort. "Is it very messy in there?" Thor asked.

"They won't be renting it for a while," Haarold answered.

That didn't make Thor feel any better. Although he was the homicide detective, there was something he found disturbing in his job that he could never admit to anyone. Thor had a weak stomach when it came to gore, so weak that he always took a few tablets of Dramamine before he went to a crime scene. The tablets prevented motion sickness and kept his lunch where it belonged as he did his job, but he still felt queasy as he examined the door of Suite 730.

Haarold had rendered the heavy walnut door useless beyond repair. Besides the two nine-millimeter bullet holes in the lock, there was a long crack in the center that ran almost from top to bottom.

Thor pushed the door open with his foot and Janus followed him into the entrance foyer of the suite. Thor had expected that most of the lights in the suite would have been blown out by the blast, but he was wrong. Lights were on in the sitting room to his left, in the bathroom to his right, and the foyer was illuminated by an ornate brass chandelier hanging from the ceiling. Directly in front of him was the master bedroom. The door was open and it was dark inside, but enough light seeped in from the foyer for Thor to see a body on the bed.

The two men put their suitcases down. Thor opened his and took out a searchlight, a camera with a flash attached, and a pair of latex gloves. "Smell anything?" he asked Janus.

"Yeah. Smoke. Burnt hair too, I think."

"Anything else?"

Janus raised his large nose in the air and sniffed a few times. "Coffee?"

"That's what I think. Strong, burnt coffee." Thor pulled on the gloves and turned on the searchlight. "First, let's take a peek at the foreign secretary." Followed by Janus, he walked into the sitting room and took a quick look around. There was no sign of any damage, so they went down the hall to the servant's bedroom. Thor shined his searchlight into the small, darkened room.

Sir Ian Smythe-Douglass had died in his pajamas and lay facedown on the floor next to the bed. Thor swung the beam around the room.

"Not much damage," Janus commented, and Thor had to agree. The windows were shattered, the rug was soaked, there were feathers everywhere, and the smell of smoke and coffee was strong, but there was no apparent structural damage. The walls and the dresser were intact, but the bed would require some work. The legs had collapsed, leaving the supporting box spring on the floor in one piece.

The top mattress accounted for the feathers. Thor knew that the Saga would pamper its guests by placing a traditional Icelandic down mattress on top of the box spring. The bomb had been there, in the down mattress among the feathers, but the limited blast damage still had to be addressed and explained.

Thor directed the searchlight beam upward and found part of the answer. There was a long depression in the ceiling above the bed.

"Shape charge?" Janus asked.

"Uh-huh. Let's get to work, starting with his wife."

Janus followed him back to the entrance to the master bedroom, but waited outside. Thor went in, his feet sinking into the wet carpet as he walked to the bed. He took a breath and shined his light on the body.

It was not as bad as Thor had expected, at least for him. It had been terrible for Penelope Smythe-Douglass, but quick. The sturdy double bed had withstood the blast and she was on her back on the center of it, lying in a pile of wet down feathers on the box spring and what was left of the down mattress. She wore a silk nightgown, but it was so blackened by the smoke that Thor could only guess at the color.

The body was intact, but her face was a mess. Blood covered her nose, mouth, and ears, and her hair was burned. Her eyes were open and staring at the ceiling, so Thor shined his light up. He knew what he would find and it was there, bloodstains on the damaged ceiling above Penelope Smythe-Douglass's head, and something else—small, black dots on the ceiling that he felt sure were burnt coffee grounds.

He stepped back and shined his light around the room. Again, there were feathers everywhere, but considering that a bomb powerful enough to kill the woman had exploded in the room, there was no structural damage that Thor could see. He knew how it had been done.

Thor brushed the feathers off the box spring and found what he expected—the Kevlar bomb blanket that had been placed under the charge in the down mattress. But there was still something missing.

Thor walked around the bed, taking pictures of the body from every angle. Then he reloaded the camera and took twelve photos of the rest of the room as Janus watched from the foyer. Satisfied that he had every portion preserved on film, he spent ten minutes looking around and memorizing every detail before he rejoined Janus. "I'm going to need some help now," Thor told him. "We have to move the body."

"Move it where?"

"Right here would be fine," Thor said, then went back into the bedroom. Janus followed him in and two minutes later they were back in the foyer with Penelope Smythe-Douglass on the floor at their feet.

She looked worse in the lighted foyer than she had in the darkened bedroom. Thor could see that both her forearms were broken, her nose was smashed, and her top row of teeth was broken. He got a towel from the bathroom and placed it next to her head as Janus watched, puzzled. "We have to roll her over," Thor told him.

"What are you looking for?"

"Pieces of black plastic."

"Black plastic?"

"Yeah, pieces of the radio-remote detonator. There's none inside the bedroom that I can see, so there have to be pieces of it in her back."

"Whatever you say."

Thor laid both her arms across her chest and together they rolled her over so that Penelope's face lay in the towel. Among the many burnt feathers melted into the fabric of the nightgown, a half-inch sliver of melted black plastic protruded from the center of her back. Looking closer, Thor could see that many smaller pieces of plastic were melted into her burned nightgown.

"You had that right," Janus said. "Now can you tell me how you knew the plastic would be there?"

"Easy. Both bombs went off at the same time, so they weren't mechanically detonated. It was done by radio. There was a radio-remote detonator tuned to the same frequency attached to each bomb in each mattress. The bomber sent the signal and that was it for Mr. and Mrs. Smythe-Douglass. Propelled them to the ceilings, but didn't do much else in the way of damage."

"How did he make the shape charge?"

"Undid the stitching in the down mattress, took out all the feathers, and then laid a Kevlar bomb blanket on the bottom, probably fashioning it so that it looked like a baking pan. Then he laid in the radio-remote detonator and a couple of strips of det cord—"

"Det cord?"

"Round strips of American C-4 plastic explosive, comes in fifty-foot rolls. It's pretty powerful stuff, but this bomber is clever and didn't use much to get the job done. Probably two strips of det cord, maybe six meters total for both bombs."

"So all the explosive force was directed upwards?" Janus ventured.

"I think so. It wasn't the explosion that killed this poor woman, although I'm sure it ruptured her eardrums. She was killed when she hit the ceiling at a couple hundred kilometers per hour, like she was fired out of a cannon."

"Pretty sophisticated," Janus commented.

"Very sophisticated, especially when you throw in the coffee. He put freeze-dried crystals in the mattress to disguise the smell of the C-4, just in case we used a bomb dog to check the room. It's an old trick the Colombians use to fool the American customs' drug-sniffing dogs, and I've heard the IRA also uses it. The coffee overpowers the smell of the explosives."

"I see. Freeze-dried crystals that don't give much of an odor until they're heated," Janus said.

"Not to us, but Brandy would smell it. It's the coffee that tells me we're not looking for an Icelander."

Janus looked relieved, but then he took a moment to examine Thor's reasoning. He didn't get it. "Because of the coffee you know that?" he asked incredulously.

"Like you said. Anybody who placed those bombs yesterday would have needed some help from the staff. Right?"

"That still makes sense. So?"

"So Brandy's been to this hotel quite a few times. Matter of fact, she's been used almost every time a foreign dignitary stayed here during the past few years. All the staff knows her and they all know that she has one unusual trait for a dog—Brandy loves coffee."

It was news to Janus. "A dog who loves coffee?"

"Loves it so much that she won't work when there's coffee around. She's got to have it. Brandy would have smelled that coffee in the bomb from the elevator and then she would have gone right for it."

"So any member of the staff looking to hide a bomb absolutely wouldn't put coffee in it?"

"Absolutely."

"Then who exactly are we looking for?"

"I can't be absolutely certain until we check the tapes from the hallway cameras, but I don't think our bomber is going to show up on any video from yesterday. I'll bet those bombs have been in those mattresses for a while."

"How long is that?" Janus asked.

"A couple of days, at least."

"Impossible. Nobody knew the foreign secretary was coming a couple of days ago. He didn't even know himself."

"He probably didn't. But, somehow, the IRA did."

THREE

Janus was under intense pressure from both the press and the British ambassador, but Thor had insisted on completing his preliminary investigation before issuing any statement. It took nine hours, so while Thor worked on in the presidential suite, the British ambassador waited impatiently in Room 728 and most members of the press corps played cards, formulated theories, spread rumors, and increased their already substantial tabs at the Saga's bar.

At ten o'clock the reporters were stirred to activity when the bodies were brought down for removal to the morgue. The medical examiner accompanied them, and as the cameras rolled, he was interviewed. The only new information they got from him was that there had been two bomb blasts, but he refused to say anything else, referring the reporters to the chief of police.

Janus had evolved into an Icelandic institution. He was very popular, highly respected, scrupulously honest, and therefore not a candidate for public mauling. It was a situation that could drive reporters to drink, and it did just that. The last time the Saga's bar had enjoyed a better volume of business was when reporters from all over the world had headquartered themselves there during the Reykjavík Reagan-Gorbachev summit in 1989.

By noon Thor was ready to leave. He had viewed the videotapes from the hallway security cameras, interviewed six members of the Saga's staff, photographed and mapped every inch of the presidential suite, collected and tagged ninety-nine items of evidence, and lifted fifty-one latent fingerprints. It was time to process his evidence, but Thor recognized he didn't have the equipment or expertise to do it properly alone. That was where Chatwick came in.

Janus needed some time to draft his press statement, so he sent Thor to Room 728 to report to Chatwick. When the young ambassador answered the door, he surprised Thor by greeting him politely and correctly in Icelandic.

Thor hadn't known that Chatwick spoke the language, but was impressed that he had taken the time and trouble to learn a difficult tongue that was useless outside Iceland and spoken by fewer than three hundred thousand people in the world. He returned the greeting in Icelandic and was invited by Chatwick into the suite.

The ambassador was informally dressed in jeans and a sport coat and had been watching the medical examiner's interview on the BBC channel. He shut the TV off before they settled into the sitting room.

First Thor had some questions for him. "Has anyone claimed responsibility for the bombings, yet?"

"Not to my knowledge."

"Has the IRA ever pulled a bombing where they didn't claim responsibility?"

"Rarely, but it's happened."

"Is it common knowledge in your country that Ian and his wife didn't get along?"

"No, I don't believe so."

"Were they ever in Dublin together?"

Chatwick looked surprised by the question, but he had the answer. "As a matter of fact, they were," he said in English. "Last year there was a fairly complicated dispute over Irish immigration to the U.K., and Sir Ian managed to resolve it to the satisfaction of both governments."

Thor followed Chatwick's switch to English. "Did they stay in a hotel or at your embassy while they were there?"

"I can't say for sure, but I'll find out. I'm assuming by these questions that you believe the IRA was responsible for the bombing?"

"That's the way it looks to me right now. What I can tell you for sure is that Icelanders weren't involved."

"I'm glad to hear it," Chatwick said. "I've always been very comfortable here."

Chatwick's stock was still climbing in Thor's estimation. "You're not surprised?" Thor asked.

"No. I don't see how you arrived at your conclusion yet, but from the outset I found it difficult to believe one of your people could have done it."

"Then I'll tell you how. I've spoken to Jónas and he tells me you requested the presidential suite for the foreign secretary at ten-thirty yesterday morning. Is that correct?"

"Yes. Sir Ian called me at ten and told me he was coming. He also asked me to make the arrangements."

"He told you it was to be an unpublicized visit?"

"Yes. He specifically said that he wanted no press."

"Did he ask you to book the presidential suite for him?"

"No, I did that on my own. He had never been here and I thought it would be a nice touch. Besides, I've dealt with Jónas before and he has a certain reputation."

"You told Jónas that the visit was confidential?"

"Yes, and he assured me that word of it wouldn't leak out from his staff."

"I'm sure it didn't. Besides Jónas, only five other staff members knew of the foreign secretary's presence here. All of them are longtime employees with a history of discretion."

"You've spoken to all five?" Chatwick asked.

"Yes, and they all say they told no one else of the visit. I believe them and I'm certain none of them have anything to do with the bombs."

"How can you be so sure?"

"Because I've seen the videotapes."

"What videotapes?" Chatwick asked.

Thor wasn't surprised that Chatwick didn't know about the hallway security cameras. They were well disguised and Jónas was always reluctant to discuss his security measures with anyone.

"Come on, I'll show you," Thor said. Chatwick followed him to the door where Thor pointed out the cameras in the hallway and explained how they operated.

"So there's a videotape showing everybody who's ever gone into that suite," Chatwick surmised.

"No, that's one of my problems."

"They don't change the videotapes?"

"Not usually. When the tape is completed the video recorder rewinds it and the camera starts taping over the old images."

"But only when there's motion in the hallway?"

"Yes. Usually about a week fits on each two-hour tape before it rewinds," Thor explained.

"So you still have pictures of everyone who was in the suite yesterday."

"Yes, I've got video on everyone who went in there yesterday, along with the time they entered and left. There's a date/time stamp on the videotape."

"So you must have a picture of the bomber."

"Maybe. What I can tell you is that the bombs were in place before yesterday."

Chatwick looked confused. "I don't see how that's possible."

"Let's go back inside and I'll explain how it is possible," Thor suggested.

Chatwick followed Thor back into the sitting room and the two men resumed their seats.

"The first person to enter the suite yesterday was Jónas," Thor said.

"He went in at ten-forty-one yesterday morning to check out the suite after you booked it. He left at ten-forty-six. At eleven-thirteen a maid went in with her cleaning cart. She dusted, stocked the bar, changed the sheets, and left at twelve-ten."

"That's it?"

"That's it. No one else went in until you arrived with Smythe-Douglass and his wife at two minutes after four yesterday afternoon. The computer hooked up to the card entry system backs that up."

"How about after we left for the meetings?"

"Nobody until you got back."

"How about the windows?" Chatwick asked.

"According to both Jónas and the maid, they were locked from the inside. They still are."

"What you're saying is that the bomber knew the foreign secretary was coming to Iceland and would be staying in the presidential suite before the decision to come here was even made."

"Hard to believe," Thor conceded, "But that's the only thing that makes sense."

"How?"

"I'm still putting that together, but I'm betting that whoever was behind the Irish claim to Rockall has to be involved."

"Someone in the Irish government?"

"Probably someone in the Irish cabinet. Somebody who hates the British, somebody connected to the IRA, somebody brilliant and diabolical. Ring any bells?"

"You just described Timothy O'Bannion," Chatwick said. "Irish minister for finance and a devout Finian."

"A Finian?"

"A leading member of the Sinn Fein party, the political arm of the IRA. He's from County Donegal, right next to Ulster."

"In the Irish Republic?"

"Yes, in the Republic, but Donegal's still an IRA stronghold."

"You think he hates the British enough to be behind something like this?"

"He always has, O'Bannion and his whole family. His brother Seamus was an IRA soldier, and there's talk that Timothy was as well."

"What do you mean, 'talk'?"

"I mean that my government has some evidence that he and Seamus were behind an ambush that killed two British soldiers in Londonderry in 1971, but it turned into a tactical defeat for the IRA. One of their men was killed during the firefight and three were wounded, including Seamus. They all managed to get away from the scene, but Seamus and another one of their wounded were captured an hour later."

"But not Timothy?" Thor guessed.

"No, not Timothy. He showed up back in the Republic with an alibi."

"I'm assuming the evidence wasn't strong enough to extradite him."

"In those days the Republic didn't extradite IRA people, so the request was never made."

"What happened to Seamus?"

"Tough case. He never talked, didn't say a word at his trial. He was convicted of murder and sentenced to life. Went on a hunger strike in the Maze Prison in 1977 and died after thirty-two days. Made himself into one of the IRA martyrs."

"I see. Is O'Bannion against the peace process?"

"He's a major obstacle and one of Smythe-Douglass's most vocal critics in the Irish government."

"Are you beginning to see my point?" Thor asked.

"I think so. This Rockall dispute between your government and mine had been festering for weeks and was bound to come to a head, sooner or later. Throw in the Royal Navy's action and Sir Ian's got an instant crisis on his hands, especially since he's the one who reportedly fanned the flames."

"Reportedly?"

"I can't admit it officially, but it's said that Sir Ian pushed through the measure declaring Rockall to be part of the British Isles. He was the MP for Cornwall, the center of our fishing industry, so he stood to gain if Rockall was ours alone. It's also said that he persuaded the prime minister to send the Royal Navy there to back up the claim."

"Aren't there quite a few Irish-born sailors in your navy?" Thor asked.

"Many seamen, and officers as well. There's also quite a few Irishmen in our fishing fleets. If O'Bannion was inclined to listen, I'm sure he would have heard of our plan to send the fishing fleet to Rockall and then protect it with the Royal Navy."

Try to protect it, Thor almost added before courtesy killed the comment. "I'm sure that plan had been brewing for weeks, so let's assume he did," he said instead. "Would O'Bannion be smart enough to predict the outcome of that encounter?"

"I'm certain he is. I don't consider myself a genius and I could have predicted it," Chatwick said. "Problem is, nobody asked me. Anyway, engineer an Irish claim to Rockall, and from the foreign secretary's viewpoint, it's a crisis that has to be resolved quickly. Maybe O'Bannion figured Sir Ian would be coming here to mend fences. If so, that's brilliant."

"Kill Smythe-Douglass and it becomes diabolical," Thor added.

"Yes, that would be diabolical if he put it all together and then figured Sir Ian would stay in the Saga's presidential suite," Chatwick agreed. "Do you have any other indicators pointing in his direction?"

"Just that the bomber was extraordinarily thorough. He planted two bombs, one in the master bedroom and one in the servant's bed. Who would expect that Smythe-Douglass and his wife weren't getting along and sleeping apart?"

"I see. If Sir Ian stayed in a hotel when he was in Dublin with his wife, it would have to be someone with connections in the hotel industry."

"Yes, someone who could quietly have had the maids questioned. Is that O'Bannion?" Thor asked.

"I don't know, but I'll find that out, too."

"Thanks."

"So now all you have to do is identify the bomber and connect him to O'Bannion, if possible."

"Identifying him could be difficult," Thor said.

"Difficult, but at least you have everybody who's been in that suite in the past weeks on video, don't you?"

"Not exactly," Thor said. "Our constable standing guard in the hallway was a problem."

Chatwick understood at once. Haarold had been in the hallway for more than two hours before the bombs went off. "How far back does the videotape go?" he asked.

"Fortunately, Janus had the cameras shut off as soon as he arrived or we'd have nothing. As it is, from the camera facing the presidential suite I've got one hour and three minutes video of our constable."

"Why's that? He was there for more that two hours, wasn't he?"

"You know Haarold?"

"Met him last night. Very impressive."

"And very unusual. Apparently, he doesn't move around much. The camera taping him in front of the suite kept shutting down for lack of motion. We still have video going back to February twenty-eighth on that one."

"How about the other camera?"

"Much better. It's over the door to the presidential suite, so it didn't get much of Haarold moving around. That tape goes back six days, to February twenty-fourth. There's a good chance we've got the bomber on that one."

"Have you watched both tapes?" Chatwick asked.

"Yes."

"Do you have a suspect?"

"I'm not sure, yet. A Canadian named Thomas Winthrop checked into the hotel on Saturday, February twenty-first, and was given a room on the fifth floor. On the following Wednesday he asked Jónas for a change to the presidential suite, said he had gotten married last month in Canada and that his wife was flying in to meet him. It's off-season, so Jónas was happy to give it to him. The bellboy brought Winthrop's luggage up and tape shows him entering and leaving the suite a total of eight times—always alone."

"His wife never showed up?"

"No. He checked out on the evening of February twenty-eighth and she doesn't appear on the videotapes, if she exists."

"He checked out of the presidential suite the day before the foreign secretary arrived?" Chatwick asked.

"Yes, but right after the Rockall incident. If Winthrop is our man, he knew that Sir Ian would be coming here before long. If so, I have to figure that Winthrop watched the hotel and saw him and his wife arrive."

"Does your immigration have a record of when Winthrop arrived in Iceland?"

"Came in on an Icelandair flight from Montreal on Saturday, February twenty-first. However, according to our immigration, he still hasn't left the country."

"Did he have much luggage?"

"Five pieces. More than enough to carry the equipment to make the type of bombs I think were used."

"So what's your plan from here, if you don't mind my asking?"

"I've got Immigration watching out for him and I've got people checking every hotel in the country."

"And if you don't find him?" Chatwick asked.

"Foreigners attract attention here at this time of year. If I don't get him in the next couple of days, I'll go public. In the meantime, I'll try and pin down the exact workings and composition of the bombs."

Thor stood up, but kept his eyes on Chatwick. He could see that the ambassador was thinking and knew what he had on his mind.

"Before you go, there's something I have to ask you," Chatwick said. "I hope you don't take it the wrong way."

It was just what Thor wanted to hear. "Go on."

"Since it was our foreign secretary who was killed, I've been instructed by my government to offer you any assistance you might require in this case. As you might imagine, we have people with quite a bit of experience investigating bombings, specifically IRA bombings."

"I don't mind a little help, as long as it's subtle," Thor said. "Frankly, I could use some specialized scientific equipment and people who know how to use it."

"We'd also be glad to help you out there. We have a mobile lab designed specifically for bomb investigations."

"That's fine with me, but I'll have to check with Janus first. He'll probably want to establish some ground rules."

"Rules like no overt presence, give help only that's asked for, no firearms, and no talking to the press?" Chatwick asked with a smile.

Thor had to smile himself. "Roger, it's a pleasure dealing with an agreeable person who understands the fine art of diplomacy. When can your people and that lab of yours be here?"

"Two hours."

Wonderful! Thor thought. All the expensive scientific equipment needed, equipment that had never been deemed necessary in Iceland, is on the runway in the U.K. and ready to go. "Two hours would be fine. I also wouldn't mind having a person who knows the IRA personnel and tactics."

"That would be Inspector Rollins. He'll also be here in two hours." Chatwick stood up and offered his hand. Thor was about to take it and thank the ambassador, but was stopped by a loud knock at the door. Chatwick went to the door and returned with Janus.

Thor could tell by one look at the chief's face that more trouble was brewing. He could also see that Janus wanted to talk to him alone, but Thor didn't think that would be polite after just having made Chatwick and his government a de facto partner in the case. "Let's have the bad news, Janus."

"There's been another murder. A girl's body washed up this morning on the beach near Heimaey."

"Murdered?" Thor asked, astonished. Three murders in one week? Impossible!

"Horribly. Body is naked and sexually mutilated. Fingers are gone and all her teeth have been knocked out."

Heimaey? That's in the Westmann Islands, about a hundred kilometers from here, Thor thought. Can there possibly be a connection? "Whoever did it doesn't want her identified," he said.

"Do you want the body brought to the morgue here?" Janus asked.

Thor put his hand in his pocket to check his Dramamine supply before answering. "I guess so."

FOUR

THURSDAY, MARCH 5TH—NEW YORK CITY

Aside from whatever protocols are described in the city charter, it is generally acknowledged that the second most powerful man in New York City government is the police commissioner. It follows that if a person possesses sufficient influence, has a police-related problem, and is lucky enough to get an appointment to see the man in charge of the largest municipal police department in the world, he or she would go for anointing to the commissioner's large, fancy office on the top floor of Police Headquarters, One Police Plaza. By tradition, the PC is never one for leaving his office to visit individual civilian problems, with two exceptions. One is, of course, the mayor. The other is the Cardinal of the Archdiocese of New York, a personage who exercises enormous (but quiet) influence on New York City politics in general and on the police department in particular.

So it was that, at the direction of Exception Number One, Ray Brunette was on his way to visit Exception Number Two. He had been to the cardinal's residence at Madison Avenue and East 50th Street many times before and didn't need anyone to show him the way. Since visits to the cardinal were always confidential and his trusted regular driver was on vacation, Brunette had elected to drive himself in an old, beat-up, unmarked car. He pulled into a garage on East 50th Street, a half block from the cardinal's residence, and tried to look inconspicuous as he gave the surprised attendant the keys.

It was no use. In good shape, six feet tall, with his trademark straight black hair, Brunette was just too easily recognizable to anyone with a TV in New York City. "Howya doin' today, Commissioner?" the attendant asked as if Brunette parked in that garage every day.

"Fine, thank you. Yourself?"

"You know. Been dealing with cheapskates all day long, but what's the use complaining?"

Brunette nodded sympathetically. "Yeah. Break your ass all day trying to do the right thing and what thanks do you get? Town's loaded with cheapskates, most of them driving Mercedes and BMWs."

"Man, you got that shit right."

With the New York formalities over, Brunette thought he was going to make it out of the garage without further fanfare. Then he noticed that the attendant had taken a disapproving interest in the unmarked car. "Mind if I ask whatcha wasting money for leaving that car here? That piece a shit's a police car, right?"

"Yes, it is."

"Then why? You can drop it anywhere and go about your business. Ain't nobody gonna give it no summons, even this funky old piece a shit."

"Really?" Brunette asked with a straight face.

"Sure. Bus stops, fire hydrants, wherever you want. Don't make no never mind."

"I didn't know that."

"Well, live and learn," the attendant said as he punched the ticket. "How long ya gonna be?"

"Maybe an hour."

"I'll have it right here, right up front. Want me to clean it up a bit for you?"

the board what wonderful, quiet residents they would be. *"Thanks for coming, but sorry and good-bye,"* was all he and Angelita had heard so far over the screams of the twins.

"Give me a little time and maybe I'll be able to come up with something for you," Chip said after listening to McKenna's litany of woe.

"That would be kind of you."

"Can't guarantee anything, you understand. Remember I'm just a bartender."

McKenna was relieved to hear that. It was Chip's usual disclaimer before he used his influence, contacted Lord-knows-who, and arranged some miracle. "Sure, Chip. I know. You're just a bartender."

"How's work going?" Chip asked.

"Not bad. Doing mostly note-passers. Easy stuff, but kind of boring."

"And no glory?" Chip asked, knowing the arrangement. The Major Case Squad got the bank robbery cases where a note was passed to the teller but no weapon was shown. The Joint Bank Robbery Task Force, composed of NYC detectives and FBI agents, took the real bank robberies.

"No, your other pals get the glory."

"Ready for something different? Still boring, but different?"

Here it comes, McKenna thought. "Sure, what is it?"

"A missing person case."

"Chip, I'm not in Missing Persons. I'm in Major Case, remember?"

"Makes no difference. This is about to become a major missing person case and you're going to be assigned to it."

"How do you know that?" McKenna asked, then instantly regretted the question. Chip just *knew*, every time, but would never reveal a source. McKenna expected nothing more than an innocent-but-reproachful look in reply to his question, but this time Chip deigned to answer.

"Because Ray's having lunch with the cardinal right now. His Eminence is laying out the problem for Ray and he's going to ask that you be assigned. Naturally, Ray's gonna agree."

Now how would Chip know that? was the first silly question that popped into McKenna's mind. I thought I was the only one who knew about the visit to the cardinal. Then he remembered the time Chipmunk had brought him and Angelita to a big-shot FBI retirement dinner. Angelita had been a little miffed, thinking that Chip's table was too far from the dais where Ray, the FBI brass, and all the politicians were seated. Then the cardinal had arrived and took his seat between Angelita and Chipmunk, and she still hadn't stopped talking about it. So instead McKenna asked, "Why would the cardinal want me assigned?"

"Because somebody heard about it, through a friend, and then somebody suggested to the cardinal, through channels, that you were the one to handle it."

So Chip assigned this case to me, McKenna realized. Good enough. "Tell me about it."

"There's an Irish girl named Meaghan Maher who works at Jameson's. She's been missing since February nineteenth. Had a fight with her boyfriend and she's gone without a trace. She's a pretty little thing, maybe a bit on the wild side."

"You mean a little bit on the loose side?"

"That wouldn't be possible. Her brother's a priest."

Sure it's possible, McKenna thought, but kept that to himself. Ray Donovan, the manager of Jameson's, was another good friend of Chip's. "Her brother wouldn't happen to know the cardinal, would he?"

"Matter of fact, he's serving one year as the cardinal's aide. He's on some sort of transfer program from his order in Ireland."

"Is she legal?"

"Not exactly. She's got a green card, though, and it's not a bad job. Even the number's good."

McKenna understood. Without illegal aliens to work long hours and exercise charm at slightly lower-than-legal wages, the entire New York restaurant industry would collapse. The first to fold would be the Irish pubs scattered throughout every Manhattan neighborhood south of 96th Street.

Current legal immigration quotas from Ireland were much lower than that necessary to round out the staffs at the Irish pubs, but that didn't stop the prospective bartenders, waiters, and waitresses from abandoning the Emerald Isle and heading for the Bright Lights. There were paper requirements to be circumvented since Immigration had begun cracking down on restaurant owners who hired people without alien registration cards stamped with a work permit. Most of the newly arrived Irish obtained one in a hurry and the more resourceful among them got two, just in case.

McKenna knew Chipmunk was telling him that the green card was a forgery, but that somewhere there was a legal Meaghan Maher who had a card with the same number. Such a card was an expensive item, so Missing Meaghan Maher was a girl with foresight and backing. McKenna saw Chip's fingerprints on that one. "Where does she live?"

"Somebody got her a studio apartment in my building. A sublet deal," Chipmunk answered, deadpan.

"Lucky, huh?"

"She's a nice, hard-working girl from a good family. She deserved a little luck" was as far as Chipmunk was going to go on that subject.

"Has it been reported to the 19th Squad?"

"Her boyfriend reported it on February twenty-third."

"Four days after she disappeared? Why'd he wait so long?"

"He's not exactly legal, either."

That shouldn't be a problem, McKenna and just about every illegal alien in the city knew. According to a mayoral executive order, city agencies are prohibited from informing INS about illegal aliens who apply for assistance or are victims of crimes. "I take it he's not too bright."

"Not a real dummy, but certainly not the sharpest knife in the drawer."

"Who caught the case."

"Walsh."

So Chipmunk's arranged a conference, McKenna realized. Greg Walsh was the old-time detective sitting at the end of the bar. McKenna considered him to be a good man and a competent investigator. "And?"

"He worked on it, but the case doesn't fall within the guidelines for further investigation. On the surface, it looks like a voluntary disappearance with no evidence of foul play. Walsh did what he could and came up blank."

Chipmunk gave the barest nod to the end of the bar and Walsh ambled over. He was dressed in a expensive three-piece suit in the 19th Squad fashion and had a case folder in his hand.

After the handshake and the pleasantries, Walsh reported. "The boyfriend calls himself Chris O'Malley. Nice kid, pretty distraught and a little emotional. Bit of a bruiser, works as a bouncer at O'Flannagan's. Surprised the piss outta me when he started blubbering right in the squad office."

"You don't think he had anything to do with Meaghan's disappearance?"

"If there is any dirty business here, no, I wouldn't classify O'Malley as a suspect. He came clean with me, even made a statement that's not in his best interests. They got into quite a tiff at her place a few days before she disappeared. He wound up smacking her."

"Any injury?"

"Just to him. He had the good sense to apologize right away and thought he had her soothed over. They climbed under the sheets to make it official and then he took a little snooze. Woke up kinda sudden when she clocked him with the vacuum cleaner."

"She hit him with a vacuum cleaner?"

"Yeah, can you believe it? I guess it was the heaviest thing she could find and still swing. Took out his uppers and loosened his molars."

"What happened then?"

"Says he smartened up quick. Apologized for putting his face in the way while she was trying to vacuum and went to the NYU clinic to get some stitches in his gums and some Darvon for the pain."

"And that was the last time he saw her?"

"Last time anybody saw her, far as I can tell."

"What was the fight about?"

"Serious stuff. They both were starting vacation together on Thursday, February nineteenth. They were supposed to hang around town for a couple of days, partying it up a bit, and then head to Florida to spend the rest of the week in the sun. Then O'Malley changed the plan and had a little surprise for her. He'd booked them to Ireland instead."

"And she didn't like that?"

"You kidding? She'd been working out for months, bought new bathing suits, had her legs waxed, and spent a fortune at the tanning parlor. This girl was ready for the sun, not the rain. But that wasn't her main concern. O'Malley wanted to bring her back to meet his parents."

"I guess she wasn't ready for commitment," McKenna guessed.

"I guess not, especially since somebody told me that O'Malley wasn't the only one in the picture."

"Who's the other guy?"

"Nobody knows."

"Not even somebody?" McKenna asked, stealing a glance at Chipmunk.

"Not even somebody," Walsh said. "Not yet, anyway."

"What else you do?"

"Checked the hospitals and morgues, put out an NCIC alarm nation-wide, asked around at Jameson's and all the Irish bars O'Malley says she liked. Got nowhere."

"Talk to Ray Donovan?"

"Sure. He's the one makes me think there's something to this. Says he wasn't too worried until she didn't show up after her vacation. Says she's a little wild, but real reliable. Never missed a day in the two years she was working for him. Never even late without a phone call and a good excuse."

"So now he's worried?"

"Real worried. Turns out his family knows her family back in the Old Sod and he's getting some pressure."

And applying some pressure, besides, McKenna thought. Chip and Donovan go back a long way together. "You talk to her family?"

"Called me every day until Justin closed the case. He went out on a limb and let me work it for a week."

McKenna wasn't surprised. The rules stated that the precinct detective squad would work on a missing person case for only three days. If the subject wasn't a minor, wasn't mentally unbalanced, wasn't the suspected victim of a drowning, or if no evidence of foul play was uncovered, then the rules clearly stated that the case would be classified as a voluntary dis-appearance and closed after the three days. If any of the mitigating factors were present, the case would be sent to the Missing Persons Squad down-town for further investigation.

McKenna knew Lt. Justin Peters, the 19th Detective Squad com-mander, and had always recognized that he would go out on a limb and bend the rules whenever he thought necessary. Keeping a missing persons case open and a squad detective assigned for a full week would have required a lot of lies on paper from Justin, a task he excelled at and maybe even relished. "So what happened then?"

"Somebody called Justin and whispered something about extraordinary connections in this case. He reopened it and sent it to the Missing Persons Squad with a suggestion they work hard on it."

"Who's got it there?"

"Swaggart."

"Swaggart? I don't know him."

"You wouldn't. He's a real zero and a boob to boot. He's been hiding out down there as long as I can remember."

"So how come Swaggart's got it?"

"I can't say for sure, but I think it's the old Peters-Mosley thing."

Of course it is, McKenna thought. The feud between Justin Peters and Lt. George Mosley, the CO of the Missing Persons Squad, was old and legendary. It had begun when Mosley was overheard telling some chief at a cocktail party that those 19th Squad detectives were nothing but a bunch of prima donnas in three-piece suits and hands adorned with diamond-studded pinky rings.

Naturally, Mosley's impromptu and ill-advised remark had found its way to Justin's ears before the party had ended and he had called Mosley, at home, the next day. Reportedly, Justin's response went something like, "Sure my detectives are prima donnas, but they deserve to be. After all, it's the 19th Squad. We cover Manhattan's politically important and very prestigious Upper East Side, and nobody pops into my squad by accident. They work hard to get here and they have to be good and work hard to stay here. As for the three-piece suits, of course, I'd throw them out if they showed up to work in anything else. And the diamond-studded pinky rings? Well, maybe."

Justin had ended the terse conversation by demanding a public apology. Mosley had unwisely balked and so it had begun. Justin never missed an opportunity to throw a few darts Mosley's way, characterizing the Missing Persons Squad as a bunch of lazy, empty suits who were hidden, sheltered, and nourished by a big-mouth, incompetent lieutenant who wasn't smart enough or man enough to clean his own house and sweep out the trash that festered and flourished there.

And so Mosley suffered, continuously. Everyone knew that Mosley wasn't in the same league as a political heavyweight like Justin Peters and all wondered why Justin didn't just squeeze the life out of Mosley and get it over with already. The more astute among them finally figured out that Mosley had become Justin's hobby, like a cat playing with a mouse for hours before it tired of the game and finally bit the helpless little thing's head off.

This case might finally end it, McKenna thought as he imagined the scenario. A case comes to Mosley from the 19th Squad, a case that, according to the rules, should have been closed. Adding insult to injury, attached to the case is a suggestion from Justin that it be thoroughly investigated. Now what would Mosley do? Why nothing, of course, McKenna realized, nothing taking the shape of Mosley assigning the case to the laziest and most useless detective he could find.

Justin has finally tired of the game, McKenna realized. The cagey squad commander suspected there was something to this case when he bent the rules and kept Walsh on it. Then he sent it to Mosley with his suggestion, knowing what Dopey's reaction would be. The case goes bad, young ecclesiastically connected Meaghan Maher turns up kidnapped or murdered, and Ray chops off Mosley's head. Game, set, match to Justin.

Then a slightly disconcerting thought hit McKenna: He realized he was carrying the axe for Justin. Oh, well. Good-bye Lieutenant Mosley. Not nice knowing you. "You got any pictures of Meaghan?" he asked Walsh.

"Plenty." Walsh reached into his case folder, took out an envelope full of photos, and passed them to McKenna. A quick pass through them told McKenna that Meaghan was a very pretty girl with some fire in her eyes and that the photos came from O'Malley. He was in a few of the shots with her and Walsh was right—he was large enough to be classified a bruiser, but to McKenna he looked like a big teddy bear. From the way O'Malley was looking at Meaghan in two of the photos, the big guy was lost in love for that red-headed little girl.

"Did you check her apartment?" McKenna asked.

"Yeah, gave it a good toss."

"O'Malley give you the key?"

"No, she never gave him one."

"Then how? The super?"

"He only had one of the keys, but this girl is real careful. She's got three locks on her door, and the two she put on are real tough ones."

"Then somebody hooked you up with a locksmith?" McKenna guessed.

The indignant look that crossed Walsh's face told McKenna he was wrong. "Hey, I don't need somebody for everything, you know. I hooked myself up with a locksmith. Guy's good, but it still took him twenty minutes to get in."

"How long to get out?"

"No time. Left those tough ones unlocked and I took the key from the super." Walsh reached into his pocket and passed McKenna a key.

"How did the place look?"

"Neat and clean."

"Clothes?"

"Plenty of clothes in the closet, underwear in the drawers, nightie under her pillow."

"Bathing suits?"

"Three. Two new ones, still have the tags on them."

"Luggage?"

"Four suitcases. Two new, two of them old and kinda beat up."

"Any pets?"

"Not even a goldfish."

"She have any credit cards?"

"Victoria's Secret."

"No Visa or MasterCard?"

"O'Malley says no."

Delicate question coming up, McKenna thought. Getting credit information is illegal without a court order, and a judge wouldn't issue one in a voluntary disappearance case. However, a good detective willing to bend the law wouldn't need a court order to scam his way past any credit bureau. "What do *you* say, Greg? Does Meaghan have a Visa or MasterCard?"

Walsh looked him straight in the eye. "I say no. This Meaghan Maher doesn't have a Visa or a MasterCard under the date of birth on her phony green card. The real Meaghan Maher with that INS number does, but she lives in Brooklyn."

"Does our Meaghan have any bank accounts?"

"She's got a checking account at Chemical under her green card date of birth. Balance of ninety-two dollars and change. Last check was her rent check, seven hundred and fifty dollars, presented to the bank for payment on February twenty-second."

"When was her rent due?"

"March first."

"Know if she ever paid that early before?"

"Sure I do. Talked to the woman she's subletting from. She says only once in the two years she's been there. Usually Meaghan's a week late getting her the rent."

McKenna noticed that the FBI agent, Timmy Rembijas, had been staring down the bar at them. Timmy had been in the FBI's JFK Task Force for so long that he had earned the nickname Timmy JFK. "What's Timmy's role in this?" McKenna asked Walsh.

"He's in a better position than me when it comes to dealing with the airlines. You know how they are about divulging their passenger lists without a court order."

"Yeah, I do, but I guess somebody asked him to check around. Unofficially, of course."

"Somebody did. From February nineteenth to yesterday there hasn't been a Meaghan Maher booked on a flight outta any of the New York airports."

Well, that accounts for the federal presence on Chipmunk's intramural team effort, McKenna thought. "Anything else?"

"Nothing. Now you know what I know."

"Everything except what your gut feeling is on this."

"Same as yours is gonna be after you snoop around and look at it awhile. Talk to everybody who knows her, and they'll all tell you that Meaghan Maher being gone doesn't make sense. She's a little wild, but she's level-headed and responsible. Besides that, she's close to her family and always kept in touch."

"You think she's dead?"

"Yeah. Hate to say it, but she's either dead or in some real serious trouble," Walsh said, then dropped the case folder in front of McKenna on the bar. "Good luck. Call me if you need anything else," Walsh said, then turned and walked back down the bar.

McKenna turned his attention back to Chipmunk. *Somebody* hadn't said a word during the whole conversation and McKenna had noticed that Chipmunk had looked bored through most of it. Nothing Walsh had said had been news to Chip. "Well, you ready to fill me in on Boyfriend Number Two?"

"What makes you think I know anything about him?"

"Chip, I know you twenty years. The whole time Walsh was talking, that blank look you're so good at left your face only once. It was when he told me about Number Two."

"You know I was gonna tell you anyway, don't you?"

"Of course."

"His name is Owen and he's probably in the military."

"Last name?"

"I don't know. Seen him a few times, but only met him once."

"Tell me about it."

"About six months ago I was at home and I ran out of smokes. I decided to go out and get some, but as I'm going down the stairs I meet Meaghan going up. She's arm-in-arm with this guy and giggling up a storm. Having a good time and about to have a great time, I assumed."

"What time was this at?"

"Maybe three A.M. Meaghan's surprised to see me, but she's brassy and she trusts me enough to introduce me to Owen. He's clean-cut, in shape, and squared away. Even had his shoes spit-shined. Then he sticks out his hand and says, 'Very pleased to meet you, sir.' That clinched it, he's a good trooper in my book."

"No other conversation?"

"No, but I could see by the way Meaghan was holding on to Owen that she really liked him."

"You ever see him again?"

"Twice. Once in the stairwell and once in front of the building. Always in the wee hours."

"When was the last time?"

"Around Christmas."

"Any further conversation?"

"No, we'd just pass and wave to each other."

"Ever talk to Meaghan about him?"

"Nope. That's not my place."

"You told Walsh about this?"

"Just that I saw her with another guy once or twice."

"You didn't give him a name?"

"No."

"Or tell him that he was in the military?"

"No."

"Why's that?" McKenna asked.

"Because I could see that Meaghan wanted to keep Owen a secret from everybody she knows. That means the people at Jameson's, that means her brother the priest, and that certainly means O'Malley. Walsh reports to too many people and word gets around. You report to only Ray."

Another reason I'm here, McKenna thought. I can see where this is heading. "I guess Meaghan figured that Owen wouldn't play too well to the folks back home."

"I'd say she's right. Meaghan's secret pal Owen is as black as my shoe."

FIVE

After leaving Churchill's, McKenna returned to the Major Case Squad office in police headquarters. It was a large, modern office on the tenth floor, but there were only two detectives there catching up on their paperwork. Everyone else was either at lunch, in court, or out working their cases. Even Inspector Dennis Sheeran, the CO of the unit, was out of the office.

That was fine by McKenna. He wanted some quiet time to go over the Meaghan case folder. He began with the photos, spreading them out on top of his desk. After studying the fourteen shots for half an hour, McKenna was sure he would know Meaghan anywhere he saw her and he had formed some impressions about what she was like. She reminded him of a Raggedy Ann doll all grown up, but still cherished by those who knew her. He put the photos back in the envelope and went through Walsh's work.

There was a lot of paper, all photocopies made by Walsh since the original reports had been sent to the Missing Persons Squad. He had been thorough in documenting his interviews of Chris O'Malley, Ray Donovan, seven Jameson's employees, six of Meaghan's neighbors, the building super, and her parents in Ireland. He had also visited four Irish bars frequented by her and had received the same story from all quarters: Meaghan was a hard-working, reliable girl with a loving family and lots of friends, and she had told none of them that she had any intention of leaving on vacation without O'Malley. All thought her disappearance suspicious, and although many had stated that Meaghan could handle herself, they all feared for her safety.

According to the information originally given by Chris O'Malley on the standard missing persons report, Meaghan was a legal resident alien, twenty years old, five-foot-four, and 115 pounds, with red hair, fair complexion, and no tattoos or noticeable scars. She had been born in Ireland, had graduated from secondary school there, and had been in the United States for three years. Her ears had been pierced for earrings, but O'Malley hadn't been sure how many times. Under the JEWELRY caption, O'Malley had reported that besides earrings she usually wore a Claddagh ring on her left hand and a crucifix on a gold chain around her neck.

During his interview with O'Malley, Walsh had gotten the truth about Meaghan's legal status and he had attached a hand-written, unofficial note to the report stating that she was an illegal alien and that she was twenty-two, not twenty-four. Her birthday was March 18th and she had been in the U.S. for two years. Walsh had also done a criminal record check on both O'Malley and Meaghan. O'Malley had been arrested for a minor assault two years before, but the case had been dismissed. Meaghan had never been arrested.

It took McKenna an hour of studying the folder before he was satisfied that he really knew everything Walsh knew on the case. By that time the office was filling up with detectives returning to document their day on paper.

Inspector Sheeran came in, took a quick look around the squad room, gave McKenna a wave, and went into his office without asking McKenna what he was up to.

A few years before, McKenna had held a political appointment as an assistant commissioner and had been, in theory, Sheeran's boss. McKenna had hated that job, finding it meaningless and unrewarding work, and had finally given up the fancy title with the nice office and the obscene salary and returned to police work as a detective. However, although Sheeran was an old friend, McKenna knew the inspector was uncomfortable supervising him. This, in turn, made McKenna uncomfortable.

The occasional mission from Brunette didn't help matters, either. Whenever somebody influential enough was scammed, robbed, or burglarized in New York City, they invariably wound up asking that McKenna be assigned their case. Most of the time Brunette ignored these requests, but not always. He believed that he had the best detectives in the world working for him, but occasionally he would drop one of those cases on McKenna.

The criteria Brunette used was still something of a mystery to McKenna, but he suspected the mayor had something to do with it. Most people Brunette could politely rebuff or tacitly ignore, but the mayor was a politician in charge of a city many people classified as unmanageable. However, His Honor was doing the impossible because he understood the political process of give-and-take: Grant a favor now and get it returned later, when needed.

Aside from what was implied in many of the newspaper columns, the mayor was the popular police commissioner's boss and both men knew it. McKenna suspected that the rule of thumb among the politically influential in town was put pressure on Brunette and you got nowhere; put pressure on the mayor and you got McKenna.

Which was good in this case, McKenna thought. Without ever having met Meaghan Maher, he had grown fond of her. He couldn't explain why in words and realized that it was unprofessional, but he had already taken a personal interest in her life and wanted to get to the bottom of her disappearance. He was growing impatient waiting for Brunette's call and was about to go through the case folder again when the phone rang.

Two minutes later McKenna was sitting in Brunette's office on the fourteenth floor, listening to his friend make the usual small talk with his feet propped up on Teddy Roosevelt's big desk. Although Brunette recognized that political influence was a fact of life that had to be dealt with, he didn't like bending his department's traditional procedures by assigning McKenna to his missions. He would eventually bring up the case as a conversation piece and wait for McKenna to express interest in it.

So they talked about the latest note-passer McKenna was working on, a guy who had robbed four banks in a month, making a total of six thousand dollars for his efforts. McKenna had identified him but hadn't yet located him. To help Brunette along, he described the case as boring and then asked how lunch went with the cardinal.

"Funny you should ask," Brunette said, taking his feet off the desk. "With St. Paddy's Day coming up, I figured he wanted to talk about ACT UP and Queer Nation, but he hardly mentioned them. Glossed right over it."

Before his meeting with Chipmunk, McKenna had also assumed that the cardinal had wanted to talk to Brunette about the two radical gay rights groups. According to ACT UP and Queer Nation, the Catholic church and the cardinal were inherently antigay. St. Patrick's Day, when the cardinal was the focus of national media attention as he presided over the St. Patrick's Day parade from the steps of St. Patrick's Cathedral, was their time of action. For the past few years, ACT UP and Queer Nation had sought publicity by disrupting church services and organizing demonstrations protesting the cardinal's perceived stand.

Everyone suspected it was a tough time for the cardinal, but he never deigned to publicly acknowledge the activities of the two groups. "I guess the cardinal had something else on his mind," McKenna stated innocently.

"Yeah, he's got an Irish aide over from Ireland. Introduced me to him and we all had lunch together."

"Nice guy?"

"A sweetheart, and sharp as they come. Cardinal told me he's gonna be a monsignor before long, figures that one day this fella might be heading up the church in Ireland."

"Really?"

"Yeah, but the cardinal also mentioned a problem the poor guy's having. He's real upset about his sister."

"Because she's missing?"

Brunette sat up straight and eyed McKenna shrewdly. "Damn! Sheeran tell you about this already?"

That was a cat out of the bag. So he's already discussed it with Sheeran, McKenna realized. Good, saves me the trouble of tiptoeing around the inspector. "No, Ray. He didn't say a word, but I already knew I had this case. Got it from a higher source, probably knew before you did."

"Higher than the cardinal?"

"Yep. I got it from Chipmunk."

SIX

Since it was almost quitting time, Lieutenant Mosley was busy clearing his desk. In front of him was a pile of COMPLAINT FOLLOW-UP reports that documented the work his detectives had done on their cases that day and he was signing them at his usual rate of six a minute. Then there was a perfunctory knock at his door and McKenna walked into his office.

The lieutenant immediately suspected he had a problem. An unannounced visit from the PC's pal could mean nothing else, so Mosley quickly ran his cases through his mind, searching for the one that had a booby trap for him inside. A few came to mind, but he couldn't attach names to them. There were just so many people reported missing in New York City, but that had never been a problem for Mosley. Experience had taught him that sooner or later, somebody found them, usually by accident.

"Good to see you, Brian," Mosley said. "What brings you here?"

McKenna didn't think that Mosley looked glad to see him at all. "I've been ordered to take over one of your cases."

In any other circumstances involving any other detective, any squad commander would indignantly shout, *"Ordered by who?"* But not with McKenna because everyone knew who the *who* was. "Good. So you'll be working for me?"

"No."

"I see," Mosely said as he mulled over the implications of McKenna's simple *"No."* "Which case?"

"The Meaghan Maher case."

"Meaghan Maher?"

"The one you got two weeks ago from the 19th Squad."

"Oh, that one. According to the guidelines, it never should have come here. Peters should have closed it, but you know him. I figured he sent it to me just to break my balls."

"That's not why he left it open," McKenna said. "Whatever the guidelines say, Lieutenant Peters was sharp enough to see that there was something to it."

That was not what Mosley wanted to hear. "There a heavyweight involved here, somewhere?"

"I never ask," McKenna lied.

"Good policy. Good thing I assigned one of my best men to it."

"Detective Swaggart?"

"Yeah, Swaggart. Very experienced man, been here for years."

"Could I speak to him?"

"Sure."

"And could you ask him to bring the case folder in?"

"You got it." Mosley picked up his phone and a few minutes later Swaggart was in the office.

Swaggart was an old-timer in his late fifties, but he looked like he had jumped out of the Mod Squad. He had muttonchop whiskers, a long, droopy mustache, and he wore a checkered polyester sports coat and frayed polyester slacks. McKenna didn't like that look in a detective. Worse, Swaggart had just been summoned into his squad commander's office and he was standing there with his top shirt button undone and his tie pulled down.

McKenna felt he was rocking on a very loose ship. After seeing Swaggart, he wasn't interested in what the man had to say. "May I see the case folder, please?"

"Not much to it. Pretty routine," Swaggart said as he handed the folder to McKenna.

It took McKenna only a minute to read because Swaggart had done only four short reports on the case. In the first he acknowledged receiving it for investigation; in the second he verified that the alarm for Meaghan

Maher as a missing person had been transmitted; in the third he described a phone call he had received from the subject's mother in Ireland, a call in which he had assured her that everything possible was being done to locate her daughter; and in the fourth he had recommended that the case be closed pending further developments. Mosley had signed each report.

McKenna was shocked. Swaggart had never once left the office to work the case. His initial shock was replaced by anger and he struggled to keep himself under control. Like Swaggart, McKenna was a detective, not a boss, and he knew it wasn't his place to offer criticism. But something had to be said. "This is it? Four reports that say absolutely nothing and case closed?"

"Yeah, pretty routine," Swaggart offered. "Remember, this case is outside the guidelines. It never should have come here in the first place."

You're right about that, McKenna thought. After all, it's people's lives we're dealing with. Their problems, worries, and concerns should never wind up in this investigative cesspool. "Lieutenant, is Detective Swaggart related to you in any way?"

"No. Why would you think that?" Mosley asked suspiciously.

"Just a thought. After looking at this case folder, I figure you must owe him something because you let him get away with it. Figured that years ago, maybe he did you a favor and married your ugliest sister."

Mosely turned red and visibly angry. His lips quivered and he looked like he wanted to shout, but then he thought better of it. He put a pleasant smile on his face and asked, "I guess you think he should have done more?"

"Much more."

"Let me explain something to you, Brian. Most people are missing because they want to be missing. Fine, but we know that they all show up, sooner or later."

"But you don't find them?"

"I've got twenty-six detectives and we get a hundred cases a day. There's procedures and we follow them. Finding someone who wants to be missing is a difficult, time-consuming job."

Too difficult for this crew with their present boss, McKenna thought. "Don't a number of them wind up as victims of crimes?"

"Not a sizable number, but it happens," Mosely conceded.

"Let's hope it didn't happen in this case. Let's hope we don't find out that this girl has been kidnapped, raped, or murdered while you're sitting on a closed case that your very experienced detective here never really worked."

"And if we do?"

"Use your imagination."

"Are you threatening me, Detective McKenna?" Mosley asked, angry and indignant.

"Yes," McKenna answered, then turned and headed for the door.

"Think you can do better, McKenna?" Swaggart shouted.

"That shouldn't be hard."

Like many other valuable investigative tools used by detectives for years, the telephone records of a subject have been officially denied to them by a host of court decisions relating to privacy. The telephone companies were forced to comply and now require a court order or subpoena before releasing subscriber information to the police. McKenna knew that he couldn't fill those requirements in this case, but that didn't concern him. Telephone companies traditionally hire retired police bosses as their heads of security, and NYNEX was no exception. Running their security operation was Steve Tavlin, an old friend who had recently retired as chief of Manhattan detectives.

McKenna got Meaghan Maher's telephone number from Walsh's reports, called Tavlin with his request, and then made himself a cup of coffee. The day shift was leaving and the night shift was reporting in, so McKenna lounged by the fax machine and exchanged pleasantries with the new arrivals while he waited and drank his coffee. He was still waiting and on his second cup when Sheeran came out of his office.

"Staying late?" the inspector asked McKenna.

"Yeah, I figure maybe nine o'clock. Got some things that need doing."

"Can I help you out with anything?"

"I'd like to use your phone. Think I'm gonna be making some international calls."

International calls could not be made from the phones on every detective's desk, but they could from the CO's phone. "Her parents?" Sheeran asked.

"That's one of them. Also hope to get a line on somebody else she's been talking to."

"Anybody in particular?"

"There's a mystery boyfriend in here somewhere and he's in the military. He hasn't been around for a while, so he's probably not stationed at any base around here."

"I guess you asked Tavlin for some help," Sheeran said.

This Sheeran's still sharp, McKenna thought.

Ordinarily, bosses never wanted to hear about the slightly illegal things their detectives did as they went about their work. "Results count, but spare me some of the details" was the usual attitude. But not Sheeran. He trusted every man in his squad to do the right thing and then competently deny it if the need ever arose. Every detective in the Major Case Squad realized that trust was a two-way street and they all felt comfortable keeping Sheeran in the loop. "Yeah, we talked," McKenna said. "He asked me to send you his regards."

"Thanks. Call me if you need anything. I'll be at home."

Right after Sheeran left, the fax started spitting paper. It lasted an hour and didn't stop until McKenna had every call Meaghan had made from home in the past year. McKenna took the paper into Sheeran's office and made himself comfortable as he went over the bills.

The last call Meaghan had made was at 1:10 A.M. on the morning of February 19th. It was an international call, so McKenna opened Sheeran's directory and turned to the page listing country calls. It was Belgium. He picked up the phone and dialed.

"Bravo Company, Sergeant Waters speaking."

Bingo! McKenna thought. Getting close to my soldier. "Yes, Sergeant Waters. This is Detective McKenna of the New York City Police Department. Could you please give me your full unit designation and tell me where you're located?"

"Yes, sir. Bravo Company, Fourth MP Battalion. We're in Brussels, Belgium."

Only one thing an American army unit could be doing in Belgium, McKenna knew. "Is your unit assigned to guard NATO Headquarters?"

"Yes, sir. Is there a problem?"

"Yes, but it's my problem, not yours. Thank you, Sergeant. You've been a big help."

"Is there anything else I can help you with?"

McKenna thought about asking Waters if there were any soldiers in Bravo Company named Owen, but decided against it. For all he knew, he might be speaking to Sergeant Owen Waters and he wasn't ready to tip his hand yet, just in case Owen had something to do with Meaghan's disappearance. Word travels fast in the military and the news that a NYC detective had called to ask about Owen would be sure to reach him. "Not yet, Sergeant. Thank you."

McKenna's next call was to Meaghan's parents in Ireland. According to her bill, she had last spoken to them three days before she disappeared. McKenna intended it to be a simple courtesy call, but figured the call was a couple of hours overdue because it was close to midnight in Ireland and the phone kept ringing. He was about to hang up when the phone was answered.

"Hello?" It was a woman's voice and she sounded like she just woke up.

"Hello, Mrs. Maher. This is Detective McKenna of the New York City Police Department." There was no response. McKenna was puzzled until he realized that Meaghan's mother was expecting bad news from the midnight call and was probably holding her breath. "There've been no new developments, but I just wanted to let you know that I've been assigned the case," he added.

"Thank God, Detective McKenna, but you scared me out of my wits," she said, relief sounding through her thick brogue.

"Sorry I'm calling so late, but we've got a time difference," McKenna said.

"Don't be sorry. Please call anytime. This wouldn't be *the* Detective McKenna, would it? Detective Brian McKenna?"

"Yes, it is. How do you know?"

"Since Meaghan's gone to America, we pick up the New York papers from time to time. We know all about you and I'm delighted that you're going to help find her."

McKenna's head was swelling. "I'll do my best, Mrs. Maher," he said.

"Was Detective Swaggart too busy? Is that why you've been assigned?"

"No, I don't think that's the case. Why would you think that?"

"Because every time we call, they always tell us that he's not in the office. They always tell us that he's busy in the field."

That lazy, lying sack of shit! Except to fill his face, Swaggart probably hasn't been out of the office in a year, McKenna wanted to scream. However, he didn't see how that would help Mrs. Maher's state of mind, so he said instead, "I've been assigned to find Meaghan because our police commissioner has taken a personal interest in this case. We're going to do everything we can and I'll call you every couple of days to let you know how we're doing."

"Wonderful! Thank you, Detective McKenna. You can't imagine what it's like for us, not knowing where she is or if she's dead or alive."

"I think I can, but it's hard to put myself in your shoes. When was the last time you heard from her?"

"That would be Sunday, February fifteenth."

McKenna already had the answer in the bills in front of him, but he had to ask. "Did she usually stay in touch with you?"

"Always. Called us every Sunday, without fail. That's one of the reasons we're so concerned."

"Has anybody you don't know called asking about her?"

"Meaghan was very popular here. Everybody's been asking about her, but we know them all."

"How about Chris O'Malley?"

"Never met him, but he's a wonderful boy. Calls every couple of days. I think he's as worried as we are."

"Will you call me immediately, day or night, if you hear anything at all?" McKenna asked.

"Of course."

McKenna gave her his work number, his home number, and his cell phone number.

"Thank you, Detective McKenna. God bless you and good luck. From this moment on, you're in our prayers," Mrs. Maher said.

Pray for yourself and Meaghan, not me, McKenna thought. The deeper I get in this, the worse it looks.

SEVEN

To avoid allegations of theft by police personnel, the rules clearly state that a relative or neighbor should be present whenever an absent resident's premises are searched. Since McKenna intended to get deep into Meaghan's life, he didn't want to air her laundry in front of her brother the priest. Whether she was dead or alive, things that Meaghan wanted kept hidden wouldn't be revealed by McKenna unless absolutely necessary. Besides, he already had somebody trustworthy who fit right into the rules.

Chipmunk had gotten off work at eight o'clock and met McKenna in front of his and Meaghan's building on East 76th Street. A minute later they were in Meaghan's small studio apartment on the third floor. There was a small kitchen and a bathroom on opposite sides of the entry hallway that led to a combination bedroom/dining room/living room. Crowded into the room was a sofa with an end table on each side and a coffee table in front, a dresser with a TV and a stereo perched on top, a small table with seating for two, a hope chest, and a built-in closet containing a fold-down Murphy bed. The two windows were adorned with bright, cheery curtains and the floor was partially covered by a throw rug that matched the colors of the curtains.

McKenna's first thought was that Walsh had understated the condition of the apartment. It wasn't just neat and clean. Except for the two-week layer of dust that had accumulated in her absence, Meaghan's apartment was spotless. His second was that the apartment had that one feature so rare and precious in Manhattan—closet space, and plenty of it. There were two closets in the main room and another long one with sliding doors in the hallway.

Meaghan's feminine touch was evident everywhere. Plants hung from the ceiling in planters at three corners of the room, a line of ceramic kittens marched across the dresser in front of the TV and stereo, a frilly linen doily was under each of the matching lamps on both end tables, a matching tablecloth of the same material covered the dining table, and two photo albums with embroidered covers were on the coffee table. On the wall over the sofa was a painting that depicted an Irish country landscape seen through the window of an old-fashioned kitchen. On the opposite wall, over the TV, were two photos in pastel blue ceramic frames. One was a shot of Meaghan as a teenager standing between a middle-aged couple in front of an Irish country cottage. The other was a photo of a smiling priest in a Roman collar.

"Some lucky guy should have married this girl already," Chipmunk commented as he looked around.

"I'm sure that thought's already crossed the minds of quite a few not-so-lucky guys," McKenna said. "I think she's sick of hearing from them."

"Why you say that?"

McKenna pointed to the phone on one of the night tables. "Because she has to be the only single girl in Manhattan without an answering machine. I would have liked to listen to who's been calling her."

"Yeah, that would have been nice," Chipmunk said. "Maybe she's got call answering with NYNEX."

"She doesn't."

"So where do we start?"

"Could you do the hope chest while I look around?"

"Sure. What are we looking for?"

"Her cancelled checks, love letters, and a photo of Owen."

"The checks should be easy, but if there's letters or Owen photos, they should be pretty well hidden," Chipmunk said. "O'Malley spent a lot of time here, so she wouldn't have left them anyplace he'd be likely to come across them."

"That's too bad, because we're here until we find them."

McKenna took off his jacket and tie and went into the kitchen. He was going through the cabinets when he heard Chipmunk yell, "Got the checks."

"That's a start. Keep going," McKenna yelled back.

The cabinets contained only four cans of ready-to-drink Slimfast, tea bags, sugar, a dinner service for four, six glasses, four coffee cups, a tea kettle, a blender, and a box of Wheaties. In the single drawer was silverware for six and a dozen take-out menus from the local restaurants.

The garbage can was empty. The stove looked new and the oven was so clean that McKenna was convinced that it had never been used.

So Meaghan's become a real Manhattan woman, McKenna surmised. Like most of the busy women in town, she didn't cook. When he checked the refrigerator, he knew he was right. It was off and empty except for a jar of peanut butter and a can of coffee. The freezer was also empty.

McKenna went on to the bathroom. It was scrubbed clean and he found nothing he considered important except for an unopened box of birth control pills. It was what he didn't find that interested him—there was no toothbrush.

The hallway closet was crammed with summer clothes and shoes, a vacuum cleaner, and suitcases. On shelves on one side of the closet were her sweaters, all neatly folded.

McKenna took the vacuum cleaner out and hefted it. It wasn't light and he smiled when he noticed that the heavy plastic cover was cracked. Chris O'Malley took quite a shot while learning his lesson, McKenna concluded. Then he took out the suitcases.

Like Walsh had said, there were four of them, two old ones and two new gray ones. The old suitcases had Montreal International Airport baggage tags attached to the handles, but it was the two new ones that interested McKenna. They were part of a matched set. One was a small overnight bag and the other was a large suitcase. He figured there were one or two smaller suitcases missing from the set. He searched the luggage, found nothing, and started on the closet.

It took a while to check the shelves, unfold and refold all the sweaters, go through all the pockets of all the clothes, and check the insides of all the shoes. It was an unrewarding task that yielded nothing about Owen, but provided another small mystery. One of the sweaters was homemade and the design on the front and back featured a Union Jack crossed with an Irish flag. Underneath, the words PEACE IN OUR TIME were embroidered. Considering the politics of most of the Irish immigrants in town, McKenna thought it was a very unusual sweater for Meaghan to own.

When McKenna returned to the main room, he found Chipmunk kneeling on the floor carefully folding a wedding dress. The contents of the hope chest were neatly arranged around him in a way that reminded McKenna of a Marine Corps footlocker inspection. There were more photo albums, an old teddy bear, two jewelry boxes, and many unopened packages of newborn baby clothes in both pink and blue. The top tray of the hope chest was where Meaghan kept her bills, cancelled checks, and receipts, all neatly arranged, and a photo framed in black of a young man wearing a British Army uniform.

Chipmunk finished folding the wedding dress and placed it in the bottom of the hope chest.

"Find anything interesting?" McKenna asked.

"Interesting? I found that our Meaghan is a girl who really thinks ahead. She's got her wedding dress ready to go, but I don't think she plans on marrying anyone soon. Better yet, she's already bought clothes for the babies she's not even close to having."

"Anything else?"

"No sign of Owen, but there is this." Chipmunk reached into the tray and handed McKenna a folded credit card receipt. "Looks like Walsh was wrong," he said. "Meaghan's got herself a Visa card."

She sure does, McKenna thought as he examined the receipt. It was in her name and Meaghan had used the card at Travel Plans Unlimited to charge eight hundred and seventy dollars the previous August. The card expired in the following October, so McKenna knew that she had had it for some time. How could Walsh be so wrong on something important like this? he wondered. That's not like him.

Walsh wasn't wrong, he concluded. "The card's in her name, but I'll bet it's not her account. Somebody who loves her gave her a credit card to use."

"Well, it's not O'Malley," Chipmunk said. "He's illegal and would have a hell of a time getting a Visa card. So that leaves her brother, her folks, or Owen."

"Hate to do this, but we gotta find out."

"Hate to do what?"

"Call Ireland. It's two in the morning there now." McKenna picked up Meaghan's phone and dialed. It rang for a while, but he didn't have to announce himself this time. "Detective McKenna?" Mrs. Maher asked.

"Yes, Mrs. Maher. Sorry to bother you again, and it's nothing else for you to worry about. There are a few things I need to know right now."

"No bother at all, but could you please do me a favor?"

"Sure. What is it?"

"Stop calling me Mrs. Maher. I'm probably not much older than you and my name's Peggy."

It was a shock to McKenna, but she was probably right. He had married late, but if he had started his family earlier in life he could have a daughter about Meaghan's age. Suddenly he felt uncomfortably old. "Okay, Peggy. It's a deal, but only if you call me Brian."

"Thank you. What do you need to know, Brian?"

"Did you give Meaghan a credit card?"

"No, she never asked for one. We're not rich and she knows we had a hard enough time getting one for ourselves."

"Did Meaghan ever come home for a visit?"

"Just once, last August for three days. She didn't have vacation, but she added two days to her weekend and popped in. It was such a wonderful surprise for us."

"Do you know what airport she left here from?"

Mrs. Maher didn't answer, and McKenna thought he knew the reason why. "Peggy, I know Meaghan is an illegal immigrant here, but that's a secret I'll keep. Besides, her legal status isn't important to me. Now tell me, did she fly out of Montreal?"

"Yes, she left from Montreal and returned the same way."

"Does she have an Irish passport or a British one?"

"What makes you think she would have a British passport?"

"Just a hunch. She knits, right?"

"She used to," Mrs. Maher said, sounding puzzled. Then she got it. "You've seen her sweater with the flags?"

"Yes, and I'm also looking at a photo of a young man in a British army uniform."

"That's my son James. He was on the *Sheffield* in the Falkland War."

The HMS *Sheffield*? That was the British ship that was hit by an Argentine Exocet missile, McKenna thought. There were horrible casualties among the British soldiers and sailors on board. He didn't want to ask the next question, but it was the logical one. "Was he killed in action?"

"Yes. It was quite a blow to us and I don't think Meaghan ever got over it. James was eleven years older than her, but he doted on her and she simply adored him. She still has a special place in her heart for soldiers, no matter where they're from."

Explains a lot, McKenna thought. Also tells me that the Maher family isn't unfamiliar with tragedy. Sure hope I'm wrong about this one shaping up, but now's not the time to dwell on it. "Well, which is it, Peg? The British or the Irish passport?"

"Both. She was born in Belfast in the North. We moved south to Dublin when she was ten, but we still have family there."

"Thank you. Now, this is important, but it's a tough one. Do you remember the luggage she had when she visited?"

"Of course I do. She had two suitcases, the same battered old suitcases she had when she first left Ireland. It was such a shame, her being so pretty and proper and carrying those old suitcases, so we bought her a nice new set of luggage.

"The gray luggage?"

"Why, yes. How do you know?"

"Because I'm in her apartment right now looking at it. How many pieces in the set?"

"Four, all different sizes."

"One more question. Does Meaghan usually take milk in her coffee and tea?"

"She wouldn't have it any other way. Very light, usually half a cup of milk whenever she had either."

"Then I have a little piece of good news for you. Meaghan wasn't kidnapped. She planned a trip. She cleaned out her refrigerator, turned it off, and threw out any open container of milk she might have had. Then she packed up two of her new suitcases and left of her own accord. I don't know where she went yet, but I'm getting some ideas."

"Can you tell me what they are?"

"Not now, Peggy. Maybe tomorrow when I know a little more. I don't want to build up any false hopes for you."

"Fair enough. Do you have a few minutes to talk?"

Mrs. Maher's few minutes turned into a half hour. She had so many questions about Meaghan's life in New York and answers to many of the questions McKenna had about the subject of his investigation. He learned that the U.S. had always fascinated Meaghan, and even as a little girl, she had always known she was coming here. She was determined to be an American. When she grew up, she had found Ireland too boring and constrained by tradition. That had hardened her resolve and she was off on her adventure.

According to Mrs. Maher, Meaghan had always been a determined and meticulous planner. She had done well enough in school, but her obstinacy and determination showed up there as well. She absolutely refused to learn a word of the required Gaelic. The ancient language fit nowhere in her plans, so she took the *F* and concentrated on the many elective speech courses she took. She wanted to lose her brogue and be able to speak like an American, and she succeeded. Her mother said she could perfectly mimic every American accent from Brooklyn to Alabama.

It all made sense to McKenna and accounted for Meaghan's choice of Montreal as her departure and entry point. She had planned well and knew the system, and McKenna had the scenario: Fly out of New York and there would be all those embarrassing inquiries from those very nosy U.S. Immigration agents when she returned. Cross the loosely guarded and fairly lax border into Canada, fly out of Montreal, and then it's a different story when she returns there. With her Irish passport, she's okay. With her British passport, she's even better and no problem for Canadian Immigration. A fellow citizen of the Empire dropping in for another visit, eh? So good to see you and welcome back.

Two hours later and Meaghan is on a bus at the U.S. border. Since she had a phony green card, McKenna was sure Meaghan had a phony driver's license as well. Show the license to the bored U.S. Immigration agent, answer a few perfunctory questions with her New York accent, and she's on her way home, back to the place she loves.

By the time McKenna finally hung up, Chipmunk had finished repacking the hope chest, had emptied the first of the closets in the main room, and was going through her clothes. "You mind doing that, Chip?"

"What's to mind? It's mindless. What do you want to do?"

"Go through her photo albums. I know her already, but I want to get right inside her head."

So while Chipmunk went through the two closets and then Meaghan's dresser, McKenna went through her life in pictures. He watched her grow up as he followed her, a tough, cute tomboy in a shantytown in Belfast, to Dublin in her teens, and finally to America.

It was in America that Meaghan bloomed. Cute became pretty and she knew it. There were photos of Meaghan at the Empire State Building, on the Staten Island ferry, at the Bronx Zoo, and at Yankee Stadium. In those shots she was enjoying herself as a spectator, but she hadn't left her tomboy heritage completely behind. There were plenty of action shots: Meaghan skiing, Meaghan in a softball uniform playing shortstop on a ladies' team in Central Park, Meaghan horseback riding, Meaghan water-skiing, Meaghan snorkeling in a blue lagoon somewhere, and Meaghan in a fencing costume, gracefully striding forward as she applied *la touché* to her opponent with her foil.

As McKenna closed the last album, he knew that there were two things Meaghan had never lacked in New York. One was clothes and the other was a photographer always ready to step forward and shoot her as the center of attention in any group or scene.

Chipmunk had finished checking the dresser and had moved the dining set aside so he could pull down the Murphy bed. As McKenna would have expected, the bed was neatly made with a homemade embroidered wool bedspread on top. Just like Walsh had said, there was a nightgown under the pillow. While Chipmunk took the bed apart and peeled off the mattress cover, McKenna browsed through Meaghan's cancelled checks.

Meaghan paid by check only when she had to, so it didn't take long to go through them. They were mostly rent and utility checks, with an occasional payment to her Victoria's Secret credit card, always marked by Meaghan PAID IN FULL on the memo line on the front of the check. There were two checks to the East Side Medical Group and five to Dr. Stanley Kramer, DDS. McKenna put one of the Kramer checks in his pocket, then replaced the photo albums and checks in the hope chest and closed it.

Chipmunk had been working hard and not complaining, but McKenna still felt guilty because he was on overtime while Chip was doing the heavy work for free. "Chip, why don't you take a break and I'll finish with the bed?" he suggested.

"Nonsense, but glad you're done snooping. Getting this mattress cover back on is going to be a two-man job."

It was, and there were a few more two-man jobs after that. Not a sign of Owen's existence had been found, but McKenna was still sure it had to be there, somewhere. So they moved all the furniture away from the walls and checked the bottom of the sofa, the table, and the dresser. Nothing, so they removed all the covers from the sofa cushions. Owen wasn't there. In the kitchen, they pulled the refrigerator and the stove out and checked behind and underneath. Still nothing.

It was eleven o'clock when they decided to take a break and think things out. Chipmunk used one of Meaghan's menus to order in Chinese food. The delivery boy was at the door in minutes. McKenna paid, and they sat at the table, each man silently thinking while they ate.

Then a thought struck McKenna. "Meaghan doesn't cook," he said.

"Yeah, so?"

"Chris O'Malley has to know that. Stove looks brand new, and I don't think the oven's ever been used."

"We checked the stove, remember?"

"I know, but that's where it has to be. She keeps no food in the apartment, so she knows O'Malley never has any reason to go there."

"So let's check again," Chipmunk suggested.

Owen was there, hiding out underneath the broiler pan in the bottom of the stove. McKenna took out the album of photos and gave it to Chipmunk without opening it.

Chipmunk did. "That's him," he said and gave the album back to McKenna.

Owen wasn't just a soldier, he was First Lt. Owen Stafford of the United States Army. The first photo was a posed five-by-seven portrait of him in full uniform with the U.S. flag in the background. Above his left breast pocket were two rows of decorations and above his right was his nametag. He was trying to look dispassionate as he stared at the camera for his official photo, but Owen couldn't pull it off. He was just too used to smiling.

"Impressive-looking guy, isn't he," Chip commented. "He's got the Silver Star, a Purple Heart, the Desert Storm Campaign Ribbon, the Panama Campaign Ribbon, and a Presidential Unit Citation."

Only one person in a thousand would recognize those medals, McKenna thought, and I've got him standing next to me. Lucky. But Chipmunk's right, McKenna thought. Owen is impressive and a good-looking man to boot. But there's something else about him shining through this photo. "Looks like a nice guy, doesn't he?"

"Must be," Chipmunk agreed. "A first lieutenant, and he called me *sir*? Makes him a wonderful guy in my book."

The next few pages of photos were wallet-sized shots showing Owen and Meaghan seeing the sights in Washington, DC, but there was only one photo in which the two of them appeared together. That one was taken on the steps of the Lincoln Memorial. Owen had his arm around her waist and was staring at the camera, but for the first time in all the photos McKenna had seen of her, Meaghan wasn't. She was staring at Owen with the same loving look on her face that O'Malley wore in the shots he shared with her.

"Looks like she's got a real case for him," McKenna said.

"Of course she does," Chipmunk said. "I knew that from the first time I saw them together."

McKenna took out the first photo of Owen, then replaced the album in its hiding spot in the broiler pan.

"We done here?" Chipmunk asked.

"No, there's just one more thing I want to do to get an idea of where she went. I want to see what clothes are missing."

"How we gonna know that?"

"Her photos. There's enough of them, so if she's wearing something in them that's not here, we can assume she took it with her."

"That's gonna take us some time to do."

"I know, but we're here and we might as well do a good job of it."

Chipmunk was right. It took another two hours of matching clothes to photos before McKenna was sure that Meaghan hadn't headed for fun in the sun. Her bathing suits and summer clothes were still there, but missing were her ski jacket, an overcoat, three sweaters, two long-sleeved suits, her cowboy boots, her brown leather gloves, and two scarfs. By the time they were done, Meaghan's clothes were strewn all over the apartment.

"Doesn't make sense," Chipmunk said. "She wanted to go to Florida."

"But she didn't. Something made her change her plans and she headed for someplace cold."

"Maybe Canada?"

"Maybe, but I'm hoping you'll find out for me."

"You want me to have Timmy JFK check for her at the Montreal air-port?"

"That's the next step, but I need something else. Could you ask him to call the Defense Department to get Owen's date of birth and social security number for me?"

"You'd have trouble getting it?" Chipmunk asked.

"I'd get it, but it would take me a while. Timmy could get it much quicker."

"Okay, I'll ask him. What else?"

"Nothing, for now. Let's put these clothes back and try to leave this place like we found it."

That took another half hour. McKenna was tired and ready to leave, but Chipmunk wasn't satisfied. "Why don't we dust and water the plants before we go?" he asked.

"Just in case she's coming back?"

"Yeah, just in case."

EIGHT

It had started off as a filthy day after a long night. After arriving home, McKenna had given Angelita a break and had spent an hour walking Shane around the apartment while the baby exercised his healthy lungs. It had taken an hour to calm Shane down and get him to sleep.

At six o'clock that morning Sean had started in. Angelita had gotten up and attended to him, but he hadn't stopped screaming for another half hour. Then Janine had come into the bedroom and McKenna had kept her amused and out of Angelita's hair until breakfast.

When McKenna had been just about ready to go to work, it was Shane again. McKenna had then changed and fed him and had been poorly rewarded for his efforts. Shane was a world-class projectile vomiter and McKenna's tie had been his target of opportunity. Shane never missed, so McKenna had changed his shirt and tie and left, glad to be out.

Before going to headquarters, McKenna called information. There was a Dr. Kramer who had his office at East 72nd Street and Second Avenue. McKenna didn't like thinking about it, but if Meaghan was dead, she had probably been dead for two weeks. In that case, her dental records would be a plus in identifying her if she was found. He called the squad office and told Sheeran he would be late, then hailed a cab and headed uptown.

The doctor was in and he had a nice practice going for himself. It was fifteen minutes before Dr. Kramer was able to see him, but the dentist recognized McKenna; after explaining the situation, McKenna was able to talk him out of Meaghan's latest set of X rays. After leaving the doctor's office, he walked to Lexington Avenue and took the train to headquarters.

McKenna had just signed in and sat at his desk when Timmy JFK called with Owen's date of birth and social security number.

"How about the flights outta Montreal?" McKenna asked.

"Nothing yet with the major carriers, but it'll take me a while to go through all the smaller ones. Why don't you give me a call this afternoon?"

McKenna took Timmy JFK's number and thanked him. Then he settled into his next task, one that wouldn't be described in any report. Because of those laws and court decisions relating to privacy, another piece of useful knowledge that cannot be legally obtained by the police without a subpoena is credit information. Once again, McKenna wasn't concerned. Fortunately, like the phone companies, banks and credit card companies are in the habit of hiring retired detectives as investigators and supervisors. McKenna called Richie White, a former partner of his who had taken a job at the Eastern District Credit Bureau after he retired. He gave him Owen's information and the credit card number from the Travel Plans Unlimited receipt and spent a few minutes on hold before White came back on the line.

"You've got something there, Brian. The billing customer on that card is Owen Stafford. Card was issued to a Meaghan Maher at the customer's request."

"Any recent activity on it?"

"She doesn't use it much. Last time was February nineteenth. Charged seven hundred and eighty-two dollars at a place called Travel Plans Unlimited in Brooklyn."

She charged a trip on the day she disappeared? McKenna thought. Looks like I was right on one thing. She took herself a vacation, but why hasn't she called anyone? Because something bad has happened to her, he concluded. "What can you tell me about Stafford?"

"Good credit rating, pays his bills on time. He's got Visa, MasterCard, and American Express. Not a big spender, but a little unusual. Looks like he does most of his charging in ladies' clothes stores."

"What's his last charge?"

"More ladies' clothes. Store called *Les Robes d'Antoine* in Brussels, Belgium. February twenty-first. Spent the equivalent of four hundred and four dollars."

So two days after Meaghan charges a big trip on his card, Owen's in Brussels buying ladies' clothes. I'm getting close, McKenna thought. "Could you send me his bills for the past year?"

"Gimme your fax number."

Fifteen minutes later McKenna was examining Owen's spending habits. Richie was right on both counts. Meaghan had used her card only four times: the two trips, once at Macy's, and once at a nail salon. And like Richie had said, Owen didn't spend much on himself. Everything was Meaghan.

Owen knew his girl and he knew what made her happy. There were purchases of ladies' clothes every month, but there were big ones the previous March and August made in Washington, DC, November in New York, December back in Washington, and the one on February 21st in Brussels. McKenna tried to read some significance into those dates. He figured that Owen had been stationed in the DC area until he had been transferred to Belgium sometime this year.

This isn't so hard, McKenna thought. Meaghan's birthday was in March, so that one's easy. The photos of them both in Washington were taken in summer, so Meaghan probably went down to visit him last August, right before she went to visit her folks. Chipmunk saw them together in November, so he treated her good while he was in town. December has to be Christmas and February 21st is also easy to figure out. Meaghan had planned to go to Florida with O'Malley, but then he had come up with that

very serious trip-to-Ireland idea and they had the blowout. It's Owen she
loves, not O'Malley, so she goes to Travel Plans Unlimited and charges some
new plane tickets on Owen's card. By February 21st, she's with him in
Brussels and he's buying her clothes, as usual. But what happened there
and why hasn't she called anyone?

I sure want to talk to Owen, McKenna concluded. But first I have to
wrap this package a little tighter.

Travel Plans Unlimited was located in the rear of a real estate agency in
the fashionable Park Slope neighborhood. It had been a short trip over the
Brooklyn Bridge to get there, but while driving McKenna couldn't help
wondering why Meaghan had traveled to Brooklyn instead of patronizing
one of the hundreds of travel agencies in Manhattan.

As soon as he walked into the tiny travel office, McKenna got his answer. It had to be the friendly service, he decided.

A well-dressed middle-aged woman was sitting at one desk talking on
the phone. A name plate on her desk said she was Terry. A casually dressed
young man was manning the other desk, talking to a male customer sitting
in a chair pulled to the side of his desk. As soon as Terry saw McKenna,
she dropped the phone and her eyes went wide. "Will you look at this,
Harry?" she said in a slight brogue. "Here I am on an ordinary Friday when
who comes walking into my shop but that famous Irish detective, Brian
McKenna himself." Then she bounced out of her chair and stood next to
McKenna. "Harry! Why are you just sitting there gaping with your mouth
open? Get the camera!"

Harry was up in a flash and into the real estate office. He returned with
a 35mm camera a moment later and took three quick shots of McKenna and
Terry shaking hands. Then Terry took three of Harry and McKenna. Finally
the customer took another three of Harry, Terry, and McKenna standing
together. That finished up the film on the roll, so McKenna assumed it was
finally over. Harry and the customer sat back down and resumed their business, but Terry wasn't through with him. "Where's your family from,
Brian?" she asked him.

"New York."

"No, I mean originally. What county?"

"I'm not sure. My family's been here a long time. My father tells me
that my great-grandfather came here during the famine in forty-eight."
Since he needed information from Terry, McKenna didn't think it the opportune moment to spoil the show and tell her that his mother's family
traced their origins to the Ukraine.

"Probably Limerick," Terry pronounced. "There's McKennas all over
County Limerick. It's a proud name, you know. And what was your mother's
maiden name, if you don't mind my asking?"

McKenna was caught off balance by the question and his mind went blank. Chiml wouldn't do, he knew, but for a moment, he couldn't think of a single name that would sound Irish enough to Terry. "Murphy," he finally told her.

"Ah, Murphy," she said, thinking. "Hard to tell, really. It's another proud name all over Ireland, but enough of that. Where do you want me to send you?"

"Terry, I'm not going anywhere myself right now. I'm here to talk to you about Meaghan Maher."

The smile left Terry's face. "Meaghan? She's not in any trouble, is she?"

"Probably. As far as I can tell, this office is the last place she was seen in New York and that was on February nineteenth."

"She's disappeared?"

"Vanished, but I've got a feeling she's in Brussels. Is that where you sent her?"

"Not exactly, but that's where she wanted to go. She came in on a Thursday, I think, and she wanted the cheapest fare she could get. But she was in a hurry and wanted to be in Brussels by Monday. *Cheap* and *hurry* don't usually go together in this business, but I searched around and found her something."

"Did she say why she wanted to go to Brussels in such a hurry?"

"She said only that she was meeting a friend over there. I never get too nosy."

"Okay, go on. What did you find her?"

"Something good. Icelandair was running a special to Luxembourg with a free weekend stopover in Reykjavík, hotel included. Even with the stay, it was cheaper than anything else on such short notice and I managed to get her booked. Saved her over six hundred dollars."

Luxembourg? Another country, but just a skip and a jump from Brussels, McKenna thought. Very smart, Meaghan. But Iceland? "How can Icelandair be so much cheaper and still provide a hotel room?" he asked.

"Simple. They do it to keep their planes in the air and stay in business. You see, the airline owns quite a few of the hotels there, but they make their money in the summer when they've got close to twenty-four hours of daylight there and nice temperatures in the sixties and seventies. Very smart destination for someone looking to beat the heat in someplace nice."

"But winter is tough on them?"

"Tough, but the airline stays alive with their specials and they get people to see the place. Once they do, they all go back. I've got customers who go all the time, even in winter. They rave about it."

Not the first time I heard that, McKenna thought. Ray also raves about the place, but I always thought he was kidding me. "You've been there?"

"In this business, I get to go everywhere," Terry said proudly. "Been there winter and summer. Love it."

"Was Meaghan happy with the arrangement?"

"Once I told her about it, she was. Since it was February, I managed to get her a little more. All-you-can-eat breakfast smorgasbord at the hotel, a snowmobile trip on one of their glaciers, and tickets to the Blue Lagoon."

"Iceland has a blue lagoon?"

"It's man-made, really. Hot water runs off one of their geothermal power plants, but it's as blue as anything you'll find in the tropics. She was happy to hear that she could go swimming there."

"Swimming in Iceland in February?" McKenna asked, astounded at the thought.

"Sure, it's usually warmer there than here. The thing to remember is that Iceland is green and Greenland is ice. Catch a nice day in February and swimming's a delightful experience at the Blue Lagoon."

And right up Meaghan's alley, McKenna thought. Snowmobiling and swimming. That accounts for her ski jacket being missing and she must have a bathing suit I don't know about. But I was wrong on one point. She wasn't shopping in Brussels with Owen on February twenty-first. She was spending her free weekend in Iceland then, but Owen knew she was coming and was buying her some welcome-to-Brussels gifts. Now it's time for that sensitive question. "Was it harder to get her a flight out of Montreal than it would have been from New York?"

Terry eyed him suspiciously. "Who said she left from Montreal?"

"Me, and we both know why. I know she's illegal, but that doesn't matter to me. If I'm gonna find her, I need all her flight information from you and I can't have you dancing around it."

Terry thought that over, then came to a decision. "You know, I wouldn't be telling this to you if you weren't a hundred percent Irish. You couldn't beat it out of me, but you must understand how hard it is for them."

"You mean the Irish immigrants?"

"Sure. They come to this country and work hard. While they're breaking their backs to earn a living, they're worrying all the time and looking over their shoulders because of those silly immigration quotas we have now. Meanwhile, we let in all those Koreans, Filipinos, and Indians and they don't have a care in the world."

Those Koreans, Filipinos, and Indians she's talking about aren't exactly a bunch of slackers, either, McKenna thought, but he didn't want to pursue that line with the very pro-Irish Terry. "How did she get to Montreal?"

"I booked her on the Amtrak overnight."

"Was that included in the seven hundred and eighty-two dollars she charged here?"

"No, she had to pay at the ticket counter at Penn Station. I booked her round-trip."

"So she left New York on Friday and was scheduled to fly from Montreal on Friday, February twentieth. Right?"

"Yes, arriving in Iceland at eight in the morning on February twenty-first."

"When was she scheduled to return?"

"That was a one-week excursion plan," Terry said, looking at the calendar on her desk. "Back into Montreal on Saturday, February twenty-eighth."

"Does she go back through Iceland?"

"Just changes planes there. Then she was booked on the overnight Amtrak again from Montreal. She should have been home on March first."

"How well do you know Meaghan?"

"As well as I know a lot of those kids working the bars and restaurants in Manhattan. Only met her twice, but one of the others must have sent her to see me. I've got a pretty good reputation with them."

"I can see why," McKenna said. "If I were in their position, I'd trust you myself."

Terry preened at the compliment. "Are you going to find her?" she asked.

"Yes. Thanks to you, I'll find her."

The way McKenna said it didn't relieve Terry's concern. "Do you think something bad happened to her?"

"Yes, I'm afraid so."

NINE

As soon as he got back to the office McKenna called Timmy JFK and gave him all the Icelandair flight numbers he had obtained from Terry.

"What do you want me to do now?" Timmy asked. "Make sure she caught all her flights?"

"Please. I appreciate you going to all this trouble."

"Anything for Chip. Besides, you're making this easy now," Timmy said. "Get back to you in half an hour."

McKenna was feeling good about his progress, but, as usual, any time there was progress on a case, paperwork had to be done. He had many complaint follow-ups to do, with each step he had taken in the investigation described on a separate report. Timmy JKF's half hour passed and he kept on typing. After an hour he had finished his paperwork and was growing apprehensive. He was just about to call Timmy back when his phone rang.

"She's in Iceland," Timmy said.

"Are you sure?"

"Certain. She left Montreal on February twentieth, as scheduled, and got to Iceland all right. She was supposed to leave there at eight A.M. on the twenty-third on flight one-ten. She never showed. I checked every flight out of Reykjavík from the time she got there to now. She's there."

"You check the other airlines?"

"That's what took me so long, but it wasn't a big problem. The only airlines flying in or out of there are Icelandair and KLM. She didn't leave on either one."

"Thanks a lot, Timmy. Any favor I can do for you, you got it."

"I know that. Hope this helps you some."

"It confuses me some, but I'll start working on this new angle," Mc-Kenna said before hanging up. Now what? he wondered, but only briefly. He knew just where to go with his problem. Ray was the one.

Brunette and McKenna had a lot in common, and one of those things was that they both had served in the Marine Corps. However, Brunette was ten years older than McKenna and had enlisted in the peacetime Marine Corps in 1954. So, while McKenna had spent almost two tours as a machine-gunner in the hills and jungles of Vietnam, Brunette had spent a good part of his four years as a spit-and-polish marine guard at the U.S. Embassy in Reykjavík, Iceland. Consequently, Brunette had loved his time in the corps because he and McKenna had experienced different problems. While Brunette might have been worried about running out of shoe polish or Brasso, McKenna's main fear had been running out of ammo.

In Iceland Brunette had become friends with a young constable. A lovable giant, but a smart, tough guy was the way Brunette described him whenever he was in a reminiscing mood. They had kept in touch over the years and McKenna had even met him once when he had visited Brunette in New York. Brunette thought it ironic that both he and Janus had risen to head their departments, but McKenna dismissed the coincidence as just another case of smart people knowing other smart people.

Before phoning Brunette, McKenna decided to call Mrs. Maher and fill her in on some of the latest developments. Sheeran was out to lunch, so McKenna went into his office and called Ireland. For the first time, his call didn't catch her asleep. "We're closer, Peggy," he told her. "I've tracked her to Iceland."

"Iceland? What would she be doing in Iceland?"

"She was on her way to Brussels to meet a friend. She was supposed to stay in Iceland for the weekend, but she never made her connecting flight. She's still there."

"Since when?"

"She got there on February twenty-first and had been scheduled to leave on the twenty-third."

"Then this really isn't good news, is it? She doesn't know anybody in Iceland."

"No, I don't consider it good news, but I promised to keep you up to date."

"Was it her secret boyfriend she was meeting in Brussels?"

The question caught McKenna by surprise. He had intended to dance around the subject for now, but Peggy already knew something. How much? he wondered. "Yes, she was on her way to meet her secret boyfriend. Did she tell you about him?"

"Never mentioned a word, and she usually tells me about all the men in her life."

"Then how'd you know?"

"Chris O'Malley. Whenever he calls, he never misses a chance to say that Meaghan being gone must have something to do with her secret boyfriend."

"How does O'Malley know about him?"

"He doesn't, for sure. He just suspects that there's somebody else in Meaghan's life and so do we. She hasn't mentioned anything about a boyfriend in over a year."

"What about O'Malley. Didn't she talk about him?"

"She used to, but not for a while. Meaghan wants to get married and have children someday, but she'd never marry Chris."

"She ever say why?"

"Because she doesn't love him anymore. She never said so, but I think it has something to do with him being illegal over there, like she is."

"So you think Meaghan would only marry somebody who's here legally?"

"No, more than that. I think Meaghan would only marry an American. She loves it there and has always thought of herself as an American. I'm certain she'd want her children to be as well."

McKenna didn't say it, but Meaghan marrying an American would make her legal and end her major problem in life. I'm sure she's already figured that out, he thought.

"Is her new boyfriend in some kind of trouble?" Mrs. Maher asked.

"Not yet. He knew Meaghan was coming to meet him, but I don't think he has anything to do with her disappearance. From what I know about him, he seems like a fine man."

"Thank God!" Mrs. Maher said, relieved. "Since Meaghan never told us about him, we were wondering if he was some kind of criminal."

"Not even close. He's a soldier, a first lieutenant in the U.S. Army. He's stationed in Brussels now."

"A soldier? Just like Meaghan to fall in love with a soldier. Can you tell me his name?"

"Owen Stafford."

"Stafford? That's not an Irish name, but Meaghan never attached any importance to where a person's family was from. But I'm still wondering why she never told us about him."

"I think she wanted it to be a surprise," McKenna said, figuring he was making the understatement of the day.

Brunette had a busy schedule that day, so it was six o'clock before he could see McKenna. After getting his reports signed and discussing the case with Sheeran, McKenna had an up-to-date case folder under his arm. He didn't believe that his friendship with Brunette provided any excuses for shoddy work or casual lapses in procedure.

"You hungry?" Brunette asked as soon as McKenna walked into his office.

"I could be, but you know I can never be sure."

"Okay, I understand. Call Angelita and find out."

Since the arrival of the twins, McKenna knew that Angelita had her hands full and she counted on help from him. He had worked sixteen hours the day before, leaving everything to her, and she had mentioned something that morning about going out to dinner together. It was tough for them to get a baby-sitter with the crew they now had at home, but if she had, he didn't want to disappoint her.

Brunette really did understand. He had met Angelita a few weeks after McKenna, when she had been a rookie cop, and they had become fast friends over the years. The Job hadn't been for Angelita, but she understood it most of the time and respected the work McKenna did, sometimes. She couldn't see losing a minute of her time with McKenna unless he had to stay late working a case she would consider important.

Over the years McKenna and Angelita had come to an understanding of what important was. One low-life drug dealer shooting another in some territorial dispute wasn't important, and his note-passer cases certainly didn't measure up. But if McKenna told her a case was important, then she knew it was and he would eventually have to give her the details.

McKenna didn't mind discussing his important cases with Angelita, and many times he looked forward to her input. She was loaded with insight, common sense, and had a true, unflattering understanding of human nature. Although he didn't talk about it around the office, more than once she had helped him by catching a point he had missed because he had been standing too close to it.

So McKenna called Angelita. For once, there was no crying in the background when she answered the phone and he felt relieved about that.

"How was your day," he asked.

"Wonderful! Janine's finally beginning to make some sense when she tries Spanish and the boys have been great. I had time to do my whole workout. Got muscles aching right now that I forgot I had."

"You still have your heart set on going to dinner?"

"I could, but what's that in your voice? Change of plans?"

How does she always know what I'm going to say before I say it? "This new case I'm working on is important and I have to talk it over with Ray. I haven't eaten a thing all day and he's hungry, so maybe we'll talk over dinner."

"Just as well. I'm close, but I haven't gotten anything definite on a baby-sitter. Where you going to eat?"

"Probably Forlini's."

"Good. Bon appétit and bring me home some of their eggplant parmigiana."

That was easy, McKenna thought. "You got it. Thanks, baby. I'll make it up to you."

"Okay, let's try this again," Brunette said as soon as McKenna hung up. "You hungry?"

"Now I'm absolutely certain of it. I'm starving."

Forlini's is an old, moderately upscale Italian restaurant located on Baxter Street in Little Italy, a few blocks from police headquarters and the courts. It is a favored eating place and watering hole among detectives, lawyers, and judges, three groups of people who are usually mutually exclusive and have nothing but disdain for one another.

In any other setting, lawyers, judges, and detectives would be quick to point out that everything wrong in society is due to the incompetence, laziness, avarice, and dishonesty inherent in the flawed characters of the other two groups. By tradition, in Forlini's they all get along and members of one group even render grudging respect to members of the other two. It has been likened to a Frenchman, an Englishman, and an Irishman having dinner together on the space shuttle while orbiting the Earth.

When McKenna and Brunette showed up at the door, they were met by Nicky, the son of the owner, and shown to their usual table in the rear. While passing though the dining room they exchanged handshakes, pleasantries, and compliments with many of the lawyers and judges eating there, about half of whom McKenna and Brunette despised.

Over dinner McKenna explained everything he had done in the case so far, leaving out nothing. Brunette had few questions. While waiting for their espresso after dinner, Brunette asked to see the case folder.

As long as there was a chance Meaghan was alive, McKenna had no desire to finish off Lieutenant George Mosley. He had been hoping that Brunette wouldn't ask to see the folder, but figured that he would. Brunette would want to know every detail about his department's case before discussing it with another sharp guy like Janus.

Brunette had been a supervisor in the detective bureau for most of his career and had reviewed thousands of case folders. He knew that whispered words can scream on paper and he had learned to see through every written attempt at ambiguity. He also knew the difference between what the rules said *could* be done in any case and what really *should* be done to solve it and put the bad guy away.

Walsh's work didn't take Brunette long to go through and he unconsciously nodded his approval as he read. Then he came to Swaggart's reports and McKenna braced himself.

It took Brunette under a minute. Then, eyes wide in disbelief, he read it again. "Good God!" was all he said before glancing at McKenna's reports and returning the folder to him.

McKenna knew that a simple *"Good God!"* from Brunette could easily translate into an enduring *"God-awful!"* for Mosley, but he didn't want to know what was going through Brunette's mind. Even in his late forties and after having spent years in homicide squads, McKenna still closed his eyes at the scary parts in horror films.

The waiter came with their espresso and Angelita's order. McKenna felt it was a good time to change the subject. "When are you going to call Janus?"

"As soon as I get back to the office."

"Tonight? Isn't it pretty late there now?"

"Makes no difference. Icelanders never know what time it is."

"Why's that?"

"Daylight for most of the summer and darkness for most of the winter. Add in that most of them work two jobs anyway and you've got people with no biological clock. Besides, it's a big country and Janus doesn't have many people. I want to get him started looking for her as soon as possible."

"Not much crime there?" McKenna asked.

"I believe that they're the most underemployed police in the world."

After returning to the office to sign out, McKenna took a cab home for a relaxing evening with Angelita. But it wasn't to be. Before he could get out of the taxi in front of the Gramercy Park Hotel, the doorman raced over with a message. Brunette wanted him back at headquarters.

McKenna realized at once that the message meant trouble on two fronts. Brunette had reached Janus and had received some disturbing news requiring immediate attention. That was bad enough, but what troubled him more at the moment was the order of eggplant parmigiana on his lap. That meant personal trouble because Angelita expected him upstairs and she hated eating alone.

McKenna thought about bringing the food up to her and offering an explanation, but decided that the coward's way out was called for this time. He gave the order to the doorman and asked him to have it brought up to Angelita, then told the cab driver to take him to headquarters.

Brunette was sitting at his desk and on the phone when McKenna walked into his office. "He's here now. Talk to you later," Brunette said before hanging up.

"Angelita?" McKenna asked.

"Yeah. Just squaring some things away on the home front for you, Buddy. Pull up a chair."

McKenna did. "Who called who?"

"I called her, figured you'd be in some trouble about coming back here."

"You had that right."

"How come you didn't tell her what you've been up to? I had to explain the whole thing to her."

"I was going to, but we haven't had a lot of time to talk in the last few days."

"Well, I told her all about it. She's interested."

Angelita thinks it's an interesting case? Good! McKenna thought. "What did she say?"

"Said she wanted you to get the guy who killed Meaghan Maher, but that's not gonna happen."

It was expected, but Brunette's statement still put a knot in McKenna's stomach. "She's dead?"

"Looks that way. On March second the body of a red-headed girl washed up on one of the big islands off the coast of Iceland. They weren't able to identify her, but they think she's connected somehow to the bombing."

The murder of the British foreign secretary and his wife in Iceland had been front-page news worldwide for a few days. McKenna had followed the story with some interest until the coverage ended, which meant to him that the investigation wasn't going well in Iceland. Just another IRA bombing that would never be solved, he had concluded. But how could Meaghan have been involved in that? Couldn't be, he decided. "When was the bombing?"

"Same day. March second, around one in the morning."

"How long had she been dead when they found her?"

"The body had been in the water for about a week, but she had been seen in the company of the guy they suspect did the bombing."

"When?" McKenna asked.

"She had dinner with him in a Reykjavík restaurant on the night of February twenty-first."

Her first night in Iceland and also the day Owen was in Brussels buying clothes for her, McKenna thought. "So the bomber killed her and blew up the Brits a week later."

"That's the way it looks. The Icelandic police have her as either another victim or an untrusted accomplice who was tortured and killed."

"Tortured?" The knot in McKenna's stomach tightened.

"Yeah. According to Janus, she was in pretty bad shape when she washed up. Her fingers had been cut off, her teeth had been knocked out, and her nipples were gone. Rope burns on her wrists and ankles, her face battered beyond recognition, bruises and burns all over her body."

"Sounds like a sex killing to me," McKenna observed."

"I agree, but apparently the Icelanders don't."

"Why do you say that? Because they're thinking that maybe Meaghan was IRA?"

"Yeah, but I can see how they made the jump. Janus must be under a lot of pressure with a double political murder on his hands."

"We're not making that jump, are we?" McKenna asked.

"You tell me, but I know that sex killings aren't the IRA style. Their people take a puritan, purely political approach to murder."

"Then the Icelanders are wrong. Unless she's been fooling everyone, including me, Meaghan wouldn't have anything to do with the IRA. Her brother was killed in the British Army and I know she doesn't hate the Brits. She's a peace-loving girl."

"Unfortunately, that's not our concern. All the Icelanders want from us is to get their body identified."

I don't like that slant, McKenna thought. But even identifying her could be a problem. No fingers, no teeth, a battered face, and a week in the water. "Okay. It's gonna be tough on everybody, but if it's Meaghan they've got, I'll get her identified."

"How? Chris O'Malley?"

"Yeah, O'Malley. He knows her well and has seen her naked, so he fits the bill. Then what?"

"Then nothing. Talk to O'Malley and send him over there. If he identifies her, you've closed your missing persons case."

McKenna saw the logic of Brunette's decision, but disagreed with it. "You and I both know that if that's Meaghan, it's not a missing persons case anymore. She's not IRA, she's a victim. One of our people has been tortured and then murdered."

"Now you sound like Angelita," Brunette said, smiling. "Think maybe you're getting too close on this one?"

Ray's right, McKenna realized. I've been violating one of the cardinal rules. "Maybe I am taking this too personal, but I think we should take a look at it."

"Technically, Meaghan Maher is not one of our people, remember? She's an illegal alien."

"Just a technicality. She's an American as far as I'm concerned. An innocent American tortured and murdered by terrorists in a foreign country. If she were Jewish and we thought the Palestinians were involved, think about what the reaction of our government would be then. Not to mention the Israeli government. The FBI, the CIA, the Mossad, and Lord-knows-who-else would all be in Iceland right now, poking around."

"You want to go to Iceland?"

"Yes."

"And do what, if it's her?"

"Just take a look at it and at least establish that she's an innocent victim."

Brunette sat back in his chair and appeared to be thinking over Mc-Kenna's request. "Janus tells me he's got his best man assigned and that he's already getting some help from the Brits," he said, but he seemed to be talking to himself as he thought.

"His best man? How good could he be?" McKenna asked.

"Janus said he's solved every murder in Iceland in the past twelve years."

So maybe he is pretty good, McKenna thought. "How many murders is that?"

"Four."

"Four? Give me a break, Ray!" McKenna said, standing up. "We don't have a man in any of our homicide squads who hasn't solved four murders this year, and we're only in March. How good can this guy really be?"

"Janus says he's good. If they had more murders, he'd solve more murders."

"I should still go."

Brunette thought a moment longer, then appeared to reach his decision. "What the hell, the cardinal's involved. Go, but there have to be some ground rules."

"I know. Be polite, ooh-and-aah over the fine work they've done so far, and don't get in the way."

"And no gun. The police there usually don't carry."

"Okay, and no gun," McKenna agreed. "But I just thought of another problem. O'Malley's also here illegally and might have a hard time getting back into the U.S."

"I'll take care of it," Brunette said simply.

Taking care of it meant talking to Gene Shields, McKenna realized. Shields was the head of the New York office of the FBI and had worked with McKenna and Brunette in the past. He was a good friend to both and a man of extraordinary influence in federal circles. "Okay, so I'll book a flight out for tomorrow?" McKenna asked.

"I've already taken care of it," Brunette said, smiling. "I've got you and O'Malley on the Icelandair flight out of JFK, leaves at eight tomorrow night."

God! I love this man, but why does he do these things to me? McKenna asked himself, then answered his own question. Ray wasn't sure if it was the right thing to do, so he used me again as a sounding board. He also wanted to see if I was as personally committed to this case as he thought I was. "I guess Janus already knows I'm coming?"

"Yeah, says he's looking forward to seeing you again. He's going to pick you up at the airport himself."

"And I guess Angelita already knows I'm going?"

"Sure. After I explained what's happened in this case so far, I waited for her to suggest it. She's smart and logical and asked the same questions you just did. She said she's not crazy about the idea, but told me that you going to Iceland with O'Malley was the only thing that made sense."

"Well thanks for that and thanks for breaking my balls so professionally."

"My pleasure. But while you're over there, please keep one thing in mind."

"I know. Officially, it's not our case."

TEN

When McKenna finally did get home, Meaghan Maher and her family were all Angelita wanted to hear about. The twins had been good all day, Janine had been a pleasure to have around, and the kids were all sleeping soundly. It was finally time to talk objectively about something important, and that was always done at the dining room table with Angelita sitting across from McKenna. No touching was the rule, just talk until the matter at hand was resolved.

Many people who knew Angelita would characterize her as difficult. This trait McKenna overlooked because, as he told himself whenever she was acting up, getting the best things in life should be difficult. Along with McKenna's love, Angelita also constantly earned his respect. She was slow to trust and disliked people in general, but individuals were a different matter. For those few she liked and admired, she would do anything. In addition, she had a finely tuned, though unorthodox, sense of justice. According to her, bad things should always happen to those who do bad things to good people. Always, no matter what.

McKenna agreed in theory, but professionalism and a desire to avoid prison kept him from acting fully in accordance with their shared beliefs. He was never one to physically abuse prisoners and was courteous to every suspect, no matter how heinous the crime. He hurt them by sending them to jail, frequently bending the convoluted judicial rules along the way to get his evidence admitted and heard by the jury.

After talking the case over, Angelita now liked Meaghan and thought she was a good person. It followed that whoever killed her was a bad person and bad things should happen to him. "You have to get the monster who did this," she told him.

Typically, Angelita disregarded not only judicial procedures, but also important things like internationally recognized police procedures, time, distance, and national boundaries. "I don't know if that's possible," he said. "The Brits have been dealing with IRA bombers and assassins for years and they haven't been having much luck."

"So? You haven't been dealing with them until now."

"Don't you see a few problems here?"

"No, I don't. An innocent person from New York has been murdered, and one thing you're good at is solving murders and tracking down the people who commit them," she said as a simple statement of fact. "Come to think of it, you're probably the best."

McKenna was introspective by nature, self-critical, and well aware of his faults and shortcomings. While never considered a braggart, he still knew he was good at what he did. But the best? "Baby, I appreciate the compliment, but I think you might be overstating the case."

"No I'm not. Ray says the same thing, told me again tonight. Said she's dead two weeks already and nobody's come up with anything. According to him, the only way to solve it is to send you to Iceland."

McKenna immediately went up another hat size, but then realized what Brunette had done. I could learn something here, he thought. Ray wanted to send me anyway, but he figured that Angelita had to be kept happy for me to operate effectively. So what does he do? Plays to the pride she has in me. So I'm going to Iceland and better yet, Angelita wants me to go.

What do I say now that won't break the bubble? he wondered. "Okay. I'm going to Iceland and I'm gonna find the man who murdered three people there," he tried, sounding as modest as he could.

"No, you're going there to find the man who killed Meaghan," Angelita said, looking at him strangely, as if she suddenly doubted his intelligence. "The other two aren't important and have almost nothing to do with it."

"The British foreign secretary and his wife aren't important?"

"No. Those were just political assassinations. They have nothing to do with Meaghan or us."

"But they were probably killed by the same man. That's not important?"

"Only if it helps you to find him," Angelita explained as if she was talking to Janine. "Don't you see that?"

McKenna didn't, at first. But then he thought about it some more, hoping it wasn't taking him too long to figure out what was patently obvious to Angelita. Finally he got it. "One has nothing to do with the other," he said. "Killing the foreign secretary and his wife was just his reason for being in Iceland."

Either Angelita broke the no-touching rule or the matter was resolved to her satisfaction. She reached across the table and took his hand. "Of course," she said, proud of him once more. "Killing the foreign secretary and his wife was just his job and makes no difference to us. It wouldn't matter if he was a truck driver or a milkman. Work is work and apparently he does well in his occupation. Meaghan Maher he killed for fun, something that probably had nothing to do with his job."

"Naturally," he agreed, as if he knew it all along. "I'm just chasing another psycho sadistic sex murderer, an animal with a sick, perverted mind who just happens to blow people up for a living."

"Right. He might be flawless in his work, but when he's at play and enjoying himself by torturing our poor Meaghan? Who knows?"

"I do. He made mistakes. They always do."

"And you'll find those mistakes and get him, right?" Angelita asked, squeezing McKenna's hand and giving him that smile he loved but hadn't seen too much, lately.

Under the circumstances, there was only one answer. "Right."

"Brian, you're so smart that I just have to love you. What do you say we go to bed?"

"And go to sleep?"

"Of course not."

McKenna was awakened at ten o'clock by Janine tugging at the blankets, but he teased her by keeping his eyes closed. He felt refreshed and well rested, although he had been only half-asleep for hours. He had first stirred when Angelita had gotten up for the 6:00 A.M. feeding, but she had kindly insisted that he stay in bed. Since he would be traveling all night and wasn't due at the office that day, he had been content to lie there, listening to the sounds of his family when they were all being good.

Then Janine tugged at the blankets again and yelled impatiently, *"Despiértate, Popí. Por favor, despiértate."*

As requested, McKenna opened his eyes wide and sat up in bed. Janine held out her arms to be picked up and he complied, hugging his show-off smart little girl with the Irish face, the Spanish complexion, and the French name.

McKenna was sure that Janine had made that major language leap in his absence during the past few days, a leap in understanding common in bilingual families. Finally, her confusion was gone. She had called him *Popí* instead of *Daddy* when she talked to him in Spanish. She was getting it straight that the same thing or person was called by different names in Spanish and English.

But he wanted to be sure. Unlike Angelita, McKenna spoke Spanish with an accent, one he didn't want Janine picking up. Sometimes he spoke to Angelita in Spanish just so Janine would think it natural that everyone spoke the language, but when he spoke directly to Janine, it was always in English. Still, he looked forward to the day she knew enough to make fun of his accent. "Has my little girl been good today?" he asked.

"*Sí, Popí. Estoy buena.*"

Now who's teasing who? McKenna asked himself. "Don't tell me that my smart little girl forgot how to speak English," he said, tweaking her nose and assaulting her pride.

"No, I didn't forget. See? I still talk English."

"Oh yeah? What's my name?"

"Daddy. Did you forget?"

Perfect, perfect, perfect! It won't be long before we're on to French, McKenna thought. "Yes, Daddy forgot his name for a minute. Good thing you remembered."

Then Janine tweaked his nose. "Fibber," she said, quite sure of herself.

Two years old and already she's got my number, McKenna thought. If she were a judge, I'd be in on my way to jail. Guess I got myself a tough eighteen years ahead raising this little girl.

Then Meaghan popped into his head and spoiled the mood. Somebody had destroyed more than one life when they killed that other tough, smart girl. McKenna winced and shuddered as he imagined himself in the shoes of Meaghan's parents. "Who do you never talk to?" he asked Janine.

"Strangers!" she shouted at once.

"My, you really are a smart little girl."

For the rest of the morning, McKenna did the things he loved doing, and it seemed that everyone appreciated having him around. He played with Janine and listened to her proudly name objects around the apartment in both Spanish and English, he had a nice breakfast with Angelita while Janine had fun destroying a coloring book with her interpretation of art, and then he fed and changed the boys, one at a time, without incident. But there were a few unpleasant tasks that had to be performed that day, and Angelita had to be told.

"I have to go out for a while," he said to her after he put Shane in his bassinet.

"I know."

"You do?"

"Sure. Someone in Meaghan's family has to be told what you think happened to her in Iceland, right?"

"Right. Go on," McKenna urged, prepared to be mystified once again by Angelita's logic and foresight.

"Therefore, knowing you, you'll go see her brother the priest. You'll tell him and he'll tell her mother."

"Right again. But how did you know that?"

"Easy. Because we both know that you're a big, soft, cowardly sissy, don't we?"

"I guess we both do," McKenna admitted as he grabbed her and hugged her. "But can we pretend every once in a while that I'm the only one who knows?" he asked, whispering in her ear.

"Okay, next time we'll pretend. I promise."

"And here's something you haven't thought of, yet. There's somebody else I have to go see."

Angelita pushed him away and stared at him with laughter in her eyes. "You mean you have to go see Chris O'Malley to ruin his life and tell him he's going to Iceland in about eight hours."

Damn!

"Please come in," the cardinal's housekeeper told McKenna. "His Eminence is expecting you."

He is? How would the cardinal know I was coming? McKenna wondered as the housekeeper showed him to a large waiting room off the entrance hallway. And how come everyone in town lately knows where I'm going before I do myself?

Has to be Ray, McKenna concluded. He called to tell the cardinal what's happened and he knows me. Like Angelita, he figured I'd rather tell the bad news to Meaghan's brother the priest than give it to Mrs. Maher.

McKenna settled into an overstuffed leather chair and waited in the old-fashioned, mahogany-paneled room. When the cardinal came in, his appearance surprised McKenna. The man in charge of the archdiocese of New York looked like an ordinary man in the street, wearing blue jeans, a flannel shirt, and loafers. McKenna stood up and the cardinal offered his hand. "Thanks for coming, Brian. And thanks for working so fast and so hard on this."

None of that kiss-the-ring stuff from this cardinal, McKenna thought as he shook the cardinal's hand. "I guess Ray told you what happened?"

"Yes, he called me this morning. Terrible thing. Just horrible."

"Did you tell her brother about it?" McKenna asked hopefully.

"I would have, but Ray told me you'd probably be around."

That's too bad, McKenna thought. I was so close to getting out of this job, and then Ray had to spoil it. "Is Father Maher up to this kind of news?"

"Nobody is, really, but he's a tough man in a sensitive kind of way. He was very close to Meaghan and we saw quite a bit of her around here. I know he misses her already, and so do I, but I'm sure he's been expecting bad news all along."

"What did you think of her?" McKenna asked.

"Delightful young lady, charming and so full of life. When Father Maher first arrived, I gave him a week off and she was here every morning to show him around the city. They had a ball together."

"Where is he now?"

"Upstairs. He's been helping me get my sermon together for St. Patrick's Day."

"Well, we might as well get this over with."

"Do you want me to stick around while you tell him about it?" the cardinal asked.

"Please. I'm not too good at this sort of thing, so I wouldn't mind if you jumped in if you see me floundering."

"Just between you and me, I'm not too good at it, either. Done it hundreds of times, but it never gets any easier to tell folks that their loved ones are dead."

Just great, McKenna thought as the cardinal left. I was counting on help from him, and now he tells me that he's a sissy like me. McKenna paced and fidgeted, trying to get his thoughts together until the cardinal returned with Father Maher.

McKenna had seen pictures of Meaghan's brother, but they hadn't accurately conveyed what he was like. He was photogenic, looking relaxed and easy-going in Meaghan's photos of him, but that wasn't the man McKenna was looking at now. He appeared apprehensive, but he hadn't forgotten his manners. "Ryer Maher," he said, offering his hand. "So good of you to come, Detective McKenna. My mother's become quite a fan of yours."

"A pleasure to meet you, but I'm afraid I've got some bad news," McKenna said, shaking the priest's hand.

"Meaghan?"

"Yes, Meaghan. It looks like she's dead. The police in Iceland have a body that matches her description and that was the last place I tracked her to."

McKenna figured that Ryer must have spoken to his mother that day, because he didn't ask McKenna what his sister was doing in Iceland, the logical next question. Instead, he asked, "How did she die?"

"She was murdered," McKenna said, hoping he could leave it at that.

He couldn't. Ryer reacted to the statement as if he had been punched. His head snapped back and he rubbed his jaw, but he remained in control of his emotions. "Did she suffer?" he asked.

Here comes the really hard part, McKenna thought. Might as well just say it and get it over with. "Yes, she suffered. She was tortured before she died."

"What was it? A sex attack?"

"I think so, but I'm going to Iceland to be sure."

"God help us!" Ryer said, more to himself than to McKenna. He remained straight and erect, but his eyes filled with tears. "Poor Meaghan. How can I tell my poor mother and father about this? How can I tell them that our Meaghan was horribly murdered by some animal, alone and so far from home?" he asked, looking to McKenna for an answer.

You got me, McKenna thought, embarrassed as he felt his own eyes filling. He looked to the cardinal for help, but that other big sissy also was close to tears.

However, the cardinal came through. "I'll tell her if you prefer, but it would be better coming from you."

"I agree," McKenna said, glad that he wasn't to be the one to do it.

"You're right, of course," Ryer said. "Can you give me the details?"

The three men sat down and McKenna told Ryer what he had learned. The priest followed McKenna's account with interest, but without a single question. When McKenna told him about Owen Stafford, he expected some reaction, but got none. McKenna concluded that Ryer knew his sister better than he had believed and got the impression Owen's race wasn't a matter of great importance to him; what was important was that Meaghan had loved Owen and he had made her happy.

Ryer's questions came when McKenna thought he had finished. "Are you going to be able to find the person who did this?"

"Officially, it's not an NYPD case, but I'm going to try. If it's any consolation, I've got the backing of our police commissioner and he's a man of some influence."

"If it helps, you also have my backing," the cardinal added. "Anything I can do to help you along, just let me know."

If it helps? Are you kidding? McKenna thought. One phone call from you to the mayor and the entire Major Case Squad is transferred to Iceland for the duration. "Thank you, Your Eminence. That's good to know."

"If you do find him, what do you think will happen to this man?" Ryer asked.

"Depends on where he goes. If he's in Ireland, maybe not much. Finding him and arresting him there might be difficult."

"No it won't," Ryer countered. "If you find that he fled to Ireland, just let me know. Even if he's with the IRA, our people have a very low tolerance for sexual psychopaths who murder young Irish girls."

"I'll keep that in mind," McKenna said.

"Now I need two favors from you," Ryer said.

"Anything."

"I would like Lieutenant Stafford's phone number. I think he should be at the funeral, if he cares to come."

"Certainly," McKenna said, happy to be relieved of another chore. He took his notepad out and gave Ryer the number of the guard company in Brussels. "What else?"

"I assume the Icelandic police will release the body so it can be shipped to Ireland?"

"I don't see why not."

"Then, I know it's a lot to ask, but could you find a good undertaker and have her embalmed in Iceland before the body is shipped? I don't want my mother to see Meaghan in the condition she's in right now. I'll pay you back, whatever it costs."

"I'll take care of it. Now I have a question for you. How would you describe Meaghan's politics?"

"Well, as you know, she can't vote here. If she could, I'd call her a Liberal Democrat."

"That's not what I mean. How did she view the political situation in Northern Ireland?"

"I don't think she even thought about it and probably couldn't care less. Meaghan thought of herself as an American. I think that if somebody pressed her for her views on Northern Ireland, she'd probably say that killing people over religion was stupid."

Smart girl, McKenna thought. "Thanks. I just had to know that."

"Why?"

"Because it's my understanding that the police in Iceland have some kind of notion that Meaghan might have been involved with the IRA."

"Ridiculous."

"That's what I said. They're probably not too bright."

ELEVEN

It had been a smooth flight, but a horrible time. McKenna had wanted to finish the book on the IRA he had brought, but that hadn't been possible with Chris O'Malley sitting next to him. The large young man had wanted to do nothing but talk about Meaghan and cry. Feeling sorry for him, McKenna had comforted O'Malley for most of the flight. By the time they landed at 8:00 A.M., McKenna was extremely uncomfortable, feeling they were the object of attention of every other passenger on the plane.

As promised, Janus was at the gate to meet them. The big man was dressed in a white suit, white bucks, and a white tie, evoking in McKenna the image of a polar bear dressed for his First Holy Communion. None of the Icelanders leaving the plane ahead of them thought Janus's appearance out of the ordinary. They all stopped to greet him so that McKenna felt like he was on a receiving line before it was finally his turn.

"Good to see you again, Janus," McKenna said.

"Thank you for coming, Brian," Janus replied. "Nice flight, I hope?"

"Not too bad," McKenna answered, then introduced O'Malley.

Janus took one look at the red-eyed O'Malley and said, "I'm truly sorry about your girlfriend. She must have been very pretty and quite a girl."

"What do you mean, *'must have been'*?" O'Malley asked. "Did he beat her that badly?"

"I'm sorry, but yes. You should prepare yourself because I think you're going to have a hard time recognizing her."

O'Malley's eyes filled with tears again, but there was still something he wanted to know. "What makes you think she was quite a girl?"

"Because the killer didn't take her easy. According to the Saga Hotel staff and from the video we have of him, she must have fought very hard. He had quite a black eye and she might even have broken his nose."

"Then I don't have to see her. That's Meaghan," O'Malley said proudly, talking from experience. "She's the toughest woman I ever met."

"I'm afraid that you'll still have to identify her, Chris," Janus said sympathetically.

"When will that be?"

"Did you eat on the plane?"

"Yes."

"Then we should wait a while. Maybe this afternoon sometime we'll go to the morgue."

Janus's simple suggestion caused a look of terror to pass over O'Malley's face and did nothing to ease the new knot developing in McKenna's stomach.

Janus led them through the terminal, stopping at Immigration and Customs only long enough for Janus to return the agents' waves. Within minutes they were in his Volvo.

"What's the plan for now?" McKenna asked.

"I'm going to take you to meet Thor. He's the man in charge of the investigation and he's here at the airport. You two will have a lot to talk about, so I'll take Chris to the hotel and you can come into town later with Thor."

"What's Thor's last name?" McKenna asked.

"Officially, he's Senior Investigating Constable Thor Eríkson, but Thor will do here. Icelanders don't use titles and last names much."

"Why not?" McKenna asked.

"Because here Thor Eríkson means only that he's Thor, the son of Erík."

Simple enough, but a man could go a long way with a name like Thor Eríkson, McKenna thought. Could be a tough name to live up to.

After a few minutes of driving, Janus slowed as he approached a gate with a U.S. Marine MP on guard. The marine saluted, then waved Janus's car through.

"We have a base here?" McKenna asked.

"U.S. Naval Air Station, the only military base in the country," Janus answered.

"What do they do?"

"Used to keep track of Soviet submarines in the North Atlantic. Now, I guess, they don't do much of anything."

"Do the Icelanders mind an American base in the country?"

"Some of them used to, but not anymore. Used to be demonstrations here about once a year protesting the foreign presence, but then somebody figured out that the base employs about ten percent of the total workforce in the Reykjavík area. Now our government is petitioning yours to keep the base open."

Janus drove through the base, then followed a service road until he came to five olive-drab trailers arranged in a circle. There was another marine MP there standing guard in the rain. He also saluted and waved the Volvo into the circle of trailers.

McKenna was surprised to see an old souped-up Mustang parked outside one of the trailers. It was the kind of car an American teenager would own.

Janus pulled in next to the Mustang. "That's Thor's car," he said, smiling and shaking his head as he looked at it. "It's his one concession to lunacy.

You'll find him inside. If you like, I'll have your luggage brought up to your room at the hotel."

"Thank you. Which hotel are we staying at?"

"The Saga, same one the bombing was in. I guess I'll see you sometime this afternoon."

McKenna got out and ran through the rain to the door of the trailer and knocked. The door was opened by a tall, blond man who was casually dressed in tan slacks and a checkered shirt. "Come in, Brian," he said. "Heard a lot about you and we're glad to have you on board. I'm Thor."

McKenna entered and saw that he was in a well-equipped mobile crime lab, almost identical to the one used by the NYPD's Bomb Squad. Besides Thor, there were another two men inside. Thor made the introductions in almost-unaccented American English, presenting Insp. Bob Hackford and Insp. Sydney Rollins from Scotland Yard.

Hackford was wearing a white lab coat, but it was Rollins who interested McKenna. He had written the foreword in the book on the IRA McKenna had been trying to read on the plane.

McKenna thought some small talk was in order before getting down to business, so he said to Thor, "I guess you've heard this before, but your English is perfect."

That drew a smile from Hackford and Rollins, but Thor looked pleased. "My gracious new colleagues here would disagree with you. They tell me I sound like a gangster from Chicago, and they might be close. I have a cousin in Milwaukee and I try to visit her whenever I'm taking one of your courses."

McKenna knew he was pushing politeness to the limit, but he just had to ask. "You've taken police courses in the United States?"

Thor didn't look offended at all. "Among other places. My government doesn't spend much money on police, but what it does spend, it tries to spend wisely. I was able to convince Janus to send me to your FBI Academy for the eleven-week course. Also been to your government's bomb course in Alabama and attended quite a few seminars in America. Matter of fact, we have a friend in common."

"We do? Who?"

"Vernon Gebreth. I went to a homicide seminar he was giving in Las Vegas and we got quite close. He talked about you and your cases all the time."

McKenna was stunned that Thor from Iceland knew Vernon Gebreth from the NYPD. Vernon had been the department's premier homicide investigator and was a good friend of both McKenna and Brunette. While still in the NYPD, Vernon had written *Practical Homicide Investigation*, a work that quickly became *the* textbook on murder. The success of the book prompted considerable jealousy from a few chiefs, so Vernon had retired to conduct his rather profitable seminar courses, teaching police from all over the world about murders, the psychology of the people who committed them, and how homicide investigations should be conducted.

If he was a student of Vernon's and if he's been to those courses, this Thor can't be quite the dummy I was expecting, McKenna thought. And he certainly doesn't look like a dummy. If anything, he looks like a giant Robert Redford in great shape.

"I'm flattered that Vernon remembers any of my cases," McKenna said, trying to sound humble.

"I think Vernon remembers everybody he's come across. He takes murder personally. Remember what he always says?"

"Sure do," McKenna answered. " ' *We work for God.* ' "

"Sort of gave me the same feeling and swelled my head," Thor said. "Getting a killer is the last act a government can do for the victim."

Careful, McKenna thought. This guy sounds like me and I'm beginning to like him. "How's the investigation here going?" he asked.

"Poorly, but we're plodding along. Knowing who Meaghan Maher is should help us. I assume you're familiar with everything that's been reported in the papers?"

"Yes, they seemed to have quite a bit."

"Difficult to hide anything from the press in cases of this scope, isn't it?" Thor asked dryly.

McKenna knew from experience that it was a classic understatement and also suspected that Thor had managed to hide a few things anyway. "I've always found it difficult, to say the least."

"Let me show you what we've got, so far."

McKenna followed Thor across the trailer to the table where Hackford was standing. On it were two small, black plastic boxes. Each one had been broken by an explosion into many burned pieces and later reassembled, but there were missing pieces from each. Also on the table was a small brass chandelier. Connected to the wires at the top of the chandelier was another black plastic box, intact and larger than the other two.

Hackford picked up one of the smaller boxes and said, "This is one of the reassembled radio-remote detonators found by Thor at the crime scene. It's American-made under military contract and is still in production."

"M1929A radio-remote detonator. I've had some experience with them," McKenna blurted out, but instantly regretted it. The look on Hackford's face changed from that of the patient instructor to the teacher surprised that one of his students might have some brains, and then to the disappointed disciplinarian contemplating how many detentions the class wise guy should get.

Oh-oh, no more showing off, McKenna thought. Don't want to spoil Mr. Stuffyface's fun. "I'm sorry. Go on, please."

"As I was saying, the transmitter supplied with this radio-remote detonator usually has an effective range of five hundred meters, at the most. Both detonators were set off by the same transmitter which is contained in this unusual device here."

Hackford moved down the table, picked up the larger box attached to the chandelier, and nodded to Thor.

"Right after the blast, Janus had anyone leaving the country at the airport detained for questioning if they had a brogue," Thor said. "However, when the body of the female washed up on Heimaey Island, I acted on the hunch that the bombing and her murder were somehow connected. That meant that the bomber had a boat. We checked the harbor and there were no foreign boats in port except for the usual commercial trawlers fueling up. But there had been one, a British sport fisherman that had left port the night before the bombing. I figured that the bomber was on board."

"Meaning he had already left the country when the bomb went off?" McKenna asked.

"Yes, but he still had to set it off. If that were the case, I knew that he had to have a relay transmitter somewhere. I looked until I found it," Thor said, pointing to the box in Hackford's hands.

"This is a very clever device," Hackford continued. "The chandelier actually serves as the antenna. Contained inside this box is a receiver hooked up to the small transmitter that sent the signal to the two detonators. It's quite sophisticated and runs on a battery that's charged by the chandelier's voltage. The bomber had a powerful transmitter on board his boat, so, when he decided he was safely away and that it was time to blow up Sir Ian and his wife, he sent the signal to the chandelier. The receiver picked it up, relayed it to the transmitter tuned to the short-range radio-remote detonators attached to the bombs, and that was it for Mr. and Mrs. Foreign Secretary."

"I assume this receiver and chandelier were in the foreign secretary's suite," McKenna said.

"No, Thor found it and it was very well hidden. Quite amazing, really. It was in a suite in the Saga Hotel that our bomber had occupied before he had the presidential suite. He had removed the chandelier and had installed this box in the ceiling among the rafters. I'm certain that he never expected it would be found."

From the way Hackford said it, McKenna got some additional information that he tucked away in the back of his mind. The Brits must have sent their best here for this investigation, he reasoned, so one of them has to be Hackford. Yet, Hackford is obviously in awe of Thor.

"How about the explosive?" McKenna asked. "I understand he used C-4 det cord, but not very much of it."

"Correct," Hackford said. "This bomber really knows his work. We've examined the burnt residue removed from the bodies, the clothing, and the ceiling. It's an old variety of C-4 without the chemical signature added in. He used less than half a pound total in both bombs to achieve the results he wanted. Never seen that before."

"Not too much structural damage?" McKenna asked.

"See for yourself," Hackford said. He opened a drawer under the table, removed an envelope, and handed it to McKenna. "The presidential suite has already been refurbished and is ready for occupancy," Hackford added.

McKenna opened the envelope and removed a stack of photographs. They were the crime scene photos taken immediately after the bombing. Shown in clear detail were the two bodies and every bit of the presidential suite, along with close-ups of every small thing the crime scene photographer considered pertinent.

Hackford, Rollins, and Thor waited patiently while McKenna went through the photos, taking his time. "Your crime scene photographer is really quite good," McKenna commented, meaning it.

"That would be Thor," Hackford said.

A homicide investigator who's also a very competent crime scene photographer? Pretty rare combination, McKenna thought, then tucked that one as well into the back of his mind. "Apparently, the bomber wanted to kill whoever was in those two beds, but he didn't want to destroy the place and piss the Icelanders off too much. I would also say that he had to have some inside information."

"Because he used two bombs?" Rollins asked, speaking for the first time.

"Yes. How would he know the foreign secretary and his wife would be sleeping in separate beds?"

"It's another question Thor's raised and he's come up with an interesting conclusion," Rollins said. "Without having anything concrete enough to report above a whisper, we have reason to believe that a high-ranking official of the Irish government is involved."

Oh-oh. Looks like another Thor fan has developed here, McKenna thought. "But not strong enough reasons to charge anyone or take to the press?" he asked.

"No. I would characterize our suspicions at this point as informed speculation," Rollins said, and left it at that.

McKenna handed the envelope of photos back to Hackford. "Could you tell me about the boat?" he asked Thor.

"Very nice one, a fifty-six-foot sport fisherman, British registry. Twin engines and all the amenities. It came limping into Reykjavík harbor on February twenty-third and docked at our pleasure-boat marina in town. The owner told the dockmaster that one of the transmissions had given out and that he would order a new one from the U.K. Said he and his mate would install it themselves when it arrived. They stayed on board and that was that."

"Do pleasure boats from the U.K. frequently stop here?"

"In the summer we get a few. Visits in the winter are rarer, but they happen."

"Did your immigration check them out?" McKenna asked.

"Yes, the dockmaster called them. An agent stopped by and checked their passports and the boat's papers, but his visit was rather perfunctory. We don't have a smuggling problem or much of a drug problem here, so there was no reason for him to be suspicious of anything. He accepted the captain's story at face value."

"How many people on board?"

"Two."

"The passports and the boat's papers were forgeries?"

"Of course. Inspector Rollins checked them out on March fourth, but they were long gone by then. They paid their bill and left the marina on the afternoon of March 1st. Told the dockmaster they were going to another marina in Grindavík to wait for their transmission."

"Where's Grindavík?"

"About ten minutes from here. It made sense to the dockmaster because their transmission would be arriving by air freight."

"Did they show up at Grindavík?"

"Yes, but by then both transmissions were working fine, of course. They stopped only long enough to fuel up and pick up a passenger."

"The bomber?"

"Yes, the bomber. He had checked out of the Saga Hotel on the night of Saturday, February twenty-eighth, right after the Rockall incident. The desk clerk called him a taxi to take him to the airport. That's where he went, but I've since found another taxi driver who took him from the airport to the hotel in Grindavík."

Of course, there had been nothing wrong with the boat's transmission, McKenna thought. That was just their excuse to hang around until the foreign secretary arrived and their passenger set the bombs. "And the bomb went off on March second?"

"Yes, at seven minutes after one in the morning, after they put out to sea."

"I take it this boat was very seaworthy?"

"Yes. According to our immigration agent and the dockmaster, it had all the best in navigation and radio equipment. The dockmaster tells me that it has two eight-hundred-gallon fuel tanks and an auxiliary four-hundred-gallon tank. That's enough to get that boat to Scotland or Ireland, if that's where they wanted to go."

"Where do you think that boat is now?" McKenna asked.

"The bottom of the North Atlantic. Inspector Rollins had every marina in the U.K. checked and the Irish government has also cooperated. The boat's not there, so I'm assuming they were met somewhere at sea by another boat."

That explains how the bomber got away, but what about Meaghan? McKenna asked himself. Her body had been in the water for about a week, so that means she had been dumped in the ocean before March 2nd. She didn't make her flight out on February twenty-third, so she was either dead or a prisoner by then. "Did the boat ever leave the marina in Reykjavík harbor before March first?"

"The dockmaster says no, but it must have," Thor said. "The marina isn't manned at night, so they must have slipped out sometime between February twenty-third and March first to dump Meaghan's body at sea."

Glad to see we're on the same wavelength, McKenna thought. "Can we talk about your bombing suspect now?"

"Arrived in Iceland on February twenty-first from Montreal carrying the valid Canadian passport of a man named Thomas Winthrop. But he's not Thomas Winthrop. At my suggestion, the Toronto police checked Winthrop's house. He was there, been dead over a week. Found him in a freezer in the basement. Tortured and finally strangled."

So the bomber arrived on the same flight as Meaghan, McKenna thought. Must be one of the reasons Thor thinks she and the bomber are connected, but I'll get to that later. "Did Winthrop live alone?"

"Yes, and rather well. He was independently wealthy and reported to be gay. He was last seen in a gay bar in downtown Toronto on February eighteenth, left with a man matching the description of our bomber."

"How old was Winthrop?"

"Forty-one, about the same age as the bomber."

"So he killed Winthrop for his passport, and then changed the picture."

"Got his credit cards, too. Charged his flight from Montreal to Iceland on Winthrop's American Express."

"When and where?"

"February nineteenth at a travel agency in Montreal. Bought a round-trip ticket with an open return."

"Did the Toronto police come up with anything else?"

"No prints, nothing we can use. Winthrop was tortured and killed in his bedroom on the second floor. I've got their crime scene photos in my office in town. Really rather grisly. Meaghan's body shows much of the same kind of torture as Winthrop's, so I sent copies of the photos of both bodies to Vernon for his opinion."

Sharp, McKenna thought. "What does he say?"

"Just sent them a few days ago, so he hasn't gotten back to me, yet," Thor said.

"Any IRA connection with Winthrop?" McKenna asked.

"No. Born in Canada, totally apolitical."

"How come I haven't read anything in the papers about this Winthrop connection?"

"At Inspector Rollins's request, the Toronto police are keeping it confidential. They haven't publicly connected Winthrop's murder to our bombing here."

"I feel we shouldn't tip our hand to the IRA about our progress," Rollins said.

"I see. Could you tell me how you think Meaghan fits into all this?" McKenna asked Rollins.

"She arrived with him on the same flight from Montreal and a person matching her description was seen with the bomber in a Reykjavík restaurant called Steikhút on the night of February twenty-first. The waiter says they arrived together and stayed talking for hours."

"Did he say they were intimate?"

"No, just friendly," Rollins said.

"Did they sit together on the plane?"

"No. He was in first class. Meaghan was in coach, wasn't she?"

"Yes, but they might have met on the plane or in either airport," McKenna said. "That certainly doesn't put her in the IRA or involve her in the bombing."

"No, but we thought that since she appeared to be Irish, there was a strong possibility of involvement on her part. Of course, that was before we knew who she was."

"Well, let's put that one to bed," McKenna said. "Meaghan is an innocent victim here. She has no sympathy for the IRA and didn't even know she was coming here until the day before she arrived. The only reason she was here at all was because Icelandair ran a package that was her cheapest way to Belgium."

"There's the matter of her passport," Rollins said. "Once you told us who she was, Thor checked with Iceland Immigration. She arrived here on a British passport. I checked that out and the address she listed on her passport application was on Ballymore Road in Belfast. The building no longer exists, but that part of Belfast is very Catholic and a real IRA bastion."

"More coincidence," McKenna said. "She's Catholic and originally from

Belfast, but nobody in her family has anything to do with the IRA. They moved to the South when she was a little girl, but she used the Belfast address later on because she needed a British passport."

"Why? If she's living in the Republic, why not just get an Irish passport?" Rollins asked.

"She did, but it's a little complicated. She's an illegal alien in the United States, but she's a good planner. Long before she moved to the U.S., she knew she was coming and also knew that having the two passports makes it easier for her to travel around and still get back into the country."

"I see, and I'm glad to hear it," Thor said. "Down the road, it should simplify our investigation somewhat."

Now for some tough questions, McKenna thought. Have to ask them in a way that won't make me sound critical of the work they've done so far. "Did you know that Meaghan was staying at the Hotel Loftleidir?"

"Only once you told us," Thor said. "After her body was found, I checked all the hotels looking for guests who had disappeared without checking out. There were none. Once Janus told me that she had been booked in the Hotel Loftleidir as part of her Icelandair package, I went back to the hotel last night and checked the room she had there. That was where she had been killed."

"How can you tell after two weeks?"

"I found a small bloodstain and two red hairs under the bed. Inspector Hackford performed some tests and confirmed that the blood and the hairs are Meaghan's. I figure that after the bomber overpowered her, he removed the box spring and mattress and laid the shower curtain over the rug underneath the bed frame. Then he stretched Meaghan out, tied her wrists and ankles to the four bed legs, and tortured her until he got tired of having fun. After that, he choked the life out of her, cleaned up, and put the bed back together."

"How did he get the body out of the hotel?"

"In her luggage. I think she had one of those pieces that you put suits in, then fold up. He put her body in there, zipped her up, and packed whatever clothes she had into her other bag. Her room faced the rear parking lot, so whatever wouldn't fit, he threw out the window."

"That must have been late at night for nobody to notice," McKenna said.

"Actually, I know now that it was around four o'clock in the morning on Sunday, February twenty-second. Then he went downstairs with the luggage and checked her out."

"Carrying Meaghan's body in one suitcase and her luggage in the other?" McKenna asked. "He must be very strong."

"Wait until you see the video we have of him. Not unusually tall, but he's a real brute."

"Does the desk clerk remember him?"

"Sure does. He had a cowboy hat on, but he also had a shiner developing under his left eye. Meaghan didn't have any room charges, so he just turned in the key and that was that. Checked her out at ten after four. Then he must have gone outside, gathered up her clothes from the ground, and threw them and her suitcase with the clothes into the Dumpster at the end parking lot. Calls a cab and he's off to the marina with Meaghan's body."

"How do you know that?"

"Because yesterday I found the cab driver who brought him there from the Loftleidir."

"Do you have any leads on who this killer is?" McKenna asked.

Thor tuned to Rollins.

"I've looked at the hotel video of him for hours, but he's not one of the IRA people I'm familiar with," Rollins conceded. "We also have a number of informants planted in the IRA and nobody knows anything about him, all of which leads me to believe he's either new or an independent contractor."

"Where do you go from here?" McKenna asked.

Hackford and Rollins looked at each other, then both turned to Thor. "As you can see, we're not doing well," Thor said. "This man didn't leave a single fingerprint in the two suites he occupied in the Saga Hotel, and it doesn't look like he made any mistakes anywhere else."

"They always make mistakes," McKenna said. "There's no such thing as the perfect crime."

"I've got just one slim hope left, and that amounts to garbage."

"Garbage?"

"Yes, garbage," Thor said. "After he checked Meaghan out of her hotel, the clerk remembers him putting the receipt in his pocket. I'm hoping he forgot about it."

"Forgot about it until when?"

"Until he returned to his suite at the Saga. If he threw it out there, I've got his fingerprints."

"You have the garbage from the Saga Hotel?"

"Not all of it. Just the paper," Thor said. "We're very serious about recycling in Iceland. The Saga staff goes through all the garbage collected from their guest's room and removes everything that can be recycled. After the bombing, I had all that saved. I have a good part of the hotel's garbage from the week before the bombing."

Pretty damn thorough, McKenna thought. Would I have had the foresight to do that? "Do you have people going through it?"

"I went through it myself once, but I didn't know what I was looking for. Now that we do, I'll go through it again."

"I can help. When do you wanna do that?"

"It can wait. Are you tired?"

McKenna didn't realize it until Thor asked the question, but he had been up all night and was exhausted. "I could use a nap."

"Then you should get one. I'll drive you to your hotel and you can get some rest before we take O'Malley to identify the body. She's in bad shape and I couldn't sleep for days after I saw her."

The knot in McKenna's stomach was back.

TWELVE

The trip to Reykjavík in Thor's Mustang covered some of the bleakest land-scape McKenna had ever seen. Thor bemoaned the fact that the airport was located in an area of lava fields in what he considered to be the ugliest part of the country. "Stick around long enough and I'll show you how beau-tiful Iceland really is," he promised McKenna.

"I haven't seen a tree, yet," McKenna commented.

"And you won't, around here. There aren't many forests in Iceland now, but there were when the Vikings first arrived and there will be again. The government has a major reforestation program going and it gets lots of popular support."

"What happened to the trees?"

"Some were cut down to build homes and ships, but most of them were burned as firewood over the centuries. That wouldn't happen today."

"Why not?"

"Because just about everything in Iceland today is heated with geo-thermal energy," Thor explained proudly. "We've got enough volcanoes and hot springs to heat and provide power for the rest of Europe, if it were closer."

Okay, enough of the small talk for now, McKenna thought. "Rollins said something about a member of the Irish government being involved in the bombing," he said. "Can you tell me what you're basing your suspicions on?"

"Be glad to, but this can't be mentioned to anyone until we get some positive proof."

"You've got a deal."

For twenty minutes McKenna heard all the reasons Thor had for be-lieving that Timothy O'Bannion was behind the bombing. McKenna mulled them over and concluded Thor was right. There was no other way the IRA could have had people in place in Reykjavík to kill the foreign secretary without the connivance of O'Bannion or a person similarly placed in the Irish government. Given his history of IRA involvement, it had to be him.

That settled, McKenna took in the scenery. The rain had stopped, the sky had cleared, dawn had finally arrived, and the character of the landscape had changed from lava fields to high, green hills. Thor turned a bend and the mountain-ringed city hugging one side of a large harbor came into view. The area surrounding the center of the city was dominated by concrete apartment buildings. Most were tall, ten stories or more, and there were expansive grassy spaces or children's playgrounds between them.

Thor turned onto a wide highway, but there wasn't much traffic. Lining the highway were stores, shopping centers, gas stations, schools, and churches. Set back from the highway were the apartment buildings. Everything was new, clean, and McKenna didn't see any graffiti or a single piece of litter on the ground. He also didn't see many people, but those he did see were casually dressed, most of them wearing ski jackets.

The closer Thor got to the center of Reykjavík the smaller the spaces between the buildings got and the older they appeared. Six stories became the norm, and then four. By the time they were in the center of town, the buildings adjoined each other. Many were made of wood and were of quaint Nordic design in colors ranging all the shades between blue and red. There was still no litter or graffiti, but there were people on the streets. Most were casually dressed shoppers or office workers. By that time, McKenna thought he was one of the few people in the country wearing a suit.

"That's where I work. Police headquarters," Thor said, pointing to a four-story modern building across the street from the bus station.

"Where do you live?"

"In an apartment building a block behind headquarters. I like to keep things convenient."

Thor drove through an area that reminded McKenna of Greenwich Village with a few differences: The buildings were lower, the streets were certainly cleaner and less crowded, the traffic was much lighter, there were no horns blaring, and McKenna didn't see a single security gate on any of the shop windows or doors. Yet, there was still a cosmopolitan atmosphere. It was what Greenwich Village should be like, McKenna decided. "Shouldn't there be more cars on the street?" he asked.

"Most of our parking is underground and many people don't have cars," Thor explained. "The buses are excellent, the fare is cheap, and you can walk from one end of the city to the other in forty-five minutes."

By then they were in an area much more formal in character. There were exclusive-looking restaurants and shops set among European-style hotels. "That's Steikhút, the place the bomber had dinner with Meaghan," Thor said, pointing to a pleasant-looking restaurant.

All of a sudden, McKenna felt very close to Meaghan at this spot so far from her home. "How far is this from the Saga Hotel?"

"We'll be there in another five minutes."

"And from the Hotel Loftleidir?"

"Ten minutes in the other direction."

"How about the marina? Where's that?"

"The harbor's four blocks from here."

So everything was close and convenient for the killer, McKenna thought. How nice for him and how bad for Meaghan.

Across a large lake and park surrounded by government buildings and formal residences belonging to the wealthy, McKenna saw the large, modern building. Lighted lettering running down the side of the building proclaimed it to be the Saga Hotel. Across the street from the hotel were many new buildings. "The National University," Thor told him.

Thor had to drive around the lake to get there and McKenna saw more different species of ducks and swans swimming around than he had imagined existed. A bellboy came over to the car and greeted Thor by name as soon as he pulled in front of the hotel. "Are there any reporters hanging around?" Thor asked.

"The usual few in the bar having their breakfast. Do you want me to park your car for you?"

"Don't bother. I'm going to be out in a minute."

"Sure," the bellboy said, opening the car door for Thor. McKenna got out and followed Thor.

It was a nice lobby, but not overly large. The decor was marble, mirrors, and glass. Thor went to the reception desk, greeted the pretty young desk clerk, and asked, "Could you call Jónas for me, please?"

"Sure, Thor. Better yet, I'll go get him for you."

"Do Icelanders usually talk to each other in English?" McKenna asked as soon as she left.

"Only if there's a foreigner present. We like to think of ourselves as polite."

"How does she know I'm a foreigner?"

"Your suit, for one. You must have noticed already, but we usually don't wear suits. Besides, both the bellboy and the desk clerk probably know who you are."

"How?"

"Icelanders are big readers, highest per capita sales of books in the world happens here. Then there's the papers. Newspapers from every major city in the world are sold in here, so I'm sure they both read the ones in English. You've had your share of coverage, you know."

"I'm flattered," McKenna said. "You also seem to be pretty well known here."

"Just a big fish in a small pond. You don't want to talk to the press now, do you?"

"Not if I don't have to. I'd rather stay low-key here. I take it you folks are also big drinkers."

"Another thing we might lead the world in. We attribute it to the long night, but you still won't see much in the way of public drunkenness here."

The desk clerk returned with Jónas in tow. He was in his forties and smiling graciously, the first person McKenna had seen dressed in a business suit in Iceland.

"So good to meet you, Detective McKenna," he said, offering his hand. "Thank you for choosing the Saga for your stay here."

"I didn't know about it before I came here, but it looks like the place I'd choose for myself," McKenna said as he shook the manager's hand.

"Thanks for saying so," Jónas replied graciously, then turned to Thor. "You wanted to see me, Thor?"

"Yes. I'd like you to try and keep the press out of Brian's hair. It would be even better if they didn't know he was here."

"I understand. I'll talk to the staff and do everything I can," Jónas said, then turned back to McKenna. "If you would just call the desk before you come down from your room or before you return to the hotel, I'll make sure there are no reporters hanging around the lobby."

"Fine, but how will you do that?" McKenna asked.

"Easy. I'll just buy them a round at the bar. They always fall for that one. Are you ready to be shown to your room?"

"Yes, thank you."

"I've given you the presidential suite, compliments of the hotel. Your luggage is already up there and Mr. O'Malley is in room seven twenty-eight. Please feel free to call me directly for anything you need."

I'm beginning to really like Iceland, McKenna thought.

McKenna had tried to sleep, but couldn't. He hadn't been able to get Meaghan off his mind and was apprehensive about seeing her in the morgue. Although he had spent years in different borough homicide squads in New York and had grown accustomed to seeing the bodies of people who had been grotesquely murdered, he had never gotten comfortable with seeing those same bodies in morgues. It bothered him being in those places where death was treated so routinely and regarded in such an antiseptic, detached manner.

Depending on the age of the victim and how they had died, sometimes seeing them in the morgue turned McKenna's stomach. He had a feeling that this was going to be one of those times and was afraid that the famous detective from New York was about to embarrass himself and the NYPD in front of Chris O'Malley and that other famous detective from nowhere. In this case, a story like that could quickly go worldwide.

McKenna gave up on sleep. He got up and walked around the large suite, looking for signs of damage from the blast. There were none, so he took a shower, then went through the selection of clothes he had brought with him. Angelita had packed nothing but suits, dress shirts, and ties, so he knew he wasn't going to be at the peak of fashion in Iceland. He put on a fresh suit, but decided against wearing a tie. He was shining his shoes at one o'clock when the front desk called. Thor had been around again and had dropped off a package for him. It was being brought up.

Another bellboy delivered the package. McKenna had been rushed through the airport so quickly by Janus that he had neglected to change any of his dollars into kronas, the Icelandic currency. He gave the bellboy five dollars and it was graciously accepted.

McKenna sat at the desk and opened the package. There was a large envelope inside with a note from Thor attached to the outside. It read:

Brian,
Enclosed are the crime scene photos and the autopsy photos from the Toronto police. They should give you some idea of what to expect at the morgue today. Also enclosed is a package of Drama-mine tablets. I find that they help to keep my stomach settled at times like this. I'll be around to pick you and Chris O'Malley up at two o'clock. Lunch is at four at my place, if you both are up to it by then.

Regards,
Thor

P.S. I already took three Dramamines and you might want to pop two before going through these photos.

So big, famous, tough-guy Thor is another sissy, McKenna thought. Good news for me, but who would have suspected that? McKenna took Thor's advice, reached into the envelope, and found the box of tablets. He took three and washed them down with a bottle of club soda from the minibar.

The photos were just as grisly as Thor had said. Winthrop had suffered excruciating pain. The first photos were of Winthrop's frozen body doubled over in his basement freezer. There wasn't much damage to Winthrop to be seen in those photos, and they were followed by a series of shots leading up to Winthrop's second-floor bedroom.

McKenna knew that the shots were taken to emphasize that there was no blood trail from the bedroom to the basement, but they told him more than that. From the furnishings, the high ceilings, and the decor in the downstairs room, it was apparent to him that Winthrop had indeed been wealthy.

The bedroom was a mess. There were belts tied to the four bedposts of the large double bed and quarts of dried blood stained the bed spread. Separate photos showed the killer's tools lying on the floor next to the bed. The scissors, the large kitchen knife, the pliers, and the hammer were all covered with blood. The killer had cut Winthrop's clothes from his body and there were separate shots of each item of clothing lying on the floor. Winthrop had been wearing a black lace bra, matching black lace panties, and black stockings, but the rest of the clothing was male. None of the clothes were bloodstained, so McKenna knew that the killer wanted his victim naked before he went to work.

There was also a photo of a broom with a broken handle. Before going any further through the photos, McKenna had a pretty good idea where the missing section of broom handle was going to show up.

He was right. The first of the morgue shots showed Winthrop lying facedown on the stainless steel autopsy table with the broken broom handle protruding from his anus. Winthrop was slight of build and had long, blond hair. The tape measure lying stretched out along the body indicated that he was five feet four inches tall. McKenna could see many cigarette burns on Winthrop's buttocks and on the back of his legs. He could also see that each of his fingers had been smashed.

With some trepidation, McKenna went on to the next photo and was shocked by what he saw. A tie was stuffed in Winthrop's mouth. His neck was bruised, showing that his ordeal had ended by strangulation, but the killer had had his way with Winthrop for some time before finally granting him the welcome release of death.

Cigarette burns and large, ugly bruises were all over the front of his body, his penis had been slit lengthwise to the base and spread open, and his scrotum had been removed. Winthrop had small, feminine breasts, but the nipples had been pulled off. His face was so bruised and battered that McKenna was certain that his mother would have a difficult time recognizing her son lying on the table, but it wasn't the overall condition of the body that had shocked McKenna. He had seen this exact type of torture before on the body of a murder victim remarkably close to Winthrop's physical condition. The description of the killer in both cases had been just as close.

As McKenna went through the rest of the photos, he wondered if it could possibly be the work and play of the same man. Or could there be two people so perverted, cruel, and insanely sadistic walking the planet at the same time? He hoped not.

In 1989, McKenna had been assigned to the Manhattan South Homicide Squad. The victim had been a slim, thirty-one-year-old transvestite prostitute named Joseph Dwyer. The body had been found by the desk clerk of the West Side Motor Inn, a flea-bag hotel used by prostitutes of all kinds to complete their business transactions. The clerk had discovered the body two hours after Dwyer and the killer had checked in and five minutes after he had seen the killer leave alone.

Dwyer had called himself Josephine Stacy Dwyer, and like Winthrop, had a fair complexion and small, feminine breasts. Strangulation had been the ultimate cause of death.

The difference between the Winthrop and Dwyer cases was the object that had been used for sexual penetration and the hair color of the victims. There had been no semen found at either crime scene, but in the Dwyer case, the killer had left an enormous white dildo protruding from his victim's anus. Winthrop's blond hair was long like Dwyer's. Dwyer had dyed his brown hair strawberry blond, which brought McKenna to another point that linked three murder cases closer together and made him think harder.

Dwyer's dyed hair was very close to Meaghan's natural color. Like Meaghan, Dwyer had also been born in Ireland, and McKenna wondered if more similarities among the three victims would come up as the day progressed.

The Dwyer case still irritated McKenna whenever he thought about it. The small, filthy room yielded hundreds of fingerprints, but none matched those of any known sex offenders. McKenna had been able to get from the desk clerk a fairly good physical description of the monster who had checked in with Dwyer, enough of a description to have the Artists Unit make up a sketch.

Then, after a week of asking around, McKenna had located Dwyer's boyfriend, Roberto Da Silva. The boyfriend had also served as Dwyer's street protection and pimp. Da Silva hadn't been the slightest bit effeminate, but he had loved his Josephine Dwyer. Loved him, but not enough to stabilize the terror and fear he had felt whenever he thought about the man who had tortured and killed his mate and best friend. It had taken McKenna two days of coaxing before he had been able to induce Da Silva to reveal the details of what had happened the night of the murder.

Dwyer had been working the stretch of Tenth Avenue on the West Side where many of the prostitutes, both females and transvestites, plied their trade. Da Silva had also been around, standing on Tenth Avenue and West 13th Street, his usual corner. One part of his job was to yell to Dwyer whenever he saw a radio car approach and the other was to protect his friend from the occasional band of drunken teenagers who sometimes cruised the area, harassing the transvestite prostitutes.

Around three in the morning on the night of the murder, Da Silva had seen a blue, beat-up Chevy Nova pull up to where Dwyer was standing. There had been one white man in the car, a good prospective customer as far as Da Silva was concerned. The man and Dwyer had talked for a moment, then Dwyer gave the signal to Da Silva that the deal had been made. Following their usual procedure for so late at night, Da Silva had gone over to get a look at the customer before Dwyer had gotten into the car.

That had been the last time that Da Silva ever saw his friend, but he had done something else that had caused McKenna's heart to skip a beat. Da Silva had memorized the plate number of the Chevy Nova.

McKenna's joy had been short-lived. The car had been reported stolen in the Bronx the night before the murder, and it had already been recovered and returned to its owner. The police had found it empty in the Woodlawn section of the Bronx.

McKenna had brought Da Silva to the Artists Unit to have another sketch made. It had been so close to the previous sketch that McKenna had felt sure he would eventually get his man.

But he hadn't. After weeks of hanging around Tenth Avenue late at night and after checking with homicide squads and sex crimes squads all over the Northeastern U.S., McKenna had been ordered by his squad commander to give up the chase. Like all unsolved homicide cases, it had been left open, but once McKenna left the Manhattan South Homicide Squad, another detective had been assigned to do the required annual report that stated, "Case open, no further results."

Then McKenna remembered something peculiar about the case and he went through the Winthrop morgue notes. By the time he put the photos back in the envelope, he was almost certain that he was once again looking for the same killer. In the Dwyer case, the victim's nipples had never been found, and neither had Winthrop's.

McKenna lay down on the bed, fully dressed, and tried to clear his head. The Dwyer case still bothered him and he usually tried not to think about it, but it was once again very much on his mind as he stretched out in the presidential suite of the Saga Hotel, three thousand miles from that other very different kind of hotel where Joseph Dwyer had suffered and died.

Worse, McKenna realized, was that because he hadn't caught that killer then in New York, Meaghan Maher had also suffered and died horribly. That thought made McKenna feel like crying. He knew that eventually, he might.

McKenna had picked up Chris O'Malley at his room, given him two Dramamine tablets, and they were waiting outside the hotel when Thor surprised them by walking out of a side door halfway down the building from where they were standing. In contrast to O'Malley's ashen appearance, Thor looked positively elated. He was carrying a clear plastic envelope in his hand and a yellow piece of paper was visible inside.

"Where you been?" McKenna asked him.

"Heaven in a garbage heap. I've got it," Thor answered, giving the envelope to McKenna.

It was Meaghan Maher's receipt from the Hotel Loftleidir. It was folded in four, but in one corner her name was typed in blue print. "What now?" McKenna asked.

"Get lucky, stay lucky. After lunch, I'm going to take this to headquarters and see if there are any prints on it. If there are, I'm coming back here to take elimination prints of all the hotel employees who had anything to do with sorting out the garbage. Last stop will be the Hotel Loftleidir to take the prints of the desk clerk who gave the killer this receipt."

"You're going to have to be really lucky if somebody else's prints didn't smudge the killer's prints, if they even are on this wonderful piece of paper," McKenna said.

"Then the good thing is, I usually am lucky."

Good detectives usually are, McKenna thought, aware that other NYPD detectives frequently swore that he was the luckiest detective on the Job.

"Ready for the morgue?" Thor asked.

"No, but we might as well get it over with. Where's your car?"

"In the lot, but we can walk if you want. It's not far from here."

"Then the walk will do us good. We'll all probably need some air by the time we leave there," McKenna said, then turned to O'Malley. "Walking okay by you, Chris?"

"Whatever you say, but you both might wind up carrying me back here."

It was smaller and cleaner than most morgues McKenna had been in, but there was no disguising where they were. Morgues around the world shared that same antiseptic smell that made McKenna's stomach jump.

The morgue attendant in the crisp and starched white uniform stood in front of the double row of large stainless steel doors with his hand on the handle of door number one. "Ready?" he asked the three men in line facing him. All nodded weakly, so the attendant swung the refrigerator door open and grabbed the handle on the stainless steel tray inside. He pulled just enough to slide the tray out three feet. The body was covered by a spotless white sheet. The attendant pulled the sheet back to expose the battered and swollen face of a red-haired young girl.

McKenna heard a gasp and then O'Malley fainted dead away so suddenly that McKenna and Thor barely had time to catch him before he fell. They lowered him to the tiled white floor and McKenna cradled O'Malley's head in his lap.

"I'd say that's a positive identification," McKenna suggested to Thor, but the big Icelander just shook his head.

The attendant left and returned a moment later with a glass of water, an ampoule of smelling salts, and a pillow. McKenna took the pillow from him and placed it under O'Malley's head. Then he took the offered ampoule and broke it under O'Malley's nose.

The effect was instant. O'Malley's eyes opened wide and he shook his head from side to side, trying to rid his nostrils of the smell. He tried to stand up, but McKenna placed his hand on O'Malley's chest. "Chris, just lie there and relax for a few minutes. Have some water before you get up," he suggested.

"You're right. Good idea," O'Malley said. He laid his head back down on the pillow and closed his eyes.

McKenna patted him on the shoulder, then stood up and took a good look at the dead girl's face. She had been scrubbed clean, so there was no blood visible, but there was no hiding the bruises on her face and around her neck. Both eyes were swollen shut, her nose was broken, and her lips sunk into her toothless mouth. Although he had seen at least a hundred photos of Meaghan Maher and would have said with confidence that he would know her anywhere, at that moment he wasn't totally sure that the battered face on the tray in front of him was hers. She had four earring holes in each ear, but McKenna needed more. He bent over and put his hand on O'Malley's forehead.

O'Malley opened his eyes and stared up at him. The morgue attendant passed the glass of water down to McKenna and he held it to O'Malley's lips. O'Malley drank half the water in the glass before he shook his head and McKenna gave it back to the attendant.

"Chris, I want you to think hard," McKenna said softly. "What is there about Meaghan's body that makes her different from every other girl in the world? What particular thing is there about her that would make you say, *That's my Meaghan, I'd know her anywhere'* ?"

O'Malley's brow furrowed in concentration, then he shook his head. "Nothing, really. Not a thing I can think of."

"No marks, no moles, no bumps, no little something?"

O'Malley thought some more, then gave McKenna the best smile he could give under the circumstances.

"Where and what is it?" McKenna asked.

"I've never actually seen it, but I've felt it," O'Malley said, his face getting redder. "She's got a little mole under her hair on the left side of her head, right behind her ear."

"Good. Thank you. Now just lie there and relax for a few minutes more." McKenna stood back up and sifted with his fingers through the red hair at the place O'Malley had described. It was Meaghan. Certainly not good news, but the positive identification made necessary the next unpleasant chore.

McKenna slid the body tray all the way out and took a deep breath. He pulled the sheet completely off and his breath left his body in an involuntary rush. As he stared down at the horribly tortured body, he felt himself get dizzy, then felt Thor's strong grasp on his shoulder.

McKenna didn't move until his head cleared. "Thanks, Thor. I'm going to be all right," he said, and Thor removed his hand. And McKenna was all right. It was the anger that helped and kept him focused on the task at hand.

It was bad, maybe even worse than it had been for Dwyer and Winthrop, McKenna decided. The body had been autopsied, but he felt that even that invasive procedure hadn't done more damage to her dead body than the killer had done to her when she was still alive. The rope burns were there on her ankles and wrists, indicating the spots where she had been tied to the bed legs. There were more burns and bruises all over Meaghan, but most of the cigarette burns were centered around her breast and vaginal areas. Her nipples had been pulled off her petite breasts and her vagina had been ripped open, but, horrible as it was to see and think about, McKenna had expected that.

What drew McKenna's attention were Meaghan's hands. All her fingers were gone from the first joint down, but they hadn't been cut off as he had expected. The bone was showing through where each finger had been, and the skin and thin muscles were shredded around it.

McKenna bent over and looked closely at her left hand, at the place where her index finger should have been. What was left of the bone of the top joint was cracked, chipped, and shaved. He picked her hand up and looked at the other side of the bone. It was in the same condition.

McKenna was sure of what the killer had done, but he didn't want to say it in front of O'Malley. The fiend had bitten her fingers off, one by one. McKenna fervently hoped that Meaghan had been dead by that time, but suspected that she hadn't been.

With Thor's help, McKenna replaced the sheet over the body, leaving just her face exposed again, then looked down at O'Malley. The big man was watching him with the most apprehensive look McKenna had ever seen.

No easy way to say this, McKenna thought as he bent over O'Malley again. "Chris, I'm sorry. It's her."

Willing disbelief showed in O'Malley's eyes. "It's Meaghan? Are you sure?"

"Yes, it's Meaghan and I'm sure," McKenna answered softly.

For a moment, O'Malley appeared to accept the news and McKenna thought it wasn't going to be as bad as he had figured it would be. But only for a moment. Then O'Malley broke down and sobbed, loudly and with abandon.

McKenna and Thor didn't say another word and let O'Malley go on until he cried himself out. It took a while, but finally he did. This time McKenna didn't bend over to speak to him. "Chris, there's something to be done here and you have to do it. I've already told you that it's Meaghan, but it's not officially her until you tell me it is. You have to stand up, look at her face, and then say, *'I know this person. I'm certain that this is the body of Meaghan Maher.'* "

"Suppose I don't do that or say that?"

"Then she can't get a proper burial, yet. She waits for her mother or her brother to come here, all the way to Iceland, just to do the hard job you should be doing for them. Is that the way it should be?"

"No. What happens, once I say it's her?"

"Then we try to forget all about it for as long as we can. We leave here, we go back to the hotel to straighten you up, and then we go to Thor's house and we try to eat because his wife is making us lunch."

"I don't think I can ever eat again," O'Malley said with conviction.

"Sooner or later, you will. Now get up and do your job like the man I know you are."

O'Malley took a moment to compose himself and stiffen his resolve, then pushed himself to his feet.

THIRTEEN

Maybe, as he had said, O'Malley would never eat again, but it was soon evident to all that eating had nothing to do with drinking. He hadn't even sat at the table as Frieda served the salmon steaks cooked in her special cream sauce, potatoes au gratin, and her homemade apples-and-rasberries concoction to Thor and McKenna. Instead, O'Malley just sat in a chair in the corner of the room, drinking Scotch straight from the bottle, saying not a word, and paying not the least bit of attention to the polite dinner conversation shared by McKenna, Thor, and Frieda. He was lost in his own world, or what was left of it.

By unspoken agreement, not a word about the bombing or Meaghan was mentioned over dinner. Instead, they talked about Thor and Frieda, how they met, and the life they had made for themselves together. It was a story so bizarre that McKenna wasn't sure, at first, that they weren't putting him on.

Ten years before, Frieda had been a fun-loving lady who made good money as a featured stripper at one of Reykjavík's hot night spots. Being enterprising, she had made a little extra money by dealing recreational drugs to her fans during her breaks in the wee hours. Eventually, this small enterprise of hers had become known to the Icelandic authorities who wink at nothing and tolerate very few slips. Thor had been assigned to investigate and bring an end to this impending collapse of public morality.

Investigate he did, and before long he had developed enough information on Frieda to accomplish his mission. But a major problem had developed. Along the way the straight-arrow Thor had fallen in love with the loose and exotic Frieda. Sometimes opposites do attract, because Frieda had also gone head-over-heels for her investigating constable, soon to be her arresting officer. They had become involved in an intolerable situation, so they had sat down to talk it over and search for some solution.

"And?" McKenna asked, waiting for the punch line.

"Really, there was no solution," Thor said simply.

McKenna thought he knew better than that. "No solution? But you're here together. How did that happen?"

"I did my job and Frieda did her time."

McKenna was astounded as he looked back and forth from Thor to Frieda, waiting for one of them to crack a smile. They didn't. "You put her in jail?" he finally asked, settling on Thor. "Are you telling me you put the woman you love in jail?"

Thor had nothing more to say, so it was Frieda who tried to explain. "I was younger and I wasn't thinking correctly about my life. I knew I was doing wrong, but I didn't care. I had no direction until I met Thor. Then I saw in him the type of person I wanted to be, but there was only one way I could be that person and still keep Thor."

"Jail?"

"Yes, jail. We had a nice dinner and Thor brought me in. I pled guilty, and then I did my two years in prison."

"Two years? Had you ever been arrested before?"

"No, I had been lucky."

"So it's two years for a first-time small-scale drug offense? You do two years for that here?"

Frieda couldn't see what it was about her sentence that was bothering McKenna, but she saw that further explanation was necessary. "Two years was what my crime called for. Our judges have very little latitude when it comes to sentencing, no matter who the prisoner knows or how sorry she is for the crimes she's committed."

"In Iceland, the law is the law," Thor said, feeling a need to explain further. "We are a very old democracy, the oldest in Europe. The elected representatives of the people enact the laws, and it's expected that they will be obeyed. If we allowed exceptions, then the people would question the fairness of our system, wouldn't they?"

Those New York drug dealers who routinely get arrested once a month better stay outta this place, McKenna thought. Things do seem simpler here and their system appears to be working fine. Maybe it *is* because everybody here knows exactly what to expect if they screw up. But two years?

"It wasn't so bad for me," Frieda said. "Thor came to visit me all the time and was there when I got out. I did my time and earned the respect of the best man in Iceland."

What's the word for this archaic *Happy Days* right-is-always-right and wrong-is-always-wrong outlook, McKenna wondered. Maybe jeepers? Yeah, that's it. Jeepers! "So what did you do after you got out?"

"Since I had already earned Thor's respect, I was soon respected by everyone. After a while, I even respected myself, so I studied and became a minister."

"A minister of what?"

"An ordained one. I'm a Lutheran minister assigned to the National Cathedral, but I don't spend much time there. The bishop is a very busy man and he uses me as an emissary, sending me to all the synods and conferences he can't attend himself. I get to do quite a bit of traveling, mostly to congregations in Norway and the U.S."

Jeepers creepers, McKenna thought. This is getting too crazy. Fortunately, Frieda thought the matter closed. She cleared the dirty dishes from the table, then went to the kitchen to make coffee and put the finishing touches on the dessert.

But McKenna had other things to think about. Since seeing the Winthrop photos and the body of Meaghan Maher, he felt a sense of ownership about the case. After all, he reasoned, he had been hunting this killer long before the Iceland bombing.

McKenna had formulated a tentative plan to catch his killer, but politics were ultimately going to be involved and the two detectives had different priorities that had to be addressed and resolved. Thor was chasing a political terrorist who, incidentally, had also murdered a young innocent girl. McKenna, as Angelita had pointed out, was chasing a sexual psychopath who just happened to blow people up for a living.

McKenna also felt that if his plan was viable, he had a better chance than Thor to catch the killer. There would have to be trade-offs with the Icelanders and the British, but first he needed more information to properly make his case to Brunette and gain his approval. "Mind if I make a suggestion?" he asked Thor.

"Certainly not. What is it?"

"Could you ask the British to go through their files and search for any unsolved sex killings committed around the same time as an IRA bombing? Anything within, say, fifty miles of the bombing."

Thor just smiled, so McKenna knew at once that he had underrated the Icelander again. "I guess you've already done that?"

"Yes, right after my first look at Meaghan. They told me they'd get right on it, but as you know, they regarded her as an executed accomplice. Their attitude changed after I got the Winthrop photos and I expect the results from my request shortly."

"You don't think they've been up front with you?"

"They've been helpful, but I'm not sure they've been completely forth-right with me."

It had been McKenna's impression that Hackford and Rollins had been quite enamored of Thor's intelligence and skill. "Why do you think they might not have come clean with you?" he asked. "Policy?"

"More a question of attitude, but I can understand how they feel. Over the years, they've come to regard these IRA bombings as their own province. Unofficially, they regard me as a talented tool to help fix something they've been working hard at for a long time."

Since McKenna wasn't being completely forthright with Thor himself, he felt a pang of guilt. He decided to come as clean as he could. "I have a plan to get this killer, but it's not fully worked out yet and I have to get my boss's views before I can tell you more. If he goes for it, it's possible we'll have some disagreements."

"Will we work them out?" Thor asked.

"That depends. Just how important is it to you where this killer goes to jail?"

"Not important at all. Iceland, Canada, the U.K., or even the States. The important thing is that this monster is dead or in jail, anywhere, and not free to kill again."

Great answer, McKenna thought, but Thor works for other people, same as me. "Do you think Janus will share your viewpoint?"

"Janus and I are old friends and we share the same views on police work. We both regard it as a vocation and feel that our decisions should be based on what is morally right, not on what is politically expedient."

"Then I was wrong. We're not going to have any disagreements," Mc-Kenna said. "That doesn't mean we're not gonna have any with Hackford and Rollins. We have to get them to forget about policy and get completely on board."

"You're going to need them for this plan of yours?"

"Probably. They must've had some of their people doing some heavy snooping around Timothy O'Bannion, but their concerns and ours aren't the same. They have to be worried about maintaining good relations with the Irish government and protecting their sources, so that's another possible reason for their lack of candor with you."

"Once you tell me where you're headed, maybe I'll speak to them about it."

"You mean if you agree with my plan?" McKenna asked.

"Yes, if Janus and I agree. Matter of fact, he'll probably be the one to speak to them. He's got a much better mad-dog act than I do."

"Fair enough."

Frieda came back in, balancing trays like a New York waitress. The coffee was good, but the dessert was one of the best McKenna ever had. Frieda had blended soft pastry, whipped cream, a smooth cheese, and a sweet strawberry preserve into something special. "What is this called?" he asked as Frieda served him his second helping.

Frieda told him, but he didn't get it, so she told him again. McKenna had an ear for languages, but he recognized that the Icelandic word for what he was eating could never be pronounced correctly by him. He didn't ask again.

Then it was time for the real dessert, the one McKenna didn't want to request when O'Malley had been awake and aware. McKenna wanted to see the image of the man who had killed Meaghan, a man he had sought long before, but he didn't think O'Malley was emotionally ready to take it in.

But there was something else nagging at McKenna's mind, a hint of uncertainty. The two things that had made him think that the same man was responsible for the murders of Dwyer, Winthrop, and Meaghan was the peculiar, vicious nature of the torture he used and the fact that the general physical description of the killer was the same in all three cases. But if the bomber in Thor's video didn't match the sketch of Dwyer's killer, then he had been going off half-cocked and his plan wasn't feasible. Worse, it would be considered stupid by anybody with half a brain.

Time to find out if I'm a dope, McKenna thought. "Let's go take a look at your video," he said to Thor.

"Go where? I've got it right here," Thor said. "He's all I've been watching on TV since the bombing."

Thor got up and McKenna followed him into the small living room. McKenna sat on the sofa, and Thor slipped a videotape into the VCR, then turned on the TV. "This is the edited version from the Saga hallway," Thor said. "Runs a little over four minutes, just shows him."

And it did, over and over, showing a stout bearded man at different times leaving the elevator and entering the presidential suite, then leaving the presidential suite and waiting for the elevator. He was shown in three different changes of clothes at opposite angles from the two hidden cameras, but he was always wearing the same cowboy hat.

The hat cast a shadow over the killer's face so that his features weren't clearly defined on the videotape, but that didn't bother McKenna. He could see enough of the man's face to determine that although he didn't have a beard when he had killed Dwyer, McKenna was looking at the same man. There were some small differences in his facial features between the video and the sketch, but there usually were. Sketches were rarely perfect, McKenna knew.

There was also the large difference that brought a smile to McKenna's face. The killer had been well tagged by Meaghan. He had first been captured on video outside the presidential suite on February 25th, three days after he had killed her, but his left eye was still blackened and the bridge of his nose was still swollen.

After a few moments it wasn't the man's face that captured McKenna's attention. It was his build and the way he walked. The killer looked and walked like Bluto, after the big brute had pounded Popeye to a pulp, but before the spinach. There was something familiar about the man. The tape ended and McKenna stared at the blue screen for a minute as Thor and Frieda watched him. "Could you run it again, please?" McKenna asked.

Thor rewound the tape and played it again, but this time Thor didn't watch it. He watched McKenna.

McKenna was too busy thinking as he watched the screen to notice Thor's interest in his reaction to the videotape. By the time the tape had ended for the second time, McKenna had formed his conclusion.

If I'm right, Ray's very wrong, he thought. This has always been an NYPD case, and maybe our most embarrassing one ever.

"Well? What's on your mind?" Thor asked.

"I think I know that man."

"What do you mean, *you know him*?"

"If I'm right, what I mean is that I've met him once or twice."

"Where?"

"In New York. He used to be a cop."

McKenna had Thor's total interest, but he didn't want to get into a long, drawn-out story embarrassing to the NYPD unless he was sure that the man in the video was Mike Mullen. One possible way to be sure was the Hotel Loftleidir receipt. If Thor could pull any latent prints off it, getting Mullen's prints for a comparison was an easy matter, but a long phone call. Mullen's fingerprint cards were still on file, but Brunette would have many questions. Again, they were questions McKenna didn't want to answer unless he was sure. The receipt was the first order of business.

McKenna and Thor left the apartment and walked the one block to police headquarters, although both felt like running there. It was six o'clock and the lab was locked, but Thor had the key. Thor turned on the lights and McKenna took a quick look around. It was a three-room affair, and it looked to be fairly well equipped. McKenna had seen police labs in all parts of the United States, and he thought that the one serving the nation of Iceland would be adequate for a small municipal police department in the U.S. "I guess your lab people don't do much business here," McKenna commented.

"Actually, I'm a big part of the lab people you're referring to, and I manage to stay fairly busy. Not like a lab technician working in, say, the New York City Police lab, but busy by our standards."

"You've seen our lab?"

"Did a one-month internship there in 1989."

What do I say to that? McKenna wondered. A man who's a good homicide investigator, who also handles their narcotics investigations, who also serves as their bomb squad, who is also a good crime scene technician and a good crime scene photographer, and now he's their main lab technician? What do I say? "How did you like it?"

"Pretty impressive, but a little chaotic."

"How is it that you're qualified to work in the lab in the first place?"

"Why shouldn't I be? I've got your equivalent of a master's degree in chemistry."

No more questions I don't want to hear the answers to, McKenna told himself. No more questions.

But McKenna couldn't help himself. He felt compelled to say something. "You know, Thor, I've never felt this way before, but I'm beginning to feel a little inadequate."

"Why? Because I wear so many hats around here?"

"That's it."

"Well, don't be. Try to keep in mind that while you're working cases and solving crimes all the time, day in, day out, I'm here bored and waiting for the next one to happen. I've got plenty of time on my hands and the total support of my boss, so I prepare myself to do everything possible to solve the next major crime."

"If and when it happens."

Thor gave a little chuckle, the first one McKenna had heard from him. "We're in Iceland, not heaven. They always happen, sooner or later."

It's beginning to seem like heaven to me, McKenna thought. "How many cases are assigned to you a month?"

"A month? Sometimes none, but then I work in the field as a crime scene technician or in here as a lab technician. That's if I'm not out of the country attending some course or seminar."

"So you're only assigned the major cases?"

"Yes, I've become a bit of a big shot here. If it makes you feel any better, what we would consider a major crime here sometimes wouldn't rate the assignment of a detective like yourself in New York."

Yeah, that's right, McKenna thought. Major crimes, that's me. I guess now's not the time to tell him that I've been spending most of my time chasing note-passers.

For the next hour, McKenna watched Thor at work. First, the Icelander removed the hotel receipt from the plastic bag with a pair of tongs and spread it out. Then he took the receipt into the dark room and photographed every section of it on both sides under ultraviolet light. After developing the photographs, he emerged from the dark room with a smile on his face. "We've got maybe five good prints on it," he announced.

The prints on the receipt still weren't visible to the naked eye, but the camera had picked them up under the ultraviolet light and Thor knew just where they were on the paper. He had circled them in pencil.

It was time for McKenna to see them, so Thor filled a flask with iodine solution, lit up a gas burner, and adjusted the setting to produce a low flame. After putting the flask on top, he waited for the heat to generate the purple iodine fumes. They rose slowly from the narrow neck of the flask and Thor held the receipt over it with the tongs, concentrating the fumes on every outlined print. Minutes later he was done and he shut the burner off.

McKenna could see that things were going well. Five purple latent prints were clearly visible inside the penciled circles on the yellow receipt. Thor clipped the receipt to a line to dry. "Should be ready in a few minutes," he told McKenna, then he picked up a phone and dialed.

"Who you calling?" McKenna asked.

"First Jónas. I want him to have whoever sorts the garbage at the Saga standing by."

The conversation with Jónas was in Icelandic and brief. "I'm so stupid," he said to McKenna after hanging up. "I should have known the people sorting the garbage would be wearing gloves."

What? Shouldn't I have thought of that, too? McKenna thought, but he felt better keeping that question to himself.

Next Thor called the Hotel Loftleidir. Another conversation followed in Icelandic and Thor wrote down a name, address, and phone number before he hung up. "The desk clerk won't be in until midnight."

"That's fine by me. Before we go to any more trouble, I've got to make a phone call."

"To New York?"

"Uh-huh. Could you give me your fax number here?"

Thor wrote it down on a piece of paper and handed it to McKenna. Since it was Sunday, McKenna first tried calling Brunette at home. There was no answer, so he next dialed Brunette's direct office number, but it wasn't Brunette who picked up. It was Camilia Wright, Brunette's secretary and one of the sharpest people McKenna had ever met. "It's Brian, Camilia. Is Ray there?"

"No, I don't expect him back for another hour. He's doing an interview for PBS."

That's good news, McKenna thought. No questions until I have the answers. "Then I need you to do me a favor, Camilia. We used to have a detective named Mike Mullen. He was the guy who—"

"I know who he was. What do you need?"

"I need you to get his personnel folder and fax me one of his fingerprint cards and his arrest report."

"You'll have it in fifteen minutes."

McKenna gave her the fax number, then read her the police lab number from the phone. "Can you have Ray call me when he gets in?" he asked.

"Will do. Is it important?"

"I hope so, but I won't know for sure until I get that print card." McKenna thanked her and hung up.

Thor took down the receipt and handed it to him. It was dry and it took McKenna only seconds to see that three of the prints were so good that he felt he could classify them himself.

While waiting for the fax, Thor didn't ask a single question. Instead, he busied himself with paperwork, invoicing the hotel receipt as evidence and documenting the lab procedures he had done on it. McKenna was a little chagrined to see that Thor was also quite a typist.

Thor didn't even look up when the fax started coming through. He continued typing while McKenna waited impatiently by the machine and even showed no interest when the transmission was complete.

McKenna wanted to do the comparison himself, but the receipt was lying next to Thor's typewriter. Thor must have read his mind because he reached into his desk drawer, took out a magnifying glass, and brought it and the receipt over to McKenna. Then, without a word, he sat back at his desk and resumed typing.

Nosiness certainly isn't one of this guy's bad points, McKenna thought. He spent ten minutes comparing Mullen's prints to the latents on the receipt, then he read the Mullen arrest report twice. When he was sure he knew every piece of information on it, he brought all the paper over to Thor. "We have a lot to talk about," he said.

"Good news or bad news?"

"Both. The man who we're looking for is a former New York City detective named Mike Mullen."

"Why is he a *former* detective?"

"He was fired after he was arrested in 1991 for shaking down quite a few high-priced call girls. He eventually jumped bail and hasn't been seen in New York since, as far as we know."

Thor's next question was so on the money that even McKenna was surprised. "Where was he assigned?"

"The Bomb Squad."

"Hold on. I'll make the coffee."

Seated on stools across from each other at the lab table, McKenna and Thor didn't pass a word until the second cup. McKenna had mentally catalogued every fact he knew in the old case, but it took some time to reconcile what he knew about Mullen with the present scenario. It didn't make sense to him, so there was only one conclusion. There was a lot about Mullen that the NYPD should have uncovered sooner in its investigation of him and his activities. McKenna didn't relish telling Thor this conclusion, but was sure he wouldn't have to. The Icelander would see it for himself.

"Mullen was an unusual case right from the start," McKenna explained. "He was born in Canada in 1952, but came south in '72 and joined our army when many young American men were heading north to dodge the draft. Spent three years and wound up being assigned to a demolition unit. Did well, rose to the rank of sergeant. He got an honorable discharge, becoming a U.S. citizen along the way. Then he joined the NYPD in 1975. Also did well with us, at first. Made detective in 1981 after just six years on the Job. He was assigned to the Bomb Squad in 1982 and was promoted to detective second grade in 1989. Then he was arrested in 1991 and surprised everyone when he jumped bail. Our Internal Affairs Division has been trying for years to track him down and get him, but he'd vanished without a trace."

"Until now," Thor observed wryly.

"Yes, until now."

"Obviously, some mistakes have been made."

Right on the money, McKenna thought. "I know."

"Feel like talking about them now?"

"No, but it has to be done. Where do you want to start, his background investigation?"

"Yes. I'm assuming your people weren't as thorough as they should have been when they conducted it."

"It was supposed to be thorough and I'd assumed until now that it was. Apparently, I was wrong."

"Because Mullen never was who he seemed to be?" Thor guessed.

"That's my bet now."

"Wasn't his original background investigation rechecked after he was arrested and jumped bail?"

"Again, I'm assuming it was, but it was never one of my cases," McKenna said, feeling embarrassed.

"What were the circumstances surrounding his arrest?"

"Beginning in 1990 our Internal Affairs Division began getting reports of shakedowns of prostitutes by someone with a detective's shield. The shield number the guy was using was 391, so they knew it was a phony. That number had belonged to a detective who had been killed in the line of duty in 1931 and it had never been reissued."

"So they knew the shield was a phony, but were they smart enough to realize they were dealing with a real cop?"

"Yeah, they knew. Mullen set it up real good and he was fairly careful, but they knew. He showed the girls he shook down that he knew too much about police procedure to be anything else."

"Tell me how he did it."

"He would check into a nice hotel, paying cash. Then he would call one of the more expensive services and have them send a girl over. He'd have all the things in his room to put the girl at ease, because every once in a while the Public Morals Division sets up a sting to close down a call-girl operation. They use undercover cops posing as traveling businessmen looking for some fun, but the girls are wise to that stunt and know what to look for in a legitimate customer before they'll talk business."

"Luggage in the room, clothes unpacked and in the closets, airline tickets on one of the dressers, some business correspondence lying around?"

"You ever do any public morals work?" McKenna asked, surprised that Thor knew the game.

"In my younger days, before I got well known here."

Must have done a pretty good job at it, McKenna thought, just like Mullen did. "Anyway, Mullen set some pretty good props. Had the luggage, had the clothes unpacked in the room, and had a rental car contract on the bed indicating he'd rented the car in a city a couple of hundred miles from New York the day before. Once the girl was satisfied that Mullen wasn't an undercover, she'd tell him how much whatever he wanted to do with her was going to cost him. As soon as she got the words out of her mouth, he'd pull out his phony shield and tell her she was under arrest for prostitution."

"But he'd give her an out?" Thor surmised.

"Yeah, he'd tell her what a shame it was that a nice girl like her making a couple of thousand a night would have to spend a couple of wasted, unpleasant days in jail."

"And she'd make an offer?"

"Yeah, but never enough. His price was always fifteen hundred to let her go. Naturally, she'd agree and he'd have her call her service or her pimp to get the money right to the room. He pulled that stunt eleven times that we know about before he was bagged."

"And probably many more that you don't know about," Thor said.

"Probably, but he was too greedy and kept at it for too long. Finally, IAD went out on a limb and started dealing directly with a couple of the services. They didn't like doing it because it appeared that the department was implicitly condoning prostitution, but they had no other way to get Mullen. The IAD people told the girls that if they were being held up by Mullen, they should ask for Benny when they called their dispatcher to have the money sent over to his room. Then the dispatcher would call an IAD team waiting in the Midtown area."

"How long did it take them to get him after that?"

"A couple of months, but then they took him in his hotel room without a whimper while he and the girl were waiting for the money to arrive. The arrest got a lot of press and caused quite a stir in the department."

"What was he charged with?"

"Grand larceny by extortion, bribery, and official misconduct. Two felonies and a misdemeanor, enough to rate a twenty-five-thousand-dollar bail. He lost that when he jumped bail and disappeared."

"You mentioned that you knew him," Thor said.

"Met him a few times before he was arrested. Once at a union picnic and once at a retirement party."

"What was your impression of him?"

"I'm gonna seem like a dope to you, but he seemed like a pretty good guy to me. He was a bruiser with a ready smile and lots of jokes. That's why his arrest caught a lot of people off guard, including me. He was popular, hard-working, and good at his job."

"He would be," Thor commented. "He was good enough to fool Meaghan and catch her off guard, and it seems to me that she was a pretty sharp girl. What were his politics?"

"I don't know."

"Any family?"

"I know I'm beginning to sound monotonous, but I don't know that either."

"I know. It wasn't your case," Thor said, smiling. "Now, just one more question. You detect any sign of a brogue in him?"

What a question! McKenna thought. I told this guy that Mullen was born in Canada, but he's not buying it. Thor's made the jump that Mullen isn't just now IRA, but that he always was, that Mullen's original background investigation when he came on the Job and the subsequent investigation after he was arrested were both shoddy or conducted by incompetents. Unfortunately, it looks like he was right. "No, I didn't hear it. He's been hiding the brogue from me and probably everyone else."

"I bet Meaghan caught it," Thor said, causing a number of speculations to jump into McKenna's mind at once. Meaghan was good at hiding her own brogue and might recognize someone else doing the same thing. Is that one of the reasons she's dead? he wondered.

McKenna's ruminations were cut short by the ringing of the phone. At that moment, it was a welcome sound. He didn't want to give Thor another *"I don't know"* to one of his questions. He got up and picked up the phone. "Detective McKenna."

"Is it him?" Brunette asked.

"It's him."

"Damn! Who else knows?"

"Just Thor and me."

"Can you keep it out of the press for a while?"

"Why? Think he'll run to someplace we can't get him?"

"Yeah, we don't want him popping up as a guest of Cuba, Libya, Iraq, or Iran."

"I'll run that by Thor," McKenna said.

"You know a guy named Dennis Hunt?"

"No."

"Well, you will. He'll be on a plane tonight with Mullen's personnel folder and the case folder on his shakedown scam and disappearance."

"Who is he?"

"Mullen's old partner in the Bomb Squad. A pretty sharp guy."

Good idea, McKenna thought. Dennis Hunt should know more about Mullen than most other people on earth. "Does Mullen have any family in town?"

"An ex-wife in the Bronx and two kids. Both boys, ages ten and twelve. She got a divorce when Mullen took off, but she's still living in her old house. Want them put under surveillance?"

"Full blown. Do her phones too, if you can."

"Consider it done. Anything else?"

"Remember the Dwyer case?" McKenna asked.

"Sure. I remember any case you didn't solve. Why?"

"Because he did that one, too."

"Good God!" Brunette said, despair in his voice. "He did a sex murder while he was still on the Job?"

"Yeah, we're gonna take a beating on this one."

"If we deserve it, we'll have to thicken our skin, put on our helmets, and take it. What's your read on it?"

"We deserve it," McKenna stated.

"Okay. Glad we got that out of the way. What else do you need? The Dwyer case folder?"

"That and anything else you can think of that I didn't."

"You got it."

"Any parting words?" McKenna asked.

"Get Mike Mullen, whatever you have to do."

It was just what McKenna wanted to hear.

———

It was another long, busy night. McKenna found that a three o'clock sunset was disorienting, and he lost track of time as he and Thor worked and planned.

The first order of business was Chris O'Malley. He was still passed out in his chair when Thor and McKenna returned to the apartment, so they carried him down to Thor's car and then up to his room at the Saga.

Next came the first of many unpleasant tasks of the evening. Thor called the medical examiner and authorized the release of Meaghan's body. Then he drove McKenna to a funeral home whose owner was a friend of his. McKenna selected a casket for Meaghan, bringing one of his credit cards to the limit. That was only the beginning. McKenna wanted Meaghan's body restored to a condition in which her mother would recognize her, but after Thor showed the mortician photos of what had been done to her, another one of McKenna's cards was maxed.

After arriving back at the presidential suite, McKenna called Father Maher. Expecting the worst while hoping for the best, Ryer Maher accepted the news stoically. "When will her body be arriving in Ireland?" he asked.

"I should be bringing her home the day after tomorrow," McKenna told him.

"You'll be in Belfast for the funeral?"

"Belfast? I figured I'd be taking her home to Dublin," McKenna said.

"Dublin isn't home, it's just where my family's living for the moment," Maher explained. "Most of our relatives are still in Belfast, and that's where our family plot is. There are generations of our people buried there."

"Okay, Belfast it is. I'll be there."

Maher graciously thanked McKenna for his work before hanging up, giving a few compliments that McKenna didn't feel he deserved.

"What next?" McKenna asked Thor.

"Janus." Thor called his boss at home and fifteen minutes later Janus joined them. The Icelandic chief was in a good mood when he arrived, but he became pensive as Thor reported on the day's developments. "You have a plan to get this guy?" he asked Thor.

"I don't, but Brian has a few things for you to consider."

Janus looked mildly surprised at Thor's statement, but it lasted only for a moment. "Let's have it, Brian."

"First of all, I've got a tough request. Both Ray and I would like you to sit on the Mullen news for a while."

"You mean not give it to the press? Not tell our sometimes vindictive reporters that you've identified the man who pulled the first political bombing in our history, not to mention the first sex murder in twenty years?"

"Yes."

"And you don't want me to tell them that this man was a New York City detective—better yet, a Bomb Squad detective. You want me to keep this news to myself, even though every reporter in the country calls me twice a day for news in this case?"

"Exactly."

"How long would you like me to sit on this?"

"As long as you can. I'd sure like to get a week of looking for him before he knows we're on to him."

"Okay," Janus answered at once. "What else?"

Now that wasn't so hard, McKenna thought. The next one should be a snap. "Thor's of the opinion that the Brits haven't been completely forthright with him."

"Of course they haven't. Why should they show all their cards to us? After all, they know the bomber isn't in Iceland and there wasn't much Thor could do to get him."

"But now things are different."

"Yes, now they are. Now we're holding some pretty strong cards."

"I agree," McKenna said. "But if we're gonna find Mullen, we need the Brits completely on board."

"What do you need from them?"

"I need O'Bannion implicated in this. I need everything they know about him."

"That might be difficult."

"Getting the information from them?"

"No, proving the connection to O'Bannion. I'm sure they've been trying to implicate him in this thing since it happened. Don't you think it would be quite a feather in their cap to publicly connect the Irish minister for finance to a terrorist bombing?"

"That's one of the problems we're gonna have with the Brits. I'm sure they attach more importance to implicating O'Bannion than they do to finding the bomber."

"But you don't?" Janus asked.

"No. I couldn't care less about O'Bannion."

"How about you, Thor?" Janus asked.

"It would be nice to get both of them, but not essential."

"What is essential?"

"Getting Mullen, if I had to choose. He's the one who murdered three people. O'Bannion would only be responsible for two of them," Thor answered, then turned to McKenna. "I guess you're planning to use whatever you can develop from Hackford and Rollins to blackmail O'Bannion."

"Yep. If the Brits have been doing their homework and if O'Bannion is involved, I'm going to pressure him into giving up Mullen."

"And then let O'Bannion off?"

"If that's the deal we make with him."

"The Brits will never go along with that," Janus said.

"Then we'll cut them out and go it alone, if that's all right with you," McKenna said.

"You mean not tell them about Mullen?"

"Not exactly. I'd like you to tell them we've got the bomber identified, but they have to play ball to get his name."

"That's a decision that's going to have to be made at the highest levels of the British government," Janus said.

"I know. I hate to put you in this position because I'm sure the proposition has to be explained to the highest levels of your government for approval first."

"When it comes to crime in Iceland, you just did that," Janus said. "And you've got my approval."

FOURTEEN

MONDAY, MARCH 9TH—KEFLAVÍK, ICELAND

McKenna had been worried about recognizing Dennis Hunt at the airport, but that didn't turn out to be a problem. He knew that Hunt had to be the man who got off the plane with Vernon Geberth at 7:00 A.M. Neither McKenna nor Thor had known that Vernon was coming.

Vernon looked good, like a retired weight lifter passing his time as a successful businessman, which was exactly what he was. He was dressed in a European-tailored suit, wore expensive Italian loafers, carried a burnished leather briefcase, sported a Florida tan, and comported himself like the man in charge.

Dennis Hunt, on the other hand, looked like somebody who worked for Vernon. As they came off the plane, he was nodding his head and paying close attention to whatever Vernon was saying to him. He was in his fifties, a tall man in reasonably good shape, but, when it came to clothes, he certainly wasn't in Vernon's league. Searching for bombs and dismantling them if and when they were found was a dirty job, and the members of the Bomb Squad weren't known as slaves to fashion. There was nothing slovenly about him, but he wore his suit like a set of coveralls and carried his old, battered briefcase like a tool box.

Vernon was warmly greeted by Thor and McKenna, and then he introduced Hunt to them. Hunt was politely deferential, but McKenna got the impression that he was uncomfortable and didn't want to be there. In contrast, Vernon was in his element—the recognized expert on murder making a house call to dispense his wisdom to the less experienced and less enlight-

ened. In Vernon's case, that meant everyone else because he had *the gift*—
he could get into a killer's head and fathom his motivation. Thirty years'
experience working homicides, an eye for detail, and a master's degree in
clinical psychology gave Vernon the ability to study crime scene photos and
then tell exactly what the killer was thinking when he did those horrible
things to his victims. "When did you find out you were coming here?"
McKenna asked him.

"Ray called me yesterday afternoon and told me what you had cooking
here. Asked me to get involved. I told him I was already involved, that Thor
had already sent me some photos of Winthrop and Meaghan. Kinda surprised him, but he offered me a free trip with expenses and here I am."

Vernon did that all the time, McKenna knew. He made his money on
his seminars, but he enhanced his reputation by helping cops solve their
difficult homicides for free.

"Did you know Mullen, Vernon?" Thor asked.

"No, never worked with him and I don't think I ever met him."

"Then you probably never did meet him," Hunt volunteered. "He was
the kind of guy you'd remember."

"How long did you and Mullen work together?" McKenna asked Hunt.

"Almost six years."

"Were you close?"

"Yeah, we were close. I would have said I knew him better than anyone,
but he still managed to surprise me."

"When was the last time you saw him?"

"April twenty-first, 1991. I drove him home from court after he made
bail."

"Did you know he was gonna run?"

The question caught Hunt by surprise and he thought a moment before
he answered. "No, but I wasn't too surprised when he did. He was facing
some time and his life was falling apart."

"Have you heard from him since then?"

"Can we talk about this later?" Hunt asked. "I worked all day yesterday,
it was a long flight, and I haven't slept in a couple of days. Today is supposed
to be my day off and instead I'm in Iceland on two hours' notice."

This guy knows something that he doesn't want to talk about, McKenna
thought. But he has to. Protecting a murderer is different than standing by
your old partner who just happens to be an extortionist, and Hunt knows that.
But I don't mind giving him the kid-glove treatment for a while. "Sure, it can
wait. We'll take you to the hotel for some food and rest. We can talk later."

After they arrived at the Saga, McKenna invited Hunt and Vernon to breakfast in the hotel restaurant. Hunt declined the offer, stating that he wanted
to shower and then order from room service before his nap.

Vernon also declined the breakfast invitation. Food and rest hadn't been his reasons for coming to Iceland. He had come to work and started right in as soon as he checked into his room. Brunette had given him the old Dwyer case folder right before the flight, but Vernon had been sitting next to a teenage girl on the plane and he had known that the crime scene and autopsy photos would have horrified her. He had done no more than browse through that case.

There was a lot to be done and Vernon preferred to work alone, so McKenna and Thor left him in his room with the three case folders and went to breakfast in the Saga's restaurant. They ate and talked for an hour and were just about to leave when Janus found them and sat at their table. "I've got some news," he announced.

"Good or bad?" McKenna asked.

"You tell me. The British government will go for your deal, but they've attached some stipulations."

"Have they implicated O'Bannion?"

"Not enough to convict him in a court of law, and certainly not in an Irish court."

"Okay, what else do they want?"

"A time limit. They say they'll give you all the assistance they can, but you've only got a month."

"So if I can squeeze O'Bannion and get some help from him, then I've got just a month to get Mullen?"

"Essentially, yes."

"And if I don't get him in that month?"

"Then they'll repudiate any deal you might make with O'Bannion and go after him."

Very clever, McKenna thought. If I get O'Bannion to cooperate, then he's implicated himself out of his own mouth. Either way, the Brits win. "Anything else?"

"If you do find Mullen, they're in on the arrest."

"No matter where I get him?"

"No matter where. They don't care about your extortion charges in the U.S. They want him before a British court."

"I don't think Ray will be real happy with that, but I guess we'll have to live with it."

"Good," Janus said, standing up. "Inspector Rollins will be at your room at three with everything he's got."

Dennis Hunt had given McKenna Mullen's bulky personnel folder, but McKenna didn't want to go over it with Thor; he preferred to examine the NYPD's dirty laundry alone. He didn't tell Thor how he felt, but the Icelander understood. After breakfast he told McKenna that he had some paperwork to catch up on. He would be back at noon to hear what Vernon had to say.

McKenna sat at the desk in the presidential suite and placed Mullen's folder in front of him. The thick manila envelope was taped and sealed with Brunette's signature scrawled across the flap. That meant two things to McKenna: Brunette had taken the time to review the folder and there were things in it that he didn't want Hunt browsing through on the flight.

As McKenna unwrapped the file, a white envelope fell out. Ray had scrawled "Bullshit" across the front of it, so he got McKenna's curiosity right away.

The envelope contained copies of Mullen's birth certificate and his high school diploma. The birth certificate verified that Michael Mullen, the first child of Thomas and Anna Mullen, had been born in L'Hôpital du Sacre Coeur in Quebec on May 23, 1952. His diploma showed that he had graduated with honors from a Quebec high school, Lycée de Ste. Anne, in June of 1970. The two documents were titled and captioned in both English and French and both were certified copies.

McKenna smiled as he replaced them in the envelope. My pal and I are on the same wavelength, he thought. Once Ray found out our Mike Mullen is an IRA bomber, he also suspects our Mullen is not the real Mullen. Ray knows that the IRA is a close-knit group who trust nobody they hadn't grown up with, so he's asking himself the same question that Thor and I asked ourselves: Why would the IRA, an organization with no shortage of bomb experts, take a chance on hiring an unknown crooked cop to pull one of their major capers? One likely answer is that whoever-he-is isn't an unknown to them. He was always IRA and always would be, no matter what he was doing or how he felt about it. Ray knows as well as I do that the IRA's motto is "Once in, never out," and they live by that simple rule.

As McKenna unwrapped the manila envelope, he saw that it actually contained two folders. The thinner one was Mullen's personnel folder. More bulky was the case folder that documented the unsuccessful hunt for the fugitive undertaken by the Internal Affairs Division. McKenna decided to start with the thinner folder.

Beginning the personnel folder were the worksheets compiled during Mullen's applicant investigation, the first order of business as far as McKenna was concerned. As he had feared, he found that it was a shoddy job. There was a lot of information; all the boxes had been checked and all the bases had been covered, but it was still a shoddy job.

As McKenna read, he learned that Mullen had taken the NYPD written test while still in the army. After his discharge he had moved to the Bronx and taken a job as an electrician's apprentice while awaiting his appointment to the NYPD. The investigator had interviewed Mullen's employer and had received a glowing report from him. He had also interviewed Mullen's neighbors in the Bronx and got much the same information. Mullen's driver's license had been verified and his driving record was checked; he had never received any moving violations, nor even a parking ticket.

Mullen had been fingerprinted and his prints had been checked nationwide and also submitted to the Canadian authorities. Once again, Mullen was found to be almost too good to be true. He had never been arrested or been in any trouble of any kind.

Mullen had been naturalized as a U.S. citizen while he had been in the army and copies of his naturalization papers were attached to his background investigation. Also attached was a copy of Mullen's DD-214, his separation certificate from the army. After inspecting it, McKenna found, as he had expected, that Mullen had been a model soldier. He had spent his entire four years in the U.S., attending the NCO Leadership Course and Demolition School during his hitch. He had earned the Good Conduct Medal and had been discharged from Fort Dix, New Jersey, in February of 1975. The investigator had located and interviewed Mullen's commanding officer at Fort Dix, a Major Schaeffer. According to Schaeffer, Mullen was one of the best soldiers he had ever seen: he was neat, well disciplined, personable, a good leader, and he knew more about explosives than anybody else in the unit. Just like everyone else interviewed, Schaeffer had thought that Mullen would make an excellent cop.

Based on what he had read in the reports, McKenna would have agreed—except for one thing: Not one person who had known Mullen before he had come to the U.S. from Canada had been located and interviewed. As far as McKenna was concerned, that glaring deficiency characterized the investigation as a shoddy affair.

As required, of course, the investigator had tried. But it had been a halfhearted attempt rife with documented excuses. The problem was that the excuses came, almost word for word, from Mullen. According to Mullen, he knew almost nobody in Canada and he couldn't provide the investigator with many Canadian references. His story was that he had grown up in an English-speaking neighborhood in French Quebec; in 1970, right after his graduation from high school, his family had moved to Toronto because French had become the official language of the province of Quebec. He gave the names of a few neighbors in Toronto and Quebec who, he said, might remember him, but he was sketchy on their addresses.

According to the investigator, virtually every English-speaking neighbor of the Mullen family had also moved. None of those mentioned by Mullen during his investigation could be located. Just weeks after the move, according to Mullen, his parents had been killed in a plane crash in the Canary Islands. Since he had no other family and knew hardly anybody in Toronto,

Mullen had told his investigator that he had come to the U.S. to start a new life in the U.S. Army.

To verify Mullen's story, the investigator had done some research on the plane crash. After finding that a Thomas and Anna Mullen had indeed been listed among the victims, Mullen had been approved as a candidate for the NYPD and his investigation had been marked complete. Three months later Mullen was in the police academy.

It was all as McKenna had suspected, with one ironic footnote. The sergeant who had supervised Mullen's investigation in 1975 was George Mosley, the same man who had supervised Meaghan Maher's botched missing persons investigation twenty-four years later. McKenna was sure that Brunette had also noticed the signature at the end of the applicant investigation report and was just as sure that Mosley's police career was rapidly coming to a miserable end. Someone had to pay the price for letting an IRA terrorist join the NYPD, and Mosley was McKenna's candidate for that dubious distinction. Worse yet, McKenna was certain that Mike Mullen was not the man's real name. There had been a Mike Mullen who had been born in Quebec and who had gone to school there, a man whose parents had been killed in a plane crash shortly after moving to Toronto, but that real Mike Mullen was not the same man who had joined the U.S. Army and the NYPD. McKenna figured that young man was probably long dead, killed for his identity.

After spending an hour going through Mullen's two-month background investigation, it took McKenna only fifteen minutes to examine the rest of Mullen's seventeen-year police career. After graduating from the academy near the top of his class, Mullen had been assigned to Fort Apache, the 41st Precinct in the Bronx. He had done well there, making many arrests and earning many medals. His sergeants had noticed and appreciated him, marking his evaluations "Excellent officer, performs above standards." His precinct CO had also noticed him and had approved Mullen's request for assignment to the Narcotics Division, thereby placing him on the fast track to the detective's gold shield.

Mullen did the rest. After two years of locking up and convicting drug dealers in Queens, he had been rewarded with the promotion and assigned to the 50th Detective Squad, once again back in the Bronx. His stay there had been short, but notable. His squad commander had evaluated him as "A hard-working, knowledgeable detective."

One year later Mullen had requested assignment to the Bomb Squad. After the required interview and aptitude testing, he had been accepted as a real find. He had then been sent to the Federal Ordnance and Training Center in Alabama for the standard three-month training course mandated for all Bomb Squad investigators throughout the country. In retrospect,

McKenna noticed that it was in Alabama that Mullen's pride caused him to step out of character. He did so well in the training that, upon graduation, his instructor had written on his evaluation, "This detective could have taught this course."

Right after his return from training, Mullen's personnel folder documented a change in his social status and address. In 1982 he had married Kathleen Murphy and they had bought a house together in the Woodlawn section of the Bronx.

McKenna found Mullen's choice of neighborhood interesting. Woodlawn was a very middle-class, very Irish neighborhood, and it was also the neighborhood in which Dwyer's killer had dumped the stolen car after the murder. If Mullen was an Irish-born terrorist looking to hide any connection to his past life, then '82 was the year he had felt confident enough in his new identity to allow himself some small solace, a return to his roots. Living in Woodlawn was as close as one could get in New York to living in Ireland.

The medical benefits records continued the story. In 1985, Kathleen delivered their first child, James, at Mount Sinai Hospital. In 1987 she was back again and left with their second boy, John. But it wasn't always a happy occasion that brought Kathleen to Mount Sinai. In '88 she had been hospitalized for treatment of a broken left forearm and a broken jaw, injuries that she had received when she had fallen down the stairs in their house.

In 1989 Mullen had been promoted to detective second grade. It was also the year in which Kathleen had her first nervous breakdown. Her treatment had required three weeks in the psychiatric ward at Mount Sinai and another four months as an outpatient.

In 1990 the city paid for a year of marriage counseling for the Mullen family, but the marriage was apparently a lost cause. Kathleen's address had remained the same, but Mullen had a new one by the end of the year. He had moved to an apartment in Woodlawn, two blocks from his home, his wife, and his kids.

In 1991, right after Mullen's arrest, the city had picked up one final tab when Kathleen had suffered her second nervous breakdown. She had spent another month in Mount Sinai and had left the day the benefits ended, the day Mullen was fired. The last items in the folder were Mullen's arrest report and his Notice of Dismissal.

All the good things that McKenna had expected to see in the personnel folder of a rising detective were there, but there was one unexpected item that caused McKenna some concern—in his seventeen years with the department, Mullen had never failed to shoot anything less than a perfect 100 during his annual pistol training and qualification.

McKenna had learned enough to recognize that the man would not be taken without a fight. Given a choice, fisticuffs with the bruiser or even a knife fight would be preferable to a gunfight with him. McKenna made himself a cup of coffee at the service bar before he opened the thick folder and began going through it.

The IAD hadn't done a much better job than the Applicant Investigation Section had done seventeen years before them. They had put in a lot of time and had generated a bundle of reports justifying their efforts, but McKenna concluded that they had failed because their hunt had been based on an erroneous assumption. IAD had figured that they were simply looking for a good cop gone bad, and that was why they had never gotten close to capturing Mullen. They had taken him at face value. Making matters worse, McKenna quickly saw that IAD had relied on his applicant investigation as a reference point, believing everything in Mosley's inept investigation long ago.

For three months after Mullen had jumped bail twenty investigators, supervised by an Inspector O'Shaughnessy, had been assigned to find him. They had taken all the logical steps. They contacted the U.S. State Department and were told that Mullen had never applied for a passport, so they had assumed that he must have been hiding out somewhere in the U.S. or Canada and had concentrated their efforts there. They had interviewed his wife and had found her to be uncooperative, so they had speculated that she might have had some idea of his whereabouts. Following that line of reasoning, they had put a tap on her phone and had surveilled her for months, but got nowhere.

It seemed to McKenna that IAD had interviewed every person who could possibly have known Mullen in New York. In the folder were the reports written following the interviews of thirty-four cops he had worked with over the years, including every member of the Bomb Squad. Each had stated that they had no idea where Mullen was.

Mullen's friends and neighbors in Woodlawn had also been interviewed, with the same results. No one had seen him or heard from him since he had jumped bail.

Mullen had been described by many who knew him as a social drinker, a man who liked to while away a few spare hours in the Woodlawn bars, so every place he had been known to frequent had also been placed under periodic surveillance. Still no Mullen. After two frustrating months, IAD had subpoenaed Mullen's banking, credit, and telephone records. What they had found led them no closer to him. Mullen had cleaned out his bank account prior to skipping, but that only yielded him two thousand dollars. At the time he still had credit cards and telephone calling cards, but wherever he was, he hadn't been using them.

By the end of the third month O'Shaughnessy had been at his wit's end. In desperation he sent two teams to Canada, one to Toronto and the other to Quebec. They had returned two weeks later without having found even one person who remembered Mullen, no less seen him.

The hunt for Mullen had been a bust, an expensive and embarrassing affair for the Internal Affairs Division. The report scaling down the investigation was near the end of the folder. O'Shaughnessy had stated on paper that the expense and manpower involved in trying to apprehend a man who was, after all, only a con artist and an extortionist, could no longer be justified. He had recommended that, pending further developments, the case be marked "Inactive, subject to annual evaluation and review." He had concluded by stating that a character like Mullen, with no apparent means of support, was bound to reveal his location by getting into trouble sooner or later. When he did, IAD would be there to apprehend him.

That was the theory, and the man who had been the police commissioner at the time had endorsed it, but it hadn't worked out as O'Shaughnessy had envisioned. For seven years the Mullen case had remained on the back burner and the annual review O'Shaughnessy had recommended consisted of nothing more than reinterviewing Kathleen Mullen, Dennis Hunt, and a few other friends of Mullen's in the department. According to the reports, they hadn't seen or heard from him and had nothing to add.

McKenna closed the folder and paced the room for a few minutes, thinking over the information he had just learned and pondering the points IAD had missed. He decided that the fugitive investigation wasn't as badly done as he had initially assumed. He acknowledged that hindsight is always more accurate than foresight and IAD had had no reason to think that Mullen wasn't what he had appeared to be in 1991.

Would I have been able to guess that if I had been assigned to the investigation? McKenna asked himself. Without having seen the Saga video, would I have been sharp enough to come to the conclusion that our Mullen wasn't the real Mullen? Maybe, but probably not, he decided. But now that I know, what else is there in those folders that IAD missed? What's in that seven-year investigation that will help me find Mullen in the week I have before he finds out I'm looking for him?

McKenna sat down at the desk again and took out all the reports written following the many interviews of Kathleen Mullen and Dennis Hunt. After the third rereading, he called Brunette.

FIFTEEN

Vernon and Thor arrived together at McKenna's room at noon, as promised. However, Vernon wasn't quite ready to give his opinion on what made Mullen tick. First he wanted to see Meaghan's body, a request Thor handled. He took Vernon to the morgue, freeing McKenna for another unpleasant task. McKenna was a detective, not a boss, and he didn't relish putting another detective's feet to the fire. However, it had to be done. It was time to talk to Dennis Hunt.

Before Vernon left, McKenna got the Dwyer, Winthrop, and Maher case folders from him. He spread the crime scene photos of the three tortured bodies on the coffee table between the two couches in the sitting room, then made a fresh pot of coffee before dialing Hunt's room.

Five minutes later, McKenna answered the knock at his door. Hunt was dressed in a fresh suit and looked better, but still uncomfortable.

"You get some sleep?" McKenna asked as he led Hunt into the sitting room.

"Some," Hunt answered, then stopped dead in his tracks as he noticed the photos spread on the coffee table. Hesitantly, he walked over to the table and stared at the photos, but he made no move to pick any of them up for a closer examination.

"But you still don't feel great?" McKenna guessed, pretending not to notice Hunt's discomfort.

"I feel miserable, but it has nothing to do with sleep," Hunt answered, still staring at the photos.

"How do you take your coffee?" McKenna asked, but Hunt ignored him as he stared down at the photos.

"How do you take your coffee?" McKenna repeated.

"Oh, sorry," Hunt answered, looking up from the coffee table. "Today I think I'll take it black."

"You got it." McKenna went to the service bar and poured two cups of black coffee. Hunt took his eyes off the photos and sat on one of the couches, dejectedly staring into space. McKenna returned with the coffee cups and placed them on the table, next to the photos. Then he sat on the other couch, facing Hunt, with the coffee table between them. "You ready to begin?" McKenna asked.

"Begin what?" Hunt asked suspiciously, focusing on McKenna.

"Begin telling the truth."

The statement hit Hunt like a punch in the gut. He lowered his eyes back to the photos and took a couple of deep breaths as he looked from one to another of the gory shots. Then he made his decision and stared back at McKenna, resigned and dejected. "I guess this is the end of my police career, but I'm ready."

"You're ready to tell me that you've been lying to IAD for years to protect Mullen?"

"I didn't think of it as lying," Hunt said defensively. "I thought of it as protecting a friend."

"Okay, let's call it fibbing," McKenna said. "But remember, if it weren't for those fibs, maybe two of those people in front of you would still be alive."

"Knowing what I know now, maybe all three of them would still be alive if it weren't for me," Hunt stated.

Three of them? How can that be? McKenna wondered, shocked by Hunt's assertion. If IAD had captured Mullen, then Winthrop and Meaghan would certainly still be alive. But Dwyer? Mullen killed him in 1989, two years before he was arrested. What could Hunt have done that could have prevented Dwyer's death?

Hunt noticed McKenna's bewilderment. He picked up one of the photos of Dwyer's body, stared at it intently, then passed it to McKenna. "Is that Joseph Dwyer?" he asked.

"That's him. Sometimes known as Josephine Dwyer."

"Then if Mullen killed him, I'm partly responsible for his death."

"How?"

"I think I'd like to talk to a lawyer before I say anything more."

"And then you'll come clean?"

"Like I said, I'm going to talk. But I'm going to be in big trouble over this."

"More trouble than just for lying to IAD?"

"Yeah, maybe lots more. I didn't realize how much more until just now, when I saw those Dwyer photos. Mullen really double-crossed me." Hunt left it at that. He picked up his cup and downed the hot coffee in four quick gulps, then placed the cup back on the coffee table and stared at McKenna.

McKenna didn't notice. He was looking at the photo of Dwyer's tortured body, trying to get the connection between Mullen, Hunt, and the victim. Nothing came to mind, not a clue. He put the photo down on the coffee table, picked up his own cup, and took a sip. It was too hot for him, so he placed the cup back on the table and stared back at Hunt. "You know I'm only a detective, just like you," he offered, seeking to place Hunt at ease.

Hunt wasn't buying it. "That's what you say, but let's not kid each other," he said, shaking his head. "I know who you are, I know your rep, and I know you're Brunette's pal. I also know I'm gonna sink on this one, but I still need a lawyer to make it official."

"You're right about me, and maybe that works to your benefit. Maybe you don't have to sink."

"What do you mean?"

"I mean that I called Brunette this morning and told him that I thought you'd been lying to IAD."

McKenna had Hunt's total interest. "Yeah? So what'd he say?"

"He said, under the present circumstances, that was no big thing. He's willing to forgive and forget, as long as you didn't do anything criminal. Tell me the truth, hop on a plane, and it's back to the Bomb Squad."

McKenna had expected Hunt to jump at the offer, but Hunt still looked uncertain. He decided to pour it on thick. "Brunette's looked at your record and liked what he saw. Says you're a little misguided if you lied to protect Mullen, but he understands loyalty and values loyal people. He sees how you'd lie to protect a friend, but knows you wouldn't lie to protect a murderer."

"Then Brunette knows me, but his deal sounds too good to believe," Hunt said, once again shaking his head.

"We can call him right now and you can ask him yourself," McKenna suggested.

Hunt thought it over for a moment before answering. "That won't be necessary. I guess I believe you."

"More important, do you trust me enough to go off the record for two questions?"

"Maybe. Lemme hear the questions first."

"Okay. First, did you know Mullen was going to kill Dwyer? Second, did you know Mullen was IRA?"

"That's it? That's all you want to know, off the record?"

"That's it, but I need the truth. If you answer yes to either one of those questions, I never heard it. We stop right here and I call Brunette and have him fly a union lawyer here for you. You trust me on that?"

"Yeah, I trust you," Hunt said, suddenly smiling from ear to ear. "No and no. No, I didn't know Mullen was going to kill Dwyer. Matter of fact, I didn't even know Dwyer was dead until I saw those photos. And no, I never knew he was IRA. Now, let's get back on the record and get this over with."

"Okay, just some preliminary questions before we get to the meat. In all the years you two were partners, didn't you ever hear a brogue from him?"

"Only when he wanted to put one on. You know, telling a few jokes over a beer or two, and then he was hilarious. He could make you think he was a leprechaun."

"I find that hard to believe," McKenna said. "Never a slip?"

"You've met him, haven't you?"

"Briefly."

"Did you catch a brogue from him?" Hunt asked smugly.

"Not that I recall," McKenna admitted.

"Enough said. If anything, he sounded like he was from Canada. Sometimes he'd slip and put *eh?* at the end of a sentence.

I guess this guy was good enough to fool just about everyone, McKenna thought. Except maybe Meaghan Maher. "He ever discuss Irish politics?"

"Only to say what was going on over there was crazy. Said he thought it would never end."

So he always stayed in character, McKenna thought. Even with his partner. "He ever strike you as homophobic?"

"I know he didn't like gays, always called them 'sword swallowers,' and he thought the AIDS epidemic was a pretty good thing. But he never made a crusade out of it, if that's what you're asking. Sometimes he'd have a good gay joke, but that was pretty much it."

"You still think so? That was pretty much it?" McKenna asked sarcastically, pointing down to the crime scene photos of Dwyer and Winthrop.

"No, I guess not," Hunt conceded.

"Okay, the preliminaries are over. Let's start with the Dwyer murder and how you fit into that."

"It's complicated, but I told Mullen that Dwyer was an agent."

"An agent? An agent for who?"

"I didn't know. Maybe the FBI, maybe ATF, maybe even the CIA. I didn't know which, but I knew that he had been infiltrated into NORAID and was probably working for one of them, either as an agent or an informer."

McKenna was familiar with NORAID, an organization formed to raise money for social work in Northern Ireland. It was widely speculated that NORAID was, in fact, an American front organization for the IRA and that the money raised was used by them to buy arms. But McKenna didn't see how it was possible that Dwyer was an agent or informer infiltrated into NORAID or how Hunt would know about it if he was. "You're going to have to start at the beginning and explain that to me," he said.

"Okay. Did you know where I was assigned before I was transferred to the Bomb Squad?"

"No."

"I was an undercover in the Intelligence Division. In '84 I was assigned to infiltrate NORAID and report on their activities."

"And that's where you met Dwyer?"

"Yep, once a week at the NORAID meetings. Sometimes more often than that if we did fund-raising duty together."

"What kind of fund-raising?"

"Stupid shit. Sometimes we'd hang out in the Port Authority building soliciting donations. It was just like panhandling, really, but you'd be surprised how much money we'd bring in."

"People would give money to you and a transvestite?" McKenna asked, incredulous.

"Lots of it. I knew Dwyer was gay, but he wasn't doing his cross-dressing act back then. He was a nice guy with a quick wit, charmed in lots of bucks. Other times we'd pick up the bottles from the Irish bars around town."

"Pick up the bottles? What does that mean?"

"NORAID had jars with labels on them soliciting contributions in most of the Irish bars. The patrons dropped in change and quite a few bills. You wouldn't think so, but it was quite a haul."

"Quite a haul? How much was that?"

"I wouldn't know, but it had to be at least five thousand a week, not counting direct contributions."

"Where would they get direct contributions from?"

"In the mail. NORAID ran advertisements and requests for contributions in all the Irish papers. According to Dwyer, they did pretty good."

"How would he know that if you didn't?"

"He did a lot of work for them, volunteering for everything. He opened envelopes in the office a couple of days a week. Before I left, he was even doing most of the accounting work and running up the totals."

"How did you know he was an agent?" McKenna asked.

"Because he was always there. The way me and a few of the other undercovers saw it, only us agents were always there because that was our job. We had to be there."

"How many agents were there?" McKenna asked.

"We couldn't be sure because there were too many agencies doing NORAID undercover work at the time and they weren't coordinating their efforts. It became sort of a running joke among us that if we hadn't been working all the time for NORAID, the whole thing would have collapsed and the IRA would have gone broke."

"How did you find out about the other agents?"

"By accident. One time I had to go to court on an old case and I met another NORAID guy there, Dennis Quinn. He was from ATF and doing the same thing I was, going to court on one of his old cases. We sat down for lunch and had a lot of laughs compiling our agent list."

"How many were there?"

"At the time I knew about another guy from the Intelligence Division and Quinn had been assigned with another guy from ATF, John McGreevy. McGreevy had told Quinn about yet another guy, an FBI agent he knew.

So me and Quinn put our heads together and that day we formed the NORAID Undercover Agents Club. Made things quite a bit easier for the members."

"How?"

"How?" Hunt asked, permitting himself a chuckle. "If we can go off the record again I'll tell you how."

"Okay, we're off. Tell me."

"First of all, you have to understand how boring those meetings were. Same old rhetoric every time, the same old suggestions, the same old boring speeches calling for more and more work. Those meetings bored us to tears and took a lot of time out of our lives. So we asked ourselves, Why should we all have to go and sit through that horseshit? See what I mean?"

McKenna did and ventured a guess. "Sure. You only needed a couple of your club members there to make a report on who was at the meeting and what was going on."

"Right. Then the rest of the club members just copied the report for whatever agency he was working for. Gave us all a few days off and some time to lead something like a normal life."

"How many members did you eventually wind up with in your club?"

"Seven."

"But Dwyer wasn't one of them, was he?" McKenna asked.

"No. We were all sure that he was working for someone, but we didn't know how to approach him. You see, there was the risk that he wasn't an agent like us, just an informer on some agency's payroll. In that case, we wouldn't want him in the club."

"Because he might inform your agencies about what the club members were up to?" McKenna guessed.

"Right. Once a snitch, always a snitch. So we left him working as hard as ever. He still was when I left the Intelligence Division in '86. Didn't see him again until '89 when I ran into him on a Bomb Squad run with Mullen."

"Where? At a NORAID meeting?"

"Nope. The plot thickens. Queer Nation had a fund raiser in the Village and some joker had taped a package to the door when they were all inside. The patrol sergeant thought it was a bomb and we were called. Mullen knew what it was right away, just an alarm clock hooked up to some highway flares. We had a couple of laughs taking it apart, but when we opened the door I almost pissed my pants. Standing in the middle of two hundred raging fags in full dress regalia was Joseph Dwyer, skirted up and dressed to the nines."

"Did he recognize you?" McKenna asked.

"Of course he did. We had spent hundreds of hours together. He looked just a little surprised to see me in my Bomb Squad coveralls, but the important thing was his reaction when I recognized him. He just gave me a

that tells us a lot about Mullen. He found that he loves inflicting pain on helpless victims and he got quite good at it by the time he got to Winthrop."

"He's been getting a lot of practice?" McKenna asked.

"I'm sure of it."

"Why does he do it?"

"A number of reasons. He's a total psychopathic sexual sadist, but sex had little to do with it in these type cases. It's power and control, not sex that propels him to torture and murder. As a matter of fact, although Mullen has two kids, I believe that now he's impotent."

"How did that happen?" McKenna asked.

"Stress and rejection, two of the prime factors causing impotency," Vernon said, then looked to McKenna. "Was he rejected by his wife?" he asked.

"Totally."

"That accounts for one factor. As for the other, stress has a cumulative effect on a person," Vernon stated smugly. "Now, think of the stress he's experienced throughout his charade on the police department and the stress he must be under now. He's a man without an identity, engaged in a dangerous business and constantly on the run and in danger of capture. That's one of the reasons he tortures and kills people—because it relieves that stress he's living under."

McKenna believed the conclusion only because Vernon had said it, but he didn't understand it. He could see that Thor was also confused, and so could Vernon.

"Think of it this way," Vernon suggested. "When he's not on his home turf the whole world is his enemy. He's a big, macho guy who always has to be polite and deferential, meaning he can never do anything that would make him stand out and possibly attract police attention. He always has to drive the speed limit, never fail to signal, and never argue with anyone in public, all of which has to increase the stress on a guy like him. You could kick sand in his face on a public beach and he'd have to smile and walk away. The only times in his life when he is in total control of the enemy are the times when he's inflicting pain on his helpless victims. And don't forget, as far as he's concerned almost everyone is his enemy."

"He'll torture anyone he can get his hands on?" McKenna asked.

"In a pinch, yes. However, I'm sure you noticed that he prefers a certain type of victim. I'm betting that the three we know about resemble his wife in stature and maybe hair color."

McKenna and Thor both nodded.

"That's his latent homosexual tendencies as well as his impotence coming out. He unconsciously identifies with the male victims, yet destroys them to preserve himself. The female victims he just hates, probably as a result of the mother-son or the marital relationship gone bad."

"I think you've got that right," McKenna agreed. "So you think that he hates his wife, that in his mind killing his victims is a substitute for killing her?"

"I think it goes beyond that. I think he hates women in general. Winthrop fell into his preferred category because of his stature and because he was effeminate, indicating to Mullen that Winthrop wanted to be a woman. That subjected poor Winthrop to special treatment, including Mullen's very painful surgical procedure that made his genitalia appear feminine. Mullen must have enjoyed working on Winthrop, almost as much as he enjoyed inflicting pain on a real woman. However, Meaghan got it worse and suffered more."

McKenna didn't want to ask, but he had to know. "What made Meaghan's treatment worse?"

"I believe she was tougher than he was used to, challenging his control of the situation. Basically, she was a threat to him. She broke his nose and probably spit in his eye. I've examined her breasts and believe that he bit her nipples off, not pulled them off as he did in the other cases. There are many jagged edges and teeth marks where her nipples should have been. I'm betting he also bit her fingers off before he killed her, bit them off one by one while she was still alive and conscious."

McKenna didn't want to think about that anymore and decided to move the discussion away from Meaghan. "If it's power rather than sex that interests him when he tortures his victims, then why does he focus on their genitalia and breasts?" he asked.

"Because he's concentrating on the parts of the body that are sexually stimulating to him, or used to be. Those are also sensitive spots where he can inflict the most pain. Remember, the more pain he inflicts, the more stress he relieves and the better he feels."

"Am I right in assuming that there should be a tortured body associated with every bombing he's done?"

"Yes. He's always under stress and he'll kill whenever he can, but if you want to pin a particular bombing on him, then look for the body of a person tortured to death a couple of days before."

"What about the nipples?" Thor asked. "Does he keep them as a trophy?"

"If he were what we call a disorganized serial killer, your opportunistic run-of-the-mill basic inadequate personality driven by a perverse and deviant sadistic sexual psychopath, then I'd say yes, he's keeping them. But he's not. He's highly organized. Therefore, I believe that he might keep them as trophies until his mission is complete, but then he probably throws them out. After all, he must travel a lot and he wouldn't want to be going through customs with somebody's nipples in his pocket."

"Then why does he take a chance on taking them in the first place?"

"Because the missing nipples form part of his 'signature.' He needs to do this, the thing that distinguishes his work from that of every other maniac's out there. You might find it hard to believe, but he's proud of his work in his own strange way."

With that statement, Vernon sat back in his chair. As far as he was concerned, the lesson was over. McKenna and Thor just stared at him expectantly.

"I guess you want more," Vernon said.

"If you please," McKenna answered. "If we're going to catch Mullen, it would sure help to know what he's really like and how he thinks when he's not torturing people, which has to be most of the time."

"That's simple," Vernon said, smiling as he stood up again, back on stage and in charge. "Although he's unusual in that sex isn't his primary motivation for killing, he fits neatly into the organized serial killer category. Whatever you need to know about him is all in my book."

"I read it all the time," McKenna said. "In fact, it's on my nightstand at home, always readily available for study as required. But please refresh my poor memory."

"No problem, but for future reference it's all in Chapters Fourteen, Fifteen, and Twenty-one," Vernon said, then resumed pacing the sitting room as he rapidly lectured in his practiced stream-of-consciousness manner. "He possesses superior intelligence, he fits well into society, he's a consummate actor, he's gregarious and out-going, he's manipulative, with good interpersonal skills, he's methodical and cunning, his victims resemble a significant female in his life, and his crime scenes reflect his controlled rage as evidenced by the restraints and torture. Frequently he will transport his victim's body to confuse the police. He's also the typical macho type that we find in many of these cases. He's in good shape, he's got a military background, and he originally selected an occupation that puts him in a position of authority. He's archetypal in that he's good with explosives and probably fascinated by them." Vernon stopped pacing and gave McKenna an inquiring glance. "I'd also bet he's extremely proficient with firearms."

"Yeah, he's archetypal," McKenna said, trying to keep his admiration for Vernon's rapid analysis out of his voice.

Vernon still took it as a compliment and allowed himself a small acknowledging smile. "Now for what you don't know about him."

"Wait a minute," McKenna said, then took out his notebook. He opened it and prepared to record the impending scraps of knowledge thrown his way.

Vernon appreciated that gesture even more. He was radiant as he resumed his pacing and rapidly made his points. "Except for his primary fixation, in this case the IRA, he's indifferent to the welfare of society. When he drives, the car will be a sedan or station wagon in good condition and meticulously clean. He has a violent temper and will hold a grudge forever if he can't respond at once. He cannot be relied upon to keep any promise he makes, but he will try to make good on any threats he makes. He's personally fearless after he conquers his stress and the threat of punishment will do nothing to alter his behavior. He is probably the firstborn son and his father held a stable, middle-class job. However, he was physically and possibly sexually abused by his mother or female parental figure. As a child he probably tortured animals, set fires, and wet the bed." Vernon stopped pacing and again faced McKenna. "You got all that?" he asked.

McKenna continued writing for a moment before he looked up from his notepad. "Yeah, got it. He was a real bad boy and a bed-wetter."

"Good, because the next part pertains particularly to you gentlemen," Vernon said, this time speaking slowly for emphasis. "Mullen makes an effort to appear friendly, like a guy you might like to know, but he's actually filled with hate. He reads all the newspapers and once he's publicly identified he'll take a special interest in whoever's handling his case. Because it will be a big, international case, he'll find it difficult to hide and will resort to disguises. In any event, he'll be desperate and near the end of his rope, maybe even fatalistic. He'll recognize you gentlemen as his adversaries in a very personal way and might try to contact you. From a psychological standpoint, he needs to cause you pain or kill you for his own mental well being. Be extremely careful, guard your loved ones, and believe nothing he says."

Class was over, but the students weren't happy.

SEVENTEEN

Inspector Rollins was punctual in the British tradition, arriving at McKenna's suite at precisely three o'clock. He obviously considered his visit to be a diplomatic mission because he was wearing a stiff, formal pin-striped suit. He sat on the sofa opposite Thor at attention, his knees together with his briefcase placed squarely on his lap. He fixed his gaze on a large manila envelope conspicuously placed on the coffee table in front of him; his name was written across the front of the envelope.

"Coffee?" McKenna asked.

"Actually, I'd prefer just plain tea, if you don't mind," Rollins answered distractedly.

McKenna was ready for that request. He had ordered tea from room service and the tray had arrived just minutes before Rollins did. He poured the tea for Rollins, then poured the plebeian coffee for himself and Thor.

McKenna sat next to Thor on the sofa, thinking that they would then get right down to business, but Rollins sat sipping his tea and not saying a word.

It was Thor who finally broke the ice. "Inspector Rollins, we've been working on a very difficult case. You've managed to impress me with your expertise and dedication and I think we've worked well together."

"We have," Rollins agreed. "I'd say we've gotten along famously."

"Good. I realize that you've followed a few of my suggestions and, as a result, you've developed some information connecting Timothy O'Bannion to the bombing. We both know that I should have gotten that information, but I didn't. I understand why and I want you to know that there are no hard feelings."

"Quite decent of you," Rollins said. "I can't say that I'd be so totally understanding if I'd have been in your position." He paused. "I want you to know that withholding that information wasn't my idea. In fact, I strongly recommended that it be given to you."

"I thought as much," Thor said.

"Thank you. I'm glad to hear that we're going to be dealing with one another as cops, not diplomats," Rollins said, nodding to both McKenna and Thor. "However, just so we all understand one another, do you mind if I reiterate the terms of our deal?"

"Not at all," replied both McKenna and Thor.

"Good. As I understand it from Janus, you've learned that the bomber had been living in the United States under an IRA cover name, but you have no idea of his present location. You believe that we can help ascertain his true identity and that Timothy O'Bannion can provide us with his location. To ensure O'Bannion's cooperation, we are to give to you certain information connecting him to the bombing here with the understanding that this information has been obtained from highly confidential sources. In return for O'Bannion's cooperation, we will not publicly acknowledge his role in the affair nor seek to prosecute him as long as the bomber is brought into the custody of Her Majesty's government by April ninth, one month from today."

"Two months, and he'll be tried in Iceland before you get him," McKenna said.

"Pardon?" Rollins said, confused and taken aback by McKenna's demand.

"Joseph Dwyer."

"Pardon?" Rollins repeated, but the confusion was vanishing and there was an edge in his voice.

McKenna picked up the envelope and took out the book on the IRA he had bought. "It was a nice foreword you wrote for this book. Very informative and it gives a little background on yourself. Says that you've been chasing the IRA for over twenty years with some success. Also says that before joining Special Branch, you were affiliated with British Intelligence in one fashion or another."

"All true," Rollins said. "What about Joseph Dwyer?"

McKenna again reached into the envelope and took out the crime scene photo of Dwyer in the hotel room and passed it to Rollins. "Our bomber did this to him, and we both know why. If we can agree to my suggested modifications to our arrangement here, this information stays with us."

"This is outrageous! I thought we already had a deal," Rollins stated, then stared at the grisly photo.

"It's only a deal after we shake on it," McKenna countered. "Until then, we're in negotiations."

"Inspector, maybe you should consider this," Thor said. "If he's tried in Iceland, I can guarantee that he will be found guilty by our magistrates in two days. During his short trial we will acknowledge the help given us by the British and American governments. There will be no demonstrations of support for him here nor will the IRA be able to portray him to our people as a political prisoner. He will receive three life sentences and eventually die in jail here with the heat turned down low."

Rollins looked up from the photo and placed it on the coffee table. "We've already considered all that and I agree that there's some merit in what you're suggesting," Rollins said to Thor.

"Substantial merit," McKenna insisted.

"All right, Brian. Substantial merit," Rollins said with a hint of a smile. "Am I to understand that if we agree to your suggested modifications, then your groundless suspicions regarding Joseph Dwyer's auxiliary employment will never be mentioned to anyone in your government?"

"Exactly. Nor will I be talking to anyone in the press about my silly groundless suspicions. You know how reporters love to inquire and speculate, but I just hate to cause trouble."

"Then I think I can easily explain the wisdom of your suggestions to my superiors," Rollins said as he offered his hand.

The three men shook on the deal, then Rollins reached into his briefcase, removed a bulky folder, and opened it.

On top was another crime scene photo documenting another one of Mullen's painful stress-relieving sessions. She had been a dirty-blond version of Meaghan Maher. The top photo was the first of many.

"Following Thor's suggestion, we've searched for unsolved sex killings throughout the world that took place around the same time as an IRA bombing," Rollins said. "What we've found is that our bomber is a particularly nasty, well-traveled bloke with an insatiable appetite for causing pain. We've come up with four cases going back to 1992 that we can definitely attribute to him. Apparently, the killings all took place a couple of days before the bombing, but in all four cases the bodies weren't discovered until after the bombing."

Rollins passed the top photo to McKenna. "That was the last one. The bomb incident was in Londonderry in November of ninety-six, but the girl was killed in Newry. That's still in the North, but about a hundred miles away from Londonderry. She was found in a ditch there four days after the incident, but she had been dead about a week."

McKenna passed the photo to Thor after looking at it only long enough to see that she had been horribly beaten and burned, that she had been strangled, and that her nipples were gone. "What do you mean by a bomb incident?" McKenna asked.

"Car bomb, six-hundred pounds of explosive placed in a car in front of police headquarters in Londonderry. It had been placed there by an IRA splinter group calling themselves the Irish Army Continuity Council, but somebody had a change of heart and called in a warning. Our troops disarmed the bomb in a controlled explosion."

"What was this girl's religion?" Thor asked, handing the photo back to Rollins.

"Nominally Protestant. Not very religious at all. She was a waitress in Newry with a bit of a reputation as a loose girl."

"Politics?"

"Totally apolitical. Not interested at all in the Troubles, as they call the conflict in Northern Ireland. The one before that is in London in December of ninety-five. The IRA blew up one of our municipal buses. Some injuries, but no fatalities. Her body was found in an abandoned row house in Liverpool." Rollins handed McKenna the next photo.

McKenna could see that Mullen had found another redhead, but he barely glanced at it before passing it on. Thor didn't even give it a glance before handing it back to Rollins.

"No more photos?" Rollins asked.

"We can do without them, for now," McKenna said. "Where was that girl from?"

"Living in London, but originally from Galway in the Republic. Catholic, politics unknown. The one before that was Bermuda, March of 1994. The Commandant of our Royal Marines was there on holiday and was the victim of a car bomb with a rather sophisticated tilt detonator. The bomb went off when he drove his car up the ramp from the hotel garage."

"Was he killed?" McKenna asked.

"No, but maybe he should have been. He was seriously maimed and horribly burned. I think that was the bomber's intention."

"And the other victim there?"

"Not at all his usual type. She was black and the youngest of the lot, just sixteen. But she got the same treatment from him, so bad that the local police started searching for a voodoo cult."

"He does have his preferences, but not all the cases will be the same," McKenna said.

"In any event, he was able to exercise his usual preference in the last case I've got to show you," Rollins said. "That was in Ottawa, Canada, November of ninety-two, a letter bomb addressed to our ambassador there. Rather sophisticated. We still don't know what the explosive was or how it was made. The envelope was X-rayed and passed through the chemical detector we had at the time. One of our security people was killed when he opened it up."

"What was the postmark?" McKenna asked.

"Toronto."

"And the victim?"

"She was last seen in a club in Kingston, Ontario, two days before the bombing. That's about halfway between Toronto and Ottawa, but her body was discovered two weeks later in the woods about thirty miles south of Quebec."

So what does all this tell us that we didn't already know or suspect? McKenna wondered. Not much, he concluded. We already knew that we were after a monster. "Did the IRA claim responsibility for all the bombings?"

"All except the Londonderry one. Like I said, that was the Irish Army Continuity Council. At the time we figured that was a splinter group, but now I believe it was the IRA after all."

"Why? Because it was the same bomber?"

"Precisely. As I recall, there was a truce on at the time, so I figure the IRA set the bomb, then made up this other group to shift the blame from themselves."

"But they still haven't claimed credit for the bombing here. Don't you find that strange?"

"Somewhat, but we know it has to be them. British target, same bomber, same MO," Rollins said. "Are you ready to go on to O'Bannion?"

"Not yet. It's important for us to agree on one thing before we go on," McKenna insisted. "There are more victims than your people have uncovered. He kills whenever he's under stress, not just before he blows something up."

"We are agreed on that, and it disturbs me deeply. However, at this point I see no reason to cloud the issue with additional inquiries to authorities in other countries that would necessarily lead to unwelcome speculation on their part."

Well said, McKenna thought. We've already got enough to hang Mullen, so why make a splash asking around? "You're right, Inspector. Let's get him first, ask around later. What about O'Bannion?"

"We don't know if he had anything to do with the other bombings, but we know he's involved in the bombing here."

"Know or suspect?" Thor asked.

"I'd say highly suspect, but everything we've learned would be termed circumstantial evidence. As Thor had suggested, O'Bannion made some indirect inquiries when Sir Ian and his wife were in Dublin last year. As a result, he knew that they weren't getting on and customarily slept in separate beds. We think that he advised the bomber to place charges in both the master bed and the one in the servant's room."

"How did he make an *indirect* inquiry?" McKenna asked.

"Is it necessary I explain that?"

"Yes. When I confront him, I have to go in with at least some real proof, not total conjecture."

"I'm afraid that could involve burning a very valuable source. Because of his background, O'Bannion was at the top of the list of people we were curious about."

"Is it someone very close to him?"

"Yes, someone very close. Someone very valuable to us in her present position."

"You're gonna have to give us the whole story and trust us not to jeopardize any operations you may be running," McKenna said.

"All right, I will. We got it from his secretary."

"Incredible!" McKenna said. "The Irish minister for finance's secretary is a British agent?"

"No, not an agent. I guess you would call her a sometime informant. She usually doesn't tell us a thing about O'Bannion's day-to-day government business, but she despises the IRA. Fortunately for us, she's managed to keep her sentiments to herself. Otherwise, O'Bannion would never have her around."

"Is she Protestant?"

"No, she's Catholic and originally from the North."

"Then her sentiments are a little unusual, aren't they?"

"Yes, unusual for a Northern Catholic. Mind you, she has no love for the Ulster Protestants. Probably has no love for us either, for that matter. But back in the seventies her sister was one of those innocent bystanders we often hear about. She was killed by an IRA explosion when they ambushed one of our patrols in Belfast."

"I see. So she reasons that if there were no IRA, then her sister would still be alive," McKenna surmised.

"I presume that's the case. In any event, her handler hears from her whenever she suspects that O'Bannion is up to something that's IRA-connected. O'Bannion is pretty careful, so we've found that sometimes she's wrong."

"But not always?"

"No, not always."

"Tell me about this time."

"Before O'Bannion was the minister of finance, he served as the minister for labor," Rollins explained. "His power base is the unions. The man who heads the Council of Free Trade Unions is John O'Rourke, a hand-picked crony of his. Our girl overheard O'Bannion asking him to have his workers in the hotel keep an eye on Sir Ian and his wife when they were in Dublin."

"So Thor was right, but that's not much to go on," McKenna said.

"There's more," Rollins stated, smiling. "On February twenty-seventh, O'Bannion was out of the office when a man calling himself Rory McGivens rang for him. He left a number and asked our girl to have O'Bannion ring him back. Since McGivens is a Northern name, she was curious. She checked the country code for the number he gave and found it was—"

"Iceland! The Saga Hotel!" McKenna said, almost shouting.

"Yes, it was here," Rollins said calmly. "She didn't know it was the Saga at the time, but she had the carbon copy from her telephone message book. She put it together after the bombing and called the number. That's when she found out it was the Saga. She also found out that there hadn't been a Rory McGivens registered here. That night she contacted her handler."

"Do you have that message slip?"

"She couldn't take a chance on tearing it out of the book, but she did Xerox it." Rollins turned a few pages in the folder in front of him before he found it and passed it to McKenna.

McKenna saw that it was a copy of a page from the standard while-you-were-out message book. In a neat feminine handwriting was the date, the time, and the simple message. McKenna noted with satisfaction that there was no room number listed next to the phone number in the message.

God, these Brits have been sitting on some pretty powerful stuff, he thought. O'Bannion knew that McGivens was in the hotel under the Winthrop name or he wouldn't have been able to reach him. And he called O'Bannion three days before the bombing, probably to report that the bombs were in place and asking if everything was going according to plan at Rockall. Now let's see what else Rollins is sitting on. "Does the name Rory McGivens mean anything to you?"

"Unfortunately, no. We've done an exhaustive review of our files and it shows up nowhere. We presume it's an alias."

"Probably, but let me show you what he looks like. Maybe that will help." McKenna reached into the manila envelope on the coffee table and took out two five-by-seven photos. One was Mullen's seven-year-old arrest photo and the other was a copy of the photo taken in uniform for his ID card when he had first joined the NYPD in 1975.

As he passed the photos to Rollins, McKenna was hoping against all odds that the IRA expert would instantly recognize Mullen and jump off the sofa in a spasm of joy. But Rollins just studied the photos intently. Then he placed them both on the coffee table.

"I guess you don't recognize him," McKenna said.

"No, I don't. I take it this man was a cop?"

"Yes. He sneaked into our department under an alias. Was with us for seventeen years before he was arrested and fired in 1991."

"What was he arrested for?"

"Shaking down call girls."

"Was he assigned to the Bomb Squad at any time?"

I'm up to my neck in sharp guys, McKenna thought. "Yes, he was."

"Interesting," the unflappable Rollins said. "I'm glad your department recognizes talent when it presents itself. I, for one, would like to hear the whole story if you'd care to tell it."

It wasn't a story McKenna relished telling, but a deal was a deal. For the better part of an hour he talked about Mullen, pointing out the pertinent parts in the fugitive's personnel folder as he explained what had happened.

Rollins listened intently throughout the account, asking very few questions and giving no indication of surprise or disapproval at Mullen's hiring by the NYPD. When McKenna finished, he had just one comment. "You're right. He was always IRA and he must be in our files somewhere. If you don't mind, I'd like to fax his fingerprint cards and photo to London."

"I'd insist on it," McKenna said. "This room comes with a fax. You can use it, if you like."

"I'd rather use the secure line at our embassy. Besides, it will give me an opportunity to explain to my superiors the amendments to the deal we've agreed on." Rollins allowed himself a small smile. "When I do that, I'd prefer to be in a place where you won't be able to hear them screaming."

"How long will it take to get a reply from London?"

"I'm sure this matter will be given the highest priority. Would it be convenient if we meet back here at nine?"

"Quite convenient," McKenna answered. "Splendid, in fact."

EIGHTEEN

Thor and McKenna decided to go out for dinner while awaiting Rollins's return, but McKenna's luck ran out in the lobby. He had forgotten Jónas's advice and had not called down to let the manager know he was leaving. There were a couple of Icelandic reporters lounging near the front door and Thor was recognized by them at once.

Worse, so was McKenna. In a matter of seconds the bar emptied out and there were six reporters between the detectives and the door, all shouting their questions.

In New York McKenna would have ignored them and pushed through to freedom as politely as he could. But they weren't in New York and that wasn't the Icelandic way. To McKenna's consternation, Thor stopped. They were captured.

At first, he tried denying being that famous Det. Brian McKenna of the NYPD. They responded good-naturedly with chuckles and guffaws, as if McKenna had just told them a real backslapper. In embarrassed desperation he turned to Thor, hoping that the Icelander would somehow handle his nation's press on his own.

Thor did handle them, but lying and denying wasn't his style. The reporters were content to let him do the talking, obviously preferring the honest local color to the devious, foreign, big-city detective. That was their mistake. Thor was cagey and told a few half truths, but no outright lies.

The first shouted questions all concerned McKenna. What they wanted to know most was, What he was doing in Iceland and did his presence have anything to do with the bombing?

Thor told them. McKenna was in the country only to investigate a New York missing persons case. He had been successful, had found his missing person, and had assisted the Icelandic police in identifying her. She was Meaghan Maher, the girl whose body had washed up on Heimaey Island the day of the bombing. According to Thor, McKenna's work was finished in Iceland and he would be leaving the next day to escort Meaghan's body to her parents in Ireland.

As for the bombing and Meaghan's murder, those cases remained a local matter under the jurisdiction of the Icelandic police.

"The murder of Meaghan Maher and the Saga bombing are connected, aren't they?" one reporter asked.

"I believe they are and I'm working on that assumption," Thor answered.

"Are you making any progress in the bombing case?" asked another.

"Yes, I believe I am."

"Have you identified the bomber?"

"I know the name he used when he was in Iceland and I know how he detonated the bombs, but I don't know yet who he really is and have no idea where in the world he is."

"Do you still believe that the IRA was behind the bombing?" asked a third reporter.

"Yes, I do, but that's all I'm prepared to say at the moment. I'm off duty now, very hungry, and just going out to dinner with Detective McKenna."

To McKenna's amazement, that was it. Try that one with the New York press, McKenna thought. Like it or not, we'd all be going to dinner together. But it was Iceland. They all thanked Thor for the interview, even shaking his hand. Then they all wrapped up their microphones, put their tape recorders in their pockets and their cameras in their cases.

All except one, that is, a crusty-looking old-timer. "Detective McKenna, would you mind answering just one question?" he asked.

Oh-oh, McKenna thought. Here we go. Thor's expertly buffaloed all but one, but that one is enough to spoil it. "No, not at all," he answered with his practiced meet-the-press, you-can-believe-me smile on his face.

"Thank you. I'm sorry, but it's a rather involved question," the old-timer said as he turned on his tape recorder.

Uh-oh, uh-oh, uh-oh! "Go ahead and ask it."

"Could you please give us your impressions of crime in Iceland as compared to the crime problems in New York?"

McKenna managed not to laugh and gave his answer.

The impromptu press conference had gone well enough, but McKenna was worried. If Vernon was right, Mullen would still be following the news in Iceland and would learn that McKenna had been assigned the Meaghan Maher case. Although Thor had deftly avoided telling the reporters that Mullen had been identified, it was just a matter of time before Mullen learned that McKenna was on his trail.

McKenna worried about Angelita, the kids, and something else that Vernon had said: Mullen would take the news personally. As he picked at his food, McKenna couldn't erase the image of Angelita being tied up and tortured by the monster. Since it was common knowledge in New York that he lived at the Gramercy Park Hotel, McKenna decided that protective measures would have to be taken at once. He voiced his concerns to Thor and the Icelander agreed. Until Mullen was in custody, great care should be taken to protect their families.

By six-thirty they had finished eating. They had two and a half hours to kill before their next meeting with Rollins, so Thor decided to go home to spend a couple of hours with Frieda.

Suddenly, McKenna envied the Icelander. He missed Angelita and had tried calling her a couple of times that day, but she had been out. He desperately wanted to talk to her just to hear her voice.

The phone was ringing when McKenna entered his suite and he got his wish. "Brian, you'll never guess what happened today," Angelita said.

Of course, she was right. McKenna never could guess, but he tried and fared poorly at the game. When he finally ran out of guesses, Angelita told him, her voice filled with excitement. "We got an apartment today, and it's beautiful. It's got three bedrooms, it comes nicely furnished, and it's in the Village on West 10th Street, right near our old place. It's not for sale, but we're getting a one-year lease."

"That's wonderful news," McKenna said, almost as excited as she was. He had wanted to buy an apartment, but they were desperate. A year would give the boys time to grow out of their screaming fits of colic and make them more acceptable prospects to a co-op board. But there was still the big New York question. "How much?"

"Guess."

Three bedrooms in the Village, furnished? What should that cost to rent, McKenna wondered. It has to be a good price or she wouldn't be so excited. "Twenty-five hundred a month," he tried.

"Nope. Fifteen hundred plus utilities."

Fifteen hundred? Wonderful! That even fits into our budget, McKenna thought. "How'd you get it?"

"The owner called me up this morning and said he heard we were looking for an apartment. Said he's a retired FBI guy with a nice job on Wall Street, but his company's transferred him to Atlanta for a year. He wasn't going to rent the place, but all he really wants is for us to watch it and take good care of it while he's gone."

"How did he hear we were looking for an apartment?" McKenna asked, already knowing the answer.

"Chipmunk told him."

"When can we move in?"

"I've already signed the lease and he's leaving tomorrow, so I guess as soon as you get back."

"No. I've got a better idea. I'd like you to pack up some things and take the kids there tomorrow. Don't tell anyone in the hotel where you're going, just move into the apartment and stay there. I'll take care of everything else when I get back."

McKenna had told her about Mullen's proclivities, so Angelita at once guessed the implications implied by McKenna's wishes. "Are we in some kind of danger?" she asked.

"Not yet, but there's a remote chance that you might be in a couple of days. I'm just trying to be careful."

"Okay, we'll do it."

"Thanks. That takes a lot off my mind. Get a phone as soon as you get in, but don't get it listed in our name."

"You want me to get us an unlisted number?

"No, let's be real careful. Any PI worth his salt can get an unlisted number and an address, so make up a name and have the phone number listed under it."

"Okay. How about Zergo Zwielich?"

"Zergo Zwielich? Who's that?"

"I don't know, but wouldn't it be nice being the last name in the phone book?" Angelita asked.

"I'm not crazy about being Zergo Zwielich, but I like it anyway," Mc-Kenna said.

They spent the next ten minutes talking about everything and nothing. McKenna felt much better after he hung up, so much better that he decided to take a run and get another good look at the city on his last night there.

Running was McKenna's usual way of relieving tension and stress. Although his age had slowed his average mileage time down by fifteen seconds over the past year, he didn't mind. He liked being in shape and still ran two marathons a year with respectable times.

McKenna ran all around Reykjavík, circling the buildings that interested him and taking his time. He was enjoying himself and had just decided that it was one of the most delightful cities he had even visited when the weather changed and revised his opinion. It had been mild, balmy, and about forty degrees for most of his run, but then a cold Arctic wind suddenly blew in and dropped the temperature by ten degrees in seconds. The wind was followed by a driving rain so cold that McKenna wondered as it stung his face why it wasn't snow. He put his head down and raced for the Saga. By the time he got there, cold and drenched, he had decided that Iceland might not be Paradise after all.

Once he was back in his suite, McKenna took a long, hot shower and put on a fresh suit. He was ready by eight-thirty and put in an order with room service for another pot of tea. He had just hung up when the phone rang again. It was Brunette. "The kids were in Belfast with their father," he said.

Belfast? That made sense to McKenna. Northern Ireland was part of the U.K., so Mullen could have taken them there from London without ever having to show a passport. Mullen would want to give his sons the heritage tour and explain their roots to them. "How do you know it was Belfast?" he asked. "Did the kids have some pictures?"

"They still do. I sent Gaspar, Fitzhughs, and Pao to do the search of Kathleen's house and they'd brought a one-on-one camera with them. After they found the pictures in the boys' room, they took duplicate photos.

There's one of the boys standing with an old man in front of a building that looks a lot like our city hall, only nicer. Fitzhughs told me it was Belfast City Hall."

McKenna marveled at Brunette's choice of personnel to do the very sensitive and illegal search. Gaspar was assigned to TARU, the Detective Bureau's Technical Assistance Resources Unit. He was an expert at wiretaps, electronic surveillance, and could open most locks in seconds without benefit of a key.

Fitzhughs and Pao were both assigned to the Major Case Squad; both were excellent detectives and close friends of his. Fitzhughs had been born and raised in Northern Ireland, so he would at once recognize any clue that the boys had been there. He also had a highly developed gift of the gab and would enable them to get out of any trouble they might get into on the mission.

On the other hand, talking was not Pao's way. The half-Chinese, half-Irish detective was the crankiest and most taciturn man McKenna knew, but that didn't bother him. Pao had often served as his partner and was completely dedicated to him. An added bonus was that McKenna was convinced Pao was one of the toughest men alive and maybe the best shot in the department, a fact to which McKenna could gladly attest. Once he had saved McKenna's life with an unforgettable shot, firing his pistol from a distance of almost two blocks and hitting a killer who was about to add McKenna to his list. "Was Mullen in any of the photos?"

"Two of them. In one he's sitting in an armchair, snoozing with his mouth open and a pistol on his lap. I'm told by Fitzhughs that it's a .357 Astra, a Spanish gun favored by the IRA. According to him, they get it from their Basque allies in the ETA."

So Mullen's always ready for action, even when he's sleeping, McKenna thought. The pistol in plain sight means that he must have explained to the kids exactly why he had to be ready. They know he's IRA, and maybe they've known it for some time. "How about the other photo?"

"It's a shot of him standing with the kids, a woman in her thirties, and the same old man in front of a new row house."

The old man is probably the kids' grandfather, McKenna thought. But who's the woman? Either a new squeeze or his sister, he concluded. "What does the woman look like?"

"Late thirties, maybe early forties, dark hair, a little on the portly side. Not bad, but she wouldn't win any beauty contest."

Sounds like the woman who picked the boys up in London, McKenna thought. "Any other souvenirs of their trip?"

"None that were found, and our guys were pretty lucky to have even found the photos. They were in an envelope taped over the door inside their closet. Mullen must have told them to be careful and closemouthed about the visit."

"He did. They wouldn't even say a word about it to Hunt, and they have to trust him by now. Did they find any phone numbers?"

"Nope. If they're still in touch with Mullen and calling him, they must have his number memorized. They also have to be calling him from a pay phone, unless he's in New York."

"How do you know that? You check Kathleen's phone records already?"

"Sheeran did. During the past seven years there have been lots of calls to a number in Londonderry, but he's established that it's the number of Kathleen Mullen's folks. He tells me that she doesn't use the phone much, and when she does it's usually a local call."

Hunt was right about Kathleen, McKenna thought. She doesn't have much of a life. And I was right about one thing, too. She is from the North. "Could you tell me about the house?"

"Sure. That was one of the things I wanted to know about, too. It's a small three bedroom. Kitchen, living room, dining room downstairs, the bedrooms and a bathroom upstairs. The furniture's not in bad shape, but our team tells me that Kathleen's not much of a housekeeper. Most of the rooms are untidy, including her bedroom, and all but one of them could use a painting."

"Which room was neat and painted?" McKenna asked, then answered his own question with a guess. "Tell me, was it the boys' bedroom?"

"You got it. They're an unusual pair and probably painted it themselves. The room's spotless, dusted, the beds are made with military corners, and everything's in its place. Looks like a barracks ready for inspection. All their clothes are neatly folded in precise rows, right down to their socks and underwear. They also do their own ironing, have an iron and ironing board in their closet and all the clothes hanging there are pressed with creases."

"Tell me they have bunk beds," McKenna said.

"That's right, with army blankets and no spreads. They must get along pretty well together. There's an extra bedroom, but apparently they'd rather share a room."

That's a very unusual attitude for brothers to have, McKenna thought. They're close in age, thirteen and eleven years old now, but I've never heard of two brothers so close that they wouldn't rather have their own rooms. "Do they have any books or magazines?"

"Nothing like any other teenagers I've ever heard of. Aside from *The Anarchist Cookbook*, the only other books they've got are on Ireland, Irish history, and the IRA. And get this—they've got a subscription to *Soldier of Fortune* magazine, piled neatly under the Irish flag hanging on the wall. They've also got a CD player in the room, but except for U2, rock 'n' roll isn't their cup of tea. It's all Irish music, including a number of Irish rev-olutionary albums. These boys are hard-core."

So Mullen already has his sons in military training, ready to take up the cause, McKenna thought. Worse, it sounds as if they like the idea. I bet they're on his side and have nothing but contempt for their mother and the way she keeps the house. If they're as mean and strong-willed as their father is, Kathleen's life must be a daily living hell. These boys bear some close watching. "Are the surveillances in place yet?" he asked.

"We tailed Kathleen to work this morning and the boys to school. Her phone's done, too."

McKenna was grateful to Brunette for the chances he was taking on this case, but he knew it wasn't necessary to express that gratitude. Both knew that if word ever got out on that illegal wiretap and the illegal bug, it was likely that Brunette would have to resign in disgrace. "I hope I'm able to bring enough home to make all that stuff you're doing legal," he said.

"At the moment, I'm not too worried about it. I trust everyone who knows about it," Brunette countered. "However, if this goes on for a while, I admit that I'd probably sleep a lot easier if you could get enough for an eavesdropping warrant."

"Will do. Buddy, I want you sleeping like a baby without a care in the world."

Thor and Rollins arrived together, right after the tea had been brought up. They were soaked, but dried off in the bathroom. Rollins, who had brought his leather briefcase out with him in the rain, placed it squarely in front of him on the coffee table next to Mullen's personnel folder and all the crime scene photos.

McKenna poured coffee for himself and Thor, tea for Rollins.

The Englishman calmly finished his tea, then placed the cup and saucer on the coffee table and smiled. "The indications are that your Michael Mulrooney is a very old friend of Mr. Timothy O'Bannion."

"Michael Mulrooney? Is that Mullen's real name?" McKenna asked.

"According to his fingerprints it is. Michael Mulrooney of Belfast, Northern Ireland. Fortunately for us, he has an arrest record with the RUC."

"The RUC? What's that?" Thor asked.

"The local police in Northern Ireland, the Royal Ulster Constabulary. They're dedicated and well trained, but highly unpopular with the Catholic population. In 1962 they caught Mulrooney throwing rocks at one of their patrols. He was arrested and fingerprinted."

"How old was he then?" asked McKenna.

"Eleven, lucky for him. Because of his age all he got was probation."

"Was he ever arrested after that first time?" McKenna asked.

"No, but not because he escaped our attention. Do you know if he has a scar on his right leg?"

McKenna didn't know, but he had the answer right in front of him. He opened Mullen's personnel folder and turned to the medical examination he had been given before appointment. It was there. "He has a circular scar on the rear of his right thigh. He told our doctors that it was the result of a skiing accident, that he got it when his leg was punctured by a ski pole when he took a fall in 1972."

"Quite remarkable that they didn't recognize it as a bullet wound, isn't it?" Rollins asked, then instantly regretted the question. "Sorry, I didn't mean to give offense," he added.

"No offense taken," McKenna said. "And yes, it really is quite remarkable that they bought his story. How did he really get it?"

"In Londonderry, 1971, during an IRA ambush of our troops."

"The same ambush you think O'Bannion was involved in, the one where his brother Seamus was captured?"

"Yes. Also captured with Seamus after that ambush was another young IRA gunman, Patrick Mulrooney."

"Michael Mulrooney's brother?" McKenna asked.

"His younger brother. Our troops report that they wounded another of the gunmen, but he got away and was never captured. According to the reports, he had been shot in the right leg."

"Did you suspect Michael Mulrooney at the time?"

"Yes, but we couldn't find him. He had disappeared."

"What happened to Patrick Mulrooney?"

"He had been seriously wounded, gut shot," Rollins said. "Wound up losing half his stomach, but he recovered sufficiently to stand trial for murder. Just like Seamus O'Bannion, he never said a word at his trial and was sent to the Maze Prison for life. And just like Seamus, he went on a hunger strike in 1977, but it wasn't quite as dramatic. With only half a stomach, he died just four days into his strike."

Rollins sat back to give McKenna and Thor some time to think over the implications of his information.

McKenna was intrigued by the relationship between Michael Mulrooney and Timothy O'Bannion. He thought over the many things the two men had in common, things that must have brought them even closer together after that fateful ambush went bad on them and their brothers. He figured that both men knew they were hot after that day, too hot to stay involved in the IRA day-to-day military operations. But once in, never out.

So what did they do? McKenna asked himself. O'Bannion became a labor leader and later a powerful politician, but he was still IRA. As his power grew in the Republic, his status must have increased in the IRA until he was one of their shakers and movers, so high in the organization that he planned and ran the Iceland bombing.

But what could Mulrooney do? After his brother was captured, Mulrooney knew he was wanted by the British for questioning. Since he was from the North, he didn't have the Southern sanctuary O'Bannion enjoyed. He had to get out of the country, but first he had to get medical attention and hide out in an IRA safe house until his leg wound healed. After that, he went to Canada and the U.S. to start over, probably with some IRA help with his initial financing and a passport. Then he became Michael Mullen.

Mulrooney was on his own and did well enough for a long time in his new identity. Well enough to fool the NYPD until now, McKenna mused. But like O'Bannion, Michael Mulrooney was always IRA.

So where do we go from here? McKenna asked himself, watching Rollins watch him. "Do you have anything on Mulrooney's family?" he asked.

"Quite a bit. His mother's dead, but his father's still alive and living in Belfast."

"How about his sister?"

"How did you know he had a sister?" Rollins asked, surprised.

"Informed guess," McKenna answered, then told Rollins about the search of Kathleen Mullen's home in Woodlawn and the photos found in the boys' closet.

Rollins took the news of the boys' visit to their father, grandfather, and aunt in Belfast as a personal affront. "Mulrooney's certainly got brass, bringing in his sons right under our noses," he observed wryly.

"He probably figured you've stopped looking for him," Thor suggested.

"Unfortunately, he's right," Rollins admitted. "I suspect his case hasn't been looked at in twenty-five years, but that's about to change. The Mulrooney family is due to get quite a bit of attention from us."

"Wiretaps and surveillance?" McKenna asked.

"We'll certainly be listening in, but I'm afraid a surveillance is impossible. They live in Ballymurphy, a very Catholic, close-knit neighborhood and a traditional IRA bastion. Any stranger there would be noticed at once. If anybody in his family has a way of getting in touch with him, he'd know that we're once again interested in him."

That prospect disturbed McKenna and he appreciated Rollins's judgment. "Well, we don't want that at this stage of the game," McKenna said.

"Suppose he's there now, staying with his folks in Ballymurphy," Thor said. "If you don't take a look at the place, we'd be missing a grand opportunity to get him."

"I suppose it's possible he's there, but I consider it unlikely," Rollins stated.

"I assume that searching that house would be a military operation, wouldn't it?" McKenna asked Rollins.

"Yes. An SAS operation, I suppose. They're quite proficient at that sort of thing."

"Then let's do it this way," McKenna said. "We'll still have the wiretap on the house. That should give us an indication if he's living there, or even visiting every once in a while. If so, your troops hit the place and it's over. But if he's not there, we leave the place alone until Janus has to release his identity to the press. That still gives us some time to find him before he knows we're even looking for him."

"That sounds sensible to me," Rollins said.

McKenna and Rollins both turned to Thor for his opinion. The Icelander was sipping his coffee, still thinking. "Then we're agreed," he said as he placed his cup on the coffee table. "I'll also go along with Brian's suggestion."

NINETEEN

TUESDAY, MARCH 10TH—KEFLAVÍK AIRPORT

The weather had improved considerably. Although it was still dark at 9:00 A.M., the temperature was in the fifties, the wind had died down, and there was no hint of rain in the air. It was a nice day to be in Iceland, but the barren volcanic landscape they passed on the way to the airport reflected McKenna's somber mood. He had arrived in an unmarked police Volvo with Rollins and Thor, following the hearse that contained Meaghan's body. McKenna knew it was going to be a long, sad day and he wasn't looking forward to it. He was dressed for the wake, wearing a white shirt, a pin-striped suit, and a dark blue tie.

There was quite a crowd at Keflavík Airport. Vernon Gebreth, Dennis Hunt, and Chris O'Malley were there for their return flight to New York, but Rollins and Thor had come to the airport just to see McKenna off. McKenna had thought they would be accompanying him to Belfast and Dublin, but both had good reasons for staying.

Thor was sure his absence would be noted and the subject of public speculation by the Icelandic reporters, especially after they learned that McKenna was also gone. They would then put unwelcome pressure on Janus for the answer and that would never do.

On the other hand, Rollins wasn't worried about leaving Iceland with McKenna. What worried him was arriving in Belfast with him. Rollins was well known there and thought that McKenna would also be recognized. Since he was sure that the IRA knew he was in Iceland working on the bombing, he saw no reason to get them wondering by showing up in their backyard with McKenna.

So McKenna was to be on his own for a while. He would keep both Thor and Rollins informed on any developments in the case, but he didn't expect to see them again until he had located Mulrooney. They both wanted to be there for that arrest, wherever it might be.

The New York flight was loaded before McKenna's, and he was grateful for that. As he waited on line to board, through the terminal's windows he saw Meaghan's casket being loaded into the cargo bay of his plane. The sight saddened and depressed him, and he was sure it would have had O'Malley bawling again.

Icelandair had no direct flights to Belfast, so McKenna had to change planes in London and didn't arrive at Belfast's Aldergrove Airport until after three. Through the terminal's window he could see that the hearse was on the tarmac next to his plane, but Meaghan was the last piece of cargo unloaded. She was on her way to the funeral home before he picked up his baggage and checked the arrival schedules. Ryer Maher's Aer Lingus flight from New York was on schedule, due to arrive in half an hour.

McKenna claimed his luggage from the baggage carousel, changed three hundred dollars into British pounds at the airport currency exchange, then went to the British Immigration and Customs section to wait. He was dreading the meeting with Ryer, so the half hour seemed like two hours as he ran through his mind all the things he would say to Meaghan's brother.

As it turned out, there wasn't much cause for concern. McKenna saw him waiting on line to clear British Customs, casually dressed in jeans, a flannel shirt, and a ski jacket, looking more like a college student than a priest.

McKenna could see that Ryer was strong and prepared to be his family's bulwark. Somehow the priest had accepted his sister's horrible death without understanding the reasons for her murder. He also stoically accepted the vigorous inspection he and his luggage received from Customs. After he was finally passed through with his two suitcases, he greeted McKenna with a firm handshake and thanked him for coming.

"It seems to me that you were the object of some special attention by Customs," McKenna observed.

"It's to be expected," Ryer answered, shrugging it off. "Don't forget, I'm traveling here from America on an Irish passport and these folks regard your country as a sort of IRA base camp and armory."

"I guess I can understand that," McKenna said.

"Were you able to find someone to make Meaghan look presentable for my mom and dad?"

It was a subject that made McKenna uncomfortable, but the question had to be answered. "I haven't seen her since the morgue in Iceland, but the undertaker I used there came highly recommended. Her body's on the way to the funeral home right now."

"And the casket? Did you get a nice one for her?"

"I thought it was nice, if there is such a thing as a nice casket."

"Maybe there isn't, but it's important to my folks. Now, how much do I owe you? And please don't be shy."

That question made McKenna even more uncomfortable, and he was shy. He shaved two thousand dollars off the price he had paid in Iceland and gave Ryer the number.

"Nonsense, too low," Ryer said. "I've heard that things are expensive in Iceland and in my business I've gotten some idea of how much these things should cost. Now, please tell me how much I really owe you."

"I already told you," McKenna stated emphatically, then decided it was a good time to change the subject. "Do you know if your folks have arrived in town yet?"

Ryer looked for a moment like he wasn't going to let McKenna off the hook, but he did. "They got in last night. They're staying at my aunt's house in Ballymurphy, close to the funeral home."

McKenna felt the hairs stand up on the back of his neck at the mention of the Mulrooney neighborhood, and a few ideas ran through his mind. "Is it far from here?"

"It's on the other side of town, but it's still not far. No more than half an hour."

"Mind if I take a ride with you to meet your folks?"

"I was hoping you'd ask," Ryer said. "I'm going to rent a car, and I can show you some of the town on the way. You have a place to stay?"

"I'm booked into the Hotel Europa."

"The Europa? Why did you pick that hotel?"

"Because I was told that it's a nice place in the middle of town."

"Well, it is nice and it is in City Centre, but weren't you told that it's probably the most frequently bombed hotel in the world today?"

"No, I wasn't. My travel agent neglected to mention that, but I don't mind," McKenna said. "Maybe staying there will give me a feel for the city."

Ryer gave McKenna a sidelong glance, then shook his head and smiled. "Suit yourself, but I can't imagine for the life of me why anyone would want a feel for this city. You're going to find that it's a pretty unfriendly place."

"That's all right, I've worked in unfriendly places before. Could we stop at the hotel on the way?" McKenna asked. "I'd like to check in and drop off my luggage before meeting everyone."

"No problem."

Ryer expected that he would be the one shuttling relatives back and forth from the funeral home, so he rented a medium-sized sedan at the airport rental agency. They found the car, put their luggage in the trunk, and headed into town.

Although it was McKenna's first visit to Ireland, he had traveled to England and had even reluctantly driven while he was there. But that was years before and almost forgotten. Everyone was driving on the wrong side of the road, including Ryer. It was disconcerting to McKenna to be sitting in the front left seat without a steering wheel and pedals in front of him.

Once they climbed onto the motorway, the Belfast skyline came into view. From a distance, it looked like a nice city—very modern and bounded by verdant cliffs on the west and a fine harbor on the east. The countryside was spectacular, overwhelmingly green and dotted with small, well-kept farms that gave way to neat suburbs as they approached the city limits. To McKenna's surprise, he couldn't see a sign of the Troubles.

During the trip McKenna performed one of the chores he had been dreading, answering Ryer's questions about the progress made in the investigation of Meaghan's death. The questions were pointed and McKenna answered them as truthfully and completely as he could. Ryer seemed especially interested in the Belfast origins of her killer, stating that the Mulrooney house wasn't too far from the house where he had grown up.

"Is it possible that Meaghan recognized Michael Mulrooney in Iceland?" McKenna asked.

"I doubt it. He was already a fugitive when she was born, and the Brits don't make a habit of publicizing the identities of the people they're looking for. They'd rather take them by surprise and unawares."

"How about you? Would you know him?"

Ryer thought the question over for a minute before answering. "I don't know the name. He's older than me, so I wouldn't have grown up with him."

"Is it possible you'd know his father?"

"Maybe if I saw him, but it's hard to say. It's been a long time since we lived here."

"How about your folks? Any chance that they'd know Mulrooney or his father?"

"Maybe, if the Mulrooneys were originally from one of the old blocks in The Lower Falls, like we were."

"What's The Lower Falls?" McKenna asked.

"What *was* The Lower Falls is a better question. There's not much left of it now. It was the old Catholic neighborhood between Ballymurphy and The Shankill."

"The Shankill?"

"A very militant, very Protestant neighborhood. In the early seventies there was a lot of terrorist activity in The Lower Falls, with both sides bombing, shooting, maiming, and murdering each other. The Catholics got the worst of it and most of the neighborhood was destroyed."

"So what happened to the rest of The Lower Falls?"

"Militarily expedient urban renewal. Since so many of the houses were damaged anyway, the Brits decided to save themselves a headache and created a barrier between Ballymurphy and The Shankill. They moved the old residents to new houses and plowed the neighborhood under. Most of it is now the Belfast DMZ."

"Was your house one of those plowed under?"

"Yes, which is one of the reasons my folks moved south. As you'll see, there's been a lot of urban renewal, most of it good. Very few of the people in Ballymurphy are living in the same old houses they were in when we lived here."

"But it's still possible your folks know the Mulrooneys," McKenna insisted.

"Maybe years ago. In any event, they wouldn't know him now. My folks have never been involved in the politics here and have always tried to put the Troubles behind them," Ryer said, apparently considering the matter closed.

But it wasn't. "It's good that they don't know him, because I wouldn't want your relatives contacting the Mulrooney family for any reason," McKenna stated. "At this point I can't afford to have Meaghan's killer aware that he's been identified and that I'll be looking for him."

"I understand, so here's what we should do. If anybody in my family asks you any questions about your investigation into Meaghan's murder, just direct them to me. I'll handle it from there."

"You'll lie to them?" McKenna asked.

"Yes, I'll lie to them," the priest stated simply. They drove in uncomfortable silence for a minute before Ryer added, "If you think that's what it'll take, I'll lie to my family and tell them we know nothing about the man who murdered my sister."

There was no further conversation between them until they arrived downtown. McKenna had not wanted to get involved just then in a discussion of the local politics with Ryer, especially since the priest's sister had been an indirect victim of the Troubles. He planned to talk to him and learn about the local situation later, possibly after the first day of the wake. But then he noticed something he considered so unusual that he had to ask about it. The shops were all open, the sidewalks were bustling with people, and the traffic was flowing smoothly, but there were no cars parked on the street.

"We're in the downtown security zone," Ryer explained. "Because of the danger of car bombs, there's no street parking allowed here. You can drop people off and pick them up, but the driver has to stay behind the wheel."

"What happens if he leaves the car?"

"Everybody runs for their lives," Ryer said without a touch of humor.

They stopped at a light in front of a building McKenna immediately recognized from Brunette's description of it. Like he had said, it looked like New York's city hall, only nicer. Belfast City Hall was the magnificent, sprawling, white Georgian building that had served as a backdrop for the photo of the Mullen boys with the old man.

There were two things about the building that McKenna felt sure hadn't been captured in that photo. One was the Union Jack, flying from the flag-pole on top of the building and flapping proudly in the breeze.

The other was the solid police presence, giving McKenna his first look at the Royal Ulster Constabulary. Two battleship gray armored police Land Rovers were parked guarding the gated entrance to the grounds. A pair of constables stood outside each Land Rover, but they weren't lounging around as New York cops were prone to do when on a fixed post outside City Hall. They stood erect and alert, eyeing traffic and every person entering the grounds. Their dark blue uniforms looked sharp and military, with a blue bulletproof vest worn on the outside as part of the uniform. One cop in each team had his hand on his holstered pistol. To McKenna, they looked distinctly unfriendly and taller than New York cops.

Inside the grounds McKenna could see more of the same. The RUC had men at each building entrance and others patrolling the grounds in pairs, and McKenna could guess why. In front of City Hall stood a tall statue of Queen Victoria, her arms regally outstretched to her loyal subjects. McKenna was sure that some of the Empire's less-than-loyal subjects in town would delight in blowing the old queen and her building to smither-eens.

McKenna saw only one more police patrol before they reached the hotel. Nobody on the street paid the RUC the slightest bit of attention and, if they hadn't been riding in armored Land Rovers, McKenna imagined from the pleasant cosmopolitan background that he could have been down-town in any city in the U.K. There was no graffiti, bomb damage, or any other sign of the Troubles visible to him.

Even the stately Hotel Europa showed no sign of bomb damage. After Ryer pulled up in front, McKenna left him behind the wheel and went into the lobby with his luggage. It looked to be exactly the type of European hotel he preferred, a study in understated elegance staffed by a courteous group of professionals.

McKenna was expected, so checking in took only minutes. He completed the registration process, got his key from the efficient receptionist, and asked her to have his luggage brought up to his room. He was surprised when he was told that his luggage would have to be searched first, but it seemed like a sensible precaution. He and his luggage were taken to a side room by two security men who expertly searched his bags before sending them up to his room. They also politely informed McKenna that all persons entering the hotel were subject to random body searches.

On his way out McKenna obtained a Belfast city map from the receptionist and was surprised to find himself wondering if she was Catholic or Protestant as he left to rejoin Ryer in the car outside.

Ryer was listening to the news on the radio. Thor's Saga Hotel interview from the day before was being aired and Ryer was listening so intently that he didn't seem to notice McKenna. Then the announcer said something that caused McKenna to listen just as intently; Martin McGuinn, an IRA spokesman, denied that the IRA was responsible for the bombing.

Could that be? McKenna wondered briefly before he dismissed the statement as a crafty piece of nonsense. No, it can't, he concluded, but we put them into a corner by linking their bomber to the murder of Meaghan Maher. She wasn't just "collateral damage," another unintended innocent bystander caught in a crossfire or killed by one of their bombs. She was a very different kind of victim, an innocent girl who was sexually tortured and horribly murdered by their bomber for reasons that had nothing to do with the IRA's cause. It's a public relations disaster for them, so they're trying to put some distance between the IRA and Iceland. They don't know just how bad it is yet, but I'm sure gonna show them. It's real bad, and that's good for me. Mulrooney's gonna pay.

The thought caused McKenna to smile. Then he noticed that Ryer was staring at him and looking confused. "Can that be? Can McGuinn be telling the truth?" he asked.

"No, it can't. McGuinn is lying. Mulrooney's IRA and always was," McKenna answered.

"Then that's a first," Ryer said, shaking his head. "McGuinn has never lied before."

"Everybody lies at least once in a while," McKenna said, but Ryer still looked unconvinced. McKenna figured it was time to again change the subject. "How many times has this place been bombed?"

"Thirty-one times, last I heard."

"They're pretty good at repairing the damage," McKenna observed.

"They've had plenty of practice," Ryer said matter-of-factly as he pulled away from the curb.

Within minutes of leaving the hotel McKenna noticed signs of the conflict. On the outskirts of the downtown area they passed a formidable new city prison, surrounded by razor ribbon and occupying an entire city block. There was a guard tower every fifty yards, each manned by two alert constables standing behind bulletproof glass as they surveyed the traffic and the sidewalk outside.

Ryer didn't have to tell McKenna when they entered the Ballymurphy neighborhood. The tricolor Irish flags flying everywhere and the graffiti announced that as soon as Ryer drove past a very old building, the Royal Victoria Hospital. Roughly spray-painted on many of the buildings were slogans: STOP THE RUC BEATINGS, UP THE IRA, and ENGLAND OUT OF IRELAND.

McKenna was used to seeing graffiti scrawled on the walls and buildings of urban American slums, but Ballymurphy wasn't a slum. If the neighborhood could be lifted up and transported to New York, it would be considered solidly middle-class. The two-story row houses looked small from the outside, but many were new and most were in good repair. McKenna was just beginning to wonder what the Catholics were complaining about when Ryer braked suddenly. A convoy of the RUC's armored Land Rovers was approaching them from the opposite direction.

"Why are you stopping?" McKenna asked.

"Safety precaution. They rarely stop and never signal for a turn. I hate when they test your brakes and reflexes by turning right in front of you."

"I guess you're not the only one," McKenna observed. All traffic in front and behind them had stopped, but the convoy didn't turn. As it passed them, McKenna counted four Land Rovers. As far as he could tell, the first two were manned by only a pair of uniformed constables, but the last two were troop carriers full of soldiers in full battle dress. There was a gun turret manned by two alert soldiers with automatic weapons at the ready on top of each on the military Land Rovers. To McKenna, the soldiers looked young, but distinctly unfriendly. "What happens if you don't stop?" he asked.

"Usually, nothing," Ryer answered as traffic resumed its flow. "However, if they turn in front of you and you wind up hitting one of their vehicles, then they presume you're IRA setting them up for an ambush. We have some very unhealthy motoring conditions here in West Belfast."

"I take it that the Catholic neighborhoods are all in West Belfast?"

"That's right. The Protestants live in East Belfast on the other side of the Shankill Road."

"How far is that?"

"About a quarter of a mile that way," Ryer answered, pointing.

"Are things any different over there?"

"I hear they are, but I couldn't say for sure. I was raised a few blocks from here, but believe it or not, I've never been there. Never even been on the Shankill Road."

McKenna had read that the Catholics and Protestants in Northern Ireland rarely mixed except in the workplace. They lived in separate neighborhoods, went to separate schools, read different newspapers, usually shopped in separate stores, and even gave birth and died in different hospitals. But a quarter of a mile? "What do you think would happen if you took a stroll down Shankill Road?" he asked.

"Maybe nothing," Ryer said. "But then again, maybe my tortured body would be discovered in a few days in some ditch outside of town. It's happened before to Catholics, many times."

"How would they know you're Catholic?"

"You mean you can't tell the difference between Catholics and Protestants here?" Ryer asked, giving McKenna an amused smile.

"No. Can you?"

"Of course. I'm from here, remember? Here in Belfast they make a science out of telling a person's religion in seconds," Ryer said. Then he made a left turn and drove a block in silence.

"You gonna tell me about it?" McKenna asked.

Ryer pulled the car to the curb and shut off the engine. "Sure, but it's going to have to wait until later. We're here."

Ryer had stopped in front of a neat row house with an Irish flag flying from a flagpole on the small front lawn next to a neatly painted sign that read:

DISBAND THE RUC
93% PROTESTANT
100% UNIONIST

"Is that your aunt's house?" McKenna asked.

"That's it. Aunt Bridgette."

"I take it that a unionist is someone who wants to keep Northern Ireland in the United Kingdom, isn't it?"

"Yeah, but the titles are a little confusing. The overwhelming majority of the Protestants here are strong unionists, also referred to as loyalists. On the other hand, those who favor becoming part of the Irish Republic are called either republicans or nationalists."

"And that would be the overwhelming majority of the Catholics here?"

"A good percentage of them, but certainly not an overwhelming majority. It's complicated, but quite a few Catholics wouldn't mind if the North remained part of the U.K. They'd just like to be treated better, that's all."

"I see. But I thought you said your folks weren't involved in the politics here," McKenna said, nodding his head towards Ryer's aunt's front lawn.

"My mom and dad aren't, and I never was either. But Aunt Bridgette and Uncle Kevin are a different story."

"Is Kevin your father's brother?"

"Far from it. Kevin Hughes and my father never really got along, but they're polite to each other these days. Bridgette is one of my mother's younger sisters."

"Is politics the reason your father and your uncle don't get along?"

"One of them. My father never condoned murder by either side, but there are two Hughes boys doing time in the Maze Prison right now and Uncle Kevin's always getting brought in for a few days on suspicion of this or that."

"Two of their sons are in prison?"

"And probably will be for a long time, unless the IRA wins."

"What are they in for?"

"They were suspected of ambushing a UDR man, but the RUC couldn't prove it."

"What's the UDR?"

"Sorry. The Ulster Defence Regiment. It's like your national guard, but much more. It's really the Protestant army. They're well armed and they're always training, even on their own time. When the Brits pull out, they're the ones the Irish Army will be up against if the country is ever reunited."

"Maybe the Brits will disband them and disarm them before they go."

"They wouldn't think of it."

"Why not?" McKenna asked. "Seems to me it would save a lot of blood-shed."

"Because the UDR is part of the regular British army and the regiment has covered itself in glory in all of the Empire's wars. They lost five thousand men in one day going over the top in the Battle of the Somme, July first, 1916. It's still a national day of mourning here."

"So I take it the IRA regularly targets the UDR men?"

"Whenever they can."

"If the RUC couldn't prove your cousins ambushed the guy, what did they get them on?"

"An Armalite was found in the boot of their car, so they got ten years apiece for weapons possession."

"Isn't the Armalite the preferred IRA rifle?"

"So I hear."

"Then I take it that your aunt and uncle are IRA sympathizers, at the very least?"

"I might go a wee bit further than that. Matter of fact, people say that Uncle Kevin and Martin McGuinn have been good friends for years."

"Besides being the IRA spokesman, just who is this Martin McGuinn?"

"He's Gerry Adams's right-hand man."

McKenna knew the name. Adams was the head of the Official Sinn Fein party, the IRA's political arm in the North. In an effort to present himself to the British and the Irish governments as a political leader rather than a terrorist, he consistently denied with a wink ever having been a member of the IRA or having taken part in any of their terrorist operations, but everyone knew that was hogwash. But neither government minded the deception; they had to deal with someone to end the madness, and Adams was the one, the only IRA voice shouting reason from the darkness. In his efforts to bring peace he would talk to anyone who would listen and had met at one time or another with President Clinton and the prime ministers of both the U.K. and the Republic.

This Uncle Kevin business and his IRA connection is getting a little complicated, McKenna thought. But is it good or bad for me? Maybe good for me and bad for Mulrooney, he concluded.

McKenna thought that Bridgette was a good-looking woman somewhere in her midforties, but her mourning clothes did nothing to enhance her appearance. She answered the door wearing an old-fashioned black dress with her graying red hair pulled back into a severe bun and her face devoid of makeup. She was wearing an apron around her waist, but even that was black.

McKenna guessed from Bridgette's outfit that she had seen more than her share of wakes and funerals. He could also see that she had been crying hard sometime in the last few hours, but she still knew how to smile. Her face lit up when she saw Ryer on her doorstep. Without saying a word, she grabbed him and hugged him hard, patting his back as if he were a child being burped.

Ryer returned her embrace and stroked her hair as he held her. Bridgette's eyes filled once again with tears, but this time they were tears of joy.

Then it was McKenna's turn, but he didn't get the same treatment. Ryer made the introductions, but Bridgette stopped him short. "I've already heard all about Detective McKenna from your mam," she said, then formally extended her hand. "Thank you for finding Meaghan and bringing her home, Detective McKenna. Our whole family is forever in your debt, so we are."

Bridgette's Belfast speech pattern caught McKenna off guard for a moment and he didn't know what to say to her expression of gratitude, so he just shook her hand and said simply, "Pleased to meet you."

"Where are my mam and da?" Ryer asked her.

"At the funeral home. They wanted some wee time alone with Meaghan before the crowd shows up."

"And Uncle Kevin?"

"He drove them there and he'll wait for them. Your mam said she'd be back soon and that I'm to take good care of you, so I am." Bridgette grabbed their hands like children and led them through the entrance hall, past the kitchen where something that smelled delicious was being prepared, and into a room that served as a combination living and dining space. It wasn't a large room, but McKenna guessed that the place would soon seem much smaller. Meaghan was to have a traditional Irish wake; bottles of whiskey and glasses lined the credenza and fifteen folding chairs from the funeral home were stacked against one wall.

Bridgette told Ryer to bring his suitcases to his cousins' old bedroom upstairs, then she went into the kitchen to make them tea. McKenna found himself alone for a few minutes and took a look around. He immediately recognized the type of handicraft and ceramic pieces that were proudly displayed on the walls and the end tables and knew where they came from. The ashtrays, the crucifix centered on the wall over the TV, the picture frames, and the small wood sculptures of old men, children, horses, and dogs all had that same look. During his police career he had frequently been in such sad homes where objets d'art made by husbands or sons in a prison handicraft shop had been the principal decorations. From the excellent quality of the pieces, McKenna concluded that the boys had been away honing their artistic skills for a few years.

On one of the end tables in a wooden frame inscribed with hearts and harps was a formal family portrait. It showed a younger, smiling Bridgette standing next to a large man who looked uncomfortable in his suit. Each had a hand on the shoulder of one of their young boys standing in front of them.

McKenna picked up the photo and studied the faces. Kevin looked like a tough guy, a solemn, confident man who was used to being in charge. However, there was nothing in the boys' appearance that suggested to McKenna that they were headed for violence and would be spending a good part of their lives in prison. They appeared to be about eight and ten, but they just looked like ordinary boys, maybe a little unhappy at being dressed up and forced to stand still, but innocent enough and without a hint of mischief on their faces.

Ryer returned quietly, surprising McKenna. He was dressed for the first time as McKenna expected a priest to look, wearing a black suit and shirt and a white Roman collar. McKenna self-consciously replaced the photo on the end table, but Ryer picked it up again and stared at it. "You're asking yourself, 'How did it happen? How did those boys grow up to do the things they did?' Right?"

"I guess I am," McKenna admitted.

"Happens all the time here. It all starts with history and it begins in the schools. You see, the Catholic children here all go to parochial schools and they're taught one version of history. The Protestant kids go to the state-run schools and they get the other version. History breeds hatred, and hatred is the dominant emotion in Ulster."

"Which side is being taught the lies?"

"Neither. Everything they're all taught is true and based on actual, sad, historical events. It's a question of emphasis, deciding which series of vicious massacres is to be taught, highlighted, and memorized for all time. The Catholic children are taught about the slaughters under Cromwell and the plantation of Ulster in 1609 by the British and the Scots. That's when the ancestors of most of our Protestants today arrived and quite forcibly ejected the Catholics from their land."

"Sixteen-oh-nine? That was long ago, just about the time those same folks colonized America," McKenna observed.

"Yes, and they did it in much the same way in your country. What it amounts to, basically, is that they threw the Indians off their land. Sometimes by trickery, more often by force, but the results were pretty much the same. The difference is that in America, nobody's seriously suggesting that the Indians be given their land back."

"And the Protestants? What are their kids taught?"

"All about 1641, the year of one of the Catholic uprisings that was centered in the North. They're told how the Catholics butchered every Protestant they could get their hands on—men, women, and children. Slaughtered about ten thousand and gave our Protestants the siege mentality that they're still holding on to."

"So what's the solution that'll end the fighting? Eliminate history as a subject in school?" McKenna asked with a touch of sarcasm.

"Unfortunately, there is no solution that will do that right now. Neither side is ready or willing to tone down the hatred and compromise with the other, so the killing is going to go on and on for some time," Ryer said with sad conviction.

Ryer's statement raised many questions in McKenna's mind, but Bridgette brought the tea service in before he could ask them. Ryer put a smile on his face and sat down on the sofa. McKenna figured that politics should be avoided in Bridgette's presence, so he did the same. The three drank their tea and talked about Ryer's work in New York until Kevin arrived with Peg and Thomas Maher. Like Bridgette, the three were dressed in the traditional mourning black. The Mahers had both been crying and looked beat, but they brightened when they saw McKenna and Ryer. They greeted McKenna just as warmly as they did their son.

On the other hand, Kevin was the picture of reserve. He was a big man who carried himself erect and without a trace of humor. He greeted McKenna correctly, but certainly not warmly, saying only, "I've heard a wee bit about you, McKenna, so I have," as they shook hands.

Then Bridgette announced that it was time for dinner and everyone took seats at the dining room table. Peg insisted that McKenna sit between her and Thomas. Kevin was seated across the table from him, saying nothing as he stared openly at him. McKenna was hungry, but felt uncomfortable.

McKenna figured that Kevin, a man with two sons in prison, didn't like cops, no matter where they were from. Or it could have been that Kevin also felt uncomfortable, and possibly even guilty, about sitting with the man who had connected his IRA with his niece's death.

However, once McKenna had dismissed Kevin's attitude as something that he would just have to endure, he still dreaded sitting casually at the dinner table with Meaghan's closest family while they talked about her life and death.

As it turned out, McKenna had nothing to worry about. After Bridgette brought in the stew, she sat down and began the conversation by bringing the Mahers up to date on what had been happening in the old neighborhood in their absence. It was the most astounding casual dinner chitchat McKenna had ever heard. Bridgette described random sectarian killings, assassinations, and maimings as casually as if she had been talking about the weather, another one of those things you can do nothing about.

McKenna and the Mahers learned that Joe McGuckin, a nice boy and a former neighbor of theirs, had been killed by British soldiers when he had tried to run his car through a checkpoint set up almost in front of their door. After his untimely death, it had been discovered by the soldiers that poor Joe, aged nineteen, had an Astra pistol, some detonators, and a detailed blueprint of the Tennant Street RUC station hidden in his stolen car.

Then there was the case of Frankie Dunne and David Kelly, another two fine kids who used to live in The Falls. The RUC had implicated the lads in three killings. From what McKenna could gather, Dunne and Kelly had been caught by the peelers after the two had gleefully treated one of the Loyalist pubs, King Billy's, to a few bursts of automatic fire from their Armalites last July 12th. The Prods inside had been busy celebrating their victory over the Catholic forces at the Battle of the Boyne, a battle that took place on July 12, 1690. Three dead, nine others shot, and the lads had been sentenced to twenty-five years and sent to the Maze Prison, where most of their mates were spending their time.

Then there was Bobby Morrisson. It was rumored that he had been seeing a Prod lass from the Crumlin Road, a real case of improper and unwise dating as far as Bridgette was concerned. He had last been seen alive leaving an Andersonstown pub in Catholic West Belfast, but he had apparently been lifted and tortured by one of the Prod paramilitary groups, because his horribly mutilated body had been found on the Belvoir Golf Course in Protestant East Belfast.

Terrence McAliskey had also been killed. Everyone knew that he had been an IRA soldier, but the Prods weren't to blame for his death. It seemed that the RUC had picked him up on one of their routine bogus trumped-up charges and Terrence had agreed to shop his friends to get out from under. He had been released by the RUC and sent out, but that hadn't been good for him. Word travels fast and hits hard in West Belfast.

Terrence's body had been fished out of the River Lagan, shot once in the back of the head.

Finally, there had been the case of Roy Fitzsimmons, an errant Bally-murphy lad who liked to watch other peoples' tellies in the comfort of his own home and drive other peoples' cars until the petrol ran out. Then he would just leave the car anywhere and lift another to take him wherever he was going. All that would have been forgiveable if Roy had been man enough to travel to East Belfast to pursue his penchant for larceny, but he hadn't. He stole from his neighbors and they knew what to do about it.

As everyone knew, complaining to the RUC would have been futile. Those blighters were concerned only with terrorism, not the crime in Bal-lymurphy, and they only appeared in the neighborhood in heavily armed convoys, backed up by the Brit soldiers. So the good Ballymurphy folks brought their complaints to the IRA and Roy was dealt with, kneecapped last August and also shot in his right elbow for good measure. Roy's pun-ishment transformed him into the scrupulously honest left-handed lad with the limp, a source of no further problems for his neighbors.

Throughout Bridgette's reporting of the neighborhood news, McKenna made a point of asking no questions nor making any comment as he enjoyed his stew. He had many, but he kept them to himself under Kevin's gaze.

After a while McKenna noticed that Thomas was paying as much at-tention to Kevin as Kevin was paying to McKenna. There was more tension in the room than he had noticed while he had been eating. McKenna re-alized that Kevin was staring at him in order to avoid Thomas's accusing gaze. As Ryer had said, the two men didn't get along, and at the moment, Thomas had quite a grievance with Kevin's politics. McKenna suspected that the only thing holding the hostility under the surface was the presence of the men's wives.

McKenna's suspicions were buttressed after dinner. Bridgette cleared the dirty dishes away by herself, with no offer of help from Peg; one of the sisters would always be there to keep their men on best behavior.

Their plan broke down over dessert, over McKenna's second piece of pie. It was a homemade peach pie with a brown-sugar crust. McKenna thought it was the best thing he had ever tasted and was plotting his third slice while he listened to Bridgette lamenting the closing of the Harland and Wolff shipyard, a move that would raise the Catholic unemployment to somewhere around 40 percent. Then, out of the blue, Thomas asked, "Detective McKenna, have you heard that Martin McGuinn has denied that the IRA is responsible?"

Suddenly, McKenna thought the pie didn't taste that good after all. "Yes, I heard that," he answered, turning to give Ryer his cue.

"Then that's the way it is," Kevin said, staring Thomas full in the face for the first time that day. "If Martin said it, then it's true, so it is."

"Bollocks!" Thomas retorted, dismissing Kevin's conviction with a wave of his hand while keeping his attention fixed on McKenna. "Besides, it's a question I'm asking to a man who knows the answer. Detective McKenna, would you be clearing this matter up for us?"

Peg was holding Thomas's arm and Bridgette grasped Kevin's, like two dog handlers straining to keep their pit bulls apart. Both women had their mouths open, but they couldn't find the commands.

"Da, I don't think Detective McKenna wants to talk about this right now," Ryer said with authority.

No good. "Mind your manners, Ryer. Remember, it's your father you're talking to, not a sniveling Sunday school class," Thomas admonished in measured tones. "I asked a question that needs answering now, not later. I've the right to know, and so does the rest of this sotted, murderous, godforsaken country."

McKenna still had his hopes pinned on Ryer until the priest gave him that sorry-but-what-can-I-do shrug, so he turned to Peg. Still no good. She was in a panic, clutching her husband's arm, but he had placed his free hand over hers.

It was apparent to McKenna that, for the moment, Thomas was in charge. All eyes were focused on McKenna. There was no way out for him; the question had to be answered. "I don't know if McGuinn is lying or not, but I do know that the man who did the Iceland bombing was once in the IRA. However, it did strike me as strange that the IRA didn't immediately claim responsibility for the bombing."

Thomas turned his full attention from McKenna back to Kevin. "What's that you folks say? Once in, never out?"

Kevin stared back for a moment, then appeared to shrink under Thomas's righteous scrutiny. "Maybe he was INLA," he offered.

McKenna thought it best to keep himself in the conversation at that point. "INLA?" he asked.

"The Irish National Liberation Army, another bunch of thugs," Thomas explained, still staring at Kevin. "It's the commie version of the IRA, so it is. Same program with a different name."

"It's not the same. I'd have none of them for mates," Kevin protested, then placed both his hands on the table in front of him, palms up. "But I'll tell you one thing, Thomas Maher. When I find out who killed our Meaghan, I swear that I'm going to kill him with these hands. IRA or no, trust me to kill him if I can."

Now what? McKenna wondered. Kevin was saying exactly what McKenna didn't want to hear and he knew what the next question would be. Then Bridgette took charge. "There'll be no more talk of killing in this house tonight, Kevin," she said, standing up as she spoke with her voice rising. "Thomas doesn't want to hear it and neither do I. No more, I say."

The leash had been yanked hard and Kevin heeled, but only for a moment. He picked up his fork and picked at his pie until Bridgette sat down again. Then he turned to McKenna and asked the question, the one with the answer that Bridgette did want to hear. "You know who did it, don't you?"

Seeing that Bridgette wasn't going to be any help, McKenna turned to Peg and found the same expectant look on her face. Once again, Ryer remembered the role he was to play and jumped to McKenna's aid. "I asked Detective McKenna the same question. He has some idea, but he doesn't know for sure who did it."

"All well and good, Ryer, but now I'm asking," Kevin said. "Do you know, McKenna?"

So much for the plan, McKenna thought. But the family has a right to know. "I know who did it, but I can't tell you right now. Soon, but not now."

"And why is that?" Kevin asked.

Time to face up to this guy, but how do I do it without stomping on his toes? I might need him and his connections later on. "Because I'm gonna get him, not you. That way there's less trouble for everybody."

Kevin glared at McKenna, then appeared to take the rebuff in stride. "Then tell me this, at least. Is he a Belfast man?"

"He once was, long ago. That's all I can tell you right now."

There was a long minute of silence. All eyes were on McKenna until Peg Maher announced, "It's time we were all getting to the funeral home. Meaghan's waiting for us."

It was as if the recess bell sounded in kindergarten. All except McKenna pushed their chairs back and stood up. Ryer gave McKenna an encouraging pat on the back and then Kevin smiled at him and said, "It doesn't take a genius to tell that I can be a bullheaded pain in the arse sometimes."

"I'm no genius, but no, it doesn't," McKenna answered cautiously.

Then Kevin offered his hand. "I understand that you're in charge and everything's to be done your way. But if you'll be needing any help from me and mine, don't hesitate to ask."

McKenna stood and formally shook Kevin's hand, knowing that he was contemplating a deal that Rollins would never countenance. "I'll be sure to keep that in mind."

"Good. And I'm hoping you'll be finding it in your heart to join us for dinner again tomorrow."

Another dinner like this one? McKenna thought. Poor Kevin's gone over the edge. Duty's been done and I'd rather spend a couple of hours picking fly shit out of red pepper with boxing gloves on and a gun to my head. "Thanks for the offer. I don't know about tomorrow, but we'll be sure to do it again sometime."

TWENTY

They took two cars to the funeral home in the adjoining Andersonstown neighborhood, with Ryer and McKenna in the rented car following everyone else. By the time they left the Hughes home, the rain had stopped and night had fallen.

There were a few things about nighttime Ballymurphy that aroused McKenna's curiosity, but only his. One thing was the sound of gunfire in the distance, but everyone else ignored it as they got into the cars. Another was the darkness; although there were streetlights lining the block, none were lit. As Ryer drove, McKenna couldn't help but notice that most of the West Belfast city streets were as dark as country roads. "Is there a problem with the electricity here?" he asked.

"No, the electric's fine. The IRA likes to work in darkness, so they shoot out the streetlights," Ryer explained, then offered his apologies for his dismal performance during the dinner show.

"You did well enough," McKenna answered. "It was a good showing against a strong cast of characters."

Then the driver of a car approaching them from the opposite direction flashed his high beams. "He's telling us that there's a police checkpoint ahead," Ryer explained.

"Is that a problem?" McKenna asked.

"No, just an unpleasant delay."

As they rounded a curve in the road, there it was. There were four constables standing in front of their two armored RUC Land Rovers, which were blocking the road. The constables were backed up by a squad of troops with automatic weapons at the ready.

Ahead of them, Kevin stopped his car, got out with his papers in his hand, and approached the constables. The Mahers and Bridgette remained in the car, all unmoving and staring straight ahead. McKenna noticed that the troops were always moving, but they managed to keep Kevin and his car under their guns. One of the constables approached Kevin's car, looked inside, but said nothing to the occupants.

It was over in under a minute. Kevin got back into his car, the Land Rover was backed up, and Kevin was waved through.

"That didn't look too unpleasant," McKenna observed as the Land Rover was placed back in a blocking position.

"That's because there's women in the car and Kevin's got local plates," Ryer explained. "We're in a different boat, two men in a car with rental plates." He reached into the glove box, took out his rental agreement, then pulled the car up to the roadblock. He shut off the engine and removed the keys.

"Good luck," McKenna told him as Ryer left the car to talk to the constables.

McKenna took his passport from his pocket, then placed his hands in front of him on the dashboard. He kept his eyes straight forward, but couldn't help noticing that at least three of the moving soldiers had rifles aimed at his head. He also saw that the constable examining Ryer's rental contract was a large and well-built sergeant, obviously a tough customer.

The sergeant returned Ryer's papers. McKenna thought everything was going fine until the constables placed Ryer against one of their Land Rovers and frisked him. That action surprised McKenna and annoyed him on both a professional and personal level. In New York, frisking a member of the clergy in full regalia would certainly be a bad career move.

Then it was McKenna's turn. Ryer remained with the other constables by the Land Rovers as the sergeant approached McKenna in the car. He looked all business and distinctly unfriendly as he gave the interior a good look with his flashlight. He ignored McKenna until he was satisfied the car contained nothing of interest to him, then he shined the light on McKenna's face.

McKenna didn't like that, either, but he kept his eyes forward and said nothing.

"Do I know you?" the sergeant asked.

"No, I don't think we've ever met."

"You an American?"

"Yes, sir."

"What are you doing in Belfast?"

"At the moment, I'm going to a wake."

"The Maher girl?"

"Yes, sir."

"Terrible business, that. What are you, one of her American relatives?"

"No, sir."

"Please exit the vehicle, slowly," the sergeant ordered.

McKenna did as he was told, then handed the sergeant his passport.

The sergeant didn't bother opening it. "Turn around and place your hands on the roof of the car," he ordered.

Once again, McKenna did as he was told and was frisked by a cop for the first time in his life. It was something else he didn't like.

"What's this?" the sergeant asked, squeezing McKenna's pocket.

"A detective's shield," McKenna answered without turning around.

It was then that the sergeant opened McKenna's passport, turning to the first page. "Good Jesus! You're Detective McKenna!" he exclaimed. "Why didn't you say so?"

"Just wanted to see how you gentlemen operated," McKenna said without moving.

"Well, turn around, man. I'm sorry about all this."

McKenna turned to find that the sergeant had his hand offered. He looked at it for a second, then shook it.

"I'm Roger Forsythe," the sergeant said.

"Pleased to meet you," McKenna answered, relieved to see that the soldiers had lowered their rifles. However, they still kept moving, circling the car.

Forsythe noticed McKenna's interest. "They're trained to present a moving target," he explained. "You'll never see soldiers here standing in one place for too long."

"I see."

"I guess all this must seem a little extreme to you, doesn't it?"

"Yes, I'll admit that it does."

"Well, don't take this as an apology, but we had eight men murdered by the IRA last year. Two of them at roadblocks, just like this one."

"I understand. I don't think I'd want your job."

"I'm not too happy with it either, but it isn't easy to get work here," Forsythe said, then waved Ryer over to the car. Ryer looked shocked when Forsythe said, "I'm sorry about your sister, Father."

"Thank you, kind of you to say so."

"Are you believing McGuinn?"

"I don't know," Ryer admitted.

"Well, I'm sorry all the same."

"Thank you," Ryer said. "Can we go now?"

"Sure."

Ryer got behind the wheel, but McKenna remained outside, measuring Forsythe.

"Is there anything I can do for you?" Forsythe asked.

"Maybe there is. What time do you get off?"

"Midnight."

"Would you mind showing me around town after you get off?"

"That depends on what part of town you'd like to see," Forsythe said suspiciously.

McKenna understood that Forsythe wouldn't want to be driving around Catholic West Belfast, especially at night. "The Shankill," he said.

"The Shankill? That's my neighborhood."

"Better yet. Will you do it?"

"Maybe, but first would you mind answering a few questions?"

"No."

"I assume by your name that you're of Irish ancestry."

"I'm half-Irish, as far as I know."

"As for that half, do you know what part of Ireland they came from?"

"No idea."

"Would you mind telling me your religion?"

"Catholic."

"Practicing?"

"Most of the time."

"What's your opinion of the Troubles?"

"I think it's crazy that people are killing each other over religion."

Forsythe considered McKenna's answer for a moment. "So do I," he said. "It's not gonna do much for my popularity, but you can meet me at the Springfield Street station at midnight."

"Thank you," McKenna said. The two men shook hands again and McKenna got back in the car.

"What was that all about?" Ryer asked after they had cleared the roadblock.

"Education. While I'm here, I might as well learn as much as I can. Get to see this crazy situation here from both sides."

"Suit yourself," Ryer said. "Wouldn't mind seeing what it looked like on the other side myself."

"You wanna come?"

"I'd like to, but I'm sure your constable wouldn't be too crazy about being seen driving a Catholic priest around The Shankill."

"You could change your clothes, you know."

"Wouldn't make any difference. In The Shankill they'd still know I was Catholic."

"You gonna tell me now how that's done?"

"Sure. In Belfast we make a science out of telling a person's religion from how he looks, how he talks, and how he walks. They'd have me in a second."

"Really? You all look and sound the same to me," McKenna said. "I know the Protestants consider themselves to be British, but everyone just looks Irish to me."

"You're wrong there. Everyone in Northern Ireland is a British citizen, but the Protestants consider themselves just as Irish as the Catholics."

That was news to McKenna. "So what are the differences?" he asked.

"Facial features, for one. The Protestants have higher cheekbones and their eyes are shaped a little differently than ours. Then there's the hair. Lots of them have sandy-colored hair and you'll notice there's a lot of red hair among the Catholics. But there's more. Catholic men and Protestant men even walk differently."

"I hadn't noticed that."

"You would, if you lived here. Catholic men walk with a light, jaunty step and the Protestants tend to swagger when they walk. They're generally bigger than the Catholics, too. More broad-shouldered."

"How about the speech?" McKenna asked. "Forsythe sounded about the same to me as Kevin did."

"Same Scotch-Irish brogue, but there are some small differences. Some people here can listen to you talk for a moment and tell what part of town you're from to within a few blocks."

"I see. What part of town you're from pins down your religion."

"Exactly."

Ryer's information gave McKenna a few things to think about and assured him that the priest had made the right decision. He shouldn't go to The Shankill with them.

An unexpected sight greeted McKenna and Ryer when they arrived at the funeral home. There was a line of people at the front door that stretched around the block.

"They're not open yet," Ryer said. "Don't open until seven."

McKenna checked his watch. Six-fifty. Then he spotted Kevin's car down the block and saw everyone get out. The Hughes and the Mahers walked to the front door, greeting many people in line along the way. Kevin knocked on the door and they were admitted.

"You wanna go in now?" McKenna asked.

"No, let's wait a little while. I'm not really looking forward to this."

"Why so many people?"

"Don't really know, but I will say I'm shocked. Maybe it's a little silent protest against the violence."

"Showing solidarity with the victim's family?"

"Maybe. Or maybe the IRA thought it was a good idea to have a crowd here."

Either suggestion sounded plausible to McKenna. He knew there was a sizable peace movement in the North that included both Catholics and Protestants. But the reason for the crowd could just as easily have been to show support for the IRA and widespread belief in McGuinn's denial of IRA involvement in Meaghan's death. In either event, he was glad for Ryer's decision to wait a while before going in to the funeral. Like Ryer, he also wasn't looking forward to seeing Meaghan's body again, especially in the presence of her family. He decided to use the time to pick Ryer's brains some more. "You know, you've never discussed your politics," McKenna said.

"That's because the situation is so hopeless up here that I don't even like thinking about it."

That wasn't good enough for McKenna. He needed more insight into what made Mulrooney tick, what hatreds had made him become the monster he was, and he was close to his quarry's roots. He could understand why Ryer wouldn't want to talk about his views on the conditions in Belfast, a place he had put behind him, but McKenna reluctantly decided to push the man for information and insight. "I don't blame you. With the IRA bombing all the public buildings and murdering every Protestant they can get their hands on, I can see how you'd want to keep it all out of your mind."

McKenna had struck a chord with Ryer. "You're right. I'm certainly sick of it all, but you should know that the UFF and the UVF have murdered way more people than the IRA has in Northern Ireland," he said indignantly.

"What's the UFF and the UVF?"

"The Ulster Freedom Fighters and the Ulster Volunteer Force, two of the larger Protestant paramilitary organizations. You'll find that they use initials for everything here."

"How many of these paramilitary organizations are there?" McKenna asked.

"Quite a few that I know of, but I really haven't been keeping track. I know that besides the UFF, there's the Ulster Volunteer Force, the Red Hand of Ulster, and lots of splinter groups that are even crazier. They're all outlawed terrorist organizations, but making them illegal hasn't slowed them down."

Much of Ryer's information was news to McKenna. He knew that the Protestants in the north were organized and very militant, but he hadn't read much about their level of violence. Why's that? he wondered. "Are the Protestant paramilitaries doing retribution killings?" he guessed.

"Supposedly. Every time the IRA blows something up, the UFF or one of the other groups goes out and murders some Catholics."

"Why do you say 'supposedly'?"

"Because, if you asked one of them, they'd tell you it's not just revenge. They like to think of their murders as a sort of population control."

McKenna had an idea where Ryer was heading, but he kept a blank look on his face to encourage the priest to keep on talking.

Ryer did. "You see, the numbers are very important here because the Brits say they'll get out when the majority wants that. Right now Catholics are about forty percent of the population, but according to the statistics, they generally have four kids while Protestant families have three. I've read projections that by the year 2010 we'll be the majority here."

"Meaning that they'd vote the Brits out then?"

"In theory, but it really couldn't happen until around 2030 when the kids get to voting age."

"And what happens then? They vote to have Northern Ireland leave the U.K. and join the Republic?"

"Maybe, but I hope not."

Ryer's statement stunned McKenna. "I thought that's what the IRA was fighting for. A united Ireland, thirty-two counties."

"That's what the IRA is fighting for, but the idea doesn't make much sense once you think about it. It would be just too much trouble and I'm sure that everyone in the South knows that. They know it, but they won't admit it."

That was another stunner for McKenna and ran contrary to everything he had heard on the subject throughout his life in New York. "Are you sure about that?" he asked.

"Certain. A united Ireland is something everyone in the Republic pays lip service to, especially the politicians from both our parties. But according to a public opinion survey I read, the Troubles in the North only place fifth on the list of national concerns in the South. Reunification is regarded as something that will probably happen eventually, but hopefully not now."

"Why's that? Because the Protestants would fight?"

"That's just one of the reasons, but it's a big one. The Protestants say they'd fight to prevent any kind of affiliation with the Republic, and I believe them. They're well armed, well trained, and just the thought of being the minority in a united Ireland drives them crazy. One of their mottos is, 'No Surrender, Not An Inch!' They've been holding all the cards for so long that they think that's the way it's supposed to be."

"So it would be a civil war?"

"One of the bloodiest imaginable. Until you get really around this town, you can't possibly have any idea how much both sides hate each other. Besides making living in the North unbearable, any attempt at reunification would also be a financial disaster for the South. Tourism just might be the biggest industry there now, so think what would happen if the bombs were going off in Dublin instead of here."

And it didn't take long for McKenna to reach a conclusion. If the paramilitaries brought the war south to Dublin and engaged in the types of terrorist bombings the IRA was doing in the North and in England, it wouldn't take long for tourism to dry up. The Irish economy would be wrecked. "Doesn't the IRA leadership recognize how bad it would be?" he asked.

"Sure they do."

"So, what's their attitude?"

"That there has to be a war for unification sooner or later, and sooner is better. Once the Brits are out, they'll be ready to go to war. They know it will be horrible, but according to them it has to be."

"You still haven't told me your position," McKenna observed. "Surely you must have some optimal solution for all this."

"No, sadly I don't. The way things are right now here, I don't think there is a solution."

"Remember, I said an optimal solution."

"Okay, here's one. If the Protestants would agree to equal rights for the Catholics, no discrimination in employment, and proper political representation, then the Catholics would agree to keep Northern Ireland as part of the United Kingdom."

That sounded simple to McKenna. "Would anyone go for that?"

"I don't think the majority of the Protestants would. Power sharing was tried here by the Protestant government in 1972, but the paramilitaries and people like Ian Paisley rebelled and brought the government down. Like I told you before, they're too used to having all the power and may never share."

"And the Catholics? Would they go for your arrangement?"

"Many of them would. The last public opinion poll was held in 1972, and at the time 39 percent of the Catholics polled stated that they preferred remaining part of the U.K. rather than reuniting with the Republic."

"What do you think the percentage would be now?"

"Probably lower since the troops arrived. They're pretty heavy-handed in the Catholic neighborhoods and have caused quite a bit of resentment against the British government. They were originally sent here to protect the minority from the majority, but since the IRA campaign the general feeling in the Catholic neighborhoods is that the troops have sided with the Protestants."

That might be because the Protestants aren't shooting at them and blowing them up like the IRA is, McKenna reasoned, but kept that thought to himself.

The funeral home had opened and the line outside had already gone down considerably as the people had moved inside. Some were already leaving, leading McKenna to conclude the scene inside must be like one of those heads-of-state wakes, with mourners lined up for a brief look at the body and a quick prayer.

"You ready to go in?" Ryer asked.

"No, but let's go."

Ryer locked the car and they walked past the line into the funeral home. A few people recognized Ryer and nodded solemnly to him on the way in. Nobody said a word.

The funeral home boasted two chapels, but Meaghan was the only one being waked and the sliding doors between them were open. More floral arrangements adorned the large room than McKenna had ever seen at any wake.

As McKenna had expected, Peg and Thomas Maher stood to one side of the coffin. The mourners on line went two by two to the kneeler in front of the coffin, stared at the body while they said a short prayer, and then got up and were greeted by the Mahers and thanked for coming. Some of the mourners then took a seat among the many rows of chairs lined up in front of the coffin, but most left to make room for others. All appeared to be going very smoothly and it looked to McKenna like the Mahers were holding up as well as could be expected.

Ryer left McKenna at the chapel door, went right to the coffin and knelt in front of it, looking at his sister's body for a few minutes as everyone in line waited silently. Then he bowed his head and sobbed silently. When he got up, he hugged his parents, then escorted them to a seat in the front row and took their place next to the coffin. He was on duty.

Then came the moment McKenna had been dreading. Ryer waved him over. He took a deep breath, squared his shoulders, and self-consciously walked to the coffin.

As McKenna stood over the coffin, he marveled at the skill of the Icelandic undertaker. He had dressed Meaghan in a white gown. White gloves disguised the fact that her fingers were missing and somehow he had also corrected her loss of teeth to such an extent that he had placed a slight smile on her face. Lying in her coffin, Meaghan looked like a young angel. However, despite all the skill lavished on her appearance by the undertaker, she still looked like a dead angel—if there was such a creature—but certainly not an angel who had been lying in a morgue freezer for the past two weeks. Still, the pitiful sight of the young girl brought tears to McKenna's eyes.

McKenna knelt and prayed, but not for Meaghan. Judging from the size of the crowd, Meaghan would receive enough prayers that evening to send her on her way. Instead, he prayed to the Old Testament vengeful God for luck and guidance in catching her killer. When he finished, he stood up and took a final look at Meaghan, fixing the sight of her forever in his mind.

McKenna wiped his eyes and stood next to Ryer who surprised him with a hug. "Thank you so much for everything you've done," Ryer whispered into his ear.

"So far," McKenna answered.

Ryer released McKenna and searched his face, perplexed. "So far?"

"There's lots more to be done," McKenna explained. "Don't thank me until I've finished my job."

"Sounds to me more like a mission than a job."

"Okay, my mission," McKenna conceded.

"Fair enough, but you should try and put that out of your mind for now. The next couple of days should be devoted only to Meaghan. It's a time for healing. Justice and vengeance can come later."

"Oh yeah? What do you think Meaghan would say to that?"

It was a question Ryer hadn't been expecting, so he took a moment to think about it. Then he smiled. "Our Meaghan had a bit of a temper. I think she'd say, *'Thanks so much for bringing me home, but don't be wasting too much precious time with this nonsense. Go get the monster who did this to me before he hurts someone else.'* That's what she'd say."

"I thought so."

"You staying for a while?"

"For a while."

McKenna left Ryer and walked around the room, inspecting the floral arrangements that had been sent. He found from the notes of condolences attached that many had been sent by persons and organizations he had expected to be represented there. There were flowers from the cardinal in New York, from the prime minister of Ireland, from the Ballymurphy Civic Association, from the Belfast City Council, from Thor and Frieda Eríkson, and from Owen Stafford.

Then there were the ones he hadn't expected. He hadn't told Ray in which Belfast funeral home Meaghan would be laid out, but his friend had found out anyway and had then passed the word. There were flowers from Ray Brunette on behalf of the NYPD, flowers from Chipmunk, and to his surprise, a nice arrangement from Brian and Angelita McKenna.

McKenna saved his inspection of the largest and most impressive floral arrangement for last. The piece was composed of green carnations arranged into a massive Irish harp, so he already suspected who sent it. Kevin was standing next to it, apparently waiting for him.

McKenna went over, nodded to Kevin, and opened the note attached to the harp. It read, *"Please Accept Our Deepest Expressions of Sympathy and Innocence"* and was signed *"Martin McGuinn."*

"Is there another note?" McKenna asked Kevin.

The question surprised Kevin, and once again, he eyed McKenna shrewdly. Then he reached into his pocket and passed McKenna a small envelope.

McKenna took it and saw that it was addressed to him. The note inside read, *"I hope you can trust me and believe me. It wasn't us and we're not responsible."* This note was also signed *"Martin McGuinn."*

McKenna put the note in his pocket and said, "You know, I wouldn't mind meeting this Martin McGuinn."

"Now isn't that a coincidence," Kevin answered straight-faced. "Someone just told me this very night that he wouldn't mind meeting you."

TWENTY-ONE

McKenna offered his apologies to Ryer, explaining that something had come up and he needed to leave. However, further explanations weren't necessary. Ryer had seen McKenna talking to Kevin and he wasn't stupid. "Something to do with my uncle?"

"Indirectly."

"Then be careful. They'll seem pleasant enough and they'll be sure to fill your head with blarney. But remember, they're killers."

"I'll be sure to keep that in mind."

Kevin and McKenna left together and waited on the corner, down the block from the funeral home. McKenna had many questions, but Kevin didn't appear to be in a talkative mood. Rather than risk rebuff, McKenna kept his silence and spent an uncomfortable fifteen minutes with Kevin before his transport arrived.

It was a black British-made taxi, the type seen on the streets of London. There were two men inside, the driver in front and a passenger in the rear who swung the door open as the taxi stopped.

"Give my regards to Martin," Kevin said as McKenna climbed into the rear seat of the cab. The driver took off before McKenna could reply.

One look around the interior of the cab disturbed McKenna. The young man sitting next to him in the backseat looked like a skinny Indiana Jones, complete with the brown leather jacket, the wide-brimmed hat, and the revolver in his hand. The only thing missing was the whip. He seemed indifferent to McKenna's presence and barely gave him a glance. His total attention was on the RUC transmissions coming over the police scanner on his lap.

Then there was the driver, another problem. McKenna put him at sixteen years old—certainly not one of the experienced IRA hard men he had been expecting. He was whistling a tune McKenna had never heard before, keeping beat with his own music by drumming the steering wheel as he drove. In under a minute McKenna was absolutely certain that he loathed the song, whatever it was.

Complicating matters were the wires hanging from the steering column and the screwdriver jammed into the ignition. Further eroding McKenna's faith in the two was the fact that although there were two supposed fare-paying passengers in the taxi, the driver hadn't thought to turn on the meter. It was a mistake that would arouse the curiosity of any competent cop they might pass.

Then a police transmission caused Indy some consternation. "Where's their Post Forty-two?" he asked the driver with anxiety in his voice.

"You got me," the driver answered, unconcerned.

"Then don't you think you should check the list?"

"Why?"

"Because the peelers are setting up a checkpoint there, that's why." To emphasize his point, Indy rapped the driver on the back of his head with his gun barrel.

The driver muttered some protest under his breath and rubbed the back of his head. But he got the point and pulled the cab to the curb. He put on the overhead light, took a folded piece of paper from his pocket, and opened it. Then he unsettled McKenna even more when he reached into his pocket and put on his glasses to read the list. "It says here that Post Forty-two is on Finaghy Road at the Motorway underpass."

"Aren't we on Finaghy Road?"

"So we are."

"And isn't the Motorway just a wee bit ahead?"

"It's not far, that's for sure."

"So, my young genius, don't you think we should be trying Kennedy Way instead?" Indy asked.

"Kennedy Way, you say? Sure, I might be able to do that," the driver answered amicably, removing his glasses and replacing them in his pocket. He made a U-turn and resumed his whistling and drumming, apparently without a care in the world.

Now, isn't this just wonderful? McKenna asked himself. Here we are, the Three Stooges, driving around Belfast, maybe lost, certainly armed, and in a stolen cab with a teenage driver who might be blind. I wonder what Ray would say to that? Better yet, I wonder how I could explain this to my new pal, Sgt. Roger Forsythe? Hanging out with these two clowns, I might be meeting him at the station long before midnight. Time to take charge.

"Why are we running around Belfast in a stolen cab?" McKenna asked.

For the first time, Indy looked at McKenna. "You talking to me?" he asked menacingly.

"Yeah, Robert De Niro. I'm talking to you."

"Because we were told to pick you up."

"Did some moron tell you two jerks to pick me up in a stolen cab?"

McKenna got the response he expected. Indy leveled the pistol at his chest. "You know, Yank, you should mind your manners."

"Oh, really? Terribly sorry," McKenna said sarcastically. "Were you told to shoot me if you felt like it or if I got out of line?"

McKenna got another response he expected, a moment of confusion before Indy regained his bravado. "Maybe. You wouldn't be the first, you know."

"Do you know who I am?" McKenna asked.

"Yeah. You're the Yank who was standing with Kevin. That's all we need to know."

"That's all you need to know?" McKenna asked derisively. "Nobody thinks enough of you to even tell you who you're picking up?"

More confusion. "Okay, Yank. Who the hell are you?" Indy asked, tapping McKenna's chest with the pistol.

"I'm the secretary general of the United Nations, but you can just call me General."

What passed across Indy's face was the exact mixture of astonishment, doubt, and bewilderment McKenna had planned. He took advantage of it and acted quickly, poking Indy's eyes with his right hand while grabbing the cylinder of the revolver so it couldn't be fired with his left. Another quick, sharp punch, this time to the Adam's apple, was all it took. Indy was temporarily blind, out of breath, and the revolver was McKenna's.

Indy tried grabbing McKenna, but wasn't strong enough. McKenna easily pushed him back, then tapped him on the forehead with the revolver. "Be quiet, be still, and you'll be all right. Understand, Sonny?" McKenna said.

Despite his condition, Indy understood. He was gasping for breath, rubbing his eyes with one hand and his throat with the other, but he did manage to nod his assent.

Then McKenna noticed that the youngster in front was fumbling for something under the seat while he drove. McKenna rapped him on the back of the head with the pistol and said, "Junior, when you finally find whatever it is you're looking for, please pass it back to me."

"Okay, General. I'm your man, so I am. No trouble coming from me this night." It took the driver a few more seconds to find his Astra automatic under his seat, but then he dutifully passed it back to McKenna.

"Now stop the car," McKenna ordered.

The driver pulled over to the curb.

There was a car parked in front of them, fifty feet ahead. "Read me the plate number off that car in front of us," McKenna ordered.

The driver looked ahead and squinted. Then he leaned over the steering wheel and placed his face to the windshield. "I can see a zero, a nine, and maybe a five."

"Okay, what I can see is that we could use some new rules. Put on your glasses, turn on the meter, and never whistle again for the rest of your life. Got it?"

"Sure, General."

The driver did as he was told, then sat waiting.

"Now drive us to wherever we're supposed to be going. If we run into a checkpoint, just stop the car."

"And then what?"

"You can try running on foot or you can surrender, I don't care which."

"We could crash the checkpoint," the driver suggested. "We've done it before, lots of times."

"But not this time. If you try it, we won't be pals and then I'll have to hurt you. Now go, and drive safely."

The driver signaled, then pulled slowly from the curb.

McKenna returned his attention to his unhappy fellow passenger. Indy's breathing was becoming more regular, but he was still rubbing his eyes.

"Can you see, yet?" McKenna asked.

Indy put his hands down and tried to focus on McKenna. "Not good I can't."

"Small price to pay for pointing guns at people. Now, what were we talking about before our disagreement?"

Indy looked at him blankly, still trying to focus.

"Oh, yeah. I remember now," McKenna said. "You were just about to tell me why you two knuckleheads picked me up in a stolen car."

"Because we don't have a proper car of our own."

"Couldn't you have borrowed a car?"

"Nobody would ever lend the likes of us their motor."

"I see that you've discovered a certain truth in life. Neither a borrower nor a lender be. Could be a source of real friction in a good friendship, don't you agree?"

It was yet another confusing moment for Indy. "Huh? Sorry, General. I don't know what you're talking about."

"Never mind," McKenna said, then he held the two guns in front of Indy's face. "Tell me, what were you going to do with these?"

"Blast some peelers, if we had to."

"Really? Haven't you noticed how heavily armed and well trained your local police and their military friends are these days?"

"They don't scare us they don't. We've been in scrapes before with the Prods."

"Then you've been lucky."

While Indy watched, McKenna unloaded both guns. The six-shot Smith & Wesson .38 revolver only had four rounds in it and the 9mm Astra, with a magazine capacity of eight rounds, was loaded only with three. "You two knuckleheads been doing a little target practice?" McKenna asked.

Indy didn't answer and McKenna knew that Indy was wondering if he stood a chance with him now that the guns were unloaded. "I know what you're thinking, Sonny, and you don't stand a chance," McKenna warned. "For you, it will be all pain and no gain, so don't make me spank you. Answer the question."

Indy decided to believe. "We find things to shoot at, things that need killing. We're patriots we are. Patriots and soldiers."

Maybe that's what they really think they are, McKenna reflected. They're young enough, probably brave enough, certainly stupid enough, and Lord knows they've got enough unreasoning hatred in them. Prime candidates to be young, dead soldiers, briefly praised and quickly forgotten while their politicians jockey for leverage and make their deals.

"You don't mind if I do you a favor and maybe save your lives, do you?"

"Suit yourself," Indy said, shrugging his shoulders.

McKenna opened his window and threw the guns out. After another few blocks, he threw the ammo out, followed by the scanner.

"That did nothing to save my life," Indy said defiantly. "We'll get more and keep on fighting."

"Too bad, but look at it this way. I just shaved ten years off your sentence if we get stopped by the RUC," McKenna said. He felt no compulsion to add that he had also saved himself a few of the hours he would need to explain away the professionally embarrassing circumstances under which he was traveling.

As it turned out, there were no further checkpoints along their route. The driver got on the motorway, and after five minutes of driving south at the speed limit they were well out of town. He signaled for a turn into a rest area, pulled in, and stopped next to a phone booth. The lights designed to illuminate the phone booth were broken and the rest area was deserted.

"Now what?" McKenna asked.

"You're to get out and wait here," Indy said.

"Wait here for what?"

"Nobody told us."

"All right. Thanks for the ride."

"General. A favor, if you don't mind," Indy said as McKenna opened the door.

"Don't mention our little disagreements to anyone?" McKenna guessed.

"We'd surely appreciate that, if you don't mind."

"Okay, but only if I can trust you to do one thing."

"Anything," Indy said hopefully.

McKenna took a ten-pound note from his pocket and offered it to Indy. "As soon as you get close to town, drop this cab off and call another taxi to take you wherever you're going. I don't want to be reading about you two tomorrow."

Indy looked at the bill, shocked at the offer. He hesitated, then took it.

McKenna was almost certain that he was throwing money away until Indy said, "It won't cost that much. Shouldn't cost more than a fiver for a taxi."

"Then save the change until the next time you need a taxi."

"That's a deal. Thanks, General."

McKenna got out and watched the taxi take off and get back on the motorway. It was dark, with the only light coming from the headlights of passing cars on the motorway, one hundred yards from where McKenna stood. He stayed next to the phone booth, figuring he was being watched and halfway expecting a call. After ten minutes of waiting, he tried the phone. It too was broken, no dial tone. As he hung up, an old commercial van pulled into the rest area and stopped just past the entrance, illuminating McKenna in the headlights.

McKenna didn't like it. While he expected to be picked up and brought to Martin McGuinn, he knew sectarian kidnappings were common in Northern Ireland and he felt uncomfortable standing there, in the middle of nowhere, alone, unarmed, and under inspection by the unknown occupants of the van. Dressed in his suit, he didn't know whether he looked Catholic or Protestant. If they weren't McGuinn's men, he was prepared to be either.

Then the van pulled forward and stopped next to him. As it passed, McKenna got a bare glimpse of the two men in the front seat. He didn't like the look of them. In contrast with his first escorts, they were in their thirties and looked like hard-bitten, legitimate tough guys. The side door opened and a female voice ordered, "Get in."

McKenna strained to see the source of the voice, but it was too dark inside. All he could see was her outline, sitting alone on a bench seat set against the side wall of the van. "First tell me my name," McKenna said.

"Why? You nervous?" she asked.

"No, just a little absentminded sometimes."

"I see. Then maybe you've forgotten that you're Detective Brian McKenna. We're here to take you to see Martin McGuinn."

"Thanks. Now I remember," McKenna said, then climbed in and sat next to her. In the darkness, he still couldn't see much more of her. Her age and facial features remained a mystery, but she was thin, dressed in slacks and a jacket, and had long hair tucked under a man's cap. The man in the passenger's seat had turned around and was inspecting him. All McKenna could see was the man's outline. He couldn't see a weapon, but felt that he was covered.

The woman took her cap off and her hair flowed down, reaching past her waist. She gave it to McKenna and said, "Please empty your pockets into the hat, then take off your shoes."

McKenna did as he was told, removing his shoes, then placing his wallet, his shield, his keys, and his money into the hat. She rummaged briefly through his things, picked up his shoes, then passed them and the cap to the man in the passenger seat. Then she stood up and began expertly frisking him as he sat there, starting at his shoulders, feeling everywhere, and missing nothing. "Please stand up," she ordered.

McKenna stood and placed his hands on the wall of the van. She completed her search, then sat down without a word. McKenna resumed his seat next to her and watched the passenger go through his wallet while the driver shone a flashlight on it, then gave McKenna's shoes a good inspection. Satisfied, he passed everything back to the woman and she handed it back to McKenna.

The driver took off and they started heading south on the motorway. After McKenna had replaced his things in his pockets and put his shoes back on, he handed the cap back to the woman. It had ear flaps inside and she pulled them down, then placed the cap securely on his head so the flaps covered his eyes. "Sorry about this," she said pleasantly.

"Think nothing of it. I understand."

"So, tell me. How's Inspector Rollins doing?"

"Fine. You know him?"

"No, but he'd know me."

"Just you?"

"No, I don't doubt that he'd know all of us."

"Is that why you didn't pick me up at the funeral home? Belfast a little hot for you?"

"No reason to go there unless we have to," she conceded.

Not knowing where he was going with his eyes covered didn't bother McKenna in the least. He had expected that, and knowing that Rollins or the RUC would recognize his new companions made him feel good, not bad. He had graduated from the expendable IRA street urchins into the hands of the professionals. "Tough business you're in," he commented.

"It's not too bad if you survive long enough to learn what you're doing. Anyway, it sure beats my day job."

"And what might that be?"

"Detective McKenna, we've just met," she protested. "You shouldn't be so nosy, asking all these questions."

"You're absolutely right. Sorry."

The next fifteen minutes passed in silence. McKenna felt the van slow down and turn off the motorway, then make a series of turns so that by the time they finally stopped, he had no idea what direction they were facing. He heard the passenger door open and felt the shift in the van as the passenger got out. Then the van pulled forward slowly and McKenna could tell by the sound of the engine echoing against walls that they were inside a garage or tunnel. The driver shut the engine off, then the side door of the van was opened. "Leave the cap on and stand up," the woman ordered.

As soon as McKenna stood, the woman took his arm. "Ready?" she asked.

"Let's go."

She guided him, holding his arm as he stepped out of the van. They walked a few steps, then climbed a short flight of stairs. She opened a door, then guided him inside and let go of his arm. He heard the door close behind him.

"You can take your hat off and sit down, Detective McKenna. I'm Martin McGuinn," a male voice in front of him said.

It took McKenna a moment to focus after he removed the hat. He was in a spotless, modern residential kitchen brightly lit by fluorescent lights. Seated at the breakfast table in front of him was a stocky, pleasant-looking man in his fifties. He was wearing a beige tweed suit and a brown tie that gave him the appearance of the perfect country gentleman. McKenna could see that McGuinn had once been one of those recognizable redheaded

Catholics Ryer had described, but no longer. His hair was thinning and graying with only red highlights left.

They were alone in the room. McKenna looked around the kitchen for a reference point, but found none. There were no notes on the refrigerator, no cute sign announcing whose kitchen it was, and the blinds on the window next to the breakfast table were drawn closed.

"Don't bother trying to figure it out," McGuinn said. "It belongs to a friend of a friend. I've never been here before, and I'll probably never be here again."

McKenna sat across from McGuinn and stared at him, waiting for the IRA spokesman to begin. But McGuinn didn't, so McKenna kept his silence, measuring the man as he returned his inquisitive stare.

"Sorry about the melodrama in the way we brought you here," McGuinn said at last.

"Think nothing of it, but I don't see how you can be much of an effective spokesman if you have to be hiding out all the time."

"Not all the time. I can give an unannounced press conference from time to time. The Brits wouldn't bother me and the RUC would have to leave me alone for the moment. As far as the Brits are concerned, publicly at least, Gerry Adams and I have been rehabilitated. They need us."

"Then who are you worried about? The paramilitaries?"

"Of course. They'd love to get a line on us. That's why we're like Yasser Arafat, never sleep in the same place two nights in a row."

"Well, if it's any consolation to you, you don't have to worry about me. I don't think it's in either of our interests to publicize my visit and answer questions about you from anyone."

"Not even Inspector Rollins?"

"Not unless I think you've brought me here to feed me a pack of lies. But that's not why I'm here, is it?"

"No, I won't be telling you any lies," McGuinn said, then changed the subject. "Tell me, how do you like Belfast so far?"

"It could be wonderful, but from what I've seen so far, I'd say you don't have to worry about me coming here on vacation."

"You don't understand the reasons behind what's going on here?"

"I understand your position and I understand the loyalists' position, but I can't see the reasons why you're killing each other over religion. It's senseless and barbaric, as far as I'm concerned."

"Surely you understand that it's more than just religion," McGuinn said.

"Religion is what started it. You're going to tell me that it's evolved into a power struggle and a civil rights struggle, but it seems to me that the hatred here is based on religion, on the way different branches of Christianity worship the same God. It's just as senseless as the way the Shiite and Sunni Muslims have been slaughtering each other for centuries."

"And it's been going on here just about as long. Maybe too long," McGuinn said, surprising McKenna. He wondered if McGuinn was just posturing for his benefit or was he talking from the heart? McKenna couldn't tell, so he sat and waited for McGuinn to continue.

"Let's concede for a moment that everybody's wrong. The Brits, the Prods, and us," McGuinn suggested. "If you had to choose, which side would you say is the least guilty?"

"I don't know enough about it, but I don't have to choose. I'm an American, remember?"

"But you're still Irish, aren't you?"

Here we go again, McKenna thought. "Yeah, I'm Irish and I'm Catholic, but so are most of the people in the South. From what I hear, lots of them don't think much of your act up here. They're not impartial, but they're not throwing bombs at anybody."

McGuinn sat back in his chair, staring at his hands on the table in front of him. "I had hoped for better from you," he said softly, more to himself than to McKenna.

"Then I guess I'm sorry, but that's the way I see it," McKenna said. "If it makes you feel any better, I think the Catholics should get a better deal up here."

"Thank you, it does," McGuinn said, smiling. "Maybe I will be able to talk some sense into you after all."

"About the Iceland bombing."

"Yes, the Iceland bombing."

"Then before you start, let's get a few things straight. I'm not working on a bombing. I'm working on a sex murder, trying to catch a maniac who tortured and murdered a friend of a friend. The bombing is incidental, as far as I'm concerned."

"Do you have a name for this maniac?"

"I know who he is, but I see no reason to tell you yet."

"You mean, first I'd have to convince you that the IRA didn't do it?"

"That would be a start, but there's more. You'd have to agree to help me catch this man and I'd have to believe you would."

"Now why would I do that?" McGuinn asked.

"Because if you don't, I'm gonna keep him publicly connected to the IRA. That's gonna give you more horrible publicity than you'd like, both here and in the U.S. Before I'm done with you, nobody in America with any kind of conscience would do a thing to help you and your people."

McKenna expected some kind of a reaction from McGuinn, but got none, leading him to believe that he had just said exactly what McGuinn had expected to hear. Then he gave McKenna a condescending smile. "Keep in mind that we never claimed responsibility for that blast, and we're not shy. If it's ours, we claim it, even if there's unexpected damage and it brings us bad press."

"Even if it kills people you didn't want to kill?"

"Yes, even then. We publicly apologize to the victim's family and accept whatever criticism we get from our people. Yet we never claimed the Iceland bombing, even before anyone knew about Meaghan Maher. As I understand it, her body wasn't discovered until hours after the blast and you didn't publicly connect her death to the bomber until yesterday. So why wouldn't we have claimed it right away if it was ours? You have to admit, it was a pretty spectacular job. Maybe one we'd be proud of."

McKenna thought that McGuinn was citing good points, all points he himself had considered before. But McGuinn had to be pressed. "It was an IRA man who did it," McKenna stated.

"Maybe I'll concede that, but it wasn't an IRA operation," McGuinn countered.

"This isn't the first sex murder he's done, and Meaghan Maher wasn't the first Irish girl he's tortured and killed for fun before a bombing."

That got a reaction. McGuinn sat up straight in his chair and stared at McKenna, not defiantly, but with a very worried look on his face. "How many others?"

"One other Irish Catholic girl, but he's killed other girls all over the world before a bombing. Counting Meaghan Maher, there's a total of five that we know of. The IRA claimed responsibility for three of those bombings, so this monster is one of yours."

"Care to tell me which bombings you're talking about?"

"Not yet. I'm not accusing you of anything in your new role as the nonviolent IRA spokesman, but I've got a feeling you might have some intimate knowledge of some of those jobs. If I told you which bombings I'm talking about, I'd probably also be telling you who I'm looking for. Maybe then we wouldn't have much more to talk about."

"Why's that? You think we'd kill him?"

"Good possibility. Sooner or later, his identity and his other crimes are gonna be released to the press, along with his connection to you folks."

"So you're thinking that we'd hang his tortured body someplace where everyone could see it?"

"I would, if I were you. It's the only way to distance yourself from those extra filthy things he's done while he was doing your dirty work."

"Would that be so bad?" McGuinn asked.

"Personally, it wouldn't bother me at all," McKenna admitted. "But that's not the way it's gonna be. I'm a cop, remember?"

"So you insist on finding this man, if you can, and arresting him."

"Exactly."

"Don't you think that would be rather inconvenient for us? If he's been involved in as many of our operations as you say he's been, he must know a lot."

"You mean that we'd put him under pressure and he'd give you all up to try and save himself?"

"You have to admit that it's conceivable," McGuinn said. "Especially if he found out we helped you in any way."

"Then you'll have to trust me. I'm after him and no one else. If I get him, he'll be tried in Iceland for three murders. We've got enough to convict him there."

"And what about the Brits? I'm sure they'll want to talk to him."

"Sure they will, but they'll have a long time to wait. They get him after he's finished serving his three life sentences in Iceland."

"Did Rollins agree to this?"

"Yeah, he did. I put him under some pressure, but he did. But there's something else you should know about the deal I made with him. I'm in charge of getting him now, but that all changes in two months."

"Then what? The Brits are in charge?"

"Yep, and he'll be tried in England. I think that would be bad for you," McKenna said, knowing he was understating his case. Watching McGuinn, he knew the man was mulling over exactly how much trouble the bomber could cause the IRA. Mulrooney would certainly be convicted of many bombings in that British court, and his extracurricular murders would be very embarrassing to the IRA. Then Mulrooney would be offered a deal to sing. "Maybe he'll sing and maybe he won't," McKenna added, icing the cake. "But the Brits will milk his activities for all it's worth, if you give them a chance. It'll be quite a show, with the whole world press there at the trial."

"Does Rollins know everything you know?"

"Yes, but it's like I told you. I'm in charge for the next two months. After that, it's Rollins's show."

McKenna watched McGuinn as the man struggled with the two possible outcomes if Mulrooney was ever caught. Neither was good for the IRA, but one was worse than the other. But McGuinn still wasn't ready to commit. "Could you tell me if you've connected this man to the Derry bomb in 1996?"

"Derry?" McKenna asked.

"Londonderry is what the Prods call the town."

"Yeah, that was him. He tortured and murdered a Protestant girl in Newry before he planted the bomb."

"That one wasn't ours," McGuinn insisted, apparently pleased with the information. "That was the Irish Army Continuity Council."

"The Brits think it *is* yours. They think this Irish Army Continuity Council was a cover you used because there was a truce on at the time."

"You know the particulars of that one?"

"Sure. Six-hundred pounds of explosives placed in a car parked outside police headquarters. Someone tipped the Brits off, so it didn't do all the damage intended."

"That someone was us," McGuinn stated. "We called it in as soon as we found out about it. We would've prevented the whole thing if we could have."

"You're gonna have to explain that to me," McKenna insisted.

"I'm willing to concede that everyone in this Irish Army Continuity Council was once in the IRA, but they're not now and we have no control over them. We're trying to exercise some, but it's a messy business."

"You know who they are?"

"We know who some are and we've been dealing with them on a case-by-case basis. Those we haven't been able to locate are no longer in the movement."

Now how do I ask him what that means without asking him if he's been ordering the murders of his dissidents? McKenna wondered. I want to keep it polite, but if I'm to believe him if he agrees to help, I have to know how serious this IRA split is. Let's try understatement. "Are you being very hard on them?"

It wasn't necessary. McGuinn was prepared to be frank. "You mean, are we killing them?" he asked.

"I guess so."

"Not unless we have to. It's hard for us to get very angry with them since they're doing the same things we were doing not long ago."

"You mean, things you might even be doing again," McKenna added.

"Maybe, but I hope not. Until Smythe-Douglass was killed, political events were moving along at an acceptable pace and we haven't done a bombing in months," McGuinn said. "We've been trying to tone down the violence and create a climate that would make serious negotiations possible."

"And now?"

"We're at a standstill. Now nobody's talking to us."

A thought hit McKenna that made one thing clear, but raised many other questions. "Smythe-Douglass wasn't in Dublin last year just to talk about an immigration problem, was he?"

"No, that was just a cover for his trip. He was there for a meeting arranged by the Taoiseach."

"What's the Taoiseach?"

"James Reynolds. *Taoiseach* is the official Gaelic title for the prime minister of the Irish Republic."

"I see. Besides Reynolds and Smythe-Douglass, who else was at that meeting?"

"Gerry Adams, meself, and two Protestant leaders whose lives wouldn't be worth a shilling if the word got out that they met with us."

"Any progress?"

"Only a little, but it was a start. At least we were all at the same table talking to each other. That was Gerry's goal, to just get the process started. Smythe-Douglass's murder came at the worst possible time for him."

"Then why didn't the IRA deny the bombing right after it happened?"

"Because we had to be sure it wasn't us, and that took some time. Gerry's in charge now, but he's in a tenuous position. Not everybody still in the movement thinks it's time to talk peace, and very few of them knew of our contacts with Smythe-Douglass. To tell you the truth, our men in the streets hate the Brits and most of them thought it was wonderful when somebody blew up Smythe-Douglass."

"*Somebody*, but not the IRA?"

"I can tell you that as an absolute fact. It wasn't us. That bombing was the most counterproductive move to our efforts imaginable."

"I believe you," McKenna stated.

"Then you'll publicly distance us from the bombing?" McGuinn asked.

"No, I'll keep you publicly connected in every way I can until I get your help."

"You're not being fair," McGuinn protested.

"I know."

McKenna had expected an angry protest to his statement, but that wasn't what he got. Instead, McGuinn just threw his hands in the air, got up, and silently paced the small kitchen.

McKenna watched him pace, realizing that McGuinn had successfully completed the transition from terrorist to politician. McGuinn didn't like it, but he had become accustomed to being leveraged in his new role. Then McGuinn sat down and looked expectantly at McKenna, as if there had been no break in the conversation.

"We're ready to talk again?" McKenna asked.

"Yes. Who's the bomber?"

"Let's make sure we've got it straight. He's not to be killed, he's to be arrested. That means that you're gonna give me all the help you can in finding him and that he's not gonna wind up in one of your safe places like Libya or Cuba."

"You've got my hand on it," McGuinn said, stretching his hand across the table.

McKenna shook it, formally sealing the deal. "Michael Mulrooney."

"Ah, so it is Mulrooney," McGuinn said. "I was afraid of that."

"You suspected it was him?"

"When I heard what a professional job that Iceland bombing was, his was the first name that popped into my mind. We wanted to talk to him straight away and we looked everywhere for him, so we did."

"So he's not in Belfast?"

"I can state as an absolute fact that he's nowhere in the North," McGuinn said, sadly but with conviction. "But even if he were, you'd have nothing to worry about. We couldn't take any sort of extreme action against him."

"Why not, if he's doing unauthorized bombings and ruining your plans."

"Because his brother was one of our famous martyrs, one of the Maze Prison hunger strikers. If we killed Mulrooney, it would tear our movement apart."

"Do you know him?"

"Of course I know him."

"Did you know him before he went to America?"

"Known him since he was a wee lad. Knew his brother, too," McGuinn said. "Patrick Mulrooney. Now there was a fine patriot for you."

"How about Michael Mulrooney? Would you say he was a fine patriot?"

"Years ago I would have, but not now. He came back from America a madman. Every one of us noticed the change in him."

"Was it that he hates women?"

"Women? My God, that's just part of it. He returned here hating everybody. Women, gays, Prods, cops, blacks, and Brits. Hates them all."

"Couldn't you see he was crazy?"

"Crazy, yes, but not unstable."

"What's the difference?" McKenna asked.

"Crazy people can't function. Mulrooney handled every job we gave him with precision. He's fearless and the best at what he does."

"You said he hates cops?"

"Now here's an interesting thing for you. He certainly hates the RUC, and he doesn't care much for the New York City Police Department. But he loves the cops there. I think he still identifies with them."

"How do you know?"

"Because when he's had a few, he loves to reminisce. Tells stories about his time in your department that would bust your gut. Leads us all to believe that you New York cops have a lot of fun."

"Sometimes it's a fun job," McKenna acknowledged reluctantly. He had a few stories of his own, but wanted to stay on track. "Is alcohol a problem for him?"

"Not Michael Mulrooney. He takes a drink every now and then, but he's the most controlled man you'll ever meet. Got a wee touch of the blarney in him and can make you laugh all night, but he's always thinking and always in control."

Everything McGuinn is saying jibes with Vernon's and Hunt's analysis of Mulrooney, McKenna thought. But he still likes New York cops? How can I use that interesting piece of information?

"Now, enough of listening to me," McGuinn said. "Where else did he murder girls?"

McKenna told McGuinn the details of Mulrooney's extra activities in London, Bermuda, and Ottawa. He offered to provide the crime scene photos for each murder, but McGuinn didn't want them. "Anything else I should know?" McGuinn asked.

"You should know that there's probably many more murders, including two he's done that I'm sure of. If I don't get Mulrooney to Iceland with your help, I'll be digging them all up for you."

McKenna could see that McGuinn didn't want to ask, but his Irish curiosity got the better of him. He wanted to know how much more McKenna knew, just in case he had to defend his organization later. "Which two?"

McGuinn's question confirmed McKenna's suspicions. Mulrooney had been a very busy lad when he had been working for the IRA. He had done more jobs for them, but the girl's bodies hadn't been discovered yet. "Well, you already know about Joseph Dwyer, don't you?"

Apparently McGuinn did, but he didn't deny that the IRA had ordered Mulrooney to kill Dwyer. "Go on."

Then McKenna told him the details of Thomas Winthrop's murder in Toronto. McGuinn's only comment was, "Men, too? Jesus, Mary, and Joseph, what's got into the man?"

"The devil, but I don't want to waste time talking about that. What are you going to do to help me find him?"

"Don't know yet, but don't worry. I'll be talking to Gerry and we're sure to come up with some ideas. You going back to New York after the funeral?"

"No, I'm going to Dublin first."

"Dublin? Why? If Mulrooney's in Dublin, we'll find him long before you could."

"That's one of the things I'm counting on," McKenna said. "I'm going to Dublin to see the man Mulrooney's been working for."

"And who might that be?"

"Timothy O'Bannion."

McGuinn looked shocked. "Timothy O'Bannion? You think the Republic's minister for finance is heading the Irish Army Continuity Council?" he asked incredulously.

It was a good performance, but McKenna had seen better during his years spent questioning thousands of people under duress, both prisoners and suspects. He felt certain he had just told McGuinn something the man already knew. "Big surprise, huh?" he asked sarcastically, leaning back in his chair.

McGuinn eyed McKenna shrewdly, then shook his head and laughed.

"I've underestimated you, McKenna. To tell you the truth, I'm not exactly shocked."

"Then why the act?" McKenna asked, but McGuinn didn't answer. He just shrugged his shoulders and gave McKenna an innocent grin.

What am I missing here? McKenna wondered. Somehow this guy knows that O'Bannion has been messing up the IRA's plans, but he didn't want me to know that he knows. Why?

Then it hit him. "How long does O'Bannion have?"

"Not long."

"Whatever's going to happen to him can't happen until I talk to him," McKenna insisted.

"You have no special place in your heart for him, do you?" McGuinn asked, studying McKenna closely.

I have to play this real careful, McKenna thought. For all I know, O'Bannion could be scheduled for death as we're sitting here. "None whatsoever," he said casually. "I consider it solely your affair."

"When's Meaghan's funeral?"

"Friday morning."

"All right, I'll see what I can do. But if I were you, I'd get to Dublin right after the funeral."

"Thank you, Martin McGuinn."

"You should thank me, Brian McKenna, because now I've got some explaining to do about this delay. You see, Kevin Hughes and I go back a long time. He had a special place in his heart for Meaghan and I liked her myself."

"You knew her?"

"When she was a wee lass. Darling girl."

"So then this is personal?" McKenna asked.

"Every once in a long while I get some satisfaction from our work, so I won't mind at all when this problem is settled. The man's no good."

"Why's O'Bannion doing it?"

"He probably tells himself that he's a patriot and that dealing with the Prods and the Brits is treason. But I think it's just blind, selfish ambition. If we can achieve a settlement with Reynolds's help, then Reynolds will be the Taoiseach as long as he likes. It's common knowledge that O'Bannion would very much like that job for himself."

That was good news for McKenna. He had found that ambitious men were more easily manipulated than true men of principle, and certainly more responsive to career-ending threats. McKenna thought that a little ambition was a good thing, but blind, selfish ambition was something else. He chided himself when he realized how pleased he was that he would be making O'Bannion's final hours miserable.

McGuinn must have read his mind. "No, he won't be missed," he said, then stood up. "Give me a number where you can be reached."

McKenna took a business card from his wallet and wrote his home number and his cell phone number on the back. He passed the card to McGuinn who pocketed it without looking at it. "Now put your hat back on, if you don't mind," McGuinn ordered.

"One more thing, and I don't want you to get the wrong idea about this."

"Yes?"

"I'm going to the Springfield Road RUC station to see a constable we met at a checkpoint tonight. He's going to show me around the Shankill."

"Why would you want to be doing that?"

"Just trying to get an education while I'm here. Thought it best to see both sides of the picture."

McGuinn thought that over for a moment. "What's this constable's name?"

"Roger Forsythe."

McGuinn looked surprised for a moment, but then he smiled. "Sergeant Roger Forsythe, you say? Now that's a piece of luck, isn't it?"

"You know him?"

"Not personally, but we make it our business to know our enemies. Know quite a bit about Forsythe, but he's something of an enigma to us. Seems to me he's only an enemy by birth, not choice."

"Tell me about him."

"Comes from what they used to call a good Protestant family until the Forsythes started favoring middle-of-the-road politics. Now they're just about ostracized. Went to college in England, but quit school to join the British army. Wound up in One Para and—"

"Sorry, but what's One Para?" McKenna asked, interrupting.

"First Parachute Regiment. Very famous unit in the British army, although most of my comrades consider it an infamous unit. They're the British army's troubleshooters, served in all of Britian's small wars, police actions, and colonial insurrections since World War II."

"Including this one?"

"Yes, including this one. Matter of fact, they're one of the British regiments stationed here now. Anyway, Forsythe was with them here, in the Falklands, and in the Gulf War. But in ninety-two, maybe ninety-three, he got out and joined the RUC. They promoted him to sergeant a couple of months ago, caused quite a bit of controversy in their ranks."

"Controversy? Why?"

"You have to understand that the RUC has a history of beating prisoners, something I can tell you from firsthand experience is true. But nobody gets beaten when Forsythe's working. He's a tough guy himself and he's not afraid to open his mouth. He won't stand for the beatings, so he's not too popular with quite a few of the other peelers."

"Beating prisoners isn't policy, is it?"

"Used to be, but now the Brits are dead set against it. Makes them look bad to the international press. We suspect they used their influence to get Forsythe promoted in the RUC as well as in the UDR. He's now also a captain in the Ulster Defence Regiment, a company commander."

"So Forsythe joined the UDR after he left the regular army?" McKenna asked, not too surprised. Staying in the reserves after joining the NYPD was also a pretty common practice.

"Course he did. Regular Prod behavior. He'll wind up collecting two pensions in his old age if he survives and we don't win. Truth is, we think he has more to worry about from his own people than he does from us."

"His policy on beating prisoners?"

"No, more than that. He won't stand for any of his men being in the paramilitaries. If he finds out, it's either quit the paramilitary or get sacked from the RUC. Matter of fact, we were considering sending him a list of the ones he doesn't know about."

McKenna wasn't shocked to learn that some of the RUC constables were in league with the outlawed paramilitaries they were supposed to be combating. The fact that McGuinn knew who those constables were didn't surprise him, either. McGuinn seemed to know quite a bit for a spokesman.

McGuinn looked at his watch in a way that told McKenna that there would be no more information forthcoming and that the meeting was definitely over.

Without another word, McKenna stood up, put his cap back on, and once again plunged himself into darkness.

TWENTY-TWO

After leaving McGuinn, McKenna was escorted back to his place in the van and they were off at once. They traveled for fifteen minutes without a word. McKenna assumed that the same three people who had taken him to the meeting were in the van with him, but he couldn't say for sure. He was again seated next to the woman; one of the people in front had opened a window and the wind had brushed her long hair across McKenna's face a few times. Because of the speed at which they were traveling, he also knew that they were on the motorway.

McKenna decided that it was time to get them talking. "Would you mind dropping me off at the Springfield Road RUC station?" he asked.

There was no answer, but McKenna could feel the tension he had just generated. For some reason he felt comfortable about that, so he waited a minute before he added, "Martin knows I'm going there."

There was still no comment from his escorts, so after a few more minutes it was McKenna who felt uncomfortable. Maybe I'm overdoing it, he thought. No reason to make these folks nervous. "Of course, you can drop me off wherever you like," he said.

"That's just what we intend to do, Detective McKenna," the woman said.

"Of course. No reason to go out of your way."

McKenna felt the van slow down and leave the motorway. He felt the motions of a few more turns before the van stopped.

"You can take your hat off in another minute," the woman told him. He heard the side door open. "Now, stand up, please, and I'll help you out."

McKenna did as he was told. Once outside, she left him and got back into the van. McKenna heard the door close and he felt foolish standing there with the hat covering his eyes, but he made no move.

"There's a phone on the wall across the street," one of the men in the front of the van said through his open window. "You can use it to call a cab."

The van took off and McKenna removed the hat. He was standing on a sidewalk in a dark residential neighborhood. There wasn't a person on the street and only a few lights showing in the houses. Across the street was a small, closed grocery store with a lighted phone booth hanging from the outside wall. McKenna walked over and saw stickers from three different cab companies attached to the side of the phone booth. He didn't know where he was, but he knew that he didn't want to be there. He picked up the phone, put in a coin, and dialed.

It was ten minutes before midnight when the taxi stopped in front of a pub a half block from the Springfield Road RUC station.

"Why are we stopping here?" McKenna asked the driver.

"It's not yet a good time to stop in front of the station," the driver said, turning in his seat to give McKenna an astonished look. "It's the changing of the shift, so the peelers and the soldiers will be real jumpy."

"So?"

The driver looked even more astonished at McKenna's cavalier attitude, but then he took it in stride. He gave McKenna a contemptuous look that told him that he considered most foreigners, including the well-dressed Yank sitting in his rear seat, to be generally stupid. "This your first time in Belfast?" he asked.

"Yes, it is," McKenna answered.

"Well then, I'll drop you off now if you like, but I don't think you'll be politely received at the moment."

"No, you're right. I think I'd rather wait."

"Good idea. If you've business in the station, why not conduct it when the peelers aren't so . . ." The driver searched for a word, apparently unsure of where McKenna's sympathies lay when it came to the RUC.

"Cautious?" McKenna offered.

The driver smiled. "I was going to say rude, overly suspicious, and very obnoxious, but cautious will do."

It didn't take McKenna long to come up with the reason for the RUC's cautious attitude during shift changes. If the IRA wanted to kill as many constables as possible in one action, why not blow up the station at the change of shift when there were twice as many of them inside?

From his seat in the rear of the taxi, McKenna could see the station to his left. The building was impossible to miss, an impressive three-story gray concrete blockhouse that was completely out of character with the residential Catholic neighborhood it dominated. The defensive arrangements included security cameras and guard towers, and the entire building was fenced off with razor ribbon. All the windows were protected by steel shutters and both the front door and the garage door were made of steel as well.

McKenna thought the structure looked more like a prison than a police station, but he could see that the security arrangements were necessary; the building was pockmarked with scars that he presumed were made by bullets fired from passing cars.

McKenna's inspection was cut short by the arrival of a squad of troops from a side street on his right. They were on foot, advancing in staggered defensive formation, and very cautious. Half of them crouched and covered the rooftops with their weapons while the other half ran to a new position of cover to permit their comrades to advance.

McKenna watched, fascinated by the precise battle techniques exercised in a residential neighborhood that seemed to offer no glimmer of resistance. The couples standing in front of the pub seemed not even to notice the troops, ignoring them totally and continuing their conversation even when two of the troops detached themselves from the squad to cover them with their automatic weapons.

The couples were used to the routine, but McKenna found it hard to be that blasé when another two soldiers approached his taxi from opposite sides, their weapons pointed at him and the driver. They said not a word, but McKenna couldn't help but notice that both soldiers had their fingers on their triggers.

Like the couples outside the bar, the driver seemed nonchalant as the rest of the squad took up defensive positions on both sides of the RUC station. He nodded to the soldier covering him and shut the engine off. But he couldn't resist turning in his seat to give McKenna a smug, knowing grin. "See what I mean?" he asked.

"Sure do," McKenna answered, hoping to end the conversation.

But the driver had more digs to get in. "If you hadn't taken my advice, it's my guess that right now you'd be pressed against that wall over there with a rifle in your back," he said, motioning with a nod of his head in the direction of the RUC station.

"Tough place to live, isn't it?" McKenna asked, fascinated at the scene unfolding in front of him.

"It's not that bad, once you get used to it. Mind your own business, I always say. Trouble only comes to nosy folks or those who wants it."

Not exactly, McKenna thought. There's always innocent victims, people like Meaghan Maher. Many of them, people caught in crossfires or blown up by accident.

McKenna's ruminations were cut short by more activity at the RUC station. The steel garage doors were pushed open by two constables and a moment later armored Land Rovers converged on the building from all directions. They made the turn into the garage at high speed with tires squealing. A minute later, fourteen of the vehicles were inside and the garage doors were closed by the constables. McKenna had looked for Forsythe among the constables in the Land Rovers, but they were going too fast for him to make out anyone.

McKenna thought it was time to go, but the driver didn't. "It'll just be another minute and things will be back to normal," he told McKenna.

What's normal here in Belfast? McKenna couldn't help but wonder as he watched the couples outside the pub. They were still talking away and hadn't expressed the slightest interest in the activities of the RUC and the soldiers.

McKenna glanced up at the soldier outside his window and looked with some difficulty past the barrel of the gun pointing at his head and into the young man's eyes. The soldier dispassionately returned his gaze, leading McKenna to believe that the man would shoot without thinking at the first perception of danger.

McKenna suddenly thought that it wasn't such a good idea to stare at the young soldier, but rather that his time would be better spent checking his fingernails and the shine on his shoes. Which was exactly what he did until the garage doors opened again and ten Land Rovers were driven out, once again at high speed. Then the soldiers abandoned their positions and ran into the garage. The constables pulled the doors closed behind them and the change of shift was complete.

The driver started up the engine and drove the half block to the front of the RUC station. McKenna paid him and got out. As the taxi pulled away, McKenna took a few moments to gather himself. He noticed that the constables manning both guard towers had some kind of automatic weapons pointed at him through the portholes. He went to the front door and tried to open it, but it was locked. There was a doorbell attached to a speaker mounted on the door and McKenna was just about to ring it when a voice sounded through the speaker. "State your business." Since he hadn't rung the bell, McKenna figured that the voice belonged to one of the constables watching him from the towers.

"I'm Detective McKenna from the New York City Police Department here to see Sergeant Forsythe," McKenna said into the speaker.

The constable didn't answer, but the door swung slowly open. It was electrically operated and there was no one in the vestibule on the other side. McKenna entered and the door closed behind him. There was another steel door at the far end of the vestibule and McKenna was walking toward it when he saw that there was a small receptionist's window built into the wall on his left. The constable there was standing behind thick bulletproof glass.

"Detective McKenna to see Sergeant Forsythe," McKenna repeated into the speaker on the wall next to the window.

"Could I please see some identification?" the constable asked.

A steel drawer emerged from the wall under the window. McKenna placed his shield and ID card into the drawer and it was retracted into the wall. The constable examined McKenna's credentials and made a log entry in the book on the desk at his side. "Please come in," he said, and the steel door on the far end of the corridor opened. He met McKenna at the door and returned his shield and ID card.

McKenna had been in hundreds of police stations all over the world and the interior of this one looked exactly as he would have expected, except for one thing. There was a sergeant sitting behind a large desk, there was a small office on the far side of the desk where two constables were seated behind computers, there was another constable on the other side of the desk manning the switchboard and the base radio, but there were no customers or any other sign of activity inherent in any other police station McKenna had ever seen. The people of West Belfast didn't bother bringing their problems to the police, and McKenna surmised that simply entering a police station would mark a person as an informer. Instead, the Catholics brought their problems to the IRA for action, leaving the RUC there with very little to do in the way of standard police work. In West Belfast, the RUC was not a police force, it was just another component of an occupying army. He was led to a small, empty room and left alone to await Forsythe.

The walls were lined with wanted posters, but they were unlike any McKenna had ever seen. There were no crimes described under the photos

of the fugitives. The captions under the photos simply stated that the subjects were wanted for "Terrorist Activities" or "Suspected IRA Involvement." Some of the photos had either APPREHENDED or DECEASED
stamped across the faces. Gerry Adams's and Martin McGuinn's old posters
were also there, but someone had drawn a line across their faces and written, "Not now wanted, hopefully later" under the photos.

McKenna wasted some time counting the posters and had reached 140
when Forsythe came in. He had changed into his civilian clothes, wearing
jeans, a cotton print shirt, and a windbreaker. Without his uniform, Forsythe
looked younger and certainly friendlier, except for one thing. Under Forsythe's windbreaker were conspicuous bulges on each side, so McKenna
was certain he was heavily armed.

"Glad you could make it, but we have to hurry," Forsythe said. "Everyone's waiting for us."

"Who's everyone?"

"All the guys who worked the evening shift. We leave here in a convoy
after work and head across town."

"Everyone lives in East Belfast?"

"Yeah, or in the suburbs north of town."

"The Protestant suburbs?"

"I see what you're getting at," Forsythe said without hostility. "You're
wanting to know if everyone who worked the night shift tonight is Protestant, are you?"

"I guess I am."

"We've got one Catholic constable assigned to this station right now.
Nice enough guy, married to a Protestant girl from a good family, but not
much of a cop."

McKenna wondered for a moment exactly what constituted a good family in Belfast, but Forsythe was in a hurry and further questions would have
to wait. McKenna followed him through the station and out the rear door.

In the rear of the station was a parking lot protected by a concrete wall
twenty feet high and crowned with razor ribbon. There was another manned
guard tower on the wall over a large steel door. Along one wall two squads
of troops were standing at attention in formation while their lieutenant
inspected their weapons. McKenna thought they looked sharp and professional.

So did Forsythe, and he had noticed McKenna's interest in the troops.
"They're from One Para. The Brits always send their best for duty here,"
Forsythe said with a touch of pride in his voice.

"They look the part," McKenna agreed and left it at that since he
couldn't afford to let Forsythe know exactly how much he knew about him.

All who had worked the evening shift were in their cars with the engines running. Forsythe led McKenna to his car, an old MG convertible in mint condition.

"Pretty small car for a guy your size," McKenna observed.

"It's my wife's car. Woke up this morning to find four flats on mine," Forsythe explained.

"IRA?" McKenna asked, feeling it was the appropriate question.

"No," Forsythe said, and left it at that. They got in the car.

The constables drove south on Springfield Road at high speed, barely slowing down for the occasional red traffic lights they passed through. At The Falls Road they turned and headed east. Minutes later, the procession passed a cleared area that was once the Catholic neighborhood of the Lower Falls before the British army had plowed it under. At that point the constables slowed their autos to normal driving speed.

"Always glad to get back to The Shankill," Forsythe announced when they had cleared the DMZ.

"On the surface, this doesn't look much different from Ballymurphy," McKenna observed, looking around. It was another middle-class residential neighborhood of small row houses, but unlike Ballymurphy, the streets were well lit. However, there was plenty of graffiti to be seen on walls and fences. It was neater than the Ballymurphy graffiti, leading McKenna to believe that the RUC didn't bother the Protestant artists much, but the hatred was still there in different messages: "No Surrender, Not an Inch," "United Kingdom, Now and Forever," and "Off the IRA." The Union Jack was painted on other fences and also flew from the flagpoles in front of many of the homes.

"The Shankill Road coming up," Forsythe said. "Heart of Protestant Ulster."

Most of the cars ahead of them turned right at The Shankill Road, toward the motorway a few blocks away. The rest continued east on The Falls Road. Forsythe was the only one to make the left onto The Shankill Road.

Belfast was not a city of wide boulevards, but McKenna had expected the "Heart of Protestant Ulster" to be somewhat grander than it was. At first glance the Shankill Road appeared to McKenna to be nothing more than an ordinary commercial strip of small stores and pubs with room for only one lane of traffic in each direction. However, as Forsythe drove on, McKenna's impression quickly changed.

First, there were the churches. There seemed to be at least one every three blocks. Most were Presbyterian, but a few other Protestant denominations were represented. Forsythe pointed to the many loudspeakers mounted in front of each church as they passed, but McKenna didn't get his point. "Evangelical preaching all day long. You're never out of earshot of the Word of God in The Shankill," he said with a smile, but it sounded like a complaint to McKenna.

Then there were the clubs. Interspersed among the small businesses were many storefront locations occupied by organizations whose signs outside proclaimed themselves to be football clubs, rugby clubs, or fraternal associations for former members of various British army units. Although every business on The Shankill Road appeared to be closed at that hour, outside each of the storefronts were groups of watchful, sullen young men. All of the lookouts paid particular attention to Forsythe's car as he passed them.

There was something illegal going on all around and McKenna suspected what it was. "Quite a sports-minded town you've got here," he commented sarcastically. "Those boys sure get up early for practice."

"Before they were outlawed, the paramilitaries used to paint their names proudly right out front and march around in their uniforms. But it's only a little different now. The worst of the thugs are still there, but membership is declining and they've been forced to change the names on their signs outside."

"So what are the lookouts watching for? The IRA or the RUC?"

"Both. It would surely be a black mark for them if the IRA shot out their windows, painted over their signs, or blew up their place and they weren't there to fight and die for the honor of their bleeding paramilitary. But what they're looking for is trouble in general, and sometimes we give it to them with a raid."

"Are there many raids?"

"It happens, but there should be more. Seems to me that they're tipped off to most of them and we usually don't come up with much. If we're to accomplish anything, we've got to get the thugs out of the RUC."

A lone RUC Land Rover passed them from the opposite direction, cruising as slowly as any police car patrolling at night would in any city in America. Forsythe pulled over to watch as the young men in front of their storefronts made a show of moving on as the Land Rover approached them.

It was the first normal bit of policing McKenna had seen since arriving in Belfast, but it highlighted one aspect of Belfast life: The police were at home in The Shankill and it wasn't necessary for them to patrol there in heavily armed convoys with military escorts. Then the second normal thing happened: The lookouts returned to their positions as soon as the Land Rover was gone.

"Those constables should have stopped and searched those blighters," Forsythe commented.

"Why do you think they didn't?"

"Maybe they're afraid of harassment if they arrest them," Forsythe offered.

"Or maybe they're sympathetic to the paramilitaries," McKenna said.

"Maybe."

"I take it that you would have stopped and searched them if you were working."

"I always do my job," Forsythe stated.

"Do you like your job?"

"Sometimes, but never when I'm working in the Catholic neighborhoods."

"You don't work there all the time?"

"If I had to do that, I'd quit. We have to spend only three months or so a year working there. The rest of the time I'm assigned to the Tennant Street station in East Belfast."

"An easier job in more pleasant surroundings?"

"The work atmosphere certainly isn't as tense and it isn't as dangerous as working in West Belfast, but actually the job is harder there," Forsythe said. "Instead of wasting time manning checkpoints all night, there's a wee bit of real police work to be done in East Belfast."

"You consider the checkpoints to be a waste of time?"

"Surely. The real hard men have spies everywhere and they monitor our radios. They know where we're going to be as soon as we do, so we never catch them at a checkpoint. What we wind up with sometimes are their dumber junior operatives driving stolen cars, carrying guns, or transporting explosives and fuses."

Thinking back on his own experiences that night made McKenna wince. Forsythe was certainly right; the RUC could have easily wound up with two of the dumbest IRA junior operatives carrying guns in a stolen car, with a New York City detective thrown in as an added newsworthy bonus.

McKenna wanted to get off that track quickly. "Do you think the situation here is hopeless?" he asked.

"Not at all. We're winning," Forsythe answered confidently. "It'll take a long time, but we'll eventually put an end to the Troubles if the Brits remain behind us."

McKenna was surprised to hear Forsythe's conclusion. It was the first optimistic forecast he had heard from either side since arriving in Belfast, but it flew in the face of everything he had learned so far. "You're winning? Are you sure?" he asked.

"Of course. British Intelligence thinks the IRA is down to maybe two hundred full-time hard men, and their financial support from you Americans is declining. Of course, before this little lull we're experiencing they were still doing all the damage they could, but they've shifted most of their terror campaign to Britain."

"Why do you think they've done that?"

"Because we filled up the Maze Prison and fought them to a standstill here. Most of the hard men wouldn't dare show their faces in City Centre or East Belfast because they know we'd be on to them straight away."

"But weren't there still plenty of bombings here before the truce?"

"Surely, but they were amateur jobs done by the young, inexperienced crowd. As usual, the Paddy Factor was at work and half the time they wound up blowing themselves up by accident, either when they made the bomb, placed it, or set the fuse."

"What's the Paddy Factor?"

"What it comes down to is that the people the IRA is using for their dirty work here are fairly inept and not too bright. Unemployed secondary school dropouts, most of them. Sure, they're a murderous-enough bunch who would shoot you in the back of the head without a second thought, but placing a bomb correctly and setting fuses is a different matter. The Paddy Factor means that if somehow it can be screwed up, then those are the fellows sure to do it. Half of the bombs now go off by accident in the Catholic neighborhoods, killing quite a few apprentice bombers in the process."

Half of them? That's too high a number to be true, McKenna thought. Unless . . . "Would the RUC or the Brits have anything to do with all these accidents?"

McKenna saw at once that he had asked a question Forsythe didn't want to answer. "Like what?" the constable asked defensively.

"Like maybe seeing to it that the IRA is supplied with defective fuses and timers," McKenna suggested.

That wasn't it, McKenna could tell from the look on Forsythe's face. "Now how would we go about doing that?" the constable asked sarcastically.

It was apparent to McKenna that Forsythe didn't know something that the Nazis only found out too late in World War II, that those folks in British Intelligence were an extremely resourceful bunch when it came to deception, high chicanery, and setting traps for their adversaries. "Maybe they found a way to blow the bombs by remote control before they could be placed," McKenna tried.

Forsythe gave McKenna a sidelong suspicious glance, but he didn't answer.

That was a pretty good guess, McKenna thought. "You gonna tell me about it?" he asked.

"Nothing to tell. That's just a rumor that's been going around, but I don't know. The Brits deny it every time it comes up."

Of course they would, McKenna concluded. Along with the bombers there would have to be additional casualties, some of them entirely innocent. "I'd sure like to hear this patently false rumor just the same," he said.

"Okay, why not? We know that these kids don't have the know-how or experience to assemble and arm their bombs at their intended target locations, so they do it at home. Since most of the bombs are blown by remote control, the rumor is that the Brits sometimes transmit strong signals on the frequencies of the radio detonators that the IRA uses."

"Now who would believe a fantastic rumor like that?" McKenna asked, even though he numbered both himself and Forsythe as believers.

"Apparently the IRA does," Forsythe answered nonchalantly. "The last three bombs in town were all detonated the old-fashioned way, with timers."

There was a silence while McKenna pondered the information he had just received. Then Forsythe yawned and McKenna suddenly felt very tired himself. It had been a long, trying day.

"Where would you like to go now?" Forsythe asked.

"Would the Hotel Europa be taking you too far out of your way?"

"Not at all. It's less than a mile from here."

"Thanks," McKenna said. He appreciated the favor, but found himself wishing his hotel was hundreds of miles from Belfast. After just one day, he was that sick of the town.

TWENTY-THREE

THURSDAY, MARCH 12TH—BELFAST, NORTHERN IRELAND

McKenna had to give the Maher family some credit, but not much. Owen Stafford had arrived at the funeral home for the last day of Meaghan's wake and the fact that he was black didn't seem to bother them. They knew that Meaghan had always considered herself to be as American as Madonna, and MTV had been available in Ireland for years. They all knew about the strange antics and customs of those daft Americans, so Thomas, Peg, Kevin, Bridgette, and Ryer initially treated Owen like family. He was an easy man to like, handsome, courteous, well-mannered, and appropriately dressed in a dark suit. His stock soared in Meaghan's family's eyes when he cried like a baby over Meaghan's body. He obviously had loved her very much and she had probably loved him, so that was good enough for them.

Owen had quite a few questions for McKenna about the circumstances surrounding Meaghan's death. McKenna answered them as best he could, and Owen took the story hard. Then McKenna had a question for him. "Why didn't you call the police when Meaghan didn't show up?"

Owen gave him the answers he had expected. He had been frantic when Meaghan hadn't arrived according to their impromptu plan and had begun making calls. For two days he had tried her apartment, and finally the police as his concern mounted. The Montreal police had been polite, but told him that they couldn't initiate a missing persons investigation on Owen's complaint since he wasn't a relative. They suggested that he have Meaghan's family contact them, but that was a problem for Owen—he didn't have the Mahers' number or address.

Owen then went on to try the NYPD and ran into the same bureaucratic wall he had hit with the Montreal police, but the Missing Persons detective who had answered the phone gave him something else to think about. He had been kind enough to add that he was too busy to investigate a case that sounded to him like a girl dumping her boyfriend.

After a week without hearing from Meaghan, Owen had figured that the detective was right—Meaghan had had a change of heart and was on vacation somewhere, he hoped alone, while she put her thoughts in order.

McKenna understood Owen's plight and his heart went out to him. Like everyone else, he spent a good part of the day consoling Owen, but then the problem arose.

It began when Ryer led the gathered family and friends in the traditional praying of the rosary before Meaghan's coffin was closed for the last time. It soon became apparent to everyone that Owen didn't know the words to the Hail Mary. They all immediately suspected that Meaghan's boyfriend wasn't Catholic, and McKenna sensed that news didn't sit well with them. During the prayers he noticed that Kevin seemed particularly interested in Owen, lost in thought as he stared suspiciously at his niece's boyfriend.

After the funeral home closed, McKenna wanted Owen to accompany him back to the hotel. However, Owen decided to accept the Mahers' invitation to the gathering of family and friends traditional after every Irish wake. McKenna certainly didn't want to go, but he went to Bridgette and Kevin's house anyway in the hope that he would be able to exercise some damage control.

He couldn't. McKenna didn't drink, but everyone else did. There was food and drinks for everyone, and more than enough to go around. For most of the night McKenna tried keeping Owen away from Kevin, but ultimately he failed. McKenna was just too much in demand and everyone wanted to talk to him. At one point he found himself telling Thomas and Ryer about his night with Roger Forsythe when, out of the corner of his eye, he saw Kevin and Owen standing in a corner of the room, deep in conversation. McKenna was worried, but their conversation seemed friendly enough, so he didn't interfere.

Toward the end of the evening, McKenna saw Kevin and Bridgette lead Peg and Thomas Maher upstairs. It looked like a family crisis brewing and McKenna feared the worst. When they didn't return, he alerted Ryer and told him his fears. Ryer understood at once. He also went upstairs, but he, too, was gone for a while.

They all came down together: Ryer, Peg, Thomas, Kevin, and Bridgette. They were smiling politely and still appeared to be the perfect hosts, but McKenna sensed the hostility between them and he could tell that the women had been crying.

Ryer approached McKenna at the first opportune moment to give him the news. "You're right. Owen's not Catholic, but it's even worse than you thought."

"He's an atheist?" McKenna guessed.

"Worse. He's a devout Presbyterian and divorced as well, so he and Meaghan had planned to get married in the Presbyterian church. According to Kevin and Bridgette, Owen's got the enemy's religion and the enemy's morals."

"Couldn't you talk any sense into them."

"I tried, and I think I smoothed things over pretty well with my folks. They're hurt and disappointed, but they'll get over it."

"But not Kevin and Bridgette?"

"No, they called me a heathen priest and a heretic when I tried. They're very old school Northern Irish Catholics and narrow-minded when it comes to marriage and religion. Remember, people kill each other over religion up here."

"But this is different. I'm sure that Meaghan and Owen weren't planning to live in Belfast," McKenna reasoned.

"Makes no difference to Bridgette and Kevin, Meaghan was still family and her marrying a Protestant would be a disgrace for them. They didn't say it, but I know they feel that God saved Meaghan's immortal soul by taking her before she could marry Owen."

"You folks are all out of your minds," McKenna said, struggling to keep his anger under control.

"I know."

During the funeral early the next morning, McKenna could see that the news of Owen's religion had become common knowledge. He noticed that everyone was icily correct in their treatment of the grieving soldier.

It promised to be a beautiful day, warm, with only a few puffy clouds in the sky, but it turned out to be a long morning. The ceremony dragged on for an hour and the cemetery was a half-hour ride away. McKenna was more than ready to put Belfast behind him by the time Ryer dropped him at his hotel. He packed, checked out, and took a taxi to the railroad station with his luggage. He found that the next train to Dublin wasn't leaving for an hour, so he went to a newsstand for a paper. He was immediately sorry that he did. The headline of the *Belfast Times* was RUC SERGEANT MURDERED, TWO OTHERS DEAD.

McKenna feared the worst. He wanted to read the story as he stood at the counter, but he didn't trust himself to remain steady. He took the paper to a coffee shop in the station, bought a cup of coffee, and sat down to read.

It was Roger Forsythe. The sergeant had been ambushed by four men shortly after midnight in front of his home after working an evening shift. His wife, Emma, had been waiting for him at the window when the attack had occurred. She had seen it all. As Forsythe had left his car, another car occupied by four men had pulled alongside. Forsythe had been ready and fired first, killing the driver and one of the passengers in the rear seat. The other two men in the front and rear seats had fired over the bodies of the dead men, hitting Forsythe at least nine times. They had then gotten out of their car, emptied their pistols into Forsythe's body, and ran west toward The Shankill Road. The car with the two bodies inside had been abandoned at the scene.

The dead men were identified by the RUC as Harold Tyrie, age twenty-nine, and Glenn Lyttle, age thirty. Both had criminal records including charges of weapons possession and assault and both had served time in prison. According to the RUC, the dead men were thought to be members of the Red Hand of Ulster, an outlawed paramilitary organization. The car used by the murderers had been reported stolen that day.

Emma Forsythe was interviewed and she detailed a series of harassing actions directed against her family over the course of the past four years. Their car tires had been slashed on three occasions, rocks had twice been thrown through their windows, and their two boys had been tormented in school by their classmates and the older boys who had constantly bullied them and called them names like "Pope Lover."

According to Emma Forsythe, her husband had been murdered by the paramilitaries because of his efforts to remove their members from the ranks of the RUC. She stated that she planned to move from Belfast as soon as possible.

Superintendent McMichael of the RUC had been interviewed and he basically agreed with Emma's assessment. He called Forsythe, "a fine man, one of the best we had," and promised quick arrests of the remaining killers. He had stated that Forsythe's efforts to rid the RUC of paramilitary members would be continued and intensified.

McKenna was saddened, stunned, and depressed by Forsythe's assassination. It heightened his feeling of relief that he was leaving Belfast, with any luck never to return. He hated the city and saw no promise in its future.

The scenery on the train ride to Dublin improved McKenna's mood considerably. The morning's promise had been fulfilled; it was a sunny day and the countryside was spectacularly green with rolling hills on one side of the tracks and the Irish Sea on the other. By three o'clock he had checked into

the Conrad Hilton Hotel, two and a half hours and a world away from
Belfast.

McKenna was pressed for time and he didn't bother unpacking. If
things ran McGuinn's way, he knew he had to see O'Bannion before the
man left his office for the day. He got directions for the Ministry of Finance
from the hotel receptionist. It was located on Merillion Square, a ten-minute
walk from the hotel.

McKenna enjoyed the trip. He had heard that Dublin was a friendly
city and by the time he arrived on Upper Merillion Street he agreed with
that assessment. People on the street nodded and smiled at him as he passed
them and nobody seemed to be in a hurry. They all looked like people he
wouldn't mind knowing.

The ministry was housed in a grand old white Georgian building. It
actually was Merillion Square, surrounding a fenced courtyard on three
sides, but it wasn't a public square. A wrought-iron fence formed the fourth
side and entry was restricted. There was a guard shack at the gate manned
by a uniformed cop. McKenna took his shield out and approached him.
"Good afternoon, Officer. I'm Detective McKenna of the New York City
Police Department and I'd like to see Mr. O'Bannion," he said, holding up
his shield.

The constable barely glanced at the shield. "The Detective McKenna?"
"The same."
"Well then, let me shake your hand. Constable John Sullivan at your
service."

McKenna put his shield back in his pocket and shook Sullivan's hand.
He had expected to be interrogated by Sullivan, but instead they talked
about the weather and how wonderful it was to be in the fine city of Dublin
on such a fine day. It was minutes before Sullivan returned to business. "I
would have been told if the minister knew you were coming, so I take it
you're not expected," he said.

"No, but it's important that I see him today. Do you know if he's in?"
"Sure he's in, but I can't let you pass without checking with his secre-
tary. Procedure, you know."
"Quite all right. I understand."

McKenna had anticipated some delay in getting to see O'Bannion. He
knew that the minister for finance would be shocked to learn that the New
York City detective working on Meaghan's murder in Iceland was on his
doorstep in Dublin wanting to speak with him. He would be worried, and
that was exactly the state of mind McKenna wanted him in. He figured that
O'Bannion would play for time to put his thoughts in order, but McKenna
knew that he would be seen. O'Bannion would want to know how much he
knew.

As it turned out, McKenna was wrong. There was no delay. The constable called O'Bannion's secretary and spoke for only a moment. She would be at the front gate shortly to escort McKenna to see her boss.

While he waited, McKenna chatted with his new friend. He learned that the police in the South were called the Garda and that in contrast to the heavily armed police in the North, they were unarmed. Sullivan stated that he had never been to Belfast and had no desire to ever go there. "I've heard that the people of the North are a strange lot, you know. Peculiar, cantankerous, and unfriendly they are."

McKenna couldn't agree more. Then Sullivan nodded toward a tall, thin woman walking across the courtyard toward them. "Now here's an exception for you," he said. "Maggie Ferguson, Mr. O'Bannion's secretary. She's a delightful person and I hear she's from someplace up North. Belfast, maybe."

A confusing suspicion formed in McKenna's mind as he watched Maggie Ferguson approach. He guessed that she was about thirty years old, but she was trying to look older. She wore a plain business suit and her red hair was pulled back into a large, severe bun. When she was standing in front of him he saw that she wore no jewelry and very little makeup. Maggie Ferguson certainly wasn't ugly, but McKenna was sure that she could be very attractive whenever she wanted to be. Her red hair was offset by the greenest eyes he had ever seen.

Ferguson offered her hand, gave him a businesslike smile, and said, "A pleasure to meet you, Detective McKenna."

In one day McKenna had learned to recognize the strange Northern accent, and it was there in a voice he thought familiar. But he couldn't be absolutely certain, so he just nodded as he shook her hand. "Would you follow me, please? I'm sure I'll be able to squeeze you in to see the minister straightaway," she said, and McKenna did, following and concentrating on her hair as she walked. He was certain that she had enough hair in that bun to reach past her waist if she undid it.

When they were halfway across the courtyard, McKenna said, "I was going to keep your cap as a souvenir, but I'd be happy to return it."

She stopped in her tracks and turned to face him. McKenna had expected shock or fear to register on her face, but all he got was a lilting smile. "Don't bother, Detective McKenna. You can keep your souvenir with my compliments. It's quite an old cap, isn't it?"

What kind of confusing mess is this? McKenna wondered. O'Bannion's secretary and Rollins's spy in the Ministry of Finance is really Martin McGuinn's IRA secret agent? It's gonna take me a while to get to the bottom of this situation, if I'm even gonna try. "What was O'Bannion's reaction to my visit?" he asked.

"We'll both find that out, won't we? He doesn't know you're here yet. It should be quite an unpleasant surprise for him."

"Briefly."

"Did you catch a brogue from him?" Hunt asked smugly.

"Not that I recall," McKenna admitted.

"Enough said. If anything, he sounded like he was from Canada. Sometimes he'd slip and put *eh?* at the end of a sentence.

I guess this guy was good enough to fool just about everyone, McKenna thought. Except maybe Meaghan Maher. "He ever discuss Irish politics?"

"Only to say what was going on over there was crazy. Said he thought it would never end."

So he always stayed in character, McKenna thought. Even with his partner. "He ever strike you as homophobic?"

"I know he didn't like gays, always called them 'sword swallowers,' and he thought the AIDS epidemic was a pretty good thing. But he never made a crusade out of it, if that's what you're asking. Sometimes he'd have a good gay joke, but that was pretty much it."

"You still think so? That was pretty much it?" McKenna asked sarcastically, pointing down to the crime scene photos of Dwyer and Winthrop.

"No, I guess not," Hunt conceded.

"Okay, the preliminaries are over. Let's start with the Dwyer murder and how you fit into that."

"It's complicated, but I told Mullen that Dwyer was an agent."

"An agent? An agent for who?"

"I didn't know. Maybe the FBI, maybe ATF, maybe even the CIA. I didn't know which, but I knew that he had been infiltrated into NORAID and was probably working for one of them, either as an agent or an informer."

McKenna was familiar with NORAID, an organization formed to raise money for social work in Northern Ireland. It was widely speculated that NORAID was, in fact, an American front organization for the IRA and that the money raised was used by them to buy arms. But McKenna didn't see how it was possible that Dwyer was an agent or informer infiltrated into NORAID or how Hunt would know about it if he was. "You're going to have to start at the beginning and explain that to me," he said.

"Okay. Did you know where I was assigned before I was transferred to the Bomb Squad?"

"No."

"I was an undercover in the Intelligence Division. In '84 I was assigned to infiltrate NORAID and report on their activities."

"And that's where you met Dwyer?"

"Yep, once a week at the NORAID meetings. Sometimes more often than that if we did fund-raising duty together."

"What kind of fund-raising?"

"Stupid shit. Sometimes we'd hang out in the Port Authority building soliciting donations. It was just like panhandling, really, but you'd be surprised how much money we'd bring in."

"People would give money to you and a transvestite?" McKenna asked, incredulous.

"Lots of it. I knew Dwyer was gay, but he wasn't doing his cross-dressing act back then. He was a nice guy with a quick wit, charmed in lots of bucks. Other times we'd pick up the bottles from the Irish bars around town."

"Pick up the bottles? What does that mean?"

"NORAID had jars with labels on them soliciting contributions in most of the Irish bars. The patrons dropped in change and quite a few bills. You wouldn't think so, but it was quite a haul."

"Quite a haul? How much was that?"

"I wouldn't know, but it had to be at least five thousand a week, not counting direct contributions."

"Where would they get direct contributions from?"

"In the mail. NORAID ran advertisements and requests for contributions in all the Irish papers. According to Dwyer, they did pretty good."

"How would he know that if you didn't?"

"He did a lot of work for them, volunteering for everything. He opened envelopes in the office a couple of days a week. Before I left, he was even doing most of the accounting work and running up the totals."

"How did you know he was an agent?" McKenna asked.

"Because he was always there. The way me and a few of the other undercovers saw it, only us agents were always there because that was our job. We had to be there."

"How many agents were there?" McKenna asked.

"We couldn't be sure because there were too many agencies doing NORAID undercover work at the time and they weren't coordinating efforts. It became sort of a running joke among us that if we hadn't working all the time for NORAID, the whole thing would have coll and the IRA would have gone broke."

"How did you find out about the other agents?"

"By accident. One time I had to go to court on an old case and another NORAID guy there, Dennis Quinn. He was from ATF and the same thing I was, going to court on one of his old cases. We for lunch and had a lot of laughs compiling our agent list."

"How many were there?"

"At the time I knew about another guy from the Intelligen and Quinn had been assigned with another guy from ATF, John McGreevy had told Quinn about yet another guy, an FBI ag little nod and a smile, but didn't say a word. Then I knew for sure that myself and all the old club members had been right. Dwyer was working at NORAID for somebody, and, for all I knew, he might have been working at Queer Nation for the same people."

"So when did you tell Mullen about him?"

"As soon as we got back down to the car."

"What was his reaction?" McKenna asked.

"He was real interested and thought it was hysterical, but I didn't know at the time if he believed me or not. He wanted to know exactly what Dwyer looked like and what he was wearing. I had to describe him to a tee before he would leave me alone about it."

"Let me guess what happened then," McKenna said. "Mullen took the rest of the night off, didn't he?"

"You got it. On the way back to the base he developed a toothache and took the rest of the night off."

"You know what he did then?"

"I do now," Hunt said. "He went back to the Queer Nation party and followed Dwyer home. Probably followed him on and off whenever he got a chance until he got an idea of his routine."

"And then he killed him," McKenna stated flatly.

"I guess so, but why like that?" Hunt asked, pointing to the crime scene photo of Dwyer.

"Because once he found out that Dwyer was spending his nights as a transvestite hooker, it gave him the perfect opportunity to torture him for information and then kill him without anyone getting suspicious. He made it look like a sex killing, not an assassination."

"Maybe, but what about these other two?" Hunt asked, pointing to the crime scene photos of Winthrop and Meaghan. "Why would he kill them like that?"

"I have a few crazy ideas, but before talking about that I'll wait to hear what Vernon has to say. For now, let's just stick to you and Mullen."

"Okay, what do you want to know?"

"Anything else you think I'd find interesting."

"At this point, I'd guess that's almost everything I know about him," Hunt said.

McKenna took his notepad and pen from his pocket. "I'm listening."

"First of all, he wasn't just my partner. Once I got to know him, he became my best friend."

"What was there that you liked about him?"

"Until he was arrested, almost everything. He was smart as a whip, hardworking, fun to be with, tough as nails, and absolutely fearless when it came to bombs. He was the star of the squad, knew more about taking bombs apart than anybody else. He was also loyal to his friends. You never had to worry about getting into trouble if you were working with Mullen, if you know what I mean."

"You mean if you broke a few rules, he'd stand by you if the bosses found out and put the heat on you."

"Exactly. He'd lie with a straight face and go to the wall with you. His motto was, United we stand, united we fall."

"Was he a family man?"

"The best, until the troubles started with Kathleen. Even after that, he still loved her and he lived for his two boys."

"The troubles? Would that be in 1990?" McKenna asked.

"No, it began sometime in eighty-eight, after Kathleen got out of college and went to work. Continued right up to his arrest, might even be the cause of it."

"You know what the troubles were?"

"I've got his version and I still halfway believe it, but there's probably more to it than that."

"Okay, give me his version," McKenna said.

"Mullen worked like a dog putting Kathleen through college. You know, watching the kids while she was in school or studying, doing all the housework and most of the cooking, besides working a second job when he was on vacation to pay for baby-sitters and tuition. With his help, she did great in school, majored in architecture. Graduated tops in her class at Fordham and landed a big job with a firm in Midtown. Before long she was making more money than Mullen and, according to him, that's when she no longer had any use for him. He thought she was running around on him at the office and it broke his heart."

"What do you think?"

"I don't think Kathleen would have done that to him. She's got too much character for that."

"So what was it?"

"Maybe an office flirtation, but certainly not an affair. But I do think she stopped loving him sometime in eighty-eight."

"After he beat her?" McKenna asked.

The question surprised Hunt. "Yeah, probably after he beat her," he said, eyeing McKenna shrewdly. "What do you know about that?"

"Less than you, I'd guess. All I know is that she somehow wound up in the hospital with a broken arm and a broken jaw, saying she took a tumble down the stairs. But that wasn't what really happened, was it?"

"No, that isn't what happened. He did it to her."

"Know why?"

"Yeah, I know why. She had been working real late on some big project in the office. The place was a mess when she got home, so she climbed on her high horse and gave Mullen the business. You know the routine, don't you?"

"You mean, 'What have you been doing all day while I've been out in the world breaking my ass for us, you lazy good-for-nothing?' "

"That's the one," Hunt said. "I think she also threw in, 'What do I need you for?' and then Mullen snapped. He's a big boy and forgets how strong he is when he gets going."

"So she gets busted up bad during a squabble. Not too smart, not too nice, and certainly not a great character sign for him," McKenna said.

Hunt didn't get it. "Don't forget, Mullen did everything around the house and usually he did a pretty good job at it," he offered in his partner's defense.

"Okay, let's not put him on trial for that right now. How do you know so much about this incident?"

"Because I saved his ass on that one. She was gonna have him locked up and you know what that means."

"Sure. He'd lose his job. It's felonious assault."

"Yeah, he would have lost it all. The job, the wife, the house, the kids. Everything gone. He was terrified, so he locked her in the bathroom and gave me a call."

"Where do you live?" McKenna asked.

"Yonkers. About ten minutes away, but I was there in five. I managed to calm things down and talk some sense into Kathleen. We all got our story straight to save his job and then Mullen and I took her to the hospital."

"And that was it?" McKenna asked.

"Yeah, that was it for a while. But things were never the same after that. It looked normal, but it wasn't."

"Because she was terrified?"

"Yeah, I guess she was."

We know now that she certainly had good reason to be terrified, McKenna thought. "Then came her first nervous breakdown. You know about that?"

"Not directly, but I know something about it."

"Where'd you get it from? Mullen?"

"No, he never mentioned a word about it and I never pressed him on it. Before she went into the hospital, it seemed to me that he was doing everything he could to make amends. He treated her like a queen, even better than he used to before the beating."

"Meaning?"

"Meaning he was always spending every spare penny he had buying her clothes and jewelry, besides doing everything else around the house," Hunt said defensively.

"And she was doing nothing?"

"No, I guess she was working a lot of hours until she lost her job."

"Too much time out of work while she was in the hospital?" McKenna guessed.

"Probably," Hunt conceded.

"Let's get back to her first nervous breakdown. What caused it and how do you know?"

"She never mentioned a word about it to the doctors or to me, but my wife went to visit her in the hospital and Kathleen whispered to her: She told my wife that sooner or later, Mullen was going to kill her. Then she went really off and said that if he couldn't kill her, someone else would do it for him."

"And I guess your wife thought Kathleen was crazy?"

"Well, she was in the psychiatric wing, wasn't she? And we both knew how well Mullen treated her and how hard he worked. It looked like classic paranoia to us and we wound up feeling sorry for him," Hunt said.

McKenna said nothing in response. He just stared at Hunt, waiting for the dawn of reason, waiting for Hunt to take some responsibility for his actions and his errors in judgment. He didn't want Hunt defending Mullen, he wanted Hunt viciously against him.

The uncomfortable silence lasted a minute as Hunt squirmed on the couch under McKenna's gaze. Finally, Hunt had to say something. "Pretty dumb, huh?" was what he came up with.

"Let's see exactly how dumb," McKenna countered immediately. "I'm betting Kathleen was born someplace on the other side. Right?"

"Yeah, she's Irish from Ireland."

"Probably from someplace in the North?"

"I don't know. I just know she was born in Ireland."

"Count on it, she's from someplace in the North. Now, she was still making good money after he busted her up the first time and she's a smart girl. Why do you think she didn't just leave him?"

"I don't know."

"You didn't know then, but you should sure know now. Why did she hang around, terrified, instead of just packing up and getting out?"

"I don't know," Hunt repeated at once.

But McKenna could see that Hunt did know, that he had figured it out. McKenna just pointed to the pictures on the coffee table in front of them and said patiently, "Look at these and tell me you're not stupid."

Hunt did as he was told, stoically looking down at the pictures, taking in first one and then another. Finally he stiffened and looked up at McKenna. "I'm not stupid."

"Prove it," McKenna said.

"After she got home from the hospital she probably made some leaving noises. Then Mullen told her who he really was and she knew what that meant. She knew that if she ever left him, he'd get her. Also knew that if she had him locked up, then someone else would get her."

"Then she wasn't crazy or paranoid?"

"No."

"Then what was she?"

"A smart, scared girl, but another victim. Maybe the only one who's still alive."

"Glad we got that out of the way," McKenna said, sitting back on the sofa. "Now, for a while I'm gonna tell you all the things that you were gonna tell me. Just stop me when I'm wrong."

In contrast to McKenna, Hunt was sitting on the edge of the sofa. "Go ahead."

"Unfortunately for Kathleen, Mullen was desperately in love with her. Because of him, they were living on one salary again, but that didn't stop him from spending every penny they had buying her things she probably didn't want and couldn't use. They're going broke, but Mullen can't help himself. He's got to win her love back and he thinks the gifts will do it. So he starts shaking down the call girls, but he doesn't save a penny of the loot. It all goes to gifts for Kathleen. After he gets nabbed, you're as surprised as everyone else. How am I doing so far?"

"That's what happened."

"Good. Now let's get to you. All this time you're sitting there at ground zero, watching him spend everything and feeling sorry for him. You should have seen it coming, but you didn't. Then he asks you for the big favor after he gets nabbed. He doesn't tell you in so many words that he's gonna run, but he wants you to keep an eye on Kathleen for him. He's—"

"Stop right there! You've got it wrong," Hunt said. "After he got locked up he couldn't care less about Kathleen. His feelings for her took a hundred-and-eighty-degree turn. He blamed everything on her."

"Does he hate her?" McKenna asked.

"I'd say so."

"You're not gonna deny now that you've been in touch with him, are you?"

"No. Like I told you, I'm gonna come clean. But it's important for you to know that it isn't Kathleen he's concerned about. It's his kids. He loves those two boys and they're crazy about him."

The kids? I should have seen that, McKenna thought. This Mullen is a macho, highly focused, dedicated guy with a one-track mind. He has to be to have pulled off the life he's led. After he got locked up he must have realized that he had failed with Kathleen, so he switched all the affection he's capable of giving to his two boys. They're his lighthouse, the only sane marker in his crazy world. "Tell me how he got in touch with you," McKenna said.

"The first time?"

"Yeah, the first time."

"In December of ninety-two my brother got a package for me."

"That was the arrangement Mullen had made with you? Everything was to go through your brother?"

"Yeah. I guess he thought they'd still be watching me, but the surveillance had been off me for a while."

Not too good a surveillance if Hunt knew about it, McKenna thought. "What was in the package?"

"Ten thousand in cash and instructions."

"Where was it mailed from?"

"New York."

"His handwriting on the label?"

"I don't think so."

"What about the instructions?"

"Typewritten and simple. Spend it on the kids, give Kathleen whatever I thought necessary to keep things running smoothly, use discretion, and don't splash it around."

"How'd you do it?" McKenna asked.

"Spent two thousand on the kids for Christmas and gave the rest to Kathleen. Five thousand right away and the rest during the year, a thousand at a time."

"What was her reaction?"

"None. No reaction at all. I guess she expected it."

"That's it? No thank you, no nothing?"

"We don't really talk anymore. You'd have to see her to understand."

"Didn't she get on with her life?"

"She's working again, but she doesn't seem to have much of a life. Listless is what I'd call her. She used to be a knockout, but she's really let herself go."

"She a redhead?"

"Used to be. How'd you know?" Hunt asked, surprised.

"Lucky guess. What color is her hair now?"

"Sort of a dirty blond. Might be her real color."

"Okay, back to the packages. How many did you get and what was the total?"

"Six packages, usually in December. Always ten thousand dollars in them, except for the one in ninety-four. That one had twenty thousand in it so I could take the boys to London to see their father."

"London? How did that work?"

"Easy. I just followed the instructions. I booked us into the Hotel Churchill and had them in Trafalgar Square by Nelson's needle at noon on the twenty-third of December. The instructions stated that a woman wearing an orange kerchief would pick them up and that's what happened."

"Did she say anything to you?"

"Not a word."

"What did she look like?"

"Maybe forty, black hair, stocky. A little plain, but not bad-looking. She just took the boys by the hand and off they went. I didn't see them again until they showed up back at the hotel on January second. Then we came back."

"Did the same woman drop them off back at the hotel?"

"I didn't see her, but I presume so."

"What about passports? You had to get the boys passports to take them to London, didn't you?"

"No, they already had them. Mullen got the boys their passports while he was out on bail."

God! How did IAD miss that one? McKenna wondered. "Where were those boys for eleven days?" he asked.

"With their father, I guess, but they wouldn't say. They came back in new clothes with new luggage, but they wouldn't say a word about it."

"Didn't you press them on it?"

"There's no pressing those two boys. They're both just like their father, tough and smart."

"You think he's in touch with them?"

"Yeah, I think so. I think he's been in touch with them for a while."

"Why's that?" McKenna asked.

"Because they didn't seem too surprised when I told them we were going to London. Neither one of them had a question about it."

"But you've got no idea how he's doing it?"

"None."

Then I'm gonna find out because those two boys are the monster's Achilles' heel, McKenna thought. "I want you to tell me everything you know about those kids."

McKenna was back on the phone to Brunette right after Hunt left. After reporting, McKenna suggested that some laws pertaining to the Fourth Amendment had to be violated.

Brunette agreed. Even if they could get a search warrant for the Mullen home in Woodlawn, that would legally require giving notice to Kathleen. That would never do, given the present circumstances. So, while Kathleen was at work and the boys were in school, the Mullen home would be thoroughly searched. McKenna had to know how Mullen was keeping in touch with his sons. It would also be nice to know where those boys had spent those eleven days with him.

SIXTEEN

McKenna and Thor sat on the facing sofas in the sitting room of McKenna's suite, talking over the Hunt interview while waiting for Vernon to arrive. The crime scene photos of the three bodies were still on the coffee table between them, consciously ignored by both men.

McKenna answered the knock at the door. The Master of Murder made his entrance with a flourish, dressed in a fresh suit and carrying the autopsy reports and his notes. McKenna resumed his seat on the sofa while Vernon pulled up an armchair and placed it near the end of the coffee table, but he remained standing as he shuffled through his papers.

It was a few minutes before Vernon tossed the papers onto the coffee table between McKenna and Thor. Class was in session as he began pacing back and forth in the spacious sitting room, his hands behind his back.

"This whole protocol is a little unusual for me," Vernon stated. "I'm usually presented with an unknown killer's work and asked to study it to ascertain his motivations. Along the way I'm frequently able to determine the killer's race, approximate age, education, socioeconomic background, sexual preference, probable occupation among a precise range of choices, certain factors he had experienced in his childhood that helped contribute to making him the fiend he is, what kind of car he's likely to drive, his personal hygiene habits or lack thereof, whether he's single or involved in a stable sexual relationship, whether he's been in the military, and many other personality traits. In short, I tell the agencies I've worked with whom they should be looking for; it's then up to them to attach a name to the person I describe, build a case against him, and finally arrest him to end the horror. When I'm working with competent investigators, it's rewarding work."

Vernon stopped pacing for a moment to direct a regal nod to Thor and McKenna, surprising them both. Kudos from Vernon were as rare as compliments from Stalin.

Vernon acknowledged their embarrassed smiles and continued his pacing. "These three cases you've given me to examine are a rare pleasure for me since we already know the identity of the killer and quite a few things about him," he said, then stopped pacing to make a point. "By the way, let me tell you that I'm convinced that the same man killed Joseph Dwyer, Thomas Winthrop, and Meaghan Maher. If necessary, I'm prepared to give expert testimony substantiating that fact."

"Vernon, I don't think that'll be necessary," McKenna said. "We have a pretty good circumstantial case linking Mullen to all three."

"Including Dwyer?" Vernon asked, surprised.

"Yeah, including Dwyer."

Vernon was accustomed to answering questions, not asking them. He sat down in his armchair, looking slightly disappointed. "Tell me about it."

McKenna did, telling about Dwyer's activities in NORAID and the encounter at the Queer Nation affair.

"Okay, so we know Mullen killed him and we know how he did it. Now let's take a good look at why he killed him," Vernon said. "If there were so many agents in NORAID, why did he single out Dwyer for assassination? Why kill one unless he could kill them all?"

"Because all the other agents were Americans working for the U.S. Government," McKenna explained. "The IRA wouldn't tangle with our government because it would kill their fund-raising efforts in America if they did. Dwyer was different. He was an Irish-born agent working for the enemy and a traitor as far as Mullen was concerned."

"The enemy? You mean British Intelligence?" Vernon asked.

"Has to be. If he had been an American agent, all hell would have broken loose with that murder. Even if he had been only an informant for one of our agencies, someone would have whispered that fact in my ear when I was investigating his murder. Then I would have known where to look for a suspect. But no one said a word to me and it wound up as an open case for nine years."

"I see," Vernon said. "British Intelligence couldn't complain about the murder of one of their agents in America."

"No, they couldn't," McKenna said. "Could you imagine the stink if it became public knowledge that a friendly foreign power was running an intelligence operation in the U.S.? The Brits had to just take it on the chin and keep their mouths closed."

"That could give us some additional leverage in our dealings with Inspector Rollins this afternoon," Thor said.

"Then we'll use it. However, I expect that Rollins will deny that Dwyer ever worked for them."

"Maybe, maybe not," Thor said. "You're looking at Dwyer as if he were a minor player, but he had to be more than that. Mullen wouldn't have jeopardized the new life and cover he had built up for himself simply to kill a minor player on some kind of revenge principle."

"You think Mullen was ordered to kill him?" McKenna asked Thor.

"Yes, once he reported to whoever he reports to about Dwyer's activities and location."

"Maybe you're right," McKenna said, again impressed with Thor's reasoning ability. "They took a big chance putting Dwyer there, so it had to be for big stakes. The IRA isn't one of our big intelligence priorities, but it is for the Brits. Dwyer was in a position to know how much NORAID was pulling in and maybe even where the money was really going."

"Let's forget Dwyer's life and get back to his death," Vernon insisted. "That's where it all began. You thought that Mullen killed Dwyer the way he did to disguise the assassination as a sex murder, and you're right. It was his first murder of this kind and he really didn't know what he was doing."

Vernon sat back in his chair, waiting for the question that had to come. It was Thor who asked it. "What makes you say that?"

"For one, Dwyer suffered and I'm sure he told Mullen everything he knew, but he didn't suffer as much as Meaghan and Winthrop did. Unlike their cases, the cigarette burns on Dwyer are not at the most sensitive parts of the body, and neither are the bruises. In fact, much of the damage done to Dwyer's body was inflicted postmortem, after Mullen had strangled him. Classic case of pathological sadism."

Vernon pointed to the photos on the coffee table. "If you'd examine the crime scene photos of Dwyer in the hotel, I'll show you what I mean."

Vernon waited a moment, but neither Thor nor McKenna made a move to pick up the photos. They were ready to believe him, so Vernon continued. "He slit Dwyer's penis and cut off his scrotum postmortem. If Dwyer had been alive when he'd done that there would have been much more blood. At the time, Mullen either didn't know what he was doing or why he was doing it. He found his activity grotesque, but he also found that it somehow sexually stimulated and excited him."

"How about the fingers and the nipples?" Thor asked.

"Dwyer's nipples were pulled off and his fingers were smashed while he was still alive. Pure torture, but it triggered Mullen's latent sexual perversion and set the stage for his later killings."

"And the dildo in his rectum? Was that postmortem?"

"In Dwyer's case, I couldn't say for sure because I don't know how sexually active he was. There wasn't much bleeding there, but if Dwyer had been a real swinger that dildo just might have been his size."

"Was Winthrop still alive when his penis was slit?" McKenna asked.

"Winthrop was alive for the whole ordeal."

"I know that Mullen wanted to make that look like another random sex killing, but why didn't he kill him first like he did with Dwyer?"

"It's a lot like sushi. Who likes sushi the first time they try it?" Vernon asked, then answered his own question. "Nobody. Yet there are many of us who acquire a taste for it and love the stuff. It's an interesting point, one

Ferguson's small smile had spread ear to ear. She's really enjoying this, McKenna saw. Wouldn't it be a bad career move for her to bring me in to see her boss, unannounced and without warning? The answer soon came to him. Under normal circumstances, of course it would. But not now. She knows that O'Bannion is not long for this world and it looks like she isn't bothered at all by his imminent demise. "You really hate him, don't you?" he asked.

"Of course he doesn't know, but I surely do. You'll probably hate him yourself in a few minutes."

"What's he like?"

"He thinks himself the grandest, smartest man in all the world and I want to be there when he finds out that he's not." That was all the information Ferguson was willing to impart for the moment. She turned and resumed walking.

McKenna followed her into the building and up a staircase to the second floor. It was a trip that took much longer than it should have. Ferguson was obviously well liked and she stopped to talk to many of the people they passed in the building on their way to O'Bannion's office. She introduced Det. Brian McKenna of the New York City Police Department to everyone she talked to, always mentioning that McKenna was on his way to speak to the minister on some official matter.

They were all civil servants and knew that when Ferguson said *official* matter, then no further questions were to be asked. Still, McKenna could see that she left everyone wondering, with their curiosities whetted. For her own reasons, she was cranking up the pressure on her boss. There would be plenty of talk, questions would be asked, and rumors were forming right before his eyes.

The office of the Republic's minister for finance was just as impressive as McKenna had expected, inside and out. The heavy mahogany double doors were at the end of the long, wide marble-lined second-floor corridor. Another constable stood outside. He smiled and respectfully tipped his hat to Ferguson, then opened the door to admit her and McKenna. Just inside was a large waiting room adorned with the standing portraits of men who McKenna guessed had been ministers for finance before O'Bannion. The room was vacant except for a receptionist sitting behind her desk in front of another set of mahogany doors. She looked quizzically at McKenna as Ferguson led him past her and through the second set of doors, but she said nothing.

Inside was Ferguson's office with a third set of mahogany doors at the far end. She went directly to those doors and stood there while McKenna looked around and tried to put his thoughts in order.

Ferguson's office was large, neat, and tastefully appointed. There was a row of books and bound budgets in a mahogany bookcase lining one wall, and mahogany-framed charts illustrating government deficits, spending and revenue projections, and tourism figures adorned the other walls. The file cabinets under the charts were also mahogany and so was Ferguson's desk. On it was a PC, a telephone, a large vase containing a dozen roses, and nothing else. Placed at a right angle to her desk was another smaller one with a fax machine, a printer, and a copy machine on top.

McKenna could see that Ferguson was efficient in her job. The furniture glistened with polish, there wasn't a scrap of paper out of place in the office, and he guessed that her desk always looked as if she was done for the day.

"Ready?" Ferguson asked, then raised her hand to knock on the door.

"Wait a minute," McKenna insisted. "Aren't you going to at least call him to let him know I'm here?"

"No."

"Then how are you going to explain this unannounced visit after I'm gone?"

"Easy. Besides being the minister for finance, Mr. O'Bannion is basically a politician with constituents from his district and important visitors from America in and out of here all day long for quick, impromptu meetings. Most of them amount to nothing more than a greeting and a photo of them shaking the minister's hand. I place a memo in the top right-hand drawer of his desk every morning that lists his visitors for the day, but he's a very busy man and hardly ever looks at it. Fridays are usually especially busy days for him and this one's been no different."

"And my name is on that list of today's visitors?"

"Yes, and I predict that, right after you leave, for once he'll look very carefully at that list."

"Won't he think that you should have told him I was coming?"

"Sure he will, but I forgot. He knows that I've been sick all day long."

"Have you been sick?" McKenna asked, knowing the answer.

"Never felt better. Now stand next to me. I want to be able to see his face when he first sees you."

McKenna did as he was told. Ferguson rapped twice on the door, then turned to McKenna and smiled. "By the way, he also keeps a pistol in the same drawer as the visitors list." Then she opened both doors inward.

Ferguson's office was large, but O'Bannion's was positively expansive and exquisitely furnished in the same Old World mahogany style, complete with mahogany floor-to-ceiling paneling. On the left was a large conference table with seating for twelve and on the right were two leather Chesterfield sofas and two matching armchairs arranged around a large, low table.

O'Bannion was seated behind his large desk at the far end of the room in his shirtsleeves with his feet propped up on an ottoman as he talked on the phone. He gave Ferguson and McKenna no more than a cursory glance, then waved his hand to acknowledge their presence before he resumed his phone conversation in hushed tones.

It's obvious that, once again, the minister has neglected to read his visitors list, McKenna thought as he stood in the doorway next to Ferguson, waiting and studying O'Bannion. He figured that the minister was somewhere in his fifties. Like Ferguson, he was very thin and his hair was his most distinguishing feature. It was thick, silver, and curly in an unruly way. With his thick mane, O'Bannion reminded McKenna of an old lion—regal, thin, and wiry, but still with some fight and bite left in him.

Then Ferguson had her fun. "Excuse me, Minister. Detective Brian McKenna of the New York City Police Department is here to see you," she announced in a loud, majordomo voice.

McKenna was sure that O'Bannion's reaction was all that she had hoped for. He looked up from his desk, wide-eyed and with his mouth open as he stared at McKenna. The phone was still at his ear, but then he hung it up without saying another word. It took him a moment to regain his composure, but O'Bannion was a professional politician, among other things, and accustomed to being placed suddenly on the spot. He put a friendly smile on his face, stood up, and said, "Please come in, Detective McKenna."

McKenna walked slowly across the room to the desk, unsmiling and keeping his eyes locked on O'Bannion's face. O'Bannion's smile remained set as he stretched his arm across his desk and offered his hand to McKenna. "I've heard quite a bit about you over the years and I confess that it's a pleasure meeting one of Ireland's most famous lost sons in person," O'Bannion said.

McKenna looked down at O'Bannion's hand and concentrated on putting a look of contemptuous disgust on his face. Just before he thought O'Bannion was about to withdraw his hand, McKenna took it and was gratified to notice that O'Bannion's palm was sweating. "Lucky for you that I'm not here to hear your confession," he said slowly, putting some pressure on O'Bannion's hand as he shook it. O'Bannion's polite smile vanished and his face assumed a look as hard and determined as the one McKenna was sporting. Then McKenna released O'Bannion's hand and wiped his own on his pants leg.

"Then exactly why are you here to see me and what can I do for you?" O'Bannion asked.

"I want you to tell me where I can find Michael Mulrooney," McKenna stated, watching O'Bannion's face closely. He saw it, a flicker of fear in the man's eyes.

"Who?" O'Bannion asked, then looked past McKenna at the door. "Thank you, Maggie. That will be all for now," he said to Ferguson at the door.

McKenna kept his eyes on O'Bannion as he heard Ferguson close the door behind her. "Surely you're not going to tell me you've never heard of the man whose brother starved himself in the Maze Prison a month after your own brother did the same."

"That was a long time ago. I remember the name now, but I surely don't know the man."

"You're lying."

"What? Detective McKenna, do you realize where you are and who you're talking to?" O'Bannion shouted, his voice dripping anger and righteous indignation.

"Certainly. I'm talking to one of the leaders of the Irish Army Continuity Council, probably the top dog. I'm talking to the man who planned the murders of the British foreign secretary and his wife in Iceland, the same man who then sent Michael Mulrooney there to carry out the plan."

"This is preposterous! Detective McKenna, you're obviously insane," O'Bannion shouted, but his voice had lost some of its bluster.

"I'm mad, but I'm not insane," McKenna retorted softly and evenly. "Fortunately for you, at the moment I'm not interested in hanging you with those murders. But I will be if you don't see things my way. I want Mulrooney for the murder you didn't plan. I want him for the murder of Meaghan Maher. Once you tell me where he is, I'm not mad at you anymore. I'm out of your life and you're home free."

"Preposterous," O'Bannion repeated, but he wasn't shouting and his voice had lost all bravado.

McKenna knew O'Bannion was thinking hard, searching for a way out and wondering how much McKenna knew. But then the fear took over and he made a decision. "Detective McKenna, I want you out of my office this instant."

McKenna ignored the order. "Bad idea and not in your best interests," he said. "Mr. O'Bannion, do you know who you're talking to?"

"I'm aware of who you are."

"Are you aware of my reputation?"

"Yes."

"I'm not going to show you my cards, but do you think I operate in the dark? Do you think I was searching around for suspects and happened to pick your name out of the Dublin phone book?"

"I don't know how you arrived at your preposterous conclusions."

"Then tell me this. Do you think I'm crazy enough to show up on the doorstep of the very powerful Irish minister for finance to threaten him with high crimes I can't prove if you force me to?"

"Would you mind telling me how you intend to do that?"

"Yes, I would mind. If you want to know how I'm going to do it, then don't tell me where Mulrooney is. If you're that stupid, the first thing I'm going to do when I leave here is call my pal, His Eminence, the cardinal of the archdiocese of New York. He's very interested in this case and even got me assigned to it. I'm sure he would love to hear about your involvement, but forget about that for a moment. I think he would be shocked to learn that the minister for finance in very Catholic Ireland is protecting a man who tortured and killed an Irish Catholic girl who happened to be a friend of the cardinal's. By the way, you should know that Mulrooney is a serial killer, that the man you're protecting has tortured and killed many young girls all over the world. He's the devil incarnate."

The wind left O'Bannion's sails and he sat down in his chair so fast that for a moment, McKenna thought he had fainted. "How many?" he asked weakly.

"Four other girls that I can prove right now, along with two gay men. Tortured and killed for fun the same horrible way he murdered Meaghan Maher. Worse for you, I'm sure there's more and I'll find out about them, too."

O'Bannion swiveled his chair to stare out the window behind his desk. McKenna decided to keep the pressure on, talking to O'Bannion's back. "I imagine the cardinal will get on the horn right away to talk to all the cardinals and bishops here. They'll be just as shocked to learn exactly what kind of man they've got running the Ministry of Finance. As I understand it, the Irish Constitution recognizes that the Catholic Church has a special position when it comes to formulating matters of policy. Besides that, there's bound to be leaks to the press, both here and in New York. You'll be headlines every day for the next month, at least, but you won't be reading them in this nice office."

O'Bannion slowly swiveled his chair back to confront McKenna. The expression on his face had changed so drastically that McKenna was reminded of Linda Blair in *The Exorcist*. He stared at McKenna with a look of pure hatred. Like Father Damian, McKenna decided to keep trying to talk the devil out of him. "Of course, the end of your political career will be the least of your problems. You'll still have me on your tail, not to mention your old IRA comrades. When word of your caper and the man you hired to do it gets out, I predict that the IRA funding from supporters in America will dry up considerably. Think of how cranky that will make your old pals. Of all people, you should know how vindictive they can be sometimes."

"Enough," O'Bannion said through clenched teeth.

"I agree," McKenna said. "More than enough. This is silly, isn't it? Just tell me where Mulrooney is and I'm gone without a whisper. I promise that he'll never know you gave him up and everything's back to normal for you."

O'Bannion's face softened until he had assumed a countenance McKenna recognized. He had seen the same confused and vulnerable look on the faces of thousands of suspects in the countless interrogations he had conducted during his career. O'Bannion was ready to deal—almost. It was time for gentle prodding and assurances.

"What happens to this man if you catch him?" O'Bannion asked.

"He'll be tried in Iceland, quickly convicted of three murders, and then he'll be sentenced to three consecutive life sentences. The Icelanders won't offer him any deals to talk and they won't entertain any suggestions from anyone else."

It appeared to McKenna that O'Bannion liked that scenario, but the minister wanted to know more. "I've read that you were in Iceland with Inspector Rollins. Does he know about your groundless suspicions concerning me?"

"He knows almost as much about your involvement as I do, but I forced a deal out of him. As long as you tell me where Mulrooney is, he and his government will leave you alone. If not, you're in the British sights bigger than Napoleon was."

O'Bannion appeared to like that answer as well. He sat back in his chair, thinking, his face a benign mask. Then he opened his upper right desk drawer and stared into it.

McKenna instantly went on guard, his body tense and ready to pounce in the event O'Bannion came up with the pistol in the drawer. But the pistol wasn't what was on O'Bannion's mind. He took the two-page visitors list from the drawer, turned to the second page, and stared at it.

McKenna knew that O'Bannion had found his name when he smiled and shook his head. "Wish I had looked at this earlier," he said, smiling wryly as he shook his head. Then he turned the list over, removed a pen from his pocket, and printed: "You must believe me. I don't know where he is right now, but I know he's planning something big on his own."

It was bad news, but McKenna almost laughed out loud when O'Bannion passed him the note. He realized that O'Bannion suspected he was wired and that the minister had said nothing during the meeting that could be used against him.

McKenna decided to play along. He grabbed the pen from O'Bannion's hand, drew a line across O'Bannion's note, and wrote underneath: "I believe you, but I don't care. I'm staying at the Conrad Hilton. You have until 7:00 P.M. to find out where he is and let me know. Have a nice life." He passed the visitors list back to O'Bannion, then turned and left the office. For effect, he made sure to close the door hard on his way out.

A changed Maggie Ferguson was waiting for him in her office outside. She was sitting at her desk with her long hair down and makeup on. McKenna was pleasantly surprised by her new look and suspected that it was intended to impress him, but he was a happily married man and never wandered. However, he did have to admit to himself that she was a very attractive woman.

"How did it go?" she asked.

"I don't know yet, but nothing can happen to your boss until after seven."

"Nothing will," she said innocently, then came up with a surprise suggestion. "Why don't you take me out to dinner later on tonight. We can either celebrate your victory or mourn your defeat together over a good meal."

Now, what does this very tricky lady have in mind, McKenna wondered. He didn't know, but he wasn't sure he could be comfortable dining with a woman who took such obvious pleasure at the imminent murder of her boss, no matter who he was and what he had done. Still, he was very curious about her double-dealing role in the affair and he had quite a few questions for her.

Ferguson noted his hesitation. "Don't tell me. You're a happily married man," she said coyly.

"As a matter of fact, I am. Very happily married."

"So am I, so you've got nothing to worry about."

Ferguson wore no rings and McKenna didn't know whether to believe her. But she is on an undercover assignment and might be telling the truth, he told himself. Then a good reason for her sudden interest in him came to mind. "Am I to be your alibi while bad things are happening tonight?"

"Why, the thought never occurred to me," she protested innocently. "Where are you staying?"

"The Conrad Hilton."

"Good choice. They have a wonderful restaurant. If you trust yourself enough, meet me there at nine."

She stood up, offered her hand, and McKenna took it. "Nine it is," he said as he shook her hand.

"Good. You want to know the best thing I've seen in a long time?"

"Tell me."

"This," she said. She removed her hand from his and deliberately wiped it on her dress.

TWENTY-FOUR

McKenna sat in an armchair in his room at the Conrad Hilton with the phone next to him and his eyes on the door, struggling with his conscience while he awaited news from O'Bannion. Twice he had dialed Brunette, but each time he had changed his mind and hung up before the first ring.

Brunette and McKenna had been friends for many years and frequently had talked each other through crises, both personal and professional. But not this time, McKenna decided. He knew Brunette well, knew his ethics and how he thought, and he felt sure that Brunette would reach the same conclusion as he had regarding O'Bannion and his fate. Therefore, Mc-Kenna saw no reason to burden two consciences with O'Bannion's impending murder.

So McKenna sat and waited. It's not our business and it's not our fight, he told himself. If the IRA wants O'Bannion, they'll get him sooner or later, so I'm right to stay out of it and not enormously complicate our position. It's a kind of justice without law, the execution of a murderer.

After a while, that sounded all right to McKenna. But there was another thing bothering him; he knew who would be responsible for O'Bannion's murder, yet he would make no move to bring them to justice. In fact, he would be having dinner with one of the conspirators while O'Bannion was being assassinated.

Once again, not our fight nor our business, he told himself. It's a war nobody understands and there's no justice in war—just casualties.

Sitting in the comfortable armchair, McKenna had almost talked himself to sleep by six o'clock. Then a sound at his door brought him wide awake and he watched as an envelope was slipped under it. He had no desire to see O'Bannion again, so he stared at the envelope for a minute before he got up and opened it. Written on a plain sheet of paper was: "He knows the IRA is looking for him and he's very angry. He's underground in New York and getting all the tools of his trade. That's all I could find out."

New York? Is that good news or bad news? McKenna wondered. He's in my own backyard, but New York is a place he also knows well. An angry Mulrooney who's loaded for bear and planning something big in New York has to be bad news, he concluded. Time to make some calls.

The first ones were to every airline serving Ireland, but McKenna hung up disappointed. He desperately wanted to get back to New York, but he couldn't get a flight out until noon the next day.

Next was Brunette. McKenna caught him at his office and gave him the news on Mulrooney. Brunette took the threat to his city stoically, and even took the liberty of congratulating himself. "If I hadn't sent you to Iceland, Mulrooney would still be here looking for trouble, but we wouldn't know about it. Wouldn't even know who he was," he said. "Forewarned is forearmed and we've got Chipmunk's and the cardinal's interest in Meaghan to thank for that."

"If we get him in time," McKenna added.

"Yeah, if we get him in time," Brunette agreed. "Of course, if we don't and he manages to blow up something major, then we're all gonna look like shit. But I'm not too worried, yet."

"You know something I don't?"

"As a matter of fact, I do. Our surveillance on his kids turned up something interesting. Thirteen and eleven years old and they've got a cell phone. The older one had it in his pocket and they were walking home from school when they took a call. Both of them talked on the phone and they seemed real excited."

We were right! His kids are Mulrooney's Achilles' heel, McKenna thought. He loves them and wants to keep in touch with them, so the phone had to come from him. "I take it we'll be listening in the next time he calls?"

"You betcha. We've got Tavlin on board and he's got all the equipment he needs in place in the Bronx. We'll be listening in. Better yet, if Mulrooney stays on the phone long enough, we've got him."

Brunette didn't have to say more. McKenna knew that in a few words, he had just described an expensive and complicated operation that would involve hundreds of detectives and Emergency Service cops, not to mention some of Tavlin's most sophisticated equipment. Once again, it was a big plus that NYNEX's chief of security was also a retired NYPD chief and a good friend. "Do we have an eavesdropping warrant, yet?" McKenna asked.

"No. We're still not exactly legal, but now we'll have enough to get one when you march before a judge and tell him what you just told me. When will you be back?"

"First available flight. Gets me into JFK at two o'clock tomorrow afternoon."

"I'll have someone there to pick you up and a judge standing by. Anything else?"

There was, and suddenly McKenna decided that it had nothing to do with conscience and friendship. As his boss, Brunette should know about O'Bannion. Whether to tell him or not was a decision he had struggled with for two days, but talking to him made it clear. Brunette was already out on a limb and authorizing illegal operations, so he had a right to know just how complicated the situation was. "O'Bannion's gonna be checking out sometime tonight. His old pals have decided that he's been a thorn in their sides for too long and too much of an embarrassment to them with the Iceland thing."

Brunette didn't answer for a moment and McKenna knew he was running all the implications of that information through his mind. In the end, it wasn't his official position that concerned him, it was his friendship with McKenna and his faith in his friend's judgment. "Have you managed to get comfortable with that?" he asked.

"Not entirely. Unlike me, O'Bannion didn't know that I was questioning him in the last hours of his life. And what did I do? Did I give him any hint or warning? No, I threatened to snitch on him to the cardinal and make the rest of his life miserable solely to gain information in this case."

"So what? Think about it," Brunette said. "If it wasn't for O'Bannion, his ambition, and his murdering ways, Meaghan Maher would still be alive. We couldn't get him and maybe the Brits wouldn't have been able to, either. I say good riddance and don't lose any sleep over it."

"I was hoping you'd see things that way, but I don't think I'm gonna be sleeping too well."

"Then take a pill, but think about this. He's an important man and there's going to be a big fuss over his demise. You will be one of the last people to have seen him alive, so the Irish cops are gonna want to talk to you."

"I hadn't thought about that," McKenna admitted. "They'll be very interested in the reasons for my visit to him and I've got nothing I want to tell them."

"Then make yourself unavailable. I need you here now and I don't want you stuck on the spot over there. If you can't come up with a story for them, get out of there and catch a New York flight out of Belfast tomorrow."

As usual, Brunette made sense to McKenna. But Belfast again? He hated that idea and searched his mind for a way to avoid going back to Belfast. "I'll have to talk to them, sooner or later, and I see a problem. I've got reservations to leave from Dublin, but O'Bannion is killed and all of a sudden I'm leaving from Belfast? Wouldn't that appear a little suspicious to any good cop looking to talk to me?"

"We'll have to talk to them, but later and on our home turf is better. We'll put our heads together and come up with a story for them."

That was McKenna's only shot and he saw there was no way out. "Okay, I'll call you back as soon as I get my new flight information."

"Good. You know, there's an upside to this situation you might not have thought of. With O'Bannion gone, your deal with the Brits is basically off. Their reason for that time limit you agreed to was that they really wanted him much more than they wanted Mulrooney."

"I thought of it, but we've still got our deal with the Icelanders," McKenna pointed out. "When we get Mulrooney, we give him to them."

"Reluctantly agreed. Talk to you later."

McKenna's next call was to Aer Lingus. He booked himself on the one o'clock flight out of Belfast the next day, but arranging transportation to Belfast proved to be a problem. He found that there were no more trains to Belfast from Dublin that evening, so he called Hertz to have a car dropped off at the Conrad Hilton. He completed his new travel arrangements by reserving a room at the Hotel Europa for late that evening and calling Brunette back to inform him of his new arrival time in New York.

Next was a call to Thor to give him the latest developments.

"New York? That's a piece of luck, isn't it?" Thor asked. "Frieda's already there, so I guess she's in for a surprise when I show up."

"I'm kind of surprised myself," McKenna said. "What's she doing there?"

"Her bishop sent her on a mission to a church in Brooklyn. It's nominally a Norwegian Lutheran church, but there are quite a few Icelanders in the congregation. Our bishop sends her about once a year to conduct a few services in Icelandic and show the flag."

"Is she there by herself?"

"No. Her trip was reported in one of our newspapers, so Janus was kind enough to send one of our best men with her. She likes this particular constable and I'm sure she'll be quite safe with him."

"Is he armed?"

"Unofficially," Thor admitted.

"Give me some information and I'll make it official, just in case. Where is she staying?"

"In Brooklyn. The Harbor Lights Motel. You know it?"

"Yes. Nice place and a good choice."

Thor gave McKenna the address and phone number of the church and the name of the constable. As McKenna expected, the church was in Bay Ridge, a middle-class Brooklyn neighborhood with a large Norwegian section.

McKenna called Brunette again with his request. No problem. A pistol permit would be issued to Constable Haarold Sigmarsson.

Then came the time for another decision: whether to keep his dinner appointment with Maggie Ferguson. He realized that his new schedule gave him the perfect excuse not to show, but his curiosity got the better of him. He wanted to know the details of the IRA's plans for O'Bannion, and since they were practically co-conspirators, he figured she would tell him. But more important, to ease his conscience he wanted to know why she hated O'Bannion so much. McKenna didn't hate him, but he hoped he could with a few good reasons from her. He figured that a little hatred would make the evening easier on his conscience.

His last call was to Angelita. He told her that things were going well and that he would be coming home.

"Great! Can't wait to see you, and wait till you see this place. You're gonna love our new home," she said. "It's so big and bright and Janine just loves it. She's already made two new friends."

"Boys or girls?"

"Girls, of course. Both her age. You know, she didn't have a single good friend when we were living in the hotel. This is much better."

"Then that's just another favor we owe Chipmunk," McKenna said. He toyed for a moment with the idea of telling Angelita about his dinner en-

gagement, but decided against it. She had always been a trifle jealous when
it came to other women even talking to her man for whatever legitimate
reason, so he figured that some things were better left unsaid in the interests
of domestic tranquillity. He didn't feel good about it, but he didn't tell her.

McKenna decided that ravishing was the only way to describe Maggie Ferguson that evening. She had changed into a short, sleeveless, high-necked
emerald green dress that complimented her tall, model-thin figure, accen-
tuated her green eyes, and perfectly contrasted with her long red hair. She
met him in the lobby and McKenna, against his will, felt perversely proud
to be seen with her when they entered the hotel's crowded dining room. If
she was with him for an alibi, she had dressed that way to make sure she
would be remembered—and it worked. All eyes were on them as they were
shown to their table.

It wasn't until they sat down that McKenna realized how hungry he
was. He hadn't eaten a thing all day, but had been so busy that he hadn't
noticed until then. They ordered their meals, and then came the part of
the procedure he dreaded whenever he ate with someone he didn't really
know. "Would you like to see the wine list, sir?"

"Would you like some wine with dinner?" McKenna asked Ferguson.

"How about you?"

"I don't drink, but feel free."

"I do, but I've already had a couple today," she admitted. "Too much
makes me crazy and I think I have to be careful when I'm with the famous
Detective McKenna."

Crazier, McKenna thought, and ordered Cokes. After the waiter left,
McKenna told her about O'Bannion's message and she looked pleased.
"Will it take you long to get Mulrooney?" she asked.

"What makes you so sure we'll get him? New York's a big town and
we've lost him there before."

"But the famous Detective McKenna wasn't the one looking for him
then," she said, smiling and dismissing his concerns. "You'll get him."

McKenna appreciated the compliments, but he was there to get background on her, not talk about himself. "Thanks. Now, are you going to tell
me how you happen to be working for British Intelligence and the IRA at
the same time?"

She didn't look surprised at his question and he wasn't surprised at her
answer. "Why should I? So you can tell your friend Inspector Rollins all
about me?"

"No, you'll tell me because you trust me not to do that. If I were to
tell Rollins anything, it would have to start with my meeting with McGuinn
and your plans for your boss."

"And you didn't do that?" she asked, but she didn't look concerned.

"It crossed my mind, but I didn't. O'Bannion can be murdered right on schedule."

"Does that bother you?"

"Yes, but I'm getting as bad as you people. In this case, murdering a murderer serves my best interests."

She feigned a pout, but McKenna just stared at her. Then she smiled and patted his hand. "Glad to be of service," she said. "I know you're not sympathetic to our movement, but I do trust you with my story. What has Inspector Rollins told you about me?"

"He told me exactly what I think you want him to believe. He said you're a Catholic girl from the North whose sister was an innocent bystander killed during an IRA ambush of a British patrol. He thinks you hate the IRA, but that O'Bannion doesn't know your true feelings. Said you're not a British agent, but from time to time you give them some information. Some of your information has not proven entirely correct, but most of it is good."

"You're right. Inspector Rollins believes exactly what we want him to believe about me. For you, I'm going to clear up some of his misconceptions. I come from a large, Republican Belfast family and we've never had an informer in our history. It's true that my sister Kate was killed during one of our operations against the British, but she wasn't an 'innocent bystander.' It was she who set off the bomb," Ferguson said proudly.

McKenna couldn't help thinking of Forsythe's term for such an event. The Paddy Factor at work. "Tell me about the ambush."

"Basic, really. Our people put a radio-detonated bomb in a curb-side sewer opening. Kate was standing on a corner with another comrade, about fifty meters away. She knew what she was doing and that should have been a safe distance. When the Brit patrol passed the sewer opening, she reached into her pocket and pressed the button on the radio detonator. The device went off, three of the enemy were killed, but Kate was hit in the chest with a lug nut from the Land Rover. Freak accident, really, but she was badly wounded. Her comrade removed the radio detonator from her pocket before the RUC and the ambulances arrived to take her to the hospital. By then she had lost a lot of blood and was unconscious.

"Because of our family background, the Brits and the RUC looked very hard at Kate and had wanted to question her when she regained consciousness. At the time, we thought there was a chance that she would pull through and Lord knows what she would tell them in her condition if she woke up. To divert suspicion away from her, my father had me make some anti-IRA statements to the press. My interviews were widely covered in the Belfast papers and the *London Times*. I was only sixteen at the time, but I was really quite good. Naturally, I cried a lot while I deplored the senseless IRA violence that had so grievously injured my innocent sister. But then Kate died in the hospital without regaining consciousness."

"So you thought that you had branded yourself as a traitor for nothing?" McKenna guessed.

"I'll have to admit that I was made to feel a little uncomfortable in West Belfast, so my father decided to send me to England. He took some of the money the Brits gave him and—"

"Wait a minute. Why did the British pay your father?" McKenna asked.

"Compensatory damages," Ferguson said, enjoying the joke. "The Brits pay the families of innocent victims of terrorist actions, so my father applied for the money. They gave him seventy-five hundred pounds. He used some of it to send me to secretarial school in London for a year. I had a knack for it and enjoyed myself there, spending their money. Graduated with honors and then I was approached by British Intelligence. They wanted me to do a little undercover work for them when I returned home."

"They recruited you as an informer?"

"Yes, and offered to pay me as well."

"Was it Rollins who recruited you?"

"No, he's too big to be one of their recruiters," she explained. "Actually, I've never met Inspector Rollins. I only found out later that my information goes to him."

"So you took the offer, or at least pretended to?"

"No, not at first. I called my father and told him about it. He went to Kevin Hughes and Kevin went to Martin McGuinn. I was told to tell the Brits that I wouldn't be comfortable working for them, but to save lives I'd be willing to pass along anything important I heard about. That was okay with them and they gave me a handler who taught me about codes and their reporting procedures and following people. Then, to make things easier for me, before I went home they arranged another press interview for me. I told the reporters that I had been wrong to denounce the IRA, that the reason for the killings was the British presence in Northern Ireland. I said that during my stay in London, I had come to like the British people—which was true—but I didn't think they knew about the terrible things their government was doing in my country. That interview appeared only as a small article in the London papers, but it was a big one in the Belfast press. When I got home I got a job as a secretary in a linen factory, but I also began working for the movement."

"Doing what?" McKenna asked.

"Little things, nothing very important. Visible things like passing out pamphlets and helping to organize demonstrations supporting our men in prison."

"So the Brits would know you were with the IRA?"

"That was the idea, both the Brits' and Martin's. Then Martin decided that it was time for me to gain some credibility with the Brits. He had some of his men plant a bomb in a car on The Shankill Road, and then he told me to contact my handler and tell him about it. I did, so the Brits found the bomb and defused it. My handler was very happy with me, but he wanted to know who planted it. I told him that I would never give names, that I just wanted to save lives. I really think he didn't know what to make of me, but that was Martin's plan. Two years later we pulled the bomb trick on them again."

"What year was that?" McKenna asked.

"Eighty-two, I think, but the payoff came in eighty-three. We were getting an arms shipment and Martin suspected that the Brits knew it was coming, but that they didn't know where. He had me tell my handler that it was coming in at Pier Nine on the Belfast Lough, so their troops and all their customs people went over there while our arms shipment was unloaded at Pier Six on the other side of the Lough."

"That hurt your credibility with them, didn't it?"

"Not too much. My handler didn't like it, but he knew that mistakes happen. Besides, as far as I know, the Brits never found out we got that shipment. But then I had some other problems. The factory I was working at closed down and the North was in pretty bad economic shape. Still is, for that matter. I couldn't get another job and the Brits offered me money once again. I refused it again and moved to the South, looking for work. At the time, O'Bannion was heading the Council of Free Trade Unions and he gave me a job interview."

"Did you know him then?"

"Knew of him, but no, I didn't know him then. But Martin did. He told O'Bannion about how helpful I had been working for the movement and told him that I was a pretty good secretary besides. I showed up for the interview dressed very nicely and he gave me a position on his staff. I liked him at first and worked hard for him. Eventually we became very close."

"Lovers?"

"Very secret lovers, for a while. He's married and that sort of thing isn't tolerated here. When he ran for the Chamber of Deputies, I helped run his campaign. When he was appointed minister for finance, I followed as his personal secretary. By then it was over between us, but I still worked hard for him."

"Why was it over?"

"Because he's a pig. He's married, but I wasn't the only other woman in his life. I found out that he's nothing more than a self-serving man without scruples."

Ah, here comes the hatred. That's what I'm here for, McKenna thought, but then the first course arrived.

Ferguson had ordered only a salad, but McKenna had ordered both the soup and the salad for himself. It looked great to him. "I don't want to miss a word of this, but I'm famished to the point where I can't concentrate with this food in front of me. Do you mind?" he asked with his fork poised over his salad.

"Not at all," she said, then checked her watch. "We've got time."

Now what does that mean? McKenna wondered, but only for a second. In no time his salad was gone while she just picked at hers. By the time he was halfway through his soup, the edge was off his hunger. Ferguson was looking at him, but she appeared to be daydreaming. "Thanks, I'm fine now," he said, and she focused on him. "You were saying?"

"What was I saying?" she asked.

"That O'Bannion's an unscrupulous pig."

"Oh, that he certainly is," she stated, once again livening up to her subject. "Just one woman on the side was never enough for him and you wouldn't believe the lies. I was a party to many of his fabrications over the years, backing up his lies to everyone. Quite often he lied when I saw no reason to, so I think that basically, he just enjoys deceit. Makes him feel grand to think he's fooling everyone."

So he cheats on his wife, then he cheats on his girlfriend, and he's no George Washington. Not my kind of guy, but I wouldn't wish him dead over that, McKenna thought. There has to be more. "Why did the romance end?"

"Because it had to. You may not believe this, but I have my morals. I think I first went with him because he can be quite charming and I was young and stupid, lonely and far from home. Besides he's fairly well off and he was good to me, for a while. He owns an apartment building in Old Belvedere, very nice section, and I got a lovely flat out of it. After a while I couldn't stand his lies and his philandering and I found somebody else."

"How did he take that?"

"The flat was gone, of course, but quite well, considering. I think we were really sick of each other. He had me transferred to another section, but I didn't mind. Then he found that he couldn't do without me. I think it's that nobody can lie for him like I can, so he asked me back and I agreed. Nothing romantic, just work."

"He knew about your connection to British Intelligence, didn't he?" McKenna asked.

"He delighted in it. He really hates the Brits and he enjoyed having me feed them information to confuse them. Some of it was true, of course, but most of it was lies right out of O'Bannion's head. Believable lies, as always, but still lies."

"But nothing to do with the IRA?"

"Oh, no. Back then, I wouldn't have told them about any of O'Bannion's work for the movement. It was just economic stuff I gave them, but they were happy just the same. We're rivals for the tourist trade, so they're quite interested in our economy."

"Then why did you tell them about his connection to the Iceland bombing?"

"Because Martin wanted me to after I told him about O'Bannion and Iceland."

Now here's a twist, McKenna thought. She still reports to McGuinn and he tells her to feed O'Bannion to their enemy, the British. Why? To distance themselves from the Iceland bombing, of course, but there has to be more to it than that. These people don't surrender one another to the British over internal politics.

Their main courses arrived, giving McKenna some time to think while they ate. He came up with some answers, but another big question. O'Bannion's a thorn in the side of Adams and McGuinn, executing unauthorized bombings, starting his own faction, killing British politicians they need, and generally screwing up their peace negotiations, McKenna reasoned. But he's an important man in the South and he shouldn't be up for a simple hit. Besides, like Mulrooney, O'Bannion's brother is one of their martyrs, so knocking him off would divide their movement. So they feed him to the Brits for some action, hoping he'll be disgraced and maybe even prosecuted. Then, when everything's going according to their plan, they decide to kill him anyway. Why do that now?

No faith in me or the Brits to do our jobs, McKenna thought, but only for a moment. Then it came to him. He put his fork down and stared at Ferguson until she did the same. "O'Bannion's death is gonna look like a suicide, isn't it?"

"Of course," she said, smiling at him as if he were one of the slow kids. "We couldn't just gun down the Republic's minister for finance, now could we?"

"Is that why you paraded me around the ministry today, telling everyone you could about me being there to see him on some mysterious official business?"

"That's exactly why. Word travels fast, and we wanted to make sure that some people knew he was under pressure. They'll all be talking after his suicide and everyone knows that you're working on the Iceland bombing. They'll reach the correct conclusion and it'll look like O'Bannion couldn't stand the pressure."

"Tell me how it's going to be done," McKenna insisted.

"Are you sure you want to know?"

"I have to know. I didn't want to talk to your police about O'Bannion's murder and I knew they'd want to talk to me, so I've made plans to leave for Belfast tonight. If your suicide plan sounds good enough to me, I'll save myself some problems and leave for New York from here."

Ferguson considered McKenna's request for a moment before she answered. "He's going to shoot himself with his own pistol in his mistress's flat tonight. He goes there every Friday night after his club meeting at the Old Belvedere Rugby Club. We have people there now, waiting inside for him with his pistol."

"How did they get in?"

"It's my old flat. I gave them the key and also his pistol. I took his gun from his desk after he left."

"What about his girlfriend?"

"She won't be there when he arrives."

"How do you know?" McKenna asked.

"Because we're friends and we have a lot in common. We had a few drinks together at O'Donoghue's Pub right before I came here. We trashed O'Bannion a bit and she drank more than I did. By now, she should have had a minor traffic accident on her way home."

"She's in jail?" McKenna guessed.

"I'm sure. The other car was driven by an American tourist who will have insisted that she be arrested for driving under the influence. The laws here are quite strict on that, so she's not going to make it home on time tonight."

"This woman is your friend?"

"Yes, and I feel bad about that part of the plan. She doesn't know she's making this sacrifice for the movement, but it's necessary."

McKenna thought that he had manipulated McGuinn, but Ferguson just made it clear to him that it was he who had been manipulated, and quite well. It was McGuinn who had made sure that he was at the ministry to see O'Bannion that day, Friday, the day O'Bannion went to see his girlfriend.

But the plan was Ferguson's, McKenna was sure. He examined it for flaws and found none. The only thing that could go wrong was that the IRA assassins could be seen either entering or leaving the flat, but McKenna considered that unlikely. If a public figure like O'Bannion had been able to slip in and out of there for years, the entrance must be protected from view. The police will be so busy handling the scandal generated by the minister for finance shooting himself in his girlfriend's flat that they won't even think of talking to me for days. "I guess I'll be staying in Dublin tonight."

Ferguson took it as a compliment. "Thank you."

"I'm still not clear on a few things. What were you doing in Belfast on Tuesday night?"

"Visiting my husband. He was the one driving the van when we picked you up and I thought it would be fun to go along."

"Didn't you think I'd recognize you today?"

"No, I guess I didn't. But that really makes no difference now, does it?"

"I guess you realize that you're gonna be out of a job tomorrow, don't you?"

"Not out of a job. I'll simply be reassigned to another office after I'm questioned by the police."

"I bet you'll have quite a bit to tell them," McKenna guessed.

"Sure will. After I talk to the police, they might not think it necessary to talk to you. I'm going to rake O'Bannion's name through the mud and I'm sure Inspector Rollins will be happy to help."

Even though she's arranged his death, her hatred of O'Bannion is going to follow him past the grave. Even that old woman-scorned theory doesn't account for this much hatred, McKenna thought. There has to be more. "I guess you don't share O'Bannion's politics," he tried.

"I surely don't," Ferguson said, obviously surprised that McKenna would even ask the question. "While Martin and Gerry Adams are working to stop the killing, O'Bannion has been using every sneaky trick he could think of to keep it going. Because of him and his ambition, it's possible that many more are going to die."

"Possible?" McKenna asked, surprised at Ferguson's choice of words. "You think there's still a chance for peace?"

"With O'Bannion gone, it's possible there can be peace of a sort. Concessions will have to be made by both sides, but maybe the time is right. It's been going on too long."

"I don't know," McKenna said. "From what I've seen and heard, I don't believe those Protestants would ever agree to unification with the South."

"Maybe they're right. But maybe this island can contain two countries living in peace, side by side."

McKenna was shocked that the IRA soldier sitting across the table from him would ever even consider such an idea. "Wouldn't that idea be considered dangerous blasphemy by your comrades?" he asked.

"By some of them, but not by Martin McGuinn and Gerry Adams. They're sensible people and they now realize that the idea of a united Ireland just isn't possible. It's a great idea to threaten the Prods with and bring them around, but it just isn't possible. I'm not a great thinker, and even I know that."

McKenna disagreed. Anyone who could put the O'Bannion plan together was a pretty sharp thinker, as far as he was concerned. "What brings you to that conclusion?" he asked.

"Simple. I've been living in the South for years now and I know that the people here don't really want us. Of course, when they're thinking with their hearts, they say they want a united Ireland. But when they think with their heads, they know they really don't. Ireland is a fairly prosperous, peaceful country, a country where the cops don't even carry guns. Why would we want to annex another country that's home to a million and a half crazy, angry Prods and where forty percent of the people are on the dole? That's the question they ask themselves in private."

They finished their dinners in silence, each lost in thought. While waiting for the check, McKenna had one more question. He hesitated before asking it because he feared the answer. But he had to know for sure. "Where is your husband tonight?"

"Sitting in a nice flat in Old Belvedere, waiting to put a bullet into the head of Mr. Timothy O'Bannion."

It was the answer McKenna had expected. "What are you going to do now?"

"I'll admit that I'm curious, so I'm going to pass by my old flat to see if my husband has done his duty yet."

That was an answer McKenna hadn't expected. After paying the check, he walked Ferguson to her car parked a block from the hotel. They formally shook hands and she drove off to check on the progress of her murderous plans.

It had turned chilly and McKenna was dressed only in his suit, but the cold outside didn't bother him as much as the cold he felt inside. He felt a need to clear his head, so he took a walk through the deserted city center.

TWENTY-FIVE

McKenna woke up the next morning, called room service, and ordered coffee and a newspaper. When the waiter arrived carrying the tray, McKenna had him place it on the table and signed the check, adding a good tip. The newspaper was folded and McKenna poured himself a cup of coffee. Then he sat down to read.

The headline shocked him. Even the best-laid plans can go awry, sometimes with horrifying results. The headline screamed that truth.

TIMOTHY O'BANNION DEAD
MINISTER FOR FINANCE KILLS SECRETARY AND HIMSELF

McKenna read on without touching his coffee. According to the article, O'Bannion had been waiting for Ferguson outside her building. Neighbors stated that when Ferguson came home at 11:15 P.M. a loud argument in the street ensued between O'Bannion and her, with each accusing the other of treachery. O'Bannion took a pistol from his belt and fired two shots into Ferguson's chest. He then turned the gun on himself and fired a single shot into his head. Both were dead by the time the Garda arrived.

The article stated that Ferguson had worked for O'Bannion for fifteen years and persons contacted at the Ministry of Finance described their relationship as "close." These same people stated that they believed Mr. O'Bannion was under some pressure at work, but the article didn't disclose the nature of that pressure.

O'Bannion was survived by his wife Margaret, age fifty-three, and a son, age thirty-one. Efforts were being made to locate and contact Ferguson's relatives in Northern Ireland.

McKenna's name wasn't mentioned in the article, but he knew that made no difference. By now, the Garda certainly knew of his visit to O'Bannion. A major scandal was brewing in the Irish press and the investigation of the circumstances leading to O'Bannion's and Ferguson's deaths would be exhaustive.

McKenna tried to imagine the reasons Ferguson's plan had backfired so tragically. He came up with three possible scenarios. The most likely was that O'Bannion didn't buy that nonsense with the visitors list. When Ferguson hadn't told him of McKenna's impending visit, he suspected that it was she who had blown the whistle on him to the Brits and set McKenna on his trail.

Another scenario could be that O'Bannion had discovered that his pistol was missing from his desk drawer. Being a practiced conspirator himself, he might have seen the implications of the theft. Again, Ferguson would be the person with whom he would want to talk about it. Unfortunately for her, that wasn't the only pistol O'Bannion owned.

The third possible scenario was the most painful one. It was possible that O'Bannion, after delivering the message to the Conrad Hilton, had then hung around the bar and had seen Ferguson arrive. It wouldn't take him long to put two and two together when McKenna met her for dinner.

In any event, despite his assurances to O'Bannion that everything would be fine as long as he gave up Mulrooney's location, McKenna now realized that O'Bannion had considered his life over. The possibility of disgrace must have loomed large in his mind, but there was something else that probably had depressed him more. His visit had convinced O'Bannion that there was nowhere else for him to go in life—no new mountains to climb and no higher position to seek. For a man with O'Bannion's all-consuming ambition, that was the worse news of all. He had decided to end it all and take the cause of his misery with him.

McKenna phoned Brunette at home and gave him the depressing news. "You think O'Bannion was planning suicide when he went to Ferguson's house?" Brunette asked.

McKenna had expected the question and knew what Brunette was thinking. "I can't be sure, of course, but that's the way it looks to me," he answered. "You wondering why he gave me the information on Mulrooney before he did himself in?"

"I have to wonder. Suppose he decided to have the last laugh on you by setting up a wild goose chase here."

"I considered that, but I don't think so. When I told O'Bannion about the things Mulrooney was doing while working for him, he was genuinely shocked. He saw the end for himself, but I think he wanted to clean up his place in history as best he could by helping us get Mulrooney."

"Maybe you even got to his conscience, if he had one," Brunette suggested.

"That's a stretch, but maybe."

"Okay. I'm gonna spend money and manpower here on the assumption O'Bannion wasn't bullshitting you," Brunette said. The two men then talked strategy for half an hour. After hanging up, McKenna had two cups of coffee before he showered, dressed, packed, and sat down to await the arrival of the Garda.

At ten o'clock Rollins called. "I hear your visit there caused quite a fuss," he said.

"It's been trying," McKenna admitted.

"I suspect it's going to be quite trying for me as well. I'm being recalled to London for consultation."

"Are you going to get any trouble out of this?"

"I doubt it. My dealings with you concerning O'Bannion have been approved at the highest levels. Have you spoken to the Garda yet?"

"Not yet."

"I must admit that it would help me tremendously in my dealings with my superiors if I knew what you were going to tell them."

McKenna did and Rollins was reasonably satisfied by the time he hung up. McKenna was also satisfied that he had gotten through the conversation without having to mention his meeting with McGuinn or the IRA's plan for O'Bannion. Just as well, he thought. In this new state of affairs, those are probably things Rollins wouldn't want to know about.

The Garda arrived at 10:30 A.M. in the person of Senior Investigating Constable Padrick O'Dougherty. He was a stocky, well-dressed man who appeared to be too young to have such an impressive title. Everything about him led McKenna to believe that he would be dealing, unfortunately, with a sharp piece of work.

After showing his credentials and introducing himself, O'Dougherty immediately began justifying McKenna's suspicions. His eyes swept the room, pausing briefly on the newspaper open on the table and on the packed suitcases on the bed. "I see I don't have to explain the reason for my visit," he said.

"No, I've been expecting you."

"Are you returning to New York today?"

"Twelve o'clock flight. I have to be leaving for the airport soon."

"This shouldn't take too long. Would you mind answering a few questions?"

"That depends. Will anything I tell you appear in the press?" McKenna asked.

"Mr. McKenna, I can only tell you that I won't be giving it to them, but in a case like this I can't guarantee anything. The whole government's shaking and the press is very interested. I can't tell you exactly what will be in the press release my superiors issue."

McKenna didn't like a few things about O'Dougherty's reply. First was calling him "Mr. McKenna," not "Brian" or "Detective McKenna." It was to be an adversarial interview and not a case of one cop talking to another. He also didn't like the fact that, in so many words, O'Dougherty had warned him that everything he said would probably end up in the press, eventually. "Suppose I don't want to tell you anything at this point?" McKenna asked.

McKenna got his first hint of a smile from O'Dougherty. "Then I might try telling you that you won't be making your flight today. But you wouldn't believe that, would you?"

"No, I wouldn't."

"Then what I will tell you is that, if you don't answer my questions, all bets are off. I will immediately phone every newspaper in town and tell them that I tried to interview you, but that you were uncooperative and refused to answer any questions. After I do that, I imagine that every reporter in New York will be waiting for you at the airport with the exact questions I want to ask you."

McKenna decided that it was an evil smile. "Let's sit down and make ourselves comfortable," he said, then led O'Dougherty to the table. Both men took seats, sitting across the table from each other. "Fire away," McKenna said.

"Pardon?"

"Ask your questions."

O'Dougherty did, starting off with the big one in a monotone voice. "What was the purpose of your visit to Mr. O'Bannion at the Ministry of Finance yesterday?"

"I was there to get from him the location and name of the person who planted the bomb in Iceland that killed the British foreign secretary and his wife. I believe that the same man killed an Irish girl in Iceland named Meaghan Maher, which is the case I'm investigating."

"You're not investigating the bombing?"

"As I've said for the record during an interview in Iceland that I'm sure you're aware of, I have no interest in the bombing except as to how it relates to the murder of Meaghan Maher. The bombing is a matter for the Icelandic and British authorities."

"What prompted you to ask our minister for finance about a man who committed a terrorist bombing in Iceland?"

"I asked him because I believe that he is the person who planned the bombing and sent the bomber to Iceland."

McKenna expected a reaction to that statement, but he got none. Instead, O'Dougherty continued with his monotone line of questioning. "Why do you believe that?"

"Because Inspector Rollins of Scotland Yard told me that he has developed information implicating Mr. O'Bannion as the man behind the bombing."

"Are you privy to that information?"

"No. He refused to divulge it on the basis that it was a British national security concern, but that didn't bother me. As I told you, I'm investigating the murder of Meaghan Maher, not the bombing."

"Shouldn't that investigation also be under the jurisdiction of the Icelandic authorities?"

"It is. My department has assigned me to assist Constable Thor Erikson of the Icelandic police in his efforts to bring the killer to justice in Iceland."

"Isn't such an arrangement unusual?"

"Yes."

"During your meeting with Mr. O'Bannion, did you accuse him of involvement in the Iceland bombing?"

"I would say that 'accuse' is too strong a word. I simply suggested to him that Special Branch had developed indications that he may be involved."

"Did Mr. O'Bannion give you the name or location of the bomber?"

"No. As a matter of fact, he vigorously proclaimed his innocence."

"You are an experienced investigator and have conducted hundreds, possibly thousands, of interviews, have you not?"

"Thousands."

"In light of that fact, did you believe Mr. O'Bannion's claim of innocence?"

"Not then, and in light of his suicide last night, certainly not now. Now more than ever I'm convinced that Inspector Rollins was right."

"Did you see Mr. O'Bannion last night?"

"No. The last time I saw him was in his office at the ministry yesterday afternoon."

"Are you aware that Mr. O'Bannion was seen in this hotel last night and that he got on an elevator that stopped at this floor?"

"No, I'm not. As I told you, I didn't see him last night."

"How would you explain the coincidence?"

"What time was he here?"

"Approximately six o'clock."

"Then I have one possible explanation. Maybe he had a change of heart and came here to give me the information I requested. Maybe he knocked on my door. Unfortunately for me, at around six I was in the shower and didn't hear a thing. I didn't answer, so he changed his mind again and took off. Did anyone see him leave the hotel?"

"Yes. He had one drink in the bar and left at approximately six-thirty."

Thank goodness! McKenna thought. O'Bannion wasn't in the hotel when Ferguson got here, so he didn't see us together. I'm not directly responsible for her death.

O'Dougherty didn't give McKenna time to dwell on the only good to come out of the interview. "You had dinner with Maggie Ferguson in this hotel at nine o'clock last night, didn't you?" he asked.

This guy has done a lot of homework in a hurry, McKenna thought. "Yes, we had dinner. We were in the dining room together from nine to approximately ten o'clock. Then she left, presumably to go home."

"Had you met Miss Ferguson before yesterday?"

"No, and it's Mrs. Ferguson. She told me she was married."

O'Dougherty paused for the first time, leading McKenna to believe that Ferguson hadn't listed her marriage with the Ministry of Finance. Her husband must be wanted or listed as an IRA member, he concluded, and she certainly wouldn't want the Ministry of Finance to know that she was married to such a man. "What was the purpose of your dinner with Mrs. Ferguson," O'Dougherty asked.

"Hunger on my part, curiosity on hers. Your Constable Sullivan at the ministry told me that she was from the North. Before my meeting with O'Bannion, I had told her that I'd just come from Belfast. After the meeting she suggested that we go to dinner so that I could tell her my impressions on the violence up there. I had nothing to do last night, so I agreed to go."

"I'm not implying anything, but Mrs. Ferguson was dressed quite attractively last night," O'Dougherty said. "It's my understanding that she usually dresses in a more demure fashion."

"You're implying quite a bit, but I should remind you that she was a married lady and I'm a happily married man," McKenna replied with an edge in his voice. "Maybe she doesn't get out much and had that dress she'd always wanted to wear."

"Sorry for the question, but you realize that it had to be asked some-time."

McKenna didn't think O'Dougherty sounded all that sorry, but he let it pass. "I understand."

"Would you mind telling me what you two talked about over dinner?"

"Just what she had planned. I don't think it's necessary that I tell you my personal views on the situation up there, but that's what we talked about. I was with her for an hour and I spent most of that time giving her my impressions."

"That's strange. Your waiter last night told me that it was Mrs. Ferguson who did most of the talking."

Ouch! Where did they get this guy from? McKenna wondered. Our waiter last night must be off duty right now, so O'Dougherty went to his home to interview him before speaking to me. I have to be real careful. "Then your waiter is wrong, but I can understand how he got this impression. As you said, Mrs. Ferguson was an attractive woman very attractively dressed. I'm sure that every time she opened her mouth, someone was watching. She did have a few things to say, mostly in response to my comments and observations."

"I see," O'Dougherty said in a manner that suggested to McKenna that he wasn't buying it. "On those few occasions she did speak, did she agree or disagree with your comments and observations?"

He's not gonna let this one go, McKenna thought, so I have to tell him something. "As I said before, I'm not going to tell you my views on the situation up there. However, I will say that, in my opinion, Mrs. Ferguson was apolitical. She deplored the violence in the North and only wished that the situation up there could be resolved, somehow."

"That's also strange. Are you aware that in 1980 she gave an interview to the press in which she expressed views that can only be characterized as pro-IRA?"

Ouch again! Who is this guy? McKenna wondered. "No, I'm not aware of that, but 1980 was a long time ago. Maybe her views have changed since then."

"Maybe, but I find it disturbing that in 1990, when Mr. O'Bannion took over the Ministry of Finance, she was given a security clearance in spite of that published interview. Do you have any idea how that happened?"

"No."

"Did she confide to you that she and Mr. O'Bannion were once lovers?"

"Certainly not, but what would make you think that?"

"Might I remind you, Mr. McKenna, that I'm the one conducting this interview and asking the questions," O'Dougherty said, but then he re-lented. "In going over the investigation that was performed for Mrs. Ferguson's security clearance, I've found a few interesting points. For instance, when she first moved to Dublin and started working for Mr. O'Bannion, she lived in a certain flat in the Old Belvedere section of town. I thought that strange because Old Belvedere is a very expensive area whose residents are not normally secretaries just arrived from the North. So I checked the real estate records and found that the building is owned by Mr. O'Bannion."

"So you concluded that they were lovers and he supplied her with the apartment, free of charge?"

"Let's just say that I'm looking into the possibility."

"Maybe he gave it to his new employee at a reasonable rent," McKenna suggested.

"That would be very generous of him, wouldn't it?"

"I guess so," McKenna conceded.

"And strange, also. Mr. O'Bannion did not have the reputation of being a generous man. Quite the opposite, actually. He was known as a bit of a tightwad. But if they had been lovers, that would account for the ease with which Mrs. Ferguson obtained her security clearance, despite some obvious impediments. Wouldn't you agree?"

O'Dougherty was taking McKenna to all the places he didn't want to go, then giving him no choice but to answer. "I guess I would agree."

"Do you believe it possible that Mrs. Ferguson was the source of the information Inspector Rollins told you about, the information he said implicated Mr. O'Bannion in the Iceland bombing?"

It was a question McKenna had expected after reading about the shouts of "treachery" exchanged by Ferguson and O'Bannion. "I guess it's possible."

"Being an experienced investigator yourself, an investigator of some renown, and knowing what I've told you and what you've read in the papers, wouldn't you agree that 'probable' would be a better word?"

McKenna had no choice. "Yes, I would. For the record, I consider it probable that Maggie Ferguson was Inspector Rollins's source of information concerning Mr. O'Bannion. Also for the record, in light of what has happened here, I think that if Mrs. Ferguson was his source, and considering how close she was to Mr. O'Bannion, then it's likely that her information was correct."

"I agree, and that's exactly the avenue I'm going to pursue," O'Dougherty stated. "Mr. O'Bannion had always been known as a vocal supporter of the IRA. There's nothing illegal about that here. However, membership in the IRA and being involved in conspiracies promoting terrorism certainly is. Whatever laws he may have violated in that regard, I'm going to find out about."

"I certainly believe that you'll do just that," McKenna said with absolute conviction.

"I now am forced to ask you a few questions that might seem offensive, but believe me, no offense is intended. I believed you when you said that both yourself and Mrs. Ferguson are happily married, but there's a matter of approximately one hour that must be addressed."

McKenna knew what was coming, the questions he had dreaded most. "Go on."

"You were seen leaving this hotel last night with Mrs. Ferguson at approximately ten o'clock. You returned alone at about eleven. I have to know what transpired during that hour you were gone."

"I walked Mrs. Ferguson to her car, saw her off, then took a walk around the city."

"Did you talk to anyone who might remember you?"

"No reason to. It was rather chilly out last night and there weren't many people on the streets."

"Which brings me to another point. When you returned to the hotel, you were wearing only a suit. No topcoat, if you see where I'm heading."

"I see where you're heading, and I resent the implication. I was not with Mrs. Ferguson after we left this hotel. As I said, she drove off and I took a walk."

"Did she say where she was going?"

"No. I presumed she was going home."

"I should tell you that Mrs. Ferguson's flat is less than a fifteen-minute drive from this hotel, yet she didn't arrive home until an hour and fifteen minutes after she left here with you. That's bound to raise many eyebrows."

I don't know where Old Belvedere is, but it has to be a ways from here. What do I say? McKenna wondered. It looks like I was swapping spit or worse with Ferguson in her car, but I can't tell this guy that she left me to check and see if her wanted IRA terrorist-husband had murdered her boss yet in his secret hideaway flat. What do I say? "Does my story raise your eyebrows?"

"Not in the slightest. I emphatically believe you took your walk and I'll state so in my report. However, I think we'll both agree that my report won't be the final word on this matter," O'Dougherty said, giving McKenna a slight sympathetic smile.

"I'm sure it won't."

"Just a few more questions, if you don't mind," O'Dougherty said, all business once again. "Was that Inspector Rollins who called you here at two minutes after ten this morning?"

This man is unbelievable! McKenna thought. He's also reviewed my telephone records and spoken to the hotel operator. She must have told him that a man with a British accent called me, so there's no use denying it. I'm sure he's got Rollins's voice on tape somewhere and he'll just have her compare the voices. "Yes, it was."

"Why did he call?"

"To tell me about O'Bannion's death, but I had already read about it in the paper."

"Not to tell you about O'Bannion's and Ferguson's death?"

"No, just O'Bannion's."

"What else did you talk about?"

McKenna knew that it was time to put his foot down, come what may. "Confidential aspects of my investigation into the death of Meaghan Maher."

"And that took thirteen minutes?"

"Yes."

"During that time, did you discuss exactly how much information you were going to give to me?"

Right on the money, McKenna thought. "No, that's not what we discussed. Besides, I don't think he even knows you."

"Of course he does. It may surprise you to know that my government has a policy of cooperating with the British government when they arrest terrorists in Great Britain. I've testified in many such cases in London and I've worked with him in the past."

Now you tell me, McKenna thought. "What do you think of him?"

"A nice man and extremely competent. However, I'm aware of his connection to British Intelligence and I'm extremely uncomfortable with the fact that it appears he was running an intelligence operation here without our knowledge or permission. After all, we are neighbors and I think that our relations with the United Kingdom might even be characterized as friendly right now."

Then it looks like Inspector Rollins has got himself a real problem, McKenna thought, especially if O'Dougherty finds out that their spy was also giving them economic information that had nothing to do with the IRA.

Still, McKenna felt the need to say something in Rollins's defense. "If Ferguson ever was a British agent, perhaps they thought that telling your government or even asking permission would compromise her effectiveness. After all, if your minister for finance was IRA, Lord knows who else in your government could also be IRA."

"I agree, but he knows that he could have come to me directly. I would have brought his request to people I know and trust."

"Would they have approved it?"

"Maybe, as long as the British government adequately assured us that the only thing they were interested in was information necessary to combat international terrorism."

Which is just why the Brits didn't go to O'Dougherty, McKenna realized. Oh well, it looks like they'll have to reap what they've sown.

"Could you just clear up a few more things for me?" O'Dougherty asked.

"If I can."

"You have a rented car in the hotel garage, yet you're leaving today. Since you rented it last night and you apparently haven't used it, why did you rent it?"

And now he's going to try to have me reap what I've sown, McKenna thought. If he knows about the car, he probably also knows about my Aer Lingus reservation from Belfast. After all, it's the Irish national airline and this guy seems to have no trouble in finding out what he wants to know. Think fast, McKenna. Think! "I was going to drive to Belfast last night and return to New York from there, but I was too tired after dinner and decided to leave from Dublin after all."

"Why would you drive two and a half hours to Belfast when our airport is thirty minutes from this hotel?"

"Because I laid out the money for Meaghan Maher to be embalmed in Iceland and I also paid for the casket. Naturally, her family wanted to re-imburse me, but it was hectic up there and it slipped all of our minds."

"So you were going to Belfast to collect a debt before returning home?"

"Yes. It's well over five thousand dollars on my credit cards and I wanted to have it by the time the bills came in."

"Very understandable and quite decent of you, Detective McKenna. That's all the questions I have for you at this point, unless you have something you'd like to add."

"As a matter of fact, Senior Investigating Constable O'Dougherty, there is something I'd like to add. That was the best interrogation I've ever seen and I feel unfortunate that I was on the wrong end of it. You're very good at what you do."

O'Dougherty really smiled for the first time since entering the room. "Thank you. Coming from you, I think that's the greatest compliment I've ever received. However, that was only an interview, not an interrogation. People tell me my interrogations are much better, but you did very well just the same. Aside from the small variances of the truth you fed me, you told me exactly what I expected to hear."

"What about those variances?" McKenna asked.

"None of them will be going in my report, so they'll certainly never find their way into the press." Then O'Dougherty reached his hand across the table and McKenna shook it. Both men got up and McKenna accom-panied O'Dougherty to the door.

"By the way, off the record and just between us cops, do you know the name of the man you're looking for?" O'Dougherty asked.

"Yes, but now he's really my problem. He's in New York," McKenna answered without hesitation.

"Did O'Bannion fold and give you that information when he came here last night?"

"Yeah, he folded. I already knew my man's name, but I didn't know he was in New York. However, I wasn't lying when I told you I hadn't seen O'Bannion here. He gave me the location in a note he passed under my door."

"I was sure he folded. Good luck and be sure to give me a call if you need anything on this end."

"You can be sure that I'll do just that."

"Good. One more thing. Could you please give my regards to Inspector Rollins when you talk to him?"

"I will, but when do you think that will be?" McKenna asked, smiling.

"About one minute after I'm gone, of course. I imagine he'll be recalled to London, so tell him I'll be ringing him at his office sometime tomorrow."

McKenna was glad to finally close the door on O'Dougherty. He felt drained after the interview, both emotionally and physically. He sat down and reviewed his session with the man. Considering that he had been worked over by a professional, he concluded that he had done as well as could be expected. Naturally, the strategy he had worked out with Rollins hadn't withstood O'Dougherty's attack, but that couldn't be helped. In order to preserve a shred of Ferguson's reputation for as long as possible, McKenna would admit no knowledge of her affair with O'Bannion. Rollins had also suggested that, to preserve her family's IRA reputation and safety in Belfast, McKenna would try to avoid mentioning her connection to British Intelligence.

McKenna hadn't shared Rollins's concern about the Ferguson family, but he couldn't tell the inspector why without revealing his meeting with McGuinn and her real connection to the IRA. In any event, he was sure that in time, McGuinn would set the record straight on Maggie Ferguson.

McKenna had felt a little guilty about not being able to reveal the McGuinn meeting to Rollins, but no longer. In retrospect, he now suspected Rollins of some duplicity in his motives. It now seemed likely to McKenna that the real reason Rollins had not wanted him to reveal Ferguson's connection to British Intelligence was precisely the reason that O'Dougherty had been so interested in it. It was another case of the British running an unauthorized intelligence operation in a friendly foreign country. Considering the security leaks inherent in the Irish situation, he could possibly forgive their actions on the terrorist front. However, he thought the British attempts at economic spying to be unconscionable and unpardonable, even though most of the information O'Bannion fed them through Ferguson was false.

With a man like O'Dougherty on the case, McKenna thought it probable that someone in British Intelligence would have to pay.

McKenna dialed Rollins's number at Keflavík Airport in Iceland. The phone rang six times and McKenna was just about to hang up when Rollins answered. "You just caught me, old boy. My flight leaves in half an hour and I was on my way out."

"I believe you know a Senior Investigating Constable Padrick O'Dougherty, don't you?"

"Yes, quite a decent fellow. Is he the one who interviewed you?"

"Yes, he was the one."

"That's too bad for us. He's really first rate, probably the best they have."

Too bad for you, McKenna thought, but didn't say. "I'm glad to hear that, because I sure wouldn't want to be grilled by someone better than him the next time."

"I understand. How much did you have to tell him?"

"In so many words I had to agree with him that Maggie Ferguson was probably IRA, that she had probably been involved in an romantic affair with O'Bannion, and that she was probably working for British Intelligence."

"That is quite a lot, but less than I would have expected with O'Dougherty on the case. Did you tell him that it was O'Bannion who planned the bombing here?"

"Yes."

"Do you think he believed you?"

"I'm certain of it."

"Well, that's one good thing to come out of it, as far as my government is concerned."

"As far as your government is concerned, O'Dougherty seemed quite angry about British Intelligence running an operation here without the Irish government's permission or knowledge. I'm certain he's going to act on his suspicions and he asked me to tell you that he'll be calling you at your office tomorrow."

"That's to be expected. He's quite right, you know, and he's got plenty to be angry about. Does he know about our economic spying?"

The lack of concern in Rollins's voice surprised McKenna. "No, not yet. Are you going to be in any trouble over this?"

"Me in trouble? Heavens, no! Long ago, I advised my superiors that I thought we should alert O'Dougherty to our operation with Ferguson and try to get the Irish government on board through him. I even went so far as to say that he should run the operation. My recommendation was endorsed by my superiors, but rejected by Intelligence. I guess they'll now have to explain their decision to someone, but that doesn't bother me."

"How about the economic spying?"

"I never wanted to accept that information. I'm on record stating my views, but I was overruled by the chaps in the Exchequer. Greedy bunch they are. No regard for rules and no sense of fair play. I'm sure that there will be hell to pay over this affair and there's bound to be political casualties. You reap what you sow, I always say, but personally I'm in the clear."

"Funny that you should put it that way, but I'm glad to hear it. Have a nice flight."

Rollins's innocence in the affair was good news to McKenna. He had liked and respected Rollins and was glad to find that his feelings were still justified.

McKenna didn't want to be late for his own flight, but he had one more phone call to make—one he had been dreading since O'Dougherty had left, but one he knew he had to make. He had to call Angelita.

Sooner or later, his dinner with Maggie Ferguson would be reported on the news and his future happiness and health depended on convincing Angelita that the only reason for the dinner was that his assignment had demanded it. That would be the easy part, he knew. The hard part would be explaining to her why he hadn't told her last night about Maggie Ferguson and the dinner.

He took three deep breaths, then dialed.

It had taken McKenna a long phone call to almost smooth things over with Angelita, so long that he missed his flight. Of course, he had admitted that he had been wrong not to tell her about the dinner with Maggie Ferguson. Wrong is wrong—period—so he would still have problems with her when he got home. Looking at things from her point of view and projecting a bit, he felt he deserved some problems because it was going to cause her problems. His dinner at a hotel with a very attractive and attractively dressed Maggie Ferguson would be reported in the New York papers with innuendo somewhere in the articles. He also realized that at least some of that coverage would focus on the lost hour.

Angelita knew him, trusted him, and would be quite certain that nothing unseemly had happened, but she would still be left to deal with questions from her family, friends, and maybe even the press. McKenna felt it wasn't fair that he had put her in that position without having given her advance notice of the dinner. He would have to pay for his bad decision. Fortunately, Angelita wasn't a woman capable of administering misery on the installment plan, so it would be over after just one night of profuse apologies coupled with a plea for understanding. He was ready to do whatever was necessary to get back in her good graces.

Then McKenna got some more bad news when he called the airlines. The next flight out that had an available seat wasn't until 10:00 P.M., leaving him with time on his hands and nothing constructive to do. The only good to come out of it was that he did get to play the tourist and wound up seeing quite a bit of Dublin after all.

TWENTY-SIX

SUNDAY, MARCH 15TH—JFK AIRPORT, NEW YORK CITY

The weather was good, the service was excellent, the cabin attendants were solicitous and friendly, and even the food was tasty, but it was still a long flight for McKenna. He had met two interesting people he had liked during the past two days and both were now dead, two victims on opposing sides of the madness. He couldn't stop thinking about Roger Forsythe and Maggie Ferguson. The more he thought about them, the more depressed he became. He was glad to be leaving the Emerald Isle and its conflicts far behind him, even though he was flying toward another major problem generated by the Troubles. The whole idea exhausted him, and he fervently wished that Mulrooney was already in irons in Iceland, doing life plus forever for his crimes.

McKenna's plane landed at JFK at 12:10 A.M. Sunday morning, ten minutes late. Sheeran and Johnny Pao were at the Customs exit to meet him. Both looked tired, but upbeat.

McKenna was happy to see Sheeran and felt honored that his boss had accompanied Pao to pick him up, but he was even happier to see Pao. McKenna understood Pao, although most people didn't. He preferred to describe the tough marksman's disposition as taciturn, while most others considered him a big grouch. But McKenna didn't mind and felt that the many pluses of working with Pao far outweighed that one minus.

"How have you been?" McKenna asked them.

"Busy," said Sheeran.

"But apparently not as busy as you were in Ireland," Pao added. "You've got one big politico dead, some grand scandals shaping up, and the governments of both Ireland and England shaking. I like it, but what the hell were you doing over there?"

"Police work, Johnny. Just police work," McKenna said lightly, but he was concerned. He had trusted O'Dougherty not to give the details of his interview to the press, but it was obvious by Pao's statement that O'Dougherty's superiors had folded under pressure from the press. "What's been on the news?"

Sheeran answered, "Quite a bit. Besides the murder-suicide, the press is reporting that the Irish police are investigating O'Bannion's role in the Iceland bombing. They're also looking into the possibility that Maggie Ferguson was either an IRA agent or a British agent, or maybe both. Besides that, the press is digging real hard over there. They've come up with two more O'Bannion girlfriends and they're making a big thing over it."

"Good God!" McKenna exclaimed. "I was lucky to get out of there before their reporters found me."

"There's more," Sheeran said. "The Irish prime minister has convened something they call a Special Panel of Inquiry. Then he summoned the British ambassador to his office and demanded that the British government provide the head of British Intelligence for questioning by the panel. I imagine that there'll be diplomatic notes flying back and forth between Dublin and London for weeks."

"Any mention of my involvement?"

Pao couldn't resist answering that one. "You kidding? You're getting more famous every minute. They got you visiting the minister for finance in the afternoon, then taking his secretary slash old squeeze slash British agent slash IRA terrorist out to dinner that night in a very fancy hotel, talking about Lord knows what. A little more than an hour after dessert, they're both grisly dead. I'd say that's some mention of your involvement, wouldn't you?"

"Johnny, you're always such a breath of fresh air."

"You know me. I'm always putting the best slant on things, trying to cheer you up."

"Do the newscasters have me as the hero or the villain in this thing?"

"The jury's still out, but you know they love you in this town. All the same, every reporter around will be trying, vying, and dying to talk to you."

That's not good news, McKenna thought as the three men walked to the unmarked car parked outside the International Arrivals Terminal. The reporters will want to know what I was doing over there and whether I've learned who killed Meaghan. I wouldn't mind defending myself, but I don't want to give them Mulrooney's name yet. Lying to reporters is bad business in this town, so the press has to be avoided for a while.

After loading his luggage in the trunk, McKenna climbed into the backseat. As Pao drove, Sheeran gave McKenna the progress made in New York. At 3:30 that afternoon Mulrooney had called his boys again on their cell phone, but this time the NYPD had been listening in. Mulrooney was going to take his sons to the St. Patrick's Day parade on Tuesday, but they weren't to tell their mother. Instead, they should dress for school, bring their books, and Uncle Jack would pick them up on the corner of Crotona Parkway and East 230th Street, two blocks from their house.

"So it's almost over," McKenna said.

"If we play our cards right, but we have to be as careful as he is. He told the kids to walk all around the neighborhood before they go to meet Uncle Jack. If they see anything that looks the slightest bit suspicious to them, they're to stand on the corner with their book bags between their legs on the ground."

Careful isn't a strong-enough word, McKenna thought. Assuming that Mulrooney's raised himself some street-smart kids, we're gonna have to be meticulous in our planning if we're gonna let "Uncle Jack" and the kids lead us to Mulrooney. "Any idea where Mulrooney was calling from?"

"Yeah. Midtown Manhattan," Sheeran answered smugly. "We also know who Uncle Jack is."

Wow! Sheeran's dying to tell me how he's so smart, but one thing at a time. "Who's Uncle Jack?"

"The owner of the cell phone the kids are using. Jack O'Reilly. According to the phone company records, he lives on 73rd Street in Jackson Heights, Queens, and he works for the Brooklyn Union Gas Company. We've got his whole life history, but more on him later. Next question."

"How do you know where Mulrooney was calling from?"

"Modern magic, and Tavlin is the magician. When Mulrooney called his kids he was also using a cell phone and Tavlin's got a program going to track down stolen phones and cloned numbers. We've got Mulrooney on East 41st Street, Fifth to Madison when he made the call. He was on the phone for less than two minutes, too short for us to get anybody there in time, but we'll be ready for him the next time he uses that phone and we'll get him if he talks long enough. Got plenty more manpower spread out all over the city now and I've got East 41st Street covered, just in case that's one of his hangouts."

McKenna was amazed. "We can do that?" he asked. "We can zero in on his phone?"

"Sure, we can do anything. We're the Major Case Squad, remember? Of course, Tavlin's given us some help that makes us as wonderful as we are. His NYNEX system is computer-controlled, triangulates Mulrooney's location from his signal strength as he moves from cell to cell or even within a cell. A map of the area he's in comes up on the screen and Mulrooney's the flashing dot in the middle. Whenever he uses that phone, all the bells go off at NYNEX and Tavlin's installed an extra terminal in our office."

"How accurate is this system?" McKenna asked.

"Half a city block, but that should be close enough."

"Who's the registered subscriber on the phone Mulrooney's using?"

"The late Thomas Winthrop of Toronto, Canada. His service was AT&T, but we've switched him to NYNEX. Mulrooney never has to worry about his phone being turned off because we'll be more than happy to pay his bill."

Figures, McKenna thought. Mulrooney took his credit cards, his identity, and his life, so why not his phone? "How about Winthrop's recent bills from AT&T?"

"Tavlin just got them for us tonight. Mulrooney didn't start using the phone until March seventh, but the calls were made from here and they're all local calls. Two calls to his kids and the rest to three different beeper numbers. After he beeps one of those numbers, he always gets an incoming call."

"Do we know who owns those beepers?" McKenna asked.

"Not yet, but we will tomorrow. The three phone lines for those beeper numbers belong to an outfit called Page America. We tried to get a hold of them to find out who they sold those beepers to, but no luck. Their office is closed till Monday."

No luck? I'd say we've had plenty of luck so far, McKenna thought. Sheeran's done great and it's time to let him shine some more. "How did it happen that you know Jack O'Reilly's life history?"

"Easy," Sheeran answered. "You know Timmy Restivo?"

Another lucky break, McKenna thought. Sheeran said that O'Reilly works for the Brooklyn Union Gas Company. "Sure I know Timmy. Retired lieutenant from Queens Homicide and now chief of security for Brooklyn Union."

"Well, I called him at home tonight. He went back to his office and brought us O'Reilly's personnel folder. O'Reilly's a meter reader, been with them for thirteen years. Married for nine years, three kids. Good worker, never a problem, but he was born in—"

"Belfast, Northern Ireland," McKenna said.

"Yes, The Lower Falls in Belfast. Timmy gave us a copy of his photo ID and we ran O'Reilly and his wife through DMV. He's got two cars, but one of them wasn't in front of his house."

"Any idea where his wife is from?"

"Certainly not Ireland. Her maiden name is Cocchi."

"We've got a surveillance on the house?"

"Yeah, and a wire on his phone. He doesn't know it, but he now has Caller ID. He called his wife at seven-ten this evening to tell her he would be home by one. He also asked if Mike had called, but he hadn't."

"Where was he calling from?"

"The Pioneer Bar, Main Street and 58th Avenue in Flushing. We sent Fitzhughs there to check it out and he found O'Reilly right away. He's working part-time as the night bartender. There's Irish flags everywhere in the bar, England-out-of-Ireland posters, loads of radical IRA songs on the jukebox, and a real Irish clientele, many of them from the other side."

"Is Fitz still inside the place?" McKenna asked.

"Yeah, he's got it good tonight, soaking up suds with the Job picking up the tab."

"Has he talked to O'Reilly?"

"Yeah, says that he's real popular, knows everybody in the place. We'll find out just who else he knows because we've got the bar phone and the pay phone tapped."

"How about eavesdropping warrants?"

"That's what you're gonna be doing now," Sheeran said, then passed a folder back to McKenna. "The applications have been typed up, the judge has been briefed, and he's waiting at home right now for you to swear to them. I kept it simple and didn't mention anything about his crimes in the rest of the world."

Pao put the interior light on and McKenna read the applications. There were six of them, all with an unsigned eavesdropping warrant attached. The applications listed the phone number to be wired, the telephone subscriber for that phone, the type of information sought, and a statement that, in the opinion of the investigating officer, this information could not be obtained by other investigative means. The information sought was "Particulars from any conversation that would disclose the location of Michael Mullen, a fugitive wanted in the State of New York for the crimes of Grand Larceny and Bail Jumping."

The applications were for the bar phone and the pay phone at the Pioneer, O'Reilly's home phone, a cell phone listed to Jack O'Reilly, and Winthrop's cell phone. The sixth application was a surprise to McKenna and told him that Brunette was taking no chances. It was for the home phone of Dennis Hunt.

Everything seemed to be going well, with the police operation entirely legal after they left the judge's Queens home at 2:00 A.M., but McKenna was still worried. Mulrooney would be captured in thirty-one hours if everything went according to the obvious plan, and possibly sooner if he used his phone again or contacted any of the tapped phones, but there was still the potential for disaster. Mulrooney was planning something big with all the tools of his trade, and was deep underground since he knew the IRA was looking for him. He had to be desperate, McKenna reasoned, especially after O'Bannion's death, and desperate men do desperate things. On the positive side, Mulrooney couldn't know yet that the NYPD was aware of his true identity and history, knew he was in New York, and was searching hard for him using all means available.

Pao took the 59th Street Bridge into Manhattan and McKenna had him stop on East 41st Street between Madison and Fifth Avenue. The deserted street was lined with high-rise office buildings and ended at the main branch of the New York Public Library on Fifth Avenue.

McKenna wanted to search for some clue as to why Mulrooney had been on that particular block, but Pao's radio crackled as soon as McKenna got out of the car. "What are you looking for, Brian?" came over the air.

McKenna recognized the voice of Joe Mendez, another one of the detectives assigned to the Major Case Squad, and realized that Mendez had been assigned to the surveillance of East 41st Street. McKenna looked up and down the block, searching for Mendez, but saw no sign of him on the deserted street.

But Mendez was still watching him. "If you need something, come on over to the library," he transmitted.

McKenna did want to talk to Mendez, so he walked toward the library on Fifth Avenue. When he got to the corner, he saw him. The usually fashionable Joe Mendez was dressed in rags and sitting on the ground under the front portico of the massive classical building. Beside him were a pair of crutches and a stuffed black garbage bag. With a show of difficulty, Mendez got up on his crutches as McKenna approached him. "Can you spare some change, sir?" Mendez asked with his grimy hand out.

McKenna thought the disguise deserved some reward, so he reached into his pocket for some change. He had a lot of it, Icelandic, British, and Irish coins, as well as American. He dropped them all in Mendez's hand.

"Thank you, kind sir," Mendez said, putting the change in his overcoat pocket. "God bless you and may all your time be overtime."

"Like yours?"

"Yes, and on behalf of the rest of the squad, I'd like to thank you for this case and the easy money. We're all on twelve-hour tours with no days off."

That *was* wonderful, McKenna knew. Time and a half was always wonderful and the well-paid first and second grade detectives of the Major Case Squad would be raking it in as long as Mulrooney was free in New York. Besides the one on East 41st Street, all the surveillances involved in keeping track of O'Reilly and the Mullen boys would be punching a sizable hole in the budget, he realized, but that was only a small part of the expense. The overtime earned by the detectives assigned around the clock to the many teams spread throughout the city would bust the budget of most of the smaller police departments in the country, and that was the easiest money of all. Those lucky detectives were doing nothing but waiting to zero in on Mulrooney should he use his cell phone again. Thanks to Michael Mulrooney, the morale of the Major Case Squad was soaring. "Who's here with you?" he asked Mendez.

"The other happy bum is Joe Sophia. He's sitting in a wheelchair and panhandling from a doorway on the other side of Madison Avenue. Tells me he was doing pretty good until the traffic died down."

"Any idea what Mulrooney was doing here?"

"None whatsoever."

"Anybody check the building directories on 41st Street?"

"I was hoping somebody would ask," Mendez said. Balancing himself on his crutches, he reached down into the garbage bag, removed a notebook, and handed it to McKenna. "As far as I could tell, there's no Irish or British organizations on the block."

McKenna thumbed through the notebook and saw that Mendez had done a lot of writing. It was almost full and contained a list of every organization and firm with offices on the block. He put the notebook in his pocket and asked, "What are you gonna do if Mulrooney shows up?"

"Take proper police action."

"Meaning?"

"Meaning I'm by myself, I'm sure he's armed, and we know he's dangerous. Just between us, I'm gonna shoot the big donkey and come up with a story later."

What would I do in the same circumstances? McKenna wondered, but only for a moment. "Good thinking, Joe."

Like Pao had said, the press certainly wanted to talk to McKenna. It was common knowledge among the reporters in town that he lived at the Gramercy Park Hotel, so McKenna had Pao drive past the place. There were news vans from all the local stations parked outside, reporters McKenna knew at the front door, and he could see through the front window that the hotel bar was doing a great business as other reporters whiled away their time in the traditional manner. It was a media circus gearing up, but the players were in the wrong tent. McKenna's rent for the month was paid, but if Angelita had followed his instructions, nobody in the hotel should know that he no longer lived there.

"Dopes," was Pao's take on the matter. "You ready to go home yet?"

Am I ready to face Angelita and spend the night explaining and apologizing? "Not entirely ready, but I've got no choice. Let's go."

It was only a half-mile drive to McKenna's new home in Greenwich Village. It was the neighborhood he had grown up in, and he liked everything about it. As Pao pulled in front of his building, McKenna noted with some satisfaction that his new location had everything that made living in Manhattan so convenient. There was a twenty-four-hour grocery store on one corner, a video rental store on the other, a Chinese laundry and dry cleaner across the street, a movie theater two blocks away, and hundreds of fine restaurants within walking distance. He was also pleased with his building, a four-story scrubbed and renovated old brownstone with new windows, a blue slate stoop, and ornate brass lamps on each side of the polished walnut front door. It was a standout beauty on a block of stately, expensive, well-maintained brownstones.

McKenna was getting his luggage from the trunk when his cell phone rang. "Do you know that Mulrooney's in New York?" Martin McGuinn asked, dispensing with all pleasantries.

McKenna knocked on the trunk and waved to Sheeran and Pao. Both men got out of the car and joined him at the trunk. "Yeah, we know he's here, but we don't know where he's staying," McKenna said to McGuinn.

"Neither do I, but do you know who he's got with him?"

"No."

"According to what I hear, two very dangerous hard men we've been looking for are with him in your city."

"Are they bombers?" McKenna asked.

"No, gunmen with loads of experience. We've been searching for them for months, but Kiernan Crowley has been hiding out in New York. Billy Ambery was with Mulrooney in Iceland. He was the mate on the boat there."

"Where are you getting this information from?"

"There used to be a man in Donegal by the name of Joe Learey who had two nice boats he put at our disposal for a price whenever we needed them. It came to our attention that one of his boats was missing, so we had a chat with him. Learey claimed that it had sunk, but we thought it curious that he hadn't made an insurance claim for it."

"Would that boat have been the fifty-six-foot sport fisherman?" Mc-Kenna asked.

"Yes, so my men talked very hard to Learey and he eventually decided to tell them the truth. He had been hired by O'Bannion and took Ambery with him to Iceland. They brought Mulrooney back with them and Learey's regular first mate met them off the Donegal coast in his other boat. They opened the sea cocks on his sport fisherman and sunk it, then took his other boat back to port. Mulrooney paid him and then Learey drove them to Shannon Airport."

"How much was he paid?"

"Three-hundred-thousand American dollars. His boat was worth about two hundred thousand, so he thought he'd made himself a nice tax-free profit for a week's work."

"How did Learey know Mulrooney and Ambery were taking a flight to New York?"

"Actually, they took a flight to Montreal. Ambery told him that New York was were they were headed, eventually."

"Why would Ambery tell him that?"

"He probably doesn't remember that he did. Learey and Ambery didn't have a lot to do while they were waiting on their boat in Iceland, so Ambery did a lot of drinking and bragging. Learey had worked for us many times, so both he and Ambery knew many of the same people."

"Including Kiernan Crowley?"

"Yes, including Kiernan Crowley. Ambery told him they were meeting Crowley in New York and that Mulrooney was planning something big there."

"Does he know what names they're using here?"

"No, and Ambery didn't know exactly what Mulrooney was planning."

"Did Learey know that he wasn't working for the IRA when he took his boat to Iceland?" McKenna asked.

"Both he and his mate claimed to the end that they didn't, but my men didn't believe them."

"I guess there's no way that Mulrooney could find out that Learey's talked to your people, is there?"

"No. Both he and his mate have had a terrible run of luck, losing two boats and their lives in a single month."

"So there's been another accident?"

"I'm sorry about it, but it was necessary. It won't be discovered for a while and I doubt if their bodies will ever be recovered. I understand that Learey's other boat went down off the Donegal coast about an hour ago."

The cavalier manner in which McGuinn described the murder of two men angered McKenna, until he realized that McGuinn had ordered the murders on his behalf to prevent word from getting to Mulrooney that the NYPD knew he was in town. It was a terrible business getting worse. "What about Meaghan Maher?"

"Learey actually cried when he told my men about her. Mulrooney brought a large suitcase on board early on the night of February twenty-first. He told them not to open it, but they had the heat cranked up on the boat and after a couple of days the suitcase started to smell. Learey opened it and was shocked when he saw what Mulrooney had done to Meaghan Maher. Neither Learey nor Ambery wanted to get caught in Iceland with her body on board, so they sneaked out of the harbor one night and dumped her body at sea."

"Why didn't they leave her in the suitcase when they dumped the body?"

"Because Ambery wanted it. He tried cleaning it, but he couldn't get rid of the smell. They realized how angry Mulrooney would be when he found out they had disobeyed his orders and opened the suitcase, so they cut it up and threw it overboard at the dock in Reykjavík harbor."

"What was Mulrooney's reaction when he found out that they had dumped the body?"

"Quite angry, at first. But they told him that the suitcase was smelling and they were afraid that someone would notice. Told him that they dumped it at sea without opening it and that calmed him down a bit."

"A bit?"

"He didn't touch Learey, but he pounded Ambery. Just one punch to the body, but he hit him so hard that Learey was sure that Ambery's got a few broken ribs. When Learey dropped them off at the airport a week later, Ambery was still walking stiff and in so much pain that he couldn't even carry his own suitcases."

"I guess Billy Ambery isn't too crazy about Mulrooney," McKenna surmised.

"According to Learey, Ambery hates him, but fears him like the devil. After they saw what Mulrooney had done to Meaghan, Ambery started drinking even more. Swore he would kill Mulrooney if he got the chance, but Learey thinks that's drunken bullshit. Says that Ambery was certainly a tough lad before Mulrooney broke his ribs, but never a match for Mulrooney."

"Can you give me any more information about Crowley and Ambery?" McKenna asked.

"Give me a fax number. I've got a few pictures and we've been making discreet inquiries for weeks. We know that both of them have relatives in New York and bogus British passports. I'll send you everything we've got."

McKenna gave McGuinn the Major Case Squad's fax number and was about to hang up when another thought hit him. "Does the name Jack O'Reilly mean anything to you?"

"No. Why?"

"Because he's mixed up with Mulrooney here."

"I don't know the man, but here's an interesting piece of information for you. She's dead now, but Mulrooney's mother's maiden name was O'Reilly. The O'Reillys were always a good republican Belfast family."

So Uncle Jack is Mulrooney's cousin, McKenna thought. He looks like a legitimate guy, but he's deep in this and getting deeper. "Thanks for the information, Martin."

"Not so fast, Brian. What about our deal?"

"You've more than fulfilled your end. As soon as this is over, there's sure to be quite a press conference and either myself or the police commissioner will announce that Mulrooney was definitely not working for the IRA when he did the Iceland bombing and killed Meaghan."

"How about the killings he did before his other bombings?" McGuinn asked.

"We won't go into detail with the press about those, but I'm sure the Brits will. Can't help you much there."

"That's all right. Our people don't believe much the Brits say anyway, so that's the least of my worries. Thanks to you and Maggie, I'm spending most of my time hiding from our own press with their questions about it."

McKenna couldn't bring himself to feel sorry for McGuinn. Instead, all through his dealings with McGuinn he had felt as if he was closing a deal with the devil. However, McGuinn had come through and the deal had to be honored. "If I can get away with it on this side of the Atlantic, I'll lie your way out of it for you," he said, then pushed his End button.

"I guess it's not time to go home yet," Pao said.

"No, let's get downtown and take a look at some information that took two more murders to get." McKenna put his suitcases back in the trunk and slammed it shut.

TWENTY-SEVEN

O'Reilly had been followed home by the time McKenna, Pao, and Sheeran arrived at the Major Case Squad office. Eddie Morgan was the detective monitoring Tavlin's computer terminal and the base radio set, but nothing was coming over the air. McGuinn's faxes had already arrived and Morgan handed Sheeran the packet of papers, but the inspector thought McKenna should be the first to read them. He handed them to McKenna and said, "Let's go into my office."

McKenna and Pao followed Sheeran in and McKenna sat at Sheeran's desk reading, with the inspector and Pao looking over his shoulder. It was soon apparent to McKenna that even more wiretaps and surveillances would have to be put in place.

Crowley was thirty-four years old and had a cousin in Woodlawn. Ambery was forty-one and had a married sister living in Levittown in Nassau County, about thirty miles east of Manhattan. McGuinn had sent the addresses for both relatives. Crowley and Ambery had both done time in the Maze Prison and somehow McGuinn had obtained their prison photos.

McKenna spent a while staring at the faxed standing prison photos of the two violent men. Both were about five foot ten, and each looked tough and in shape as they glared back at the camera. Like Mulrooney, they wouldn't be taken without a fight. McGuinn had also provided photocopies of the front page of the forged British passports Ambery and Crowley had been using as well as a list of aliases the two had used in the past. There were many of them, and though it would have been nice to track the men through credit cards, they apparently had none.

McKenna gave all the fax sheets to Sheeran and he handed the package to Pao.

"How many copies you want made?" Pao asked.

"I think everyone on this case should have it, so we're gonna need at least a hundred."

Is it possible we've got a hundred men working this case? McKenna wondered. "Where did you get all this manpower from?" he asked Sheeran.

"Thirty-two from our squad, another twenty from the borough Homicide Squads, and the rest from the Joint Terrorist Task Force."

The Joint Terrorist Task Force was staffed by city detectives and federal agents from the FBI and ATF. Their commander reported to Gene Shields, so McKenna was glad to hear of their involvement. He knew that federal help would be necessary to get Mulrooney extradited quickly and spirited to Iceland after his arrest, which brought another thought to mind. "Inspector, do you mind if I use your phone?"

"International call?"

"Two. Iceland and London. I've made some promises, so we're gonna be getting some company for the showdown."

McKenna reached Thor at home and told him about the plan to capture Mulrooney on St. Patrick's Day. Thor would be arriving at JFK at 9:00 P.M. on Monday and he would have with him an extradition request from his government.

Rollins was another story. It was 8:00 A.M. in London when McKenna called, but Rollins was already at his desk on Sunday in New Scotland Yard. However, Rollins wouldn't be able to make it to New York by St. Patrick's Day. Instead, he would be spending the rest of the week testifying before closed parliamentary committees about the role of British Intelligence and Special Branch in the O'Bannion-Ferguson affair. He presumed that his government would soon be putting as much distance as possible between their two agencies and anything connected to Mulrooney, O'Bannion, or Ferguson. Rollins thought that the British government would now be quite content to have Mulrooney rotting away and incommunicado in an Iceland prison.

When he finished his calls, McKenna went upstairs to Brunette's office on a hunch. It was three-thirty in the morning, but Brunette was in and sleeping with his head on his desk cradled in his arms. He woke up as soon as McKenna closed the door. He looked tired, with bags under his red eyes, but he still had a smile for McKenna. "Welcome home, buddy. What brings you here at this hour?"

McKenna pulled up a chair across from Brunette's desk. "Some new stuff on Mulrooney and a request," he said.

"Okay, let's start with the request. What is it?"

"I'd like Pao or two other tough guys assigned to my house whenever I'm not there."

"You're taking Vernon's opinion on what to expect from Mulrooney very seriously, aren't you?" Brunette asked.

"Sure am. He can't know where I live now, but I don't want to take any chances. He'll try reaching out for my family if we manage to put his back to the wall."

"Okay, you've got Pao. What else?"

"We're gonna be waking up that poor judge again for two more eaves-dropping warrants," McKenna answered, then told Brunette about the information he had received from McGuinn and of Thor's impending arrival.

"Can you think of anything else we should be doing?" Brunette asked.

"Just one thing. We should get down to Missing Persons and find out if they've got any young girls reported missing recently."

"I've already done that, but I was sort of hoping you wouldn't have burdened your mind thinking of that."

"I have a hard time thinking of anything else. If Mulrooney's running true to form and he's planning something soon, a young girl is going to be kidnapped, tortured, and then killed. He might even have her now."

"He doesn't, as far as we know. I made Justin Peters the new CO of Missing Persons and he's on top of it."

So Mosley's gone already, McKenna thought. I wonder what Brunette did to him, but I've already heard about enough murders for one night. "I was thinking that maybe we should go public on Mulrooney," McKenna said. "Big as he is and conspicuous with whatever's left of the shiner Meaghan gave him, somebody here would have to remember seeing him."

"Why go public now and risk scaring him out of town when we're so close to getting him?"

"Maybe if we publicize his picture and warn the public, we could wind up saving some young girl's life."

"Maybe, but if he runs and gets away, what then? He'll be under pressure and he'll kill again—maybe again and again until somebody else finally stops him. But that decision might be out of our hands before long, anyway."

"Why's that? You getting any indications that the press knows something's up?"

"I've already had calls from the *News* and the *Post*, but that was inevitable. I stonewalled them, but I can't keep that up for much longer."

"What put them wise?"

"I had Mulrooney's picture shown at every hotel in town and they found out about it. Somebody from one of the hotels blabbed to some reporter and made the rest of the press curious."

"What do they know so far?" McKenna asked.

"Just that we're looking real hard for somebody, but they don't know who yet. Sheeran's told everybody working the case that their lives would be over if they whispered anything in their favorite reporter's ear, but I still think we've been lucky that it hasn't been leaked already."

"You're right, and it can't last forever," McKenna agreed. "If Mulrooney starts talking on his phone again, the press is sure to pick up our radio traffic as we track him down."

"So can we agree on this? We don't have long before the press is on to us, but let's keep it under wraps as long as we can," Brunette suggested, then looked at his watch. "If we can last another twenty-nine hours, we've won. Better yet, we might even get lucky and get him before he goes to pick up his kids."

"Or before he kidnaps another young girl," McKenna added. "You think there's a shot of that?"

"Why not? We've been lucky so far."

"I'll agree that we've gotten a lot to go on, but that information has made us indirectly responsible for three murders and a suicide."

Brunette leaned back in his chair and eyed McKenna shrewdly. "Your conscience is really acting up, isn't it?"

"This case has it working overtime," McKenna admitted. "I don't know when I've felt more miserable or unsure of myself."

"Then clear your mind and get that conscience in check. You keep doing just what you've been doing and leave the hard thoughts to my conscience. That's my job."

"Isn't yours bothering you?" McKenna asked.

"Killing me, but it's performing exactly to specifications. Heavy's the head that wears the crown and the throbbing conscience comes with the territory."

"Okay, you've got my vote. We'll keep the wraps on as long as we can."

McKenna didn't know why, but something Brunette had said worked. He left Brunette's office exhausted, but confident and feeling better than he had felt for days.

TWENTY-EIGHT

The apartment was lovely, but McKenna hadn't been able to enjoy it. After spending a long two hours with Angelita, she had eventually forgiven him and permitted him to get a few hours' sleep. Angelita was up with the kids before him, but she managed to keep them reasonably quiet. He was up at nine, still tired, and had gotten dressed and eaten breakfast by the time Pao arrived at ten.

Like McKenna, Angelita was another one of the few people in the world who understood and liked Johnny Pao, but McKenna had neglected to mention that Pao would be staying and the reason for his assignment. That took some embarrassed explaining to her while Pao stood by listening with a noncommittal look on his face, but Angelita saw the wisdom of having Pao around until Mulrooney was captured. She was making Pao breakfast while

he watched the kids when McKenna left for headquarters in Pao's unmarked car.

Sheeran was already back at work by the time McKenna arrived, and
Eddie Morgan was still manning the base radio set. After signing in, Mc-
Kenna went to Sheeran's office. "Anything been happening?"

"Lots," Sheeran said. "Mulrooney's been using his phone, but we
missed him."

"We get any more information?"

"Some, and it leads to a lot of speculation. I'll play you the tape."
Sheeran took a cassette player from his drawer and placed it on his desk.
"First call was at eight-nineteen this morning. He called Ambery's sister."
Sheeran turned the machine on and McKenna heard the phone ringing in
Levittown. A woman answered. "Hello?"

Then McKenna heard Mulrooney's voice with the Northern brogue
ringing through. "Hello, Margaret. It's Mike. Is Billy there?"

"No. He didn't come by last night, so I was thinking he was with you.
He was supposed to pick up the rest of his stuff," Margaret answered, also
with a Northern brogue.

"It wasn't me he was with, but you'll be seeing him soon enough."

"I surely hope so. That worthless sod's been owing me a quid for over
a week and I could sure use it now. Can you do something about that,
Mike?"

"Don't worry, I'll tell him to take care of it."

"Thanks. Seems you're the only one he pays any mind to. I can't even
get him to see a doctor and I know he's hurting."

"I'll take care of that as well. Bye." The call ended and Sheeran shut
off the cassette player.

"Do we know where he was when he made that call?" McKenna asked.

"That's part of the problem. He was in Staten Island and moving fast,
in a car and headed north on the West Shore Expressway. Nobody figured
Staten Island, so we had only three teams there this morning. Closest one
was at least five miles behind him on the expressway, but I had the other
teams waiting for him at the Verrazano-Narrows Bridge toll plaza in case
he was headed to Brooklyn. His next call was a minute later to one of the
beepers, so there's no audio on it. Just the sound of Mulrooney punching
in the last two digits of his phone number. Kiernan Crowley answered the
beep at eight-thirty-two and he's been up to something."

"Where was Mulrooney then?"

"Unfortunately, Elizabeth, New Jersey. He must have used the Goethals
Bridge to cross over, so he beat us this time. We had no teams in Jersey."
Sheeran turned the cassette player back on. First came the sound of two
beeps as Mulrooney punched the last two digits of his number into

his phone, and then came the incoming call. It was another Northern brogue and a short conversation. "Kiernan here. Where do you want to meet?"

"Where are you now?" Mulrooney had asked.

"A pay phone in the Bronx."

"You get the van?"

"Yeah, I got it."

"Any problems?"

"Not a one. I don't think they'll even miss it for days."

"Good. Meet me at Billy's at noon."

"How about Billy?"

"He should be there by then," Mulrooney said, then ended the call.

Sheeran turned off the cassette player. "What do you think?" he asked.

"They've stolen a van from a corporation big enough to have many of them, so I'd have some good people handle the investigation if any large corporation reports one of their vans stolen."

"I've already put that process in motion. We're going to be notified immediately by the Alarm Board if that happens," Sheeran said. "Are you thinking he's gonna load up that van with explosives and park it near a place owned by people he doesn't like?"

"Maybe. He pulled the same stunt in Londonderry, but if it's a car bomb, it sets my mind at ease a bit."

"Why?"

"Because I was worried he was going to pull some stunt at the St. Patrick's Day Parade to impress his kids. Now I'm thinking that he's planning something else we might be in a position to prevent. We got the British UN embassy covered good, haven't we?"

"That and their ambassador's apartment, their consulate, and the British Airways office in Rockefeller Center. I have enough people there to grab them in case they try to drop a van in front of any of those places, but we should have them all captured by noon."

McKenna checked his watch. It was ten-forty-five. "Shouldn't we be leaving now?" he asked. "Even on a Sunday, Levittown's got to be at least an hour away."

"By car it is, but by chopper it's only fifteen minutes. Ray's got one standing by for us at the Wall Street Heliport."

"How about manpower?"

"Five teams waiting at the Nassau County Eighth Precinct, about a mile from the house, but there's a problem. I had to tell the Nassau PD something and they weren't happy about us pulling a major operation in their bailiwick. They insisted on supplying the heavy weapons teams and their Bomb Squad."

"And the surveillance on the house? It has to be difficult to watch it from a residential neighborhood like that without being noticed."

"That was the easiest part. I went through the Personnel Record File and found we've got a detective from the Queens Robbery Squad living right across the street from the sister's house."

"What's his name?"

"Her name," Sheeran corrected. "Detective Lisa Marchese. She and her partner are now assigned to the case, watching the house."

"Does Lisa know Ambery's sister?"

"For years. Even met our pal Billy once when he visited a couple of years ago and said she saw him there last week. He looked loaded and was walking real stiff."

"What does Lisa think of her neighbors?"

"Thinks the sister's nice enough, but her husband's an oiler, Billy's a wise guy, and their kids are spoiled rotten."

"How old are the kids?"

"Nine and eleven. They went to church with their father this morning and now they're at an amusement park with him. The only one home right now is Margaret, so there shouldn't be much of a problem if our boys show up."

"We got a warrant for the house?" McKenna asked.

"Getting it right now. Anything I missed?"

"As usual, Inspector, you haven't missed a thing."

McKenna had twice had bad helicopter experiences and he hated flying in them, but the trip to Levittown went fast enough. He and Sheeran were on the ground in the large parking lot behind the Nassau County Eighth Precinct by eleven-thirty. The NYPD helicopter, the five unmarked NYPD cars, the three Nassau County PD Emergency Service trucks and their large Bomb Squad bomb disposal truck had been noticed by the local residents and were drawing quite a crowd of local people.

The Nassau County cops blocked off their parking lot, but Sheeran wasn't happy with the picture and figured it was only a matter of time before the press arrived. Worse, he knew that he had very little control over the Nassau cops and what they would tell the press, so he, McKenna, and ten NYPD detectives spent the better part of the next hour sidestepping questions from the Nassau County cops and an increasingly annoyed and very skeptical Nassau County chief.

The party line dictated by Sheeran and followed by his detectives was that information had been developed by Scotland Yard that a group of wanted IRA terrorists might be meeting in the house at noon. According to Sheeran, that was all they knew.

The Nassau cops weren't buying it and the situation became increasingly uncomfortable. McKenna and Sheeran both realized that many fences would have to be mended once Mulrooney was captured.

The agony was ended at 12:35 P.M. by Mulrooney himself. Sheeran and McKenna were sitting in the back of one of the NYPD unmarked cars, hiding from the Nassau County chief and talking to two detectives from the Joint Terrorist Task Force when a transmission came from Morgan over the radio. "Headquarters Base to all units. Be advised that the subject just dialed a beeper number."

Both Sheeran and McKenna reached over the front seat to grab the radio lying on the dashboard, but Sheeran got to it first. "Squad CO to Headquarters Base, you got a location on the subject?"

"Manhattan, Inspector. He wasn't on long enough to get a definite location, but he's in a cell bounded by Fifth Avenue and Seventh Avenue, 23rd to 27th Streets. Any units close enough to respond?"

There were four teams left in Midtown. All answered and were on their way to the area.

Now what the hell is he doing in Manhattan when we're all waiting for him here? "They're meeting at Billy's Topless Bar, West 24th and Sixth," McKenna shouted.

"Of course they are," Sheeran shouted back, just as loud. He keyed the radio and transmitted. "Squad CO to all responding units. Set up outside Billy's Topless Bar, West 24th Street and Sixth Avenue."

The four units acknowledged the order, and then Sheeran asked over the air if there were any Emergency Service units available in Midtown to assist with heavy weapons. ESU Truck One-three and Truck One-five were available and responding with heavy weapons.

Sheeran threw the radio back on the dashboard, left the car, and ran to the helicopter with McKenna close behind him. Less than a minute later the pilot had them in the air and headed for Manhattan. McKenna had left his radio on the seat in the helicopter and they heard the teams and the Emergency Service units report in. All were in position outside the bar. Sheeran ordered that a team be sent in to have a beer and check the place out, and that drew a chuckle from McKenna. He imagined that there would be no shortage of volunteers for that assignment.

Cisco Sanchez and Bobby Garbus from the Major Case Squad won the job and the helicopter was over Queens before they reported back. "Team Fourteen to Squad CO."

Sheeran recognized the voice. "Go ahead, Cisco. What have you got?"

"Sorry, Inspector. I've got nothing at all. They might've been in there, but they're gone now. You want me to go back in and ask around?"

"Negative. Have all units return to their assigned areas. I want everybody ready in case his beep gets answered," Sheeran transmitted, then turned to McKenna. "That was strike two for today, but I've got a feeling we're gonna get a few more pitches coming our way."

"And I've got a feeling that O'Reilly's the one he beeped. Ambery and Crowley are with him, so the other beeper has to be O'Reilly's. Know where he is right now?"

"Uh-huh, tending bar at the Pioneer. We've got a unit watching the place, so let's see if you're right," Sheeran said, then keyed the radio. "Squad CO to the unit with the meter reader."

"Team Nineteen. Go ahead, Inspector."

"Let me know if your man makes a phone call."

"You're right on the money, Inspector. We can see him through the window and he's on the phone."

"Headquarters Base to Squad CO. The subject's getting that incoming call."

"Where is he?"

"West Side in the Fifties and heading north up Eighth Avenue, but we've got no teams there yet."

"Damn! What a fiasco!" Sheeran said to McKenna. "He's in the Fifties and our teams are still way behind him in the Twenties."

"Team Twenty-one to Squad CO. O'Reilly just hung up."

"Headquarters Base to Squad CO. The subject's done with his call. Total conversation time, twenty-four seconds. He's not much of a chatterbox."

"Anything interesting?"

"I'd say so. The subject wanted O'Reilly to bring both suitcases when he picks up the kids tomorrow morning."

"That's not good news, but at least it's not strike three," McKenna said. "I'll bet he's got kids' clothes in those suitcases and he's planning on snatching his boys, so whatever he's planning is gonna happen soon. Maybe we should be talking to one of the auxiliary players now."

"Which one?"

"Maybe Mrs. O'Reilly would be interested in learning what kind of a man her husband has for a cousin. Jack is doing pretty good in this country, so maybe we should offer him a chance to help us out before he gets in too deep."

"I don't know," Sheeran said, shaking his head. "We'd be taking quite a chance ourselves on that one. I'd prefer to wait and grab Mulrooney when Jack delivers the kids."

Should we? McKenna asked himself. Mulrooney's desperate, on the move, meeting with his pals, and set to blow up something big. We've got most of the bases covered, but he can still ruin our plan by killing people and causing damage between now and then. What's the right thing to do right now?

Sheeran's sharp and in charge, so I should be playing his plan, McKenna decided. "You're the boss," he said.

"Really?" Sheeran answered, smiling and patting McKenna on the back. "Let's try this one out. You tell me what you want done and that's what I'll recommend we do."

That wasn't what McKenna wanted to hear. He sat thinking and worrying until the helicopter landed at the Wall Street Heliport.

Mulrooney made no further calls from his cell phone that afternoon and none of the other wiretaps turned up anything of interest, so McKenna spent three hours at the office typing up his reports documenting his week's activities. He had been a detective a long time and knew that his reports were always considered in the Detective Bureau to be respectable models of ambiguity. He documented most of the information he had obtained and every source except McGuinn, but was loose enough in his reports to leave himself some latitude if he would have to testify in the case.

McKenna thought that prospect unlikely. The next time Mulrooney saw the inside of a New York courtroom should be his last before he was dragged back to Iceland, but the reports would enter the public domain after the case was over and, by tradition and procedure, had to be compiled anyway.

Missing from his reports was the meeting with McGuinn, but all the information McKenna had learned from him was there with one exception—there was no mention made of the murders in Donegal. McKenna attributed the rest of McGuinn's information to Maggie Ferguson, although it pained him to think that her death had certainly helped him write credibly through some of the hard parts in his reports. He mentioned nothing about the plot to kill O'Bannion and her part in it.

In short, on paper everything he and the NYPD had done was entirely legal and he had fulfilled all the deals that had brought him to that point. There were never any illegal wiretaps and no inside police knowledge of any nasty murder plots anywhere. All his good guys shone through as being very good and eminently believable and all his bad guys were indeed despicably bad.

McKenna brought his reports into Sheeran's office. As was his custom with McKenna, Sheeran merely glanced at each report before signing it.

McKenna suddenly realized that he'd had enough for a while. He was depressed, worried, jet-lagged, and bone-tired. "If it's all right with you, Inspector, I'm gonna give Pao a break. I'm going home."

"Glad to hear it. Me, too."

TWENTY-NINE

Thanks to the *Iceland Weekly*, Mulrooney thought it fate that Frieda would be his. The newspaper was designed to stir foreign interest in the country as well as keep the many Icelandic émigrés working abroad informed on events at home. Mulrooney had found Iceland to be a pleasant but rather dull place and he had no intention of ever returning there, but he was one of the newspaper's most dedicated readers. The coverage of the bombing in the recent issue was still extensive two weeks after the event, a fact that surprised and gratified Mulrooney. He attributed this focus to a lack of any other real news in the nation, but the issue contained a few bonuses for him; there was a feature article on Thor, one of his opponents.

After poring over the article, it was apparent to Mulrooney that this Thor was something of a national hero and the slant of the article was that as a matter of course, Thor would eventually bring the bomber to justice. Mulrooney was amused by this viewpoint, but he was also astonished to learn how much the small-time detective had uncovered. He had found the relay transmitter hidden in the chandelier of Room 530, he knew about Mulrooney's escape by boat, and he had also firmly tied the death of Meaghan Maher to him. Mulrooney had thought that none of those things would have been discovered, but Thor had done it. He was intrigued by this Icelandic detective, and just as intrigued by his wife.

There was a photo of Frieda, and Mulrooney thought her to be a striking woman. The newspaper devoted a half page in telling her history, a woman who had elevated herself from obscure sleaze to the pinnacle of respectability in Iceland, a minister in the national church.

Frieda's choice of husband and occupation had placed her squarely in the enemy's camp, as far as Mulrooney was concerned. She was a Protestant minister married to the man who thought he was going to get him. As he read the article, Mulrooney thought it would be amusing to somehow turn the tables on Thor. Then fate dealt Mulrooney an ace. The end of the article listed all the countries Frieda had traveled to during her ministry and stated that she would be conducting services at the First Norwegian Church of Brooklyn on Sunday, March 15th, today, the very morning Mulrooney read the article. Fate, Mulrooney was sure. Of all the places in the world for her to be, she was in the very city he was in. He felt an inner need to take some action.

The first thing Mulrooney did was call the First Norwegian Church. He learned that Frieda had already conducted a service at 9:00 A.M., but she would also be conducting an evening service in Icelandic at seven-thirty. Perfect timing, as far as Mulrooney was concerned. He was parked a half block from the church when Frieda left the small parsonage at seven-fifteen, but he was in for two surprises.

The first surprise was Frieda herself. She was very tall, possibly six feet, and she carried herself erect with an almost-military march as she walked. Although she was dressed in a black clerical cassock, Mulrooney thought she looked more like a professional basketball player than a minister. She exuded an air of confidence, maybe even superiority, that Mulrooney found exciting and alluring. She was something different, but just what he needed at the moment. As he briefly relished her appearance, he found himself wondering how Frieda sounded when she whimpered.

As Mulrooney had expected, she was accompanied by another minister. He chatted away as they walked and Frieda merely nodded a few times to acknowledge his presence. Mulrooney was parked too far away to hear any of the conversation, but he was amused that the minister had to look up to talk to Frieda. What Mulrooney hadn't expected was the second man. He was a giant, a full head taller than Frieda, but he formed no part of the conversation as he trailed behind Frieda and the minister. He was a watchful fellow, unsmiling, looking up and down the block as he walked. For reasons Mulrooney couldn't fathom, Frieda had a bodyguard.

Mulrooney had originally intended to take in the service, but the presence of the bodyguard ruled out that course of action. He was bound to be noticed in the small church during a service conducted in a language he didn't understand, and that wouldn't do with a bodyguard around. So Mulrooney waited in his car during the service, thinking and wondering. Why did Frieda have a bodyguard? The only conclusion he could draw was that Thor knew more about him than had been reported in the press, which had to mean that McKenna knew more about him. How much more? he wondered, but didn't waste much time worrying about it. Frieda would tell him.

The service ended at eight-thirty, and the first two people out the front door were Frieda and her bodyguard. The big man stood ten yards away from Frieda, watching, while she greeted the worshippers leaving the church. It seemed to Mulrooney that she knew many of them and they obviously held her in awe as they waited in line to speak with her. A few stopped to talk to the bodyguard, but he was a man of few words. His eyes never left Frieda as he barely acknowledged their greetings.

Mulrooney liked his style and relished the challenge represented by the man. He had always thought that feats accomplished easily were hardly worth doing, but this Frieda affair was shaping up as a worthwhile project. His adrenaline was flowing as Frieda, the bodyguard, and the other minister returned to the parsonage.

The three were out again in fifteen minutes. The minister had changed into a suit, but the change in Frieda was dramatic. She was wearing jeans, penny loafers, white socks, and a fur jacket, and she had her blond hair in a ponytail. Mulrooney knew she had to be in her thirties, maybe even her forties, but she looked like a teenager to him—a very exciting teenager. She was the farthest thing from a minister he had ever seen and he found himself longing to see her bound, naked, terrified, and in pain.

There was a two-car garage separating the church from the parsonage and the minister went in to get the car, leaving Frieda and her bodyguard standing on the sidewalk. Mulrooney ducked under the dashboard as the bodyguard surveyed the street. Frieda was talking to him, but he appeared to be ignoring her as he concentrated on his surroundings. He opened the front passenger door for Frieda when the minister pulled up in the large Oldsmobile, took a final look around, and got into the backseat.

Mulrooney followed them at a prudent distance. Fortunately for him, there was enough traffic to enable him to stay at least three cars behind the Oldsmobile and he wasn't noticed. The minister drove to Rizzo's, a restaurant with its own parking lot, and the three entered as Mulrooney watched, parked a block away. They were out again just after ten o'clock and Mulrooney followed the Oldsmobile to the Harbor Lights Motel, a perfect location as far as he was concerned. The upscale motel was located near the service road of the Belt Parkway, it had its own parking lot, and judging from the number of cars parked there, it didn't appear to be anywhere near full occupancy. He watched as the minister pulled away after dropping off Frieda and her bodyguard. She went into Room 137, the corner unit, while the bodyguard stood in front of Room 136, having a smoke.

Mulrooney parked in the lot of a shopping center a block away and returned in time to see the bodyguard enter Room 136.

The hotel clerk was at his desk at 4:30 A.M., enjoying a small snooze, when he felt something hard and metallic pressed against his forehead. He knew he was in real trouble even before he opened his eyes to stare at the man across the desk from him. When he did, his terror abated slightly. Though a large pistol with a silencer attached was at his head, the brute holding the gun and leaning across the desk was smiling and appeared to be congenial. The clerk had been robbed twice before during his ten years of working the night shift, but this man didn't seem as bad as those other crack-crazed robbers.

"You feeling cooperative this morning?" Mulrooney asked.

"Especially cooperative, sir. The place is yours, anything you want."

"Then this should be fairly easy for you. What's your name?"

"Issac Markman."

"Issac, I want you to give me the pass key, I want you to draw a diagram of Rooms 136 and 137, and I want you to give me your car keys. Would you do all that for me?"

"Anything. The pass key's in the desk drawer in front of me," Issac said without moving. "There's a pen and paper in there, too."

"That's good for both of us."

Five minutes later Issac attached a note to the front door of the office as Mulrooney watched. It read "Family Emergency—be back in two hours." Issac turned out the lights and locked the office, then the two walked down the motel's exterior walkway to Room 136. Mulrooney's gun was out of sight, tucked into the front of his pants under his jacket, but that meant nothing to Issac. He knew the man could easily snap him in half.

Mulrooney returned the pass key to Issac and took out his gun again. "Open the door, Issac," he ordered softly.

"I'm not going to do it if you're going to kill them. I won't be party to murder," Issac whispered, trembling as he stared into Mulrooney's eyes. "If you're going to kill me, do it now."

Mulrooney's smile broadened as he measured the small man in front of him. "Issac, I'm not going to kill anyone unless I have to. I just need some information from them. Once I get it, I'm out of your hair and out of their hair."

"Honest?" Issac asked, wanting to believe.

"Honest Injun. Let's get this over with."

Issac turned and inserted the key into the lock. He swung the door open as far as he could and everything was as Mulrooney had expected. The room was dark and the security chain was on.

Mulrooney suddenly gave Issac a hard shove from behind. The force broke the security chain, swung the door wide open, and propelled Issac into the room. There was a single gunshot, a muzzle flash, and Issac moaned as he fell to the floor.

From the door, Mulrooney fired three times at the source of the muzzle flash, his silenced pistol making more noise than he would have liked. Then he stood back, outside the room, and listened. The only sound he heard was Issac's labored breathing. Without entering the room, he reached into it and turned on the lights. He was satisfied at the sight that greeted him as he peered in. Issac was on the floor, shot in his left side. The bodyguard was sitting up in bed, his revolver still in his hand, eyes open in surprise, and dead with three holes in his chest.

Mulrooney entered, shooting Issac in the head as he stepped over him. He stopped at the connecting door between Rooms 136 and 137, took another gun from his belt, stepped back, and kicked at the doorknob. The door swung open to reveal Frieda getting out of bed in the lighted room. Mulrooney was disappointed to note that she was wearing a flannel granny nightgown. He fired once and the tranquilizer dart lodged in her back. She tried to pull it out, but couldn't reach it. She gave up and turned to face him, her eyes already glassing over.

"Lay down and don't scream," Mulrooney ordered, but she ignored him as she began to wobble. Mulrooney crossed the room and stood in front of her. She raised her hand to hit him, but the drug was taking effect and slowing her reflexes. He easily avoided the blow and pushed her onto the bed. He waited and watched. Within a minute, Frieda's breathing became regular. Her eyes were open, but she was unconscious and would be for half an hour.

Mulrooney went outside and placed DO NOT DISTURB signs on the door-knobs of both rooms. He left the door of Room 137 slightly ajar, then walked across the street and waited. He was mildly concerned that someone might have heard the bodyguard's shot, but after ten minutes he realized he had succeeded. No police. He whistled merrily as he walked to his car for his toolbox.

THIRTY

MONDAY, MARCH 16TH—GREENWICH VILLAGE

McKenna was up with Angelita at 6:00 A.M., one minute after the twins had loudly announced that they were awake, hungry, and ready for a new day. McKenna was in synch with their feelings. He felt well rested, recharged, hungry, and ready to get back to work. But first came the chores.

After the morning routine of changing diapers, feeding, burping, vom-iting, howling, feeding again, and changing diapers again was over, the twins decided that their father and mother had suffered just about enough for one session. The little devils went back to sleep, smiling and looking like angels in their bassinet.

Then Janine felt it was her turn to act up. Most of her toys and dolls had been left in the hotel and she had already filled all her coloring books with her artwork. She was bored and in a tizzy, feeling neglected and jealous of all the attention her new brothers had already received that morning, but Angelita knew how to deal with the situation. While McKenna made break-fast, Angelita sat with Janine in front of the TV, watching a PBS bilingual children's show.

Everything's going to be okay today, McKenna thought as he flipped flapjacks in the kitchen and listened. Janine was in the living room, squealing with delight as she watched her show. She had all the answers and knew all the words in both Spanish and English, and Angelita was being lavish in her praise of their smart little girl.

But McKenna was wrong. The day started going bad when he went out for the papers after breakfast. The *Post*'s banner headline was MCKENNA DINES MATA HARI AND . . . He paid for the paper and stood in front of the newsstand, reading.

Maggie Ferguson, a cog in the Troubles during her life, had been transformed by the tabloids into a superspy by her death. It was her picture under the headline that gave McKenna his first inkling that he was in for another tough day. A tourist had been especially impressed by her looks and he had snapped a photo of her while she had been standing in the lobby of the Conrad Hilton waiting for McKenna. Unfortunately, he had turned out to be a photographer with a sensible touch of greed; he had sold his photo to the Belfast, Dublin, and London tabloids.

The *Post* had also gotten into the deal, and in a rare departure from its black-and-white format, ran the photo on the front page in full color as a U.S. exclusive. A file photo of McKenna's face was placed as an inset in the corner of the Ferguson photo.

Maggie Ferguson had looked exceedingly beautiful in her sexy green dress in the last hours of her life. McKenna was certain that photo wasn't going to play well at home, but after reading the article inside, he knew that would play even worse.

The British and Irish reporters had been working hard, delving deep, cashing in favors, and putting on the pressure—so much pressure that they had gotten both Martin McGuinn and the British minister for defense to admit that Maggie Ferguson had been one of their agents. McGuinn had stated that he had heard from one of his unnamed sources that Ferguson had been an IRA agent infiltrated into British Intelligence. On the other hand, the minister for defense had claimed the opposite. Maggie Ferguson had been a British agent inserted into the IRA.

The Irish minister for home affairs had also been interviewed, and he scathingly denounced both the British and the IRA roles in the affair. He was disturbed that one or both had knowingly placed an agent in the Irish Ministry for Finance, an action he termed despicable. He promised that his government would get to the truth through its Special Panel of Inquiry and that appropriate diplomatic responses would be made.

Maggie Ferguson had certainly shaken up her world as she left it, McKenna thought. As he read on, he became more convinced that she had also shaken up his. It was implied in the article that it had been his fancy dress-up dinner with the beautiful spy that had brought matters to a head. The press had apparently also leaned heavily on the Garda, and some high-ranking Irish police official had collapsed under the pressure; the reasons for McKenna's visit to Dublin were spelled out, almost word for word, from his interview with O'Dougherty.

McKenna thought that his account regarding his walk after seeing Ferguson off at the hotel was taken at face value by the reporter, but the blockbuster and the reason for the suggestive headline were contained in the final three paragraphs of the article. They were rife with innuendo seemingly designed to ruin McKenna's life and reputation.

The first paragraph stated that although McKenna had claimed in his statement to the Irish police that Maggie Ferguson was happily married, concerted efforts by the press and the Garda had failed to turn up her supposed husband. The second paragraph disclosed that Ferguson's body had been autopsied and evidence of very recent sexual intercourse was present. The third described McKenna as married, the father of three children, and living at the Gramercy Park Hotel. The article closed by saying that although McKenna was back in town, all attempts by the press to contact him for interview or comment had failed.

McKenna was beside himself as he folded the paper and started walking. A prime example of the Paddy Factor at work, he thought. Maggie Ferguson leaves me to see if her husband has murdered her boss yet. There's no evidence of police activity outside O'Bannion's girlfriend's secret flat because O'Bannion isn't there. He's waiting outside Ferguson's flat to murder her. So what does she do? She knows she's looking good, she's had a few drinks so she's feeling good, she knows her girlfriend won't be around because she's in jail, she knows her husband is inside, probably tense and nervous, and she knows that O'Bannion's secret flat is, after all, a very nice place. So she parks her car and stops in for a calming quickie with the husband she hardly ever sees. Probably right in O'Bannion's bed, half an hour before her own life ended, she ruined mine!

McKenna searched for a way out. There were only two people in the world to whom he could tell his version of events, but feared that only one of them would believe him. He knew he could count on Brunette, but he realized that he wasn't so sure about Angelita when he noticed that he was walking away from his apartment with the newspaper, not toward it.

He stopped on a corner and stood reading the article again. It didn't get any better the second time around, but there was one bright spot that had nothing to do with his personal situation: No mention had been made of Mulrooney, which meant that none of the hundreds of cops working the case had blabbed to their favorite reporter.

One thing McKenna was sure of—he was not yet ready to bring the papers home. He stepped into the street and hailed a cab.

An hour and a half after he had left on his simple errand, McKenna brought the paper home to Angelita. Pao was there already, looking apprehensive, so McKenna knew that he had already read the *Post*. "Where have you been? We've both been worried sick about you?" Angelita said, so McKenna also knew that Pao hadn't mentioned the article to her.

"I took a cab to Health Services in Queens."

"Health Services? What for?" Angelita asked.

"To get a certified sample of my blood. It's on its way to Ireland right now."

"A blood sample? What for?"

McKenna placed the *Post* on the kitchen table. "Because there's an article in there that strongly hints that I had sex with Maggie Ferguson right before O'Bannion killed her. My blood sample will set the record straight."

Angelita sat down and stared at the page one photo of Ferguson for a full minute. Then she looked up at McKenna and she didn't look happy. "Passably pretty, huh?"

They were the exact words he had used to describe Maggie Ferguson to Angelita when he had finally told her about the dinner. He couldn't come up with an appropriate reply, so he and Pao just stood there shuffling their feet while Angelita read on.

When she had finished, she gave McKenna the shock of his life. She folded up the paper and flipped it across the kitchen and right into the trash can, a perfect ten-foot shot. McKenna had expected tears and a tantrum at the very least, but she just looked up at him, dry-eyed. "This is going to make things difficult for us for a while, but we both know what happened."

"You've figured it out already?" McKenna asked, prepared to be amazed once again at Angelita's reasoning powers.

"What's to figure out? Your sex-starved Maggie Ferguson saw that she couldn't have my husband, so she went over to O'Bannion's and threw her dopey husband a boff before she went home to die."

I love this woman! McKenna thought as he marveled at Angelita's intelligence, her faith in him, and her basic, though somewhat flawed, understanding of the complex situation. But then another interpretation of events had to be endured.

Pao, who couldn't possibly have had any idea what Angelita had been talking about, felt compelled to offer his support in his own way. "Yeah, that dumb nympho. I hope she managed to pass her horny husband one of her diseases before O'Bannion did her in."

Both Angelita and McKenna just stared at Pao, amazed and open-mouthed, not knowing what to say. Angelita was the first to laugh, but only beating McKenna by a second. He joined her, with Pao standing there straight-faced and wondering what he had said to provoke this round of merriment.

Sheeran was sitting on McKenna's desk, waiting for him, when McKenna arrived. The five detectives in the office all had their faces buried in copies of the *New York Post* and none of them seemed to notice McKenna. He stopped in front of his desk and Sheeran stood up and put an arm around McKenna's shoulders.

"Listen up, everybody. I've got an announcement to make," McKenna shouted.

Everyone looked up from their newspapers, all seeming to notice Mc-Kenna for the first time.

"I'm only going to say this once, and you can believe it or not," Mc-Kenna stated loudly. "I did not at any time boff Maggie Ferguson, nor did I even think of doing so."

All except for Cisco Sanchez continued staring at McKenna. He, instead, dramatically held his front page of his newspaper at eye level, looking from that knockout Maggie Ferguson photo to McKenna over and over while everyone watched him, center stage. Then he reached his conclusion and voiced the group's sentiments. "For heaven's sake, Brian! Why not? I sure would've."

And that was the simple truth of the matter. Cisco sure would have, everyone knew, but Cisco wasn't done with his analysis of the situation. He stood up and continued in rapid fashion. "I would have boffed her so long and so hard that O'Bannion would have died of old age waiting for her to come home. I would've saved the lovely señorita's life and ruined her for other men, as is my custom. If I had been the one in Ireland with this luscious Maggie Ferguson, she would now be alive and happily listed among the countless—"

"Thank you, Cisco," Sheeran said, but the way he said it left no doubt in anyone's mind that Cisco had just received a direct order to sit down and shut up.

Cisco did, but it was to a round of polite applause. Everyone watched as Cisco, whistling happily, took a pair of scissors from his desk and cut Maggie Ferguson's picture from the front page of his newspaper, taking special care to cut away the inset of McKenna's face from the photo. He then placed the photo on his desk and admired it lovingly for a moment. He stopped whistling only for the moment it took him to bend down and kiss the Ferguson photo. Then, whistling again, he placed it with special care in his top desk drawer.

All this time Cisco was seemingly oblivious to the attention he was getting. He stopped whistling and looked around the room at everyone looking at him. "What?" he asked innocently.

It was Sheeran who answered. "Cisco, I hate to be the one to break the news to you, but it seems to me that you're in love with a dead girl."

"Everyone knows that Cisco is not stupid, Inspector," Cisco replied indignantly. "He doesn't just look at the pretty pictures in the papers like many dumb detectives he knows. No, Inspector, Cisco reads the papers and knows all the hard words. So naturally Cisco knows that lovely Maggie Ferguson is untimely dead, but everyone knows that Cisco is a hopeless romantic and that Maggie Ferguson will live in his heart forever."

Everyone didn't know precisely that but everyone, including Sheeran and certainly McKenna, did know one thing through unfortunate experience: When Detective First Grade Cisco Sanchez got on his high horse and started speaking of himself in the third person, he was especially unbearable, but impossible to beat in any verbal contest.

All looked to Sheeran with bated breath, silently awaiting the inspector's response, and all were relieved when Sheeran wisely surrendered. "All the same, Cisco. I want to be the first to offer my condolences on your loss."

"Thank you, Inspector. Cisco graciously accepts your condolences, but he has a question. Who here could ever be foolish enough to think that a smart man like Brian McKenna would ever consider trying to boff one of Cisco's girls, especially his current lucky favorite?" Cisco played his eyes around the room, looking for a taker. "Stand up, you dummy, whoever you are, so Cisco and his pal Brian can expose your stupidity to the world."

It was suddenly and universally resolved that McKenna had indeed been telling the truth. Cisco gave him a smile and a regal nod, but remained seated as he busied himself with the *Times* crossword puzzle.

Minutes later, Cisco was the only one still seated. McKenna was at the end of the receiving line, accepting expressions of sympathy and support from everyone else until Sheeran dragged him into his office, closing the door behind them. Sheeran looked uncomfortably serious and McKenna guessed what was on his mind. "You've heard from a Constable O'Dougherty of the Irish police, haven't you?"

"Yes, I have," Sheeran said, obviously surprised. "He called for you this morning. You weren't here, so I took the call."

"And he asked you to tell me that I didn't have to, but he would appreciate it if I could send him a certified blood sample?"

"Exactly."

"Well, I don't want to talk to him right now. Could you do me a favor and call him back for me?" McKenna asked.

"Sure. What do you want me to tell him?"

"That a sample is already on the way to him, air express."

"You knew O'Dougherty was going to call this morning?"

"Hoped he would. It's gonna end a lot of uninformed, unwise speculation when they compare my blood to the semen found in Maggie Ferguson."

"Why don't you stop some of the speculation now and give a statement to the press right now?" Sheeran asked.

"Because I wouldn't give them the satisfaction and they wouldn't believe me anyway. I'd rather wait until they get the news from the other side."

"Not a bad idea, but I don't know if I'd be able to stand the kind of pressure you're gonna be under while you're waiting to be vindicated."

"No pressure because Angelita's behind me, so let's get down to real business. Have we gotten that beeper information from Page America yet?"

"I sent Mendez and Sophia to their office with a subpoena. They should've been back already, so they might've run into a problem."

Right on cue, there was a knock at the door. Joe Mendez and Joe Sophia came in. They had learned from Page America that Jack O'Reilly had purchased the three beepers and they had a three-page printout that listed all the return phone numbers that had been paged into them. They had also thought to stop by Tavlin's office to get the location of the phones and had written it next to each number.

"It's mostly pay phones, but there's a few interesting ones in there," Mendez explained. "There's Mulrooney's cell phone, O'Reilly's house, the Pioneer Pub, and a new player in Woodlawn. Lady by the name of Brenda McDermott, residence of 889 East 220th Street, apartment 4A. Tavlin says she's had the phone for five years."

McDermott? Where have I heard that name recently? McKenna wondered. Then it came to him. "She's probably connected to Crowley. The name he's using on his bogus British passport is Kiernan McDermott."

After Mendez and Sofia left, Sheeran and McKenna went over the list of the locations of the pay phones. The beepers had been in use since O'Reilly had signed on with Page America on March 6th. Three of the pay phones in Woodlawn had been used more than once, and two of those were located in Irish taverns. The other was on the street. Every other number that had been paged to only once was on the street in Woodlawn, Midtown, Jackson Heights, or Levittown.

"So, what do you think?" Sheeran asked.

"They certainly like to stay in touch with each other, which tells us that they're not together all the time," McKenna said. "Probably living in different places. I'd say we have to put a few more surveillances and another wire in place."

"You're right. The wire on Brenda McDermott and the surveillances on her place and the other three Woodlawn phones," Sheeran said, looking very unhappy.

"What's the matter?" McKenna asked. "I'm the one who has to type up the applications and go to court for another eavesdropping warrant."

"What's the matter is that I'm running out of people. We're stretched to the limit, everybody's on overtime, and none of our regular cases are getting worked. Now we've got another wire and four more surveillances and I don't know where I'm gonna get the manpower from."

It was a complaint McKenna had never heard before. In a department of forty thousand people with four thousand detectives, getting enough people to work any mission on overtime had never been a problem. "How many people we got working on this now?"

"I stopped counting at a hundred and twenty."

"Can't you raid the precinct squads for more people?"

"I could, but then our operation here would be common knowledge all over the Job. It wouldn't take the press long to find out what we're up to."

"How about the Intelligence Division?"

"They've already offered me ten people, so maybe I can squeeze twenty out of them by tomorrow. Makes no difference, I'm still gonna have to start cutting corners now to keep all the surveillances and the Brit locations covered."

"Glad I'm not the boss," McKenna said. "Mind if I use your phone to make a few more international calls?"

"Go ahead. You going to find out who Brenda McDermott is for us?"

"Gonna try." His first call was to Peg Maher in Dublin. He got Kevin Hughes's phone number in Belfast and called him.

"What can I do for you, McKenna?" Hughes said bluntly.

"Can you get a hold of Martin McGuinn right away?"

"No, I'd say not. After they cornered him last night, he's hiding again from the press, thanks to you."

McKenna ignored the implied criticism. "Okay. Maybe you can help me. Do you know a Brenda McDermott?"

"I don't think so. Why?"

"How about Kiernan Crowley? Do you know him?"

"Used to know him, but heard he's off to America. Is he running with Mulrooney?"

McGuinn had told Kevin about Mulrooney, McKenna realized, but knew the secret was safe with him. "He sure is, and he's set to cause us some problems."

"Ah! Then I'm thinking that it might be his ex-wife, Brenda, who you're asking about. But that Brenda's last name was never McDermott. She was a MacAlary before she was a Crowley. Good republican family."

McKenna promised himself that he would scream if he ever again heard somebody say *"good republican family."* "Why is she his *ex*-wife? What happened between them?"

"Kiernan surely loved that woman, loved her so much that he divorced her before he went to the Maze to do ten years. Told her she had to get on with her life. I'd heard that she'd gone to America some years back."

"Did she love him as much as he loved her?"

"It looked to me like she did."

"Do you know what she's doing here?" McKenna asked.

"Working hard at being one of your illegal immigrants, I imagine. That would account for the phony name she's using. But I can tell you this. She was a nurse when she was here, and a damned good one."

"Thanks, Kevin. You've been a big help," McKenna said, then hung up.

"Brenda's a nurse and the love of Crowley's life," he told Sheeran. "Now, if you don't mind, I'll leave you to your misery and go visit our judge."

"And then?"

"That's it for me today, Inspector. I'll take a break and then I'm picking up Thor at the airport at nine. After dinner with him, I'm going to try to get another good night's sleep."

"Before you go, I've got a question for you."

"Shoot."

"I was wondering if you know who stuck it to Maggie before O'Bannion killed her," Sheeran said.

"I do, and I'll tell you right now, but only if you insist. In any event, I promise to tell you later."

"Why not right now? Because I wouldn't want to know?"

"Exactly. If I told you now, I'd have to tell you everything. Believe me, I don't want you sharing the burden I'm carrying."

"Then when?"

"Probably when we're both older, grayer, and wiser, but certainly before they close the box on either one of us. We'll sit down over a couple a drinks and I'll explain the whole thing to you."

"But you don't drink," Sheeran observed.

"I will then. Special occasion and Irish whiskey for both of us, one time."

"When's *then* gonna be?"

"When there's finally peace in Ireland and nobody cares about the filthy things people like you and I knew and did during their long, miserable, bloody, little war."

"That's a deal," Sheeran said, then both men got a shock when Brunette walked in, an extraordinary event. Cops, detectives, and bosses went to see the police commissioner, he never went to see them. The look on Brunette's face screamed Bad News.

Suddenly, McKenna received a horrible premonition. "Frieda?" he asked.

"Yes, Frieda and Haarold Sigmarsson. He got them both," Brunette said.

"Where?"

"The Harbor Lights Motel in Brooklyn. He did the night clerk, too."

"Is it bad?" McKenna asked, feeling foolish as soon as he asked the question.

Brunette knew what he meant. "Horrible, I'm told. He had his way with her for a long time."

"Who's there now?" Sheeran asked.

"Brooklyn South Homicide and the ME. I told them to leave everything in place until you get there."

The thought of going to this particular homicide scene sickened Mc-
Kenna and he searched for a way out. He stood there, speechless, as he
ran questions and excuses through his mind. Prime among the questions
was: How did Mulrooney find her? but the answer came to him quickly.
The monster had read about her visit in the Icelandic press and had followed her from the church to the hotel. How much had Frieda told him?
was another quick question, but that answer was also apparent. Under the
kind of torture Mulrooney loved administering, she told him everything she
knew—meaning he now knows that we're on to him.

The excuses McKenna came up with lacked the quality of the questions.
He had to go to Brooklyn. He took a deep breath and turned to Sheeran.
"Ready?"

"Not for this, but let's go."

THIRTY-ONE

McKenna thought he was prepared for the worst, but he wasn't. The crime
scene was more horrible and more bizarre than anything he had ever wit-
nessed before. Frieda was naked on the bed, her wrists and ankles bound with
strips of torn sheets, gagged with cloth torn from her flannel nightgown. Her
ears, her fingers, and her nipples were gone, her vagina was spread open and
slit to her navel, her teeth had been knocked out, and cigarette burns covered
her face and body. Cut into her upper chest was a bloody message inscribed
in small letters: "Thor, this is one tough woman you had. Thank you."

There were additional affronts to Frieda's dignity perpetrated by Mulrooney. He had ripped out her tongue and inserted it in her rectum and
he had positioned the bodies of Haarold Sigmarsson and the night clerk as
silent spectators to Frieda's torture and death. They were seated in chairs
on either side of the bed, each with a Coke in one hand and a candy bar
in the other, a smile fixed upon their faces.

Sheeran had ordered all the many detectives, bosses, crime scene tech-
nicians, and ambulance attendants from the room when he and McKenna
had arrived, so the two men were the only live people there. "How can I
show Thor this?" McKenna asked.

"It's horrible and I'm glad I'm not in your shoes, but I'm going to break
some rules to make it a little better," Sheeran stated. He went to the door
and called the Brooklyn South Homicide commander into the room. Lt.
Ronnie Perugine was a tough guy, famed for his competence and respected
for his press connections.

"How did we find out about this?" Sheeran asked.

Perugine explained, quickly and concisely. The desk clerk had last been seen alive at 4:10 A.M. when he had rented a room to a couple from Ohio. At 5:55 A.M. a 62nd Precinct unit responded to the motel on the complaint of another prospective guest. The cops took the note on the door at face value and advised the man to seek accommodations at another hotel. He did, but another 62nd Unit was back at 8:05 A.M., called by the relieving day clerk. According to him, Issac Markman was reliable, a long-time employee, a man who would never leave the motel unattended. He had called Markman's wife and she had no knowledge of his whereabouts.

The cops were perplexed but not overly concerned since Markman's car was missing and all the night's proceeds were still in the register. They conducted a cursory inspection of the premises, found nothing amiss, called Markman's wife, and asked her to come to the station house to prepare a missing persons report.

The bodies were discovered by one of the motel's maids at 11:05 A.M. She had disregarded the DO NOT DISTURB sign, knocked on the door, received no answer, and fainted dead away after entering Room 137. No one else had been interviewed since all the motel's other guests had already checked out by the time the detectives arrived. In short, Perugine was convinced he was facing a difficult investigation, made even worse because out of the blue, he had already received a call from the PC on the case, the press was straining for information on the sensational killings, and now the CO of the Major Case Squad was standing in front of him, asking him questions. "It looks like I'm in for a tough time on this one," Perugine stated at the conclusion of his report.

"Yes, you are, but not as tough as you think," Sheeran said.

"Pardon?"

"It's not your case, it's a Major Case Squad investigation."

"Great, especially since you've already got half my men working for you. But why is this burden being lifted from me, if you don't mind my asking?"

"Because we know who did it and we're going to get him. Now, how much does the press know?"

"So far, just what they've got from our radio. They know we've got a very gruesome scene in here, two dead men and a horribly tortured woman."

"Then here's what I want you to tell them. Nothing, except for the identities of the victims. Nothing about motive. Nothing about Haarold Sigmarsson being an Icelandic cop. Nothing about the message carved into her chest. Nothing. You got it?"

McKenna could see that it was the toughest order Perugine had ever received. Nothing to his many pals in the press? How would he pull that off? McKenna wondered.

So did Perugine, but he appeared to take it in stride. "Okay, but let me tell you a few things you may not realize. First of all, I didn't know the guy was a cop until you told me. Second, I have no idea of motive or why you're here taking my case. Third, you just ruined the rest of my life. Having reporters mad at you can be very damaging to a career."

"Then tell your pals in the press that it's all my fault," Sheeran suggested. "I've got one more thing for you. Do you know a good funeral director?"

"Sure. Timmy Burns at Cooks. He's the best and a retired cop besides."

"Good. Then he gets the woman as soon as we leave. She's a cop's wife. I want her cleaned up and presentable by tonight."

"She doesn't go to the morgue?" Perugine asked, shocked at this breach in procedure."

"No, straight to Cooks is where she's going. This is a special case and she was a special person. Can you do that?"

"You tell me to do it, I do it. I take it this killer isn't going to be arrested and this case isn't going to court, is it?"

"No."

"But you are going to get him?"

Sheeran nodded to McKenna for the answer.

"If it takes me the rest of my life," McKenna stated simply, but both Perugine and Sheeran realized he had just taken a solemn oath. McKenna was going to slay the monster or die trying.

Perugine would make the notification to Mrs. Markman, but the job of telling Thor about Frieda and Haarold fell to McKenna in an unexpected way. The phone rang in Room 137 just as Sheeran and McKenna were leaving, and McKenna picked it up. "Brian?" Thor asked, surprised to hear McKenna's voice.

"Hello, Thor," McKenna said, a chill running up his spine.

Thor caught something in McKenna's voice. "Is Frieda there?" he asked, a trace of alarm in his voice.

"Yes, she is, but I've got some very bad news for you."

"Mulrooney got her?" Thor asked, guessing at the worst.

There was only one possible answer and no way to soften the blow. "Yes."

"Did he make her suffer?"

"Yes," McKenna answered, his eyes fixed on Frieda's tortured body.

"Horribly?"

"Yes."

"As bad as Meaghan?"

"Yes."

"And Haarold?"

"He got him, too, but Haarold didn't suffer."

There was a long pause and McKenna couldn't think of a thing to say to fill it. "Did Mulrooney make any mistakes, anything that will bring us closer to getting him?" Thor asked, all business.

"None that I can see."

"I'm at Keflavík Airport now and my flight leaves in ten minutes, so I'll have to ask Janus to notify Haarold's wife for me. You still picking me up at JFK tonight?"

"I'll be there."

"Thank you. Keep working hard and stay focused. I'll see you tonight," Thor said, then hung up.

"Well?" Sheeran asked.

"That man is righteous ice, an avenging knight with a mission. I wouldn't want to be Mulrooney right now," McKenna said, then hung up the phone.

As usual, court was crowded and it took McKenna forever to get in to see the judge and get his eavesdropping warrant for Brenda McDermott's phone signed. Also as usual in this case, the wire was already in place well before the warrant was signed, so it really didn't matter. But McKenna didn't get a break and he had to rush to the airport to pick up Thor in time at nine o'clock. He made it and was parked in front of the terminal when Thor came out carrying two suitcases.

McKenna didn't know what to say to the man as he got out of the car and opened the trunk, but Thor removed the burden from him. "How you holding up?" Thor asked.

"Not well. Yourself?"

"I'm going to be fine until we get him. After that, I can't say. Where is she?"

"In a funeral home in Brooklyn."

"Not the morgue?"

"No, not the morgue."

"Thank you," Thor said. He placed his suitcases in the trunk and McKenna closed it.

"Tell me everything, Brian. Please, leave nothing out. I can take it," Thor said as soon as they got into the car. "Tell me what he did to my Frieda and then take me to the funeral home."

It was something McKenna had been dreading, but he did as Thor asked.

Although the funeral home was closed by the time they got there, Timmy Burns was waiting for them in front of his place. He was solicitous and caring, the perfect professional funeral director. "I'm sorry to have put you to this trouble," Thor said, surprising both Burns and McKenna.

"I was happy to be of service," Burns answered as soon as he recovered.

"Please take me to Frieda and then I'd like to be alone with her for a while," Thor said.

McKenna waited outside while Burns took Thor into the funeral home. After a few minutes, Burns joined McKenna outside and they both waited for an uncomfortable half hour while Thor did whatever he was doing inside with Frieda. Under the circumstances, small talk seemed inappropriate, so both men kept their thoughts to themselves. When Thor finally emerged, McKenna thought he looked even bigger and stronger than usual. Thor was a very tough man.

"I don't know how I'll ever be able to repay you for the kindness you've shown," Thor said to Burns and offered his hand.

Once again, Burns didn't know what to say. He shook Thor's hand without comment and looked relieved when McKenna and Thor got into the car.

McKenna had many questions on his mind, but he didn't voice them as he headed toward Manhattan. After an embarrassing ten-minute silence, Thor said, "You're wondering how much Frieda knew about Mulrooney, aren't you?"

"Yes, I am. It's something we have to talk about."

"She knew everything I know about Mulrooney, but I know my Frieda. She told him nothing. He tried his best to get it out of her, but he still doesn't know that we know he's Mike Mullen."

Anyone else who could have seen Frieda's tortured body would have doubted Thor's sanity upon hearing his opinion on Frieda's ability to withstand pain, but not McKenna. He knew Thor, he knew Frieda, and he took Thor's statement at face value; Mulrooney still doesn't know the NYPD is on to him and listening in on his phone calls. It was the only news with the slightest hint of promise McKenna had received that day.

McKenna drove to the Plaza Hotel on Fifth Avenue and Central Park South and parked across the street. There was a mounted cop on post there and McKenna gave him the car keys and asked him to keep an eye on the car. No problem.

Thor checked in and then insisted McKenna join him for dinner in the Edwardian Room. McKenna was surprised that Thor could think of food after the day he had just been through, but he took it in stride since the Edwardian Room was the Plaza's best restaurant and one of his favorite places to eat.

McKenna thought he would be consoling his friend while they both enjoyed a fine dinner, but it wasn't to be. Rollins called his cell phone just as their salads arrived.

"You might have some trouble brewing on your end," Rollins said. "Mulrooney called his father for what sounded to me like a final farewell. Said he might never see him again."

"How did his father take that?" McKenna asked.

"He's hard, almost like he expected it. Wished his son luck and told him to do his duty. Said he was proud of him, but warned him that traitors in the IRA were looking for him."

"What was Mulrooney's reaction to that?"

"Said he already knew about the traitors and he was being careful, but there's more. The old man mentioned something that really interested Mulrooney, and I think you'll find it quite interesting as well. Seems that there's two men missing in Donegal, a boat captain named Learey and his first mate. This Learey had two fine boats and they're also missing."

Have to play this one close, McKenna thought. "Would one of those boats have been a fifty-six-foot sport fisherman?" he asked.

"I'm still trying to find out for sure, but I think that's a safe assumption. What's more important to you is that Mulrooney told his father that he didn't believe in accidents. He said he smelled a rat."

McKenna was getting a call-waiting beep. "Thanks for the info, Inspector, but I have to go. Somebody else is waiting to tell me the same things you just did."

"Really? How?" Rollins asked.

"I'll explain it all later," McKenna said, then switched to the waiting call.

"We've got problems," Brunette said.

"I know. I got it from Rollins's wire on the father in Belfast. It looks like Mulrooney's getting suspicious."

"Worse than that. I think Frieda talked and he's on to us."

"She didn't."

"How can you be sure?" Brunette asked.

"Thor's sure she didn't talk, so I'm sure."

"Well, that's the only bright spot in a dismal picture, but listen to this. After Mulrooney called his father, he called Dennis Hunt. Said he wanted a meeting right away to give him more money for his kids. I haven't heard the tapes yet, but either Hunt blew it or we did. Mulrooney never showed, but I have a feeling he was there, watching us set up to take him."

A lot's been happening since I left the office, McKenna realized. Sheeran would have called me with any news as it happened, but he's home sleeping. "When did Mulrooney call his father?" McKenna asked Brunette.

"About two and a half hours ago. Eight-twelve."

"Did he use Winthrop's phone?"

"Yep. He was someplace in Fort Lee, New Jersey, when he called."

"And when did he call Hunt?"

"Half hour later. Eight-forty-six, again with Winthrop's phone. By then he was in Yonkers. He told Hunt to meet him in a gas station at McLean Avenue and the Bronx River Parkway at nine-thirty."

McKenna knew the area. It was well lit, right on the NYC-Yonkers border, but was residential and not too busy at nine-thirty at night. "Did Hunt call you or did you just get it off the wire on his phone?"

"I'm happy to say he called me at headquarters, but I was home. The duty chief gave him my home number and I authorized the operation after I spoke to Hunt. We had six teams in the Bronx and Mulrooney had given us enough time to set them all up in a hurry, so I told Hunt to go meet him. It was my call and my mistake."

"Where are you now?" McKenna asked.

"McLean Avenue, but I'll be on the way to the office in a minute. Where are you?"

"The Edwardian Room. I was getting ready to have a late dinner with Thor, but we need a damage control meeting. I have to return my car to headquarters anyway, so we'll meet you there as soon as I pay the check for the dinner we're not having."

"No, finish dinner and meet me after. I want to listen to those tapes by myself, first. Then I think I'm gonna need a little while to get my story straight for you."

Now isn't this a switch? McKenna thought. For the first time in the long history of the NYPD, the police commissioner is worried about getting his story straight for one of his detectives. "Don't worry about it, Ray. If the chance to get Mulrooney tonight had come my way, I would have made the same decision you did. I'd have jumped at the chance and we'd be in the same shape."

"Nice of you to say so, but I don't know," Brunette said dejectedly. "Now I need a big favor from you."

"Anything."

"See if you can find a way to leave Thor at the hotel. He's already seen enough of our dirty laundry and I don't want him peeking into this mess I've made tonight in the mood he must be in."

McKenna looked across the table at Thor. The big man was eating his salad, appearing calm, content, and uninterested in McKenna's phone conversation and the consternation it was causing him. He caught McKenna staring at him, gave him a wink, and resumed eating his salad.

This Thor is one cool character, McKenna thought. He must know from listening in that we're in trouble with this case, but he's too polite to show his concern with our mistakes. "I'll see what I can do, but it won't be easy," McKenna told Brunette, then pressed End.

"This salad is really very good," Thor said, then paused. "Could you please give my regards to Commissioner Brunette and explain to him that I'm too tired to meet him tonight. I need some rest and some time alone, so tell him that I want to look my best when I meet him."

Meaning you want us to look *our* best when you meet him, McKenna thought. This guy is almost *too* tough, *too* polite, and *too* astute to be true, thank God. "Okay, I'll tell him."

"Better get started on that salad or you won't be finished with it when our steaks arrive."

When McKenna arrived he found Brunette at his desk looking dejected. A cassette player was on the desk in front of him. "How's your pal Thor holding up?" he asked.

"On the surface, unbelievably well, but I get the feeling I'm witnessing a controlled nuclear explosion when I look at him."

"Do you trust him to perform without going crazy?"

"Absolutely. The time to worry about him is when this is all over. Until then, he's still a big plus for us."

"Then that's when we'll worry about him, when all this is over," Brunette said, considering that matter closed. "Now on to the most recent disaster. After listening to the tapes and thinking hard, I can't come up with a single excuse. Mulrooney set us up and we should have known better."

"You sure? It wasn't Frieda, but maybe something else spooked him," McKenna offered, seeking to console his friend.

Brunette was in no mood to be consoled. "Just listen to the tape."

McKenna took a seat and Brunette turned on the machine. The call from Mulrooney to his father had gone just as Rollins had described, but McKenna could hear the suspicion in Mulrooney's voice when he had said, "Da, I think I smell a rat."

The call to Hunt was next and Hunt's wife had answered. "Hello, Mrs. Hunt. This is Lieutenant Finan," Mulrooney had said, without a brogue and using the name of the CO of the Bomb Squad. "Is Dennis there?"

"Hold on, Lieutenant. I'll get him for you."

There was a pause before Hunt had come on the line. "Yeah, Lou. What can I do for you?"

"Hello, Dennis me boy. How are you?" Mulrooney had asked, but the Northern brogue was now there, strong.

There was a pause before Hunt had answered and McKenna could imagine Hunt's surprise at hearing Mulrooney's voice. "Fine. Is that you, Mike?"

"Sure it's me. You busy at the moment?"

There was another pause before Hunt had answered. "Kind of. Where are you?"

"I just got into town, but I could be to your place in half an hour."

"You're in New York?" Hunt had asked, and McKenna could hear the terror in his voice.

"Sure I am. Just leaving the airport and looking to spend some time with an old friend," Mulrooney had answered cheerfully.

"Mike, I don't know what you're up to, but leave me out of it. Please, leave me out of it," Hunt had pleaded.

"Why? You don't think they're still watching you, do you?" Mulrooney had asked, sounding unconcerned.

"No, of course not. You're gone and forgotten after all these years," Hunt had answered, but McKenna didn't think he had sounded convincing at all.

Mulrooney hadn't seemed to notice. "All right, I'll tell you what. If you're worried, I'll meet you someplace else in your neighborhood. Seems to me I remember a gas station at McLean and the Bronx River Parkway. That place still there?"

"Yeah, it's still there."

"Good. I should be there by nine-thirty."

There was another pause before Hunt spoke. "What is it you need from me?"

"Same as always. I've got some money for Kathleen and the kids that I want you to pass on to them."

"Okay, but couldn't we make it a little later? I just got up and it'll take me a while to get myself together."

"And here am I, always saying what a good pal Dennis Hunt is, never thinking of himself and always ready to do a friend a favor. I don't care what you look like when you get there, but I'm a little pressed for time. Can I count on you for this one last favor?"

"Yeah, Mike. You can always count on me. Don't worry, I'll be there," Hunt had said before hanging up.

Brunette shut the cassette player off. "Dopey, huh?"

"We know now it was a mistake, but not necessarily dopey," McKenna said. "Remember, hindsight is always twenty-twenty."

"Not good enough and I'm responsible. I never should have authorized that operation without hearing the tape. Unless I'm dopier than I think, I would've seen he was setting us up to see how hot he was and how much we knew."

"Who was our commander on the ground?" McKenna asked.

"Kotowski, but the blame's not his. Tonight was his first night working this case, so he doesn't know Mulrooney like Sheeran does."

McKenna considered Capt. Abe Kotowski to be sharper than most bosses in the Bureau, sharp enough to deserve his place as XO of the Major Case Squad, but not as sharp as Sheeran. Unfortunately in this instance,

Sheeran couldn't be there all the time, so Kotowski always worked opposite hours from him when a big operation was running. "Can you tell me how it all went down?" McKenna asked.

"Kotowski was in Midtown when the base notified him of the phone call. He hadn't heard the tape either, but he knew that he had to get to the Bronx in a hurry. He radioed the teams and got them on the way, and then he called me for permission to proceed. I gave it and—"

"Gave it, just like you should have," McKenna said.

Brunette smiled sardonically at McKenna. "Thanks. I gave it and things started going bad at that point. Now, imagine Mulrooney's there right after he finishes talking to Hunt. He was probably hiding in the woods by the Bronx River Parkway, watching the gas station. Next thing he sees is a car pull up to the station and two guys wearing suits get out. He certainly knows what cops look like, so he's not surprised when our two men go into the gas station to talk to the two guys working there. Then he sees them all go into the back, but what do you think he sees when they all come out again?"

"Two miserable detectives dressed as gas station attendants and two gas station attendants proudly wearing their new suits."

"Exactly. Then another team pulls up and two more guys in suits take the two new guys in suits and both cars out of there in a hurry. That's all Mulrooney had to see, if he even waited around that long. He calmly walked a couple of blocks to his car, humming to himself and secure in the knowledge that he's smarter than the police commissioner of the city of New York."

"Then that's too bad for him, 'cause he's not. He's been caught before by IAD, by people who certainly aren't as smart as you. But I think you're still not giving him enough credit."

"I'm not?" Brunette asked. "What I think I just told you is that I'm ready to build an altar for this guy to sacrifice chickens and goats to him, so what am I missing?"

"I've seen how the IRA operates in Northern Ireland, so I'm sure he hung around in the woods for a while longer while the rest of our teams were setting up."

"Doing what?"

"Playing with his scanner. There had to be lots of radio traffic between the teams while they were setting up, and he knew there would be. He hung around long enough to pick up the strongest radio signal, the one closest to his location. Now he's got our exact frequency and he's listening in."

"You're right, Brian," Brunette said, looking very unhappy. "Mulrooney *is* listening in and that's sure gonna make things tougher for us."

"Only at first. We can't contact the teams we've got out there right now and tell them to change frequencies because he'd know right away. We've got to wait until the tour change, which is when?"

"Four A.M. You thinking of running a little disinformation campaign on him?"

"Sure am. I hear that the FBI's got some radios that operate on frequencies so high that they can't be picked up by ordinary police scanners."

"They do," Brunette said. "I'll call Gene Shields at home and get all the radios he can spare."

"If you can. Then everybody working after four this morning should be using an FBI radio, but Mulrooney won't know that. We need lots of voices up here after four to lull him into a false sense of security. We can't let him know that we've changed frequencies on him."

"Okay, you and I will write the script. But he knows we know that he's our Mike Mullen and he has to figure that we're watching his wife and kids."

"Now he does, so tomorrow's operation is gonna be a bust. But I'd still watch his kids real closely in case he tries to snatch them from under our noses."

"We'll sure be doing that. Seems to me that the only connections to Mulrooney we've got left are Jack O'Reilly, Ambery's sister, Brenda McDermott, and Winthrop's phone."

"That's it, but now he's really suspicious and looking real close at everyone and everything," McKenna said. "Let's make sure we do nothing that tells him we're still here, working hard, and in the game."

"If there still is a game. Since he knows we're on to him, maybe he'll clear out and go blow up something in somebody else's city," Brunette said, almost sounding hopeful.

"Not this boy. You heard that farewell message to his father. He's out with the IRA, and with O'Bannion gone, there might no longer be an Irish Army Continuity Council to hide him out. He's got very few places in the world left to run to, so this is it for him—End Game, win or lose."

"Since he knows we know who he is, there's no longer any reason to keep the press in the dark. We've still got time to make the morning editions, so by tomorrow morning I'm gonna have his face plastered on the front page of every paper in town. I'm also going to connect him to the killings in Brooklyn and give some details about the horrible things he did there. By the time I'm done tonight, Michael Mulrooney will be the most-wanted man in the history of this city."

"Are you gonna tell them about all the other bombings and killings we've connected him to?"

"Might as well take all my medicine in one dose. I'm gonna have to tell them that one of our fired detectives, somebody we've been looking for and haven't been able to find, has been doing bombings and horrible murders all over the world. Then you can give them the details and pay back your debt to McGuinn. Exonerate his IRA and distance them from Mulrooney any way you like."

"Good idea, but could you do me a favor?"

"Sure."

"Could you leave me out of this midnight press conference of yours? You do all the explaining and I promise that I'll read every word you say in the morning papers."

"You really want to leave me up there explaining and answering questions all by myself?"

"Yeah, and I'd really owe you if you'd do that."

"Yes, you really will. They think they've already given you your lumps and now it's my turn. I'm in for a real bruising."

THIRTY-TWO

ST. PATRICK'S DAY—JACKSON HEIGHTS, QUEENS

McKenna had been right. As far as Michael Mulrooney was concerned, he was in End Game. He felt refreshed after his fun with Frieda, but it hadn't helped as much as he had hoped. She had given him pleasure, but no information of any use to him. His world was closing in on him and he didn't care, except for one thing: He was determined to spend some time with his kids before it was over.

Before the episode on McLean Avenue, he had been reasonably certain of his plans. He would do his work and then leave with his boys. He had three expertly made passports under a clear family name, three airline tickets good for any flight from Boston to Bangkok, and enough money to last them for years in Thailand.

Now things were different, but he would still show them, just as he had shown Thor that Michael Mulrooney wasn't a man to be trifled with. Another big part of *them* was Brian McKenna, but he was unsure of his feelings toward the famous detective. He had met McKenna once or twice and liked him. McKenna hadn't been famous at the time, but he had enjoyed a good reputation in the department as a smart cop, a hard worker, and still a guy who could always be counted on to do the right thing. Those were all points in McKenna's favor because Mulrooney still liked NYC cops and deep down, still considered himself to be one of them.

However, Mulrooney's affection for The Finest didn't include IAD or the hierarchy, those self-righteous bosses who had looked down their noses at him and had shamed and hounded him out of the Job, the city, and the country. Them he hated, but that was another point in McKenna's favor. He knew that McKenna had once been forced to join the hierarchy, but had found a way to leave the weasels to become a cop again.

Of course, fate had made Mulrooney and McKenna enemies and placed them on opposite sides of the fence, but Mulrooney didn't mind. Having a worthy enemy to combat and outthink was one of the true pleasures in life, but Mulrooney never underestimated his opponents; he had decided to learn exactly how much McKenna knew about him before he proceeded with his mission.

That quest for knowledge had brought Mulrooney to his cousin's neighborhood at one o'clock in the morning, prepared for battle if need be. Wearing a long-haired wig, he had driven his stolen car at the speed limit down 73rd Street. He saw nothing suspicious on O'Reilly's block. There was nobody hanging around the deserted residential street and nobody sitting in any of the parked cars, but a brown commercial van parked at the curb a block away from the house aroused his interest. He had seen no one in it as he had passed, but knew that meant nothing. He had worked many surveillances himself during his time in Narcotics, frequently operating from a van that looked just like that one. Those vans came equipped with handy gadgets like periscopes, battery-operated heaters and coffee pots, and even Porta-Potties—all features designed to keep the detectives hiding in the back comfortable, alert, inconspicuous, and most important, inside.

Mulrooney decided to investigate further. He removed his wig and drove around the block and down 34th Avenue. As he approached 73rd Street, he shut off his lights and engine and coasted into a parking spot provided by a fire hydrant near the corner. He could see the van parked a block and a half away, so he opened his windows and watched it through his binoculars. From experience, he knew the one drawback inherent in the design of those surveillance vans. All those fancy gadgets were powered by a separate set of batteries, but on long surveillances through chilly nights, the engine had to be started from time to time to keep the heater battery charged and the temperature inside just right. It *was* a chilly night, so Mulrooney watched, listened, and waited with one scanner tuned to the Major Case Squad frequency and the other tuned to a published frequency he already knew, the regular band used by the local 114th Precinct.

Fifteen minutes later, one of Mulrooney's questions was answered. He saw a small puff of smoke drift from the van's exhaust pipe and even heard the engine crank loudly for a moment before it caught. After learning about his old partner Dennis Hunt, he was only mildly surprised to find that the

NYPD also had his cousin under surveillance. In fact, his first thought was that those detectives should get their van tuned up every once in a while.

Although he wasn't quite sure of Hunt's role and thought it possible that Hunt's phone was tapped without his knowledge, he didn't suspect treachery on O'Reilly's part. Rather, he attributed the NYPD presence on 73rd Street to good police work by Brian McKenna.

But how had McKenna found out about O'Reilly? Hunt didn't know he even had a cousin in New York, so he couldn't have tipped off McKenna. Only one other way came to mind, but Mulrooney wanted to be sure. He decided that further investigation and action was called for. He screwed his silencer onto his pistol and inserted the weapon into the large breakaway shoulder holster under his long overcoat. It was time to take a stroll and create some excitement for the detectives in the van.

Mulrooney had a general destination in mind and he arrived at it by walking a circuitous route. Five minutes later he was standing under a traffic light at 74th Street and 33rd Avenue, around the corner from the van. He waited patiently for a target to present itself, but the streets were deserted with no traffic in sight. Then an opportunity came from an unexpected quarter. A gray-haired white man wearing pajamas, a robe, and carrying a garbage bag left his house eight doors from the corner. He looked at Mulrooney for a second, then brought his trash to his garbage can at the curb.

It was an easy shot, but it was also a heavily Irish neighborhood and Mulrooney had time. He saw no need to kill some kindred soul from the Old Sod on St. Patrick's Day unless he had to, so he walked toward the man.

The old man stopped with the lid to his garbage can in his hand and some alarm showing on his face as he watched Mulrooney approach. He relaxed a bit when Mulrooney smiled and said, "Excuse me, sir. Could you tell me where Jack O'Reilly lives?"

"Sorry. Don't know the man, but I can tell you he doesn't live on this block. I've been living here forty-two years and I know everyone here."

"Thanks anyway. Sorry to bother you," Mulrooney said, then turned and walked back toward the corner. No brogue, so he turned, drew his pistol, and quickly fired one muffled shot when he heard the old man replace the lid on the can. Mulrooney was quite pleased with himself as the man slumped to the ground. It was a clean head shot, so the old man died without making a sound.

Mulrooney waited for a moment, looking up and down the street, and then another opportunity presented itself. He heard a car coming down 33rd Avenue and the light was red. The old Cadillac stopped at the light and Mulrooney could see that the sole occupant was the driver, a black woman in a nurse's uniform. No need to ask her any questions, he thought.

He raised his pistol and fired again. The bullet made some noise as it broke through the driver's-side window, entered her left ear, and lodged in her brain. She fell across the front seat.

However, there was a small problem. The woman's foot had slipped off the brake as she died and the car glided slowly across the intersection and hit a parked car. There was some noise as a result of the minor collision, but the sound still fell within acceptable parameters as far as Mulrooney was concerned. He liked showing off a bit, so for the sheer fun of it, he ran around the intersection shooting at the traffic lights. Nineteen seconds and twelve bullets later he had shot out each red, yellow, and green signal on each side of the traffic light.

That will give McKenna something to consider, Mulrooney thought as he reloaded. Fourteen targets hit and only fourteen shell casings lying on the ground. He holstered his gun and calmly resumed his stroll.

It took another five minutes for Mulrooney to return to his car, but he was gratified not to hear the sound of sirens as he walked. He again sat watching the van through his binoculars and listening to his scanners. If the detectives inside were any good, they would have two radios and would be monitoring two frequencies—the Major Case Squad's and the 114th Precinct's. He didn't have long to wait. As he had expected, it was the 114th's dispatcher who first got the news. "In the 114th Precinct, we have a report of two persons shot on the street at 74th Street and 33rd Avenue. One-fourteen units to respond?" came over his local scanner.

Three 114th Precinct units radioed the dispatcher that they were responding, and Mulrooney heard the sound of many sirens in the distance. The next transmission he heard pleased him and justified his faith in his detectives. "Team Nineteen to Headquarters Base."

"Go ahead, Team Nineteen."

"We're getting a report over the division radio of two persons shot at 74th Street and 33rd Avenue, right around the corner from us. Request permission to respond."

"Go ahead over and take a look, Team Nineteen. Let us know if it has anything to do with the subject."

"Will do."

Mulrooney was happy that the two detectives had decided to leave their van parked and run around the corner to his new crime scene. Everything was going according to plan. It looked like only one team had been assigned to the surveillance of O'Reilly's house for the slow evening hours, but one thing concerned him slightly. If this is Team Nineteen, exactly how many men does McKenna have hunting for me? he wondered. Must be hundreds.

He smiled. He's going to need them all if he's ever to get me, he thought. He opened the briefcase on the seat next to him and removed a small object he was very proud of, one half of his latest and greatest invention. It was a black metal rectangular box, about the size of a pack of cigarettes, and he had made many of them. There was a magnet attached to one flat side, the number 28 was painted on the other side, and a switch with a tiny LED light was on top. As the 114th Precinct patrol sergeant was reporting to the dispatcher that there were two dead civilians, both shot through the head, Mulrooney flipped the switch and the LED light shone a bright green. It was time to bring fun to a higher plane.

Mulrooney put his wig back on, started his car, and turned onto 73rd Street. As he passed 33rd Avenue, from the corner of his eye he caught a glimpse of many police cars a block away at his crime scene. When he got to the surveillance van, he stopped alongside and got out of his car. It took him only seconds to attach the magnet on his device to the gas tank of the van, and then he was back in his car and on his way again. He passed O'Reilly's house, drove four more blocks, and parked.

For another ten minutes Mulrooney waited in his car, listening to 114th Precinct units at 33rd Avenue and 74th Street request the medical examiner, the crime scene unit, and the duty captain. All were on their way, but Mulrooney was growing impatient. It was close to two o'clock and he had to meet Ambery and Crowley at three to complete the night's work. Then came the transmission he had been waiting for. "Team Nineteen to Headquarters Base," sounded through his Major Case Squad scanner.

"Go ahead, Team Nineteen."

"We're back on location."

"Those shootings have anything to do with our man?"

"There's a good chance of it, Base. One thing we can tell you is that there's a murderous marksman loose in this neighborhood. We're breaking out the big guns, so let us know anything you hear on your end."

"Will do, Team Nineteen."

Mulrooney opened his briefcase again and removed the other half of his invention. It had once been an ordinary cellular phone before he had modified it to fit his needs. He turned it on and the small LED screen lit up. Then he punched in the numbers 2 and 8 and they showed up on the screen, but were replaced by a seven-digit number after he pressed the Recall button. He put his invention on the seat next to him, then took Winthrop's phone from his pocket, turned it on, and dialed the information number for Washington, DC.

"Directory Assistance. What listing?" a mechanical voice asked.

"I'd like the home number for the British ambassador to the United States, please."

It took a moment for a real voice to come on the line. "I'm sorry, sir. The number you requested is unpublished. Would you like the general information number for the British Embassy?"

"No, that's all right. I just thought he'd like to know that a brown van on 73rd Street is going to blow up seconds from now," Mulrooney said. He turned off his phone, then picked up his invention again and looked in his rearview mirror. He was too far away to make out the van at the moment, but knew he'd be able to see it shortly.

"Team Nineteen, Team Nineteen, get out of the van! He's close to you and he's got it wired to blow!" came over the Major Case Squad scanner, again and again.

That transmission clearly answered Mulrooney's second question. Ah, McKenna, you do have my phone. You're a cagey bastard, so you are, he said to himself as he kept his eyes glued to his rearview mirror and his finger poised over the Send button of his invention. "Kill them, don't kill them? Kill them, don't kill them?"

Mulrooney decided not to kill Team Nineteen after all. He figured the two detectives would be miserable enough toiling over paperwork for the next month, at least.

"Team Nineteen to Base, we're clear. We're clear and running," was the transmission Mulrooney heard before he pressed his Send button. Then he saw the van in his rearview mirror, brightly and briefly.

THIRTY-THREE

McKenna knew there was a big problem brewing when the racket woke him and Angelita at two-twenty in the morning. The phone on his nightstand, his cell phone in its charger on his dresser, and his beeper somewhere in his dark bedroom had all gone off at once. Worse, the din woke up the twins and they started wailing.

McKenna got up and rushed for his cell phone. "Sorry to wake you up, buddy, but we've got big problems," Brunette said, but McKenna could hardly hear him.

"Hold on a minute, Ray."

The phone on the nightstand stopped ringing, so McKenna knew Pao had picked it up in the living room. Angelita got up and found the beeper, still attached to his belt on his pants hanging in the closet. Then she picked up the twins and cradled them, one in each arm, trying to calm them down.

McKenna took the phone into the living room. Angelita had insisted that Pao sleep over since he would be returning shortly anyway, but Pao was up now, dressed in a pair of McKenna's pajamas, listening on the phone, and writing in his notebook.

"Okay, Ray. What's wrong?" McKenna asked.

Brunette told him about the murders and the explosion that had taken place in O'Reilly's neighborhood.

"Any other injuries?" McKenna asked.

"Fitzhughs and Sullavan are having trouble hearing, but they're not going sick. Aside from that, there were another two parked cars destroyed and some windows blown out on the block."

"So he knows we've been listening in on him and he knows we've been watching O'Reilly," McKenna said.

"Yeah, and he also knows we can track his location whenever he's using his phone. The base told Fitzhughs and Sullavan that he was close when he dialed Washington information."

"Worse than that, I'm sure he's eventually gonna suspect that we've got all those phone numbers from Page America."

"That means we're wasting time watching Ambery's sister, Brenda McDermott, and those pubs in Woodlawn. They'll never go near those places again."

"They won't go near Margaret's house, I'll give you that," McKenna said. "But I think we can still get lucky with Brenda McDermott. I don't think Mulrooney knows we've got her number."

"Why wouldn't he? It's on the Page America list and he's called it himself three times."

"I'm sure he knows Brenda, but if I'm right, he doesn't know her phone number. I think Mulrooney thought he was calling a pay phone when he called Crowley at Brenda's place.

"You're gonna have to explain that one to me," Brunette insisted.

"Okay, bear with me. Mulrooney can't be certain that we know he has Crowley or Ambery with him or that we know who they are. He suspects that the IRA did the boat captain in Donegal, and he might even suspect that either Learey or his mate told them about him and Ambery before they died. But he can't be sure. He knows we're watching Ambery's sister right now because he called her himself this morning and he knows we're monitoring his calls. But that doesn't mean we know who Ambery is. Maybe all we really know is that Mulrooney's connected somehow to somebody named Billy."

"All right, but if he thinks about the pagers, then he also has to know that we'll find out about Crowley's connection to Brenda McDermott," Brunette reasoned.

"Not necessarily. Mulrooney can't suspect we know about Crowley because he doesn't know that Ambery got drunk in Iceland and told Learey about him. Like McGuinn said, Ambery was so drunk that he probably doesn't remember himself that he told Learey about Crowley. Now, except for the calls to Brenda's number and O'Reilly's number, what do all the rest of those beeper calls have in common?"

"They're all beeped to pay phones."

"Right. I'm figuring that Mulrooney told Ambery and Crowley to always use pay phones, just to be safe. Now Ambery hates Mulrooney, but he's afraid of him. Besides, Mulrooney knows his sister and has her number. So every time Ambery wants to get in touch with either of the other two, he goes to a pay phone—even if he's at his sister's house in Levittown. He gets up and goes out."

"I see where you're going," Brunette said. "Crowley doesn't always follow the plan. When he's at Brenda's and he's either tired or just doesn't feel like going out, he beeps them to Brenda's phone. When they return his call, he tells them that he's at a pay phone."

"Like maybe he did this morning when he returned Mulrooney's beep," McKenna said. "He told Mulrooney that he was calling from a pay phone, remember? If that call shows up on Brenda's phone records, we'll know I'm right."

"On two counts. If you're right, Crowley disobeyed orders and Mulrooney can't suspect we know about Brenda. I'll have Tavlin check on her local usage first thing in the morning, but where does that leave us? Once Mulrooney tells them that we know about his phone and the beepers, Crowley would be crazy to go near Brenda's again."

"That's if Mulrooney tells them."

"You think he won't?"

"Why should he? He's the one who screwed up by using Winthrop's phone, and he thinks Crowley and Ambery have been following his orders to the letter. He thinks there's no danger if all we've got is pay phone numbers to go on, so why would he admit his mistake to his underlings?"

"Buddy, you could be right again," Brunette said. "Maybe all is not lost because of one thing. I'm beginning to believe that you're so far into his head that you know what he's going to do almost before he does himself."

"Yeah, I'm into his head, but it's not a nice place to be. It's pretty grimy in there."

"So where do we go from here?" Brunette asked.

"I'm going to Jackson Heights. I think it's finally time to talk to the O'Reillys. They're in for quite a horror show when I show them the pictures of what Mulrooney's done."

"Then you'll be meeting Sheeran there. I woke him up right before I called you. I'll have somebody pick you up and take you there."

"What about you? Shouldn't the police commissioner be making an appearance at the scene of a terrorist bombing?" McKenna asked.

"Yes, but I can't tonight. I just got home when this happened and that press conference really tired me out."

"Was it that bad?"

"I don't know what they'll print, but they went into a real feeding frenzy on me when I told them who Mulrooney was. You can imagine the questions."

McKenna could. "You didn't tell them that we'd get Mulrooney before he blew something up, did you?"

"Not in so many words. That was one of the many questions I tried to sidestep. What I did say was that there was a chance we'd get him before then, but Mulrooney has just proven me wrong. I'm sure the mayor is going to be on my ass for that one during the whole parade."

"I didn't know you were marching with him in the parade," McKenna said.

"Then you're the only one. He announced it last week while you were away. Of course, he might withdraw the invitation after he reads the morning papers. His Honor might not wanna be seen with me in public."

"Go to bed, Ray. You're so tired that you're hallucinating. You always make him look good and he always wants to be seen with you."

"You're right. Good night."

It had taken McKenna only a short time to shower, shave, and dress, but longer than he had wanted to explain to Angelita why he had to leave her alone again with the two howling boys. In the end, Angelita had understood and then she had gone even further, telling him to quit dragging his feet on the case and get Mulrooney.

When McKenna was ready to go, Pao told him that Cisco had already been waiting downstairs for him for ten minutes. Then he tore two pages from his notebook and handed it to McKenna. "This all I need to make me look brilliant when I get there?" McKenna asked.

"Not exactly brilliant. It's just everything that dumb fuck Kotowski knows so far," Pao answered.

McKenna knew Pao well and wasn't surprised at the reply. Captain Kotowski wasn't a bad guy, he just hadn't made it with Pao. Very few did. In many ways, Pao was like those German shepherd war dogs who could establish absolute loyalty to only a limited number of handlers. Every other person was the enemy as far as Pao was concerned, a danger to be snapped at or bitten whenever they got close. McKenna was proud to be included in Pao's small circle, but every once in a while he felt like scratching Pao's ear to calm him down.

McKenna was at the front door when he realized he had forgotten the briefcase containing his case folder. He went back into the bedroom to get it. The twins had calmed down a bit, but Angelita was still holding them as she rested in bed. Janine had woken up and had crawled into bed with them. McKenna tarried a moment longer to give all another kiss goodnight.

Cisco Sanchez was the picture of the successful detective: Well dressed and well groomed, he always carried himself proudly, like the man in charge. He was a flamboyant man-about-town who thought he was the best detective in the NYPD, which meant, according to Cisco, that he was the best detective in the world. Unfortunately for the many bosses who despised him, Cisco frequently solved difficult cases and got his man so often that they sometimes begrudgingly had to wonder if Cisco was right.

Unlike most of the bosses, McKenna liked Cisco, appreciated his many talents, and used them whenever he could. The two men were close friends, so close that McKenna didn't mind that Cisco sometimes treated him as the detective who was so lucky with his cases that he qualified as the only legitimate Pretender to the Throne.

As soon as he got into the car, McKenna knew he was in for it. "So, Big-Shot, Very-Lucky Detective McKenna thinks he can leave His Majesty, Most-Excellent Detective Cisco Sanchez, waiting in the car like a common lackey, huh?"

"Sorry, Cisco. If I had known it was you down here, I would've rushed down in my pajamas."

"Lucky for you, Cisco accepts your humble apology. Unfortunately, Cisco now has to make up for wasted time, so prepare for liftoff," he said, then attached the magnetic red light to the roof of the car.

Besides skydiving, hang gliding, scuba diving, ski jumping, semiprofessional boxing, womanizing with many jealous, high-strung Spanish ladies, and every other sport Cisco could think of to kill himself in his spare time, he was also a stock car racer of some local renown. "Never been in an accident, but probably caused hundreds of them," was the way McKenna liked to characterize Cisco's driving. He fastened his seat belt, braced himself, and closed his eyes until they were on the East River Drive, siren blaring and headed north toward the Triborough Bridge at terrifying speed. When the G-forces pressing McKenna into his seat abated, he turned on the overhead light and read Pao's notes. It was an account of what the Queens detectives had learned so far, what specialized units were on the scene, and which department big shots were there or en route.

The Crime Scene Unit and the Bomb Squad were there, but the two famous luminaries from those units hadn't yet arrived when Pao had taken the notes. Lt. Simon Finan, the CO of the Bomb Squad and the NYPD's leading expert on explosives, lived far Upstate. Det. First Grade Joe Walsh, universally recognized as the Crime Scene Unit's leading expert on processing evidence and the NYPD's leading ham and glory hound, had been at a conference at the Sheraton Hotel in Midtown where he had been hosting, entertaining, and dazzling crime scene detectives from departments all over the country.

The top brass was represented by the duty chief, but conspicuously absent from the list was the chief of detectives. McKenna figured that Brunette had told him to stay home—Sheeran was to be the man really in charge.

McKenna memorized the particulars on the victims. Quenton Bachmann, age sixty-eight, had been last seen by his wife, Emily, in their living room. They had been watching a late movie on TV when she had fallen asleep. She had been awakened by the sound of sirens and had looked out her front door to see the police standing over the body of her husband of forty-two years. She had identified the body for the officers, had calmly answered some questions, apparently in shock, and then had suffered her first heart attack. She was in Elmhurst Hospital in critical condition.

Jessy Banks, age thirty-nine, was a nurse and had worked the four-to-twelve shift at Elmhurst Hospital. She had stayed at the hospital working until 1:30 A.M. because her relieving nurse had come in late. At the time of her death she had been on her way to her mother's house on 69th Street to pick up her two children, Shawn, age five, and Debra, age three. Her body had been discovered by Robert LeGrand, a passing motorist. He had stopped to render assistance at what he had first thought was a minor traffic accident. He called 911 on his cell phone at 1:49 A.M.

Jessy's husband, Jerome Banks, was a civilian tow truck operator for the NYPD. He had been working at the time in Manhattan, assigned to tow cars from the Fifth Avenue parade route. He was relieved from duty and was being brought to the scene by the department chaplain.

No witnesses to the double homicide had been uncovered so far by the Queens detectives.

Department van 5988 had been destroyed by the explosion at 1:58 A.M. Most residents of 73rd Street had been awakened by the explosion and many of them were on the street. Included in the crowd were Jack O'Reilly and Dorothy O'Reilly, still being watched by Fitzhughs and Sullavan.

McKenna put the notes back in his pocket as Cisco shut off the siren and slowed down at the Triborough Bridge toll plaza. He showed the NYPD vehicle identification plate to the tollbooth attendant, and McKenna was shocked to hear the man say, "Hiya, Cisco. You going to the explosion?"

"Yeah, Blackie. Somebody has to solve these crimes."

"You're the one for the job. Go get him," Blackie said, and waved them through.

Cisco brought the car up to normal driving speed and McKenna couldn't help but notice that he didn't turn the siren back on. Cisco had that casual look on his face and McKenna recognized the signs: Cisco wanted to talk, but he had to be asked for his advice. First some casual conversation, then to the heart of the matter, McKenna decided. "You know many tollbooth attendants?" he asked.

"Cisco knows many of his subjects, the high and mighty as well as the low and seemingly insignificant. He spends much time making the rounds in his kingdom."

"How long you been working?"

"Since four yesterday morning."

"Aren't you tired?"

"Cisco never rests while there are evildoers afoot disturbing the peace and tranquillity in the realm, which brings me to another point," he said, dropping the act. "There is a recent, ugly rumor making the rounds that this wonderful, easy overtime is going to be cut."

"How recent is this rumor?"

"About an hour and fifteen minutes. It started roughly two minutes after Mulrooney blew up 5988, but it's based in fact. Kotowski's had someone call most of the guys who were supposed to come in at four A.M. Told them to stay home and await further instructions."

McKenna saw the point at once. Everyone working knew from the Base's last transmission to van 5988 that Mulrooney now knew his phone was being monitored and his location tracked. So why have all those very expensive detectives on overtime cruising the city doing nothing but snoozing in shifts while waiting for Mulrooney's next call, the call he probably wouldn't be making? Or is it the call he *shouldn't* be making? McKenna wondered. "You think he's gonna use that phone again?"

"Certain of it."

"Wouldn't that be a rather stupid thing for him to do?"

"No, it would be an arrogant thing for him to do and totally in keeping with his character. It would only be a stupid thing for him to do if he knew we had all our units concentrated in the place logic dictates he's going to be tomorrow."

"Midtown?"

"Exactly. That's where he's gonna make his call from, right before or after something blows up in honor of good old St. Patrick. He'll want to rub our noses in the dirt to show us we can't do nothing about him."

"Why would he do that?"

"Because he's angry at us. Maybe not at us, but at the bosses directing us. He knows now that we're going to prevent him from taking his kids, so he's angry and frustrated. He's the kind of guy who always acts on his anger, eventually."

McKenna was surprised to hear Vernon's assessment of Mulrooney repeated by Cisco. "What makes you such an expert on his character?"

"I do a lot of talking and reading. I've talked to a lot of the old-timers who knew him, and I've read all your reports and all Sheeran's notes."

"You raided Sheeran's office?"

"Do it all the time. He keeps all the good case stuff in his bottom right desk drawer, behind that puny lock," Cisco explained. "Did you know that he writes down everything he knows, hears, or suspects about a case?"

"No."

"Well, he does. Hears something new and he runs in his office and closes the door. Writes down everything he heard and then makes these diagrams. Very neat and very pretty. Facts go in square boxes, suspicions go in rectangles, witnesses are underlined, and suspects go in circles. Then he draws lines and arrows connecting everything the way he sees it. When he's done making his diagram, he studies it to make sure he's got it right."

That Sheeran had a system didn't surprise McKenna. He knew Sheeran as a dedicated, hard worker and an organized kind of guy who seemed to have the facts at his fingertips on all the cases his squad was working. But McKenna was sure that Sheeran wouldn't want his successful system to be general knowledge among his troops. "Does he know you've been reading his stuff?"

"Of course he does. Even offered to give me a key once, but that would take the fun out of it."

"Why does he put up with it?"

"Because every great once in a while I'm able to help him out with his notes. For instance, a few times he didn't properly consider some facts, didn't attach the proper importance to them, so I underlined them for him. One time he even had all his arrows pointing at the wrong suspect, a guy who turned out to be a minor accomplice, but a very good witness for the State. I erased his arrows and pointed them in the right direction for him."

"He never says anything to you about this?"

"Of course not. He's a sharp guy, sharp enough to accept good advice from a competent source and then keep his mouth shut. After all, in this Job it can never look like the troops are telling the bosses what to do, can it?"

"No, it never can. How many people know what you've been up to?"

"Since I started, it was only two—me and Sheeran. As of this moment it's three, but that's the limit."

"I guess you like Sheeran, don't you?" McKenna asked.

"Brian, he's the best boss I ever worked for. I'm not supposed to know this, but he protects me from other bosses who want to kill me when I sometimes get too crazy, irritating, or annoying for their plebeian tastes."

Sometimes too crazy? McKenna thought. Try most of the time, Cisco.

The secret relationship between Cisco and Sheeran suddenly made clear to McKenna one thing that had many other detectives perplexed; the newest car in the unit was always assigned by Sheeran to Cisco. When the crybabies grumbled, Sheeran stated simply that Cisco had never had an accident and kept his car in great shape, which was certainly true. Cisco's car was always spotless and once a week he came in early to wax and polish it.

There was one more question McKenna had for Cisco. "What did you think of my reports?"

"Pretty good. They almost looked like something I would write."

McKenna was content with probably the greatest compliment Cisco had ever given another detective.

THIRTY-FOUR

Cisco parked at 33rd Avenue and 76th Street, which was as close as he could get. Radio cars, unmarked cars, Emergency Service trucks, press vans, fire trucks, and ambulances jammed the blocks in front of them. McKenna picked up his briefcase and they got out of the car, headed through the cars for 74th Street.

Police barriers had been placed across 33rd Avenue halfway between 74th Street and 75th Street. A crowd of civilians, many dressed in their pajamas and overcoats, stood pressed against the barriers on one side and five uniformed cops were spread out on the other side. Many reporters also stood on the other side of the barriers, along with a few cops and detectives. All were looking up at the Det. Joe Walsh show. McKenna and Cisco stood back and decided to take in a bit of the performance.

A Con Edison cherry picker was parked in the middle of the intersection under the traffic light and Walsh was on his way up, expertly operating the basket. He stopped just where he wanted to, right at the face of the light and inches from it. In under a minute he had the face of the light off, and then he put on a pair of heavy rubber gloves and a miner's hat with a light affixed to the front. With a large pair of felt-tipped tweezers, he probed inside the traffic light while press photographers on the ground snapped away. He removed a spent bullet with the tweezers, examined it briefly, then put on the finishing touch. He took a magnifying glass from his pocket, held the bullet at eye level, and examined it through the glass, his face set in his practiced look of perfect concentration. It was a perfect photo opportunity, and the press took advantage of it, illuminating the intersection with flashes.

Then Walsh shook his head. He wasn't pleased; either the bullet was deformed or he felt the photographers might still have some film left. He put the bullet in his breast pocket, removed another spent bullet, and repeated his examination process. There were fewer flashes going off, so this time Walsh decided to be pleased. He nodded his head and the crowd said "Ahh," and a few even clapped.

Walsh refrained from taking a bow as he surveyed his fans, and then he saw McKenna. "Detective McKenna! I'll be right down to explain to you what happened here," he shouted down to McKenna, then took off his miner's hat and operated the controls to lower the basket.

I think that sometimes I hate that man, McKenna thought, but he revised his opinion as every eye in the crowd turned toward him and the reporters rushed over. I'm now certain that I hate Joe Walsh most of the time, McKenna concluded.

McKenna and Cisco stepped forward, the crowd parted, and they were under the barriers. However, in New York the press rarely gives way when they have questions to ask. McKenna knew all the old-timers among the reporters and even counted some of them as friends, but he stopped only long enough to say, "Inspector Sheeran will be here shortly and I'm sure he'll be giving you a statement on what happened here tonight. I won't be making any statements."

Most of the old-timers believed McKenna and backed away. He knew only a few of the younger reporters, but they obviously believed nothing anyone said and kept their microphones thrust in front of McKenna's face while they shouted questions. Many of the questions were for information concerning his exact relationship with Maggie Ferguson, and McKenna thought many of them were rudely put. He didn't answer, he just looked straight ahead, and with Cisco running interference, pushed for the sanctuary offered by the secondary line of defense, the yellow crime scene tape stretched across the street and sidewalk. Once under the tape, the reporters were behind them and Joe Walsh was in front of them.

Walsh was a big, gregarious man in his late fifties. He was sixty pounds overweight, but he had a full head of curly gray hair that still made him a rather striking figure. He was smiling and had been expecting a good review until he saw McKenna's face. "I know, Brian," he said, offering his hand. "Sometimes I even hate myself."

"Then why do you do it?" McKenna asked, ignoring Walsh's outstretched hand.

"Who knows what incredible sickness makes a man want to be on the front page of every paper every day?"

"Maybe you're not sick. Maybe you're just a big scumbag," Cisco suggested.

"No. I've examined that possibility and I'm happy to say that's definitely not it," Walsh said, not looking at all offended. "My wife still likes me most of the time, my kids love me, and my grandchildren adore me. They're all very discerning people and I'm sure they would have told me

I was a scumbag if indeed I was. It must be something else that afflicts me, but what?"

McKenna knew that Walsh was still hamming it up for the cameras. He wanted to end the soliloquy and get to work, but knew the only way to do that was to shake Walsh's hand in another photo opportunity. He did, and Walsh held McKenna's hand until the flashes stopped.

Walsh knew better than to offer his hand to Cisco, but he appeared content with what he had. "Want me to show you around and tell you what happened?"

Definitely not, McKenna thought as he imagined the scene. Walsh would parade him around in full view of the photographers behind the yellow tape, pointing at this and that as he instructed his pupil on the wonders to be learned when a crime scene was expertly processed. "Why don't you just tell me what happened," McKenna suggested, then walked slowly toward the intersection and away from the cameras.

Walsh and Cisco followed McKenna to Jessy Banks's car. She was still there, spread across the front seat of her car, eyes open and a bullet hole in her ear. There was very little blood visible, so McKenna knew that the bullet hadn't gone through her skull.

"The killer's using a 9mm Beretta model 92 with a Czech-made sound suppressor attached," Walsh said. "He practices all the time, and he's using reloads with reduced charges. He fired fourteen rounds, twelve of them quickly while he was on the move, and he hit what he was aiming at fourteen times, which is pretty remarkable. The sound suppressor and the reduced load should've considerably reduced the accuracy of the Beretta."

McKenna accepted Walsh's analysis at face value. He couldn't imagine how Walsh had arrived at his detailed conclusions in such a short period of time, but he had worked with Walsh enough times to recognize that the man was right, that Walsh just *knew.*

However, Cisco couldn't accept it. "How do you know he was using a silencer? Because nobody heard the shots?"

"Sound suppressor," Walsh said, correcting Cisco. "Silencers exist only in the movies and there's really no such thing. Just the action of the slide of the pistol moving back and forth when the weapon is fired makes quite a bit of noise and it's impossible to completely eliminate the noise the bullet makes when it leaves the barrel."

"Okay, what makes you so sure he's using a sound suppressor? While I'm at it, what makes you so sure of most of the bullshit you just told us?"

"Elementary, my dear Cisco. The shell casings tell me it's a 9mm, and there's fourteen of them. The Beretta Model 92 holds fifteen rounds and it's one of the few automatics made that has a barrel protruding from the slide, so it's one of the few 9mm guns where the barrel can be threaded to accept a sound suppressor."

Walsh took one of the spent bullets and the magnifying glass from his pockets and handed them to Cisco. "Take a look. You'll notice that rifling marks on the bullet run clockwise, 1.35mm apart. That's a Beretta. You'll also notice there's a bit of steel wool and burnt fiber on the bullet. That's residue it picked up on its way through the sound suppressor. The fiber looks like Egyptian cotton to me, and that's the material the Czechs use in their sound suppressors."

Very impressive, McKenna thought, but Cisco still hadn't had enough. "And the reduced loads? How do you know about that?" he asked.

"Even more elementary, my dear Cisco, so pay close attention. First, a bullet ordinarily leaves the barrel of a Model 92 at 1,280 feet per second, much too fast and making too much noise to be muffled by any sound suppressor made. Second, fired at close range, that bullet would go right through the head of anybody it hit. Both our victims here still have a bullet in their heads. Third, a full load 9mm parabellum bullet would be quite deformed after hitting the steel in the traffic light. The bullet in your hand is only slightly deformed."

Cisco couldn't help himself. He had to look down at the bullet and he obviously didn't like what he saw. The bullet was in perfect shape.

"See what I mean?" Walsh asked.

Cisco didn't answer, but that didn't bother Walsh. "Where was I?"

"Fourth, I think," McKenna said.

"Ah, yes. Fourth, the fourteen spent shell casings lying all around the crime scene have multiple ejector marks on them, indicating to a reasonable person that the killer is a target shooter and a reloader. These shell casings have been used many times. In my humble opinion, this time he reloaded them with only enough powder to produce a muzzle velocity of approximately eight hundred feet per second, close to the minimum muzzle velocity necessary to ensure that the slide on the Model 92 will fully retract every time. Fifth, as you walk around the intersection, you will note that the ejected shell casings on the ground are spread around. As a highly experienced expert, I inferred from their position that the killer fired at the traffic light quickly while walking around the intersection. Have I answered your questions, Cisco?"

"Yes," Cisco said sheepishly.

"Do you feel the need for any further instruction?"

"No."

"And has this little chat enabled you to reach any conclusions?"

"Just one I already knew. Joe Walsh, you are a big, fat windbag."

"I'm not that fat and you haven't reached the proper conclusion. That might prove unfortunate for you in the event you meet up with this killer," Walsh said, then turned to McKenna. "Brian?"

"Don't get into a gunfight with Mulrooney," McKenna answered.
"Exactly."

The scene around the corner on 73rd Street was equally crowded with cops, bosses, and detectives surrounding what was left of van 5988, lying on its side and badly burnt. The cars that were parked in front of and behind the van had also been destroyed by the explosion and resulting fire. Reporters and photographers were on the far side of the yellow crime scene tape and curious civilian onlookers were on the other side of the barriers.

Lieutenant Finan had arrived and was at work inspecting the underside of the van. Dennis Hunt was also nearby, scraping samples from a sheet-metal piece of the van lying next to a tree that had been damaged by the fire.

"Can you tell me what he used to do this?" McKenna asked Finan.

"Nothing to it. He magnetically attached a small metal box containing C-4 to the side of the gas tank. Then he detonated it by radio. Not much C-4 in the device. Most of the damage you see here was caused by the gas tank exploding. Fitzhughs tells me they had half a tank."

"You can tell all that already?" McKenna asked, amazed.

"Yeah, we got lucky on this one. We've got a good piece of his device," Finan answered, and led them over to Hunt. "That's a piece of the bottom of the left rear quarter panel," Finan said. "What you see welded to it is the top of the device's casing."

McKenna could see it, a rectangular piece of metal that had been welded by the heat of the explosion to the underside of the rear quarter panel. "How do you know it was C-4 he used?" McKenna asked.

"I've been in this business a long time, Brian. It's supposed to be odor-less, but I can smell it," Finan answered, touching his nose.

"Really?"

"Every time, but we've already done a field test on the residue left on that piece of metal. Burnt C-4," Finan answered. He took a screwdriver from Hunt and used it to pry the piece of bomb casing from the sheet metal. It came off easily and Finan examined it, then gave it to McKenna. "Looks like we might be having quite a few of these explosions around town, he said.

McKenna could see what he meant. Some of the black paint was still on the case, as well as the number 28. "You think he's got another twenty-seven of these?" McKenna asked.

"I think that's a distinct possibility," Finan answered, then bent down. Something small on the ground had caught his interest. He picked it up and examined it in the palm of his hand.

McKenna was amazed that Finan had even seen the tiny piece. "What do you think it is?" he asked.

"I know what it is," Finan answered. "It's the frequency chip from the radio receiver in the device. It's burned and wrecked, but that's what it is."

The frequency chip gave McKenna something to think about, a glimmer of hope. He had an idea, but he hadn't fully worked it out when Sheeran arrived with Fitzhughs. "Is Gaspar working?" McKenna asked Sheeran.

"Yeah, but he's getting off at four. You need him?"

"I'm not sure yet, but maybe. Could you have him hang around?"

"I'll take care of it."

McKenna told Sheeran what he had learned from Walsh and Finan, then presented a problem. "Cisco feels that Mulrooney's arrogant enough to use his phone again. Captain Kotowski's been cutting the manpower coming in at four, but maybe they should all come in and be concentrated in Midtown tomorrow."

"I agree," Sheeran said. "I'll make sure it happens. What next?"

"I want to talk to the O'Reillys right now."

"Okay. Do you want Cisco to give you a hand?"

"Sure. I could always use a hand."

"You want us to bring them into the One-fourteen?" Fitzhughs asked.

"No. We really don't have much on Jack and nothing at all on Dorothy, so I'd rather talk to them in their house. Are they still out here?"

"Yeah, both of them. They've got their kids up and with them, too. You'll spot her right away. She's got rollers in her hair under a kerchief and she's wearing a white robe with big red roses all over it."

"What routine do you want to use on them?" Cisco asked. "Good Guy–Bad Guy or Smart Guy–Dumb Guy?"

McKenna didn't like either of them. He thought Good Guy–Bad Guy had been overplayed, and he suspected the role Cisco had in mind for him if they used the Smart Guy–Dumb Guy routine on the O'Reillys. "How about Good Smart Guy–Good Smart Guy?" he asked.

"Naw, that would never work. Far as I know, it's never been done."

"Okay, we'll do Good Guy–Bad Guy. Would you mind being the bad guy?"

"Mind? Are you kidding? It's my favorite role," Cisco said. He turned and walked under the crime scene tape and over to the police barriers. There were four cops at the front of the barriers and a crowd of civilians on the other side watching the police at work. Dorothy was right in front, wearing her robe and standing next to her husband. Each was holding one of their children, two girls who appeared to be three or four years old.

McKenna thought Dorothy wasn't a bad-looking woman, but taller than most and big-boned with a swarthy complexion. On the other hand, Jack looked every bit an O'Reilly. He had brown hair, a ruddy complexion, but was a head shorter and twenty pounds lighter than his wife.

One of the cops manning the barriers had a megaphone and Cisco took it from him. "Listen up," Cisco ordered through the megaphone he held two feet from Dorothy's face. "Which of you people knows the monster who murdered those two innocent people around the block and caused all this damage here?"

From where he stood McKenna could see that Dorothy's and Jack's only reaction to Cisco's question was a look of annoyance prompted by their proximity to the megaphone—they didn't know what Cisco was talking about.

"You're not listening, people," Cisco said, again into the megaphone. "What I'm asking is which one of you people knows that filthy, murdering Michael Mulrooney, Mike Mullen, or whatever he's calling himself around here."

That got a reaction from both Dorothy and Jack. Their faces contorted into a look of sheer terror. Jack put his daughter down, but held the girl's hand.

Then Cisco closed the lid on them. "Dorothy, step forward. The great and powerful Oz wishes to speak with you and he will not be kept waiting."

Dorothy took a pitiful half step forward. Jack let go of his daughter's hand, then turned and ran right into Detective Sullavan's arms.

The first thing McKenna did was place the O'Reilly children in the care of two female cops. Then they walked Dorothy and Jack around the corner to show them the bodies of Jessy Banks and Quenton Bachmann. The O'Reillys were still terrified, and the sight of the bodies of the two innocent victims added horror to their emotions.

"Are you sure Mike did this?" Jack asked after McKenna replaced the blanket covering Bachmann's body.

"Certain," McKenna said. "He ended the lives of these two people merely to create a distraction so he could blow up the van assigned to the detectives watching your house. He might've also caused another death here. The wife of this poor man had a heart attack when she saw what Mulrooney had done to her husband."

"Don't be giving us that shocked act," Cisco added. "You knew all along that Mulrooney's a stone-cold killer. Known it for years."

"Sir, you're wrong," Jack said. "You've gotta believe me. I knew that years ago he'd been involved in some military actions against the British and might have killed some of their soldiers, but I never suspected he'd do something like this."

"Yeah, I bet," Cisco said sarcastically.

"How long have you been watching us?" Dorothy asked.

"Quite a while," McKenna answered. "Watching and listening. We have a tap on your phone. Also have all the phones wired at the Pioneer."

The tap and the surveillance had actually been on for less than two days, but the O'Reillys had no way of knowing that. McKenna and Cisco watched as the O'Reillys' minds raced over every phone conversation and every action of theirs since Mulrooney had arrived in the country.

"That's right. We've got you good," Cisco said.

"I don't know what you could have me for," Dorothy said. "Are we under arrest?"

"That depends on you," McKenna stated. "If you tell me that you'll cooperate and if I believe you, then we'll go to your house and have a long chat. You'll tell me everything you know about Mulrooney and then you won't be charged with a thing. You can put your kids to bed and go to sleep yourselves."

"Then there's the other option, the one I'd prefer," Cisco snarled. "If you decide not to cooperate or if I catch you in a single lie, I'm gonna clap the handcuffs on tight on both of you and drag you to Central Booking myself. Put those snotty-looking kids of yours in a foster home where they'll stay while they're waiting for you to get out of jail. If Mulrooney blows up something big tomorrow or kills anyone else, I can guarantee that they'll be waiting a long time before they see Mommy and Daddy again."

"We don't know what Michael's planning," Dorothy said. "Matter of fact, we don't know if he's even planning anything."

"I don't believe a word of that," Cisco said.

"Wait a minute, Cisco," McKenna insisted for the O'Reillys' benefit. "She could be telling the truth. They might just be innocent dupes."

"You dopey enough to believe them?" Cisco asked, also for the O'Reillys' benefit.

"I'm not dopey. All I'm saying is that it's possible she's telling the truth. We should hear them out before I decide, and you shouldn't jump to conclusions. You're always looking to lock people up on every trumped-up charge you can come up with."

"Works for me. Gets me to Central Booking every day, making lots of overtime. The extra money I make locking up these two would just about cover the price of a new punching bag I've been looking at."

"Excuse me, sir. What would we be charged with?" Jack asked meekly, addressing McKenna.

"I'd have to listen to all the tapes of your phone conversations before I decide, but I'd say harboring a fugitive and conspiracy to commit kidnapping for starters."

"Kidnapping?" Jack asked, confused, but Dorothy looked even more confused than he did.

"Yeah, that's what it's called when you agreed to help Mulrooney take his kids from Kathleen Mullen, the lawful custodial parent," Cisco said.

"I didn't think it was anything that serious," Jack said. "This thing is just snowballing on us. Can I speak to my wife privately for just a moment?"

"No, you can't," Cisco said. "Don't want you two getting your story straight together, and I want an answer from each of you right now. What's it gonna be? Central Booking for black coffee and salami sandwiches or your house for tea and crumpets?"

"Will the IRA find out if we talk to you?" Jack asked.

"Yes, but that's not bad for you," McKenna said. "Mulrooney's no longer in the IRA and has been outlawed by them. Whatever he's doing here he's doing on his own. Do you know who Martin McGuinn is?"

"Of course," Jack answered.

"Well, if you don't believe me, we can call him up and you can ask him yourself."

"That won't be necessary. We believe you," Dorothy said. "If you don't get Michael, will he find out that we talked to you?"

McKenna could see that Dorothy was terrified at that prospect. "No, he won't. I can promise you that you'll never be called to testify in this case."

Dorothy and Jack exchanged a glance and a nod. "Let's all go to my house for some tea and crumpets," Dorothy said, stealing a glance at Cisco. "I don't know much that will interest you, but I think my husband might have a lot on his mind that he wants to talk to you about. Then he has some explaining to do to me after you're gone."

THIRTY-FIVE

McKenna believed the O'Reillys were going to come clean, but didn't want them alone together until they did. With that in mind, Cisco and he accompanied them upstairs when they put their kids to bed. Then Dorothy made a pot of tea and, to McKenna's surprise, actually warmed some crumpets. They filled the four chairs surrounding the square table in the O'Reillys' small, neat dining room. Jack sat next to his wife at one corner, with Cisco facing Dorothy and McKenna facing Jack. Dorothy had set the table and the tea pot and crumpets were there in front of them.

To ensure the O'Reillys' complete cooperation, McKenna had a few minutes more of unpleasantness in store for them. Bad Guy Cisco administered the extra torture before they put anything in their stomachs.

"Just in case you still have some sympathy for good old Mike floating around somewhere in the back of your minds, I want you two desperados to take a good look at what he does for fun when he isn't blowing up things for Ireland," Cisco said. He opened McKenna's briefcase, took out the folder containing the crime scene photos of Meaghan Maher and the other victims, and passed it to Dorothy. "Take a deep breath and open it up," Cisco ordered.

Dorothy did and she looked at Meaghan's photo, but only for a second. She turned pale, trembled, then got up and ran for the bathroom. All could hear her retching, but Cisco didn't want to waste any time waiting for her. He gave the folder to Jack. "Your turn, tough guy. The first one you'll see is an Irish Catholic girl named Meaghan Maher. That sick monster tortured her for fun before he finally strangled her, just like he did with the rest of the victims you're gonna be looking at."

"Jesus, Mary, and Joseph help us," Jack said under his breath as he stared at the photo of Meaghan's battered body. As he went through the rest, he too turned pale and his hands became unsteady. "I can't believe Mike did all these horrible things," he said as he closed the folder.

"Believe it," McKenna said. "He did it and I can prove it. It'll be in all the papers tomorrow."

"Why would he do it?" Jack asked.

"Like Cisco said, he's a sick, cruel monster. He does it because he enjoys doing it."

"I can't believe it," Jack repeated, shaking his head, but McKenna could see that he did believe it.

When Dorothy returned from the bathroom, she looked spent, pale, and weak. Cisco took the folder from in front of Jack and placed it in front of Dorothy. "Take a look," he commanded. Dorothy ignored him, keeping her eyes front and her hands on her lap.

Cisco reached across the table and opened the folder. "Look!" he ordered sternly.

Dorothy looked down at Meaghan's photo, but McKenna could see that her eyes weren't focused on it. Cisco removed the photo, exposing the one underneath, but Dorothy screwed her eyes tightly shut. "I've seen enough!" she shouted.

"I think she has seen enough, Cisco," McKenna suggested.

"I don't think so," Cisco said. "This is good reality training, like we gave the Germans after the war. They all had to go to the movies and see films showing all of the horrible things Hitler had done in their name."

"I know, but she's had enough. Please, Cisco. Leave her alone," McKenna said, playing his role to the hilt.

"Okay. Have it your way," Cisco said with reluctance in his voice. He closed the folder and put it back in the briefcase.

"Is it gone yet?" Dorothy asked, her eyes still closed.

"Yeah, Dorothy. It's gone. You can open your eyes now," McKenna said. "Let's eat, and then we'll talk."

Dorothy opened her eyes to glare at her husband. "I can't believe you

let that man in our house! You even let him play with our children, for
Christ's sake! What the hell were you thinking?"

"I'm sorry. You gotta believe me, I didn't know about any of this. How
could I know?" Jack said weakly.

"How couldn't you know?" Dorothy countered. "You've known him all
your life, haven't you? What kind of judge of character are you?"

"Not a good one, I guess. I'm sorry."

Dorothy glared at her husband a moment longer, then got up and
poured tea for everyone. The O'Reillys were deep in thought with Jack
avoiding Dorothy's gaze. McKenna had two crumpets and Cisco had three,
but the silent O'Reillys didn't touch theirs.

"Okay, here's what we're gonna do," McKenna said loudly, startling the
O'Reillys. "I'm gonna question Dorothy first while you, Jack, wait in the
bathroom until we need you. Just to keep things honest, I'm going to take
you both down to headquarters tomorrow and have you polygraphed. If we
come up with any lies or any inconsistencies in your stories, our deal is off.
Understand?"

"Yeah, we understand. But shouldn't we be talking to a lawyer first?"
Jack asked.

"If you want," Cisco said. "You can call him from your cell in Central
Booking."

"No, that's all right," Jack said. He got up and Cisco escorted him to
the bathroom. When Cisco returned and took his seat, McKenna began.
"How long have you known Michael Mulrooney, Dorothy?"

"A long time. I knew him when he was a cop and he was one of the
ushers at our wedding, but I thought his name was Mike Mullen back then.
He and my husband were always close and Jack used to be very proud of
him."

"They're cousins?"

"Yes. Mike's mother was Jack's mother's sister."

"When did you find out who he really was?"

"After he got arrested and took off."

"How did you find out?"

"Jack's sister came over from Ireland for a visit. We were having a
couple of drinks one day while Jack was at work. She said she had seen
Mike in Belfast, which surprised her because she knew he was wanted by
the police there. I asked her what for, and she told me that Mike had been
involved with the IRA when he was younger and had been wounded in a
gunfight with the British army. He got away and was sent to Canada to hide
out. His brother Patrick was also wounded, but he was captured. He was
one of the hunger strikers, starved himself to death. Then I asked her how
he could've gotten on the cops if he was a wanted man and I got her to
tell me that Mullen wasn't his real name. He was Mike Mulrooney."

"What was your reaction to that?"

"I was in shock. I almost couldn't believe it, but I knew it was true. My husband had been lying to me for years. That caused the biggest fight in our marriage until the one we're going to have when you leave."

"What was his excuse?" McKenna asked.

"He told me a whole line of silly things about oaths and secrecy in the IRA. Said he was honor bound to tell nobody about Mike, that the man was a real patriot. He also hinted that somebody would get us if I said anything about it to anybody. I figured it was none of my business and the man is his cousin, so I kept my mouth closed like he wanted."

"Did you like Mike?"

"Until now I did. He had me fooled. He was a very funny man, always had a good joke to tell. He was also very generous, even bought us this dining room set we're sitting at."

"Didn't your opinion of him change after he was arrested here?"

"Not really. If anything, I felt sorry for him and liked him more. You have to know his wife and the kind of pressure he was under. He worshipped that woman and he really loved his kids. Best father I've ever seen, but after a while Kathleen wanted nothing to do with him. He spent every penny he could get his hands on buying her things, but she ignored him and never showed any thanks. I don't think he spent a penny of that money he got from those prostitutes on himself. I think it all went for gifts to Kathleen."

"Did you hear from him after he disappeared?"

"No, not a word. But then we ran into him in Bermuda, of all places. It was quite a shock for both Jack and me but we wound up having a wonderful time for three days."

"What was he doing there?"

"Living high on the hog. He was staying at the Sonesta Beachfront and he had a suite under the name of William Winters. He'd been there for a week when we got there and had lots of money."

"Was he still there when you left?"

"Yes, he said he had to stay on, but we both knew better than to ask why by that time."

"Were you in Bermuda before or after the commandant of the British Royal Marines was wounded so badly in that bombing there?"

"We left four days before that."

"You knew that Mulrooney was IRA and that it was him who did the bombing, didn't you?"

"I knew he was with the IRA and I strongly suspected that he did it."

"Didn't that change your opinion of him?"

"Have you ever been to Northern Ireland?" Dorothy asked.

"Yes, I've been there."

"Then you should know how crazy it is over there and how badly they treat the Catholics. It's a war and Mike is a soldier in it. According to Jack and his sister, a very brave and dedicated soldier."

"Maybe he's brave and maybe he's dedicated, but he's a lot of other things. Do you know that folder with all those pictures you don't want to look at?"

"Yes," Dorothy answered apprehensively.

"In it are pictures of a sixteen-year-old black girl he tortured and murdered in Bermuda, maybe even while he was there with you. Would you like to see those photos now?"

"No, and I won't look if you try to show them to me."

"Don't worry, I won't try. Now tell me, when did you see him again?"

"About a week ago, but I knew he was in New York."

"How?"

"Jack started wearing a beeper and I asked him about it. He told me that Mike had come into the Pioneer one night while we was working there. They had some beers and Mike had asked Jack to buy him three beepers and a cell phone for his kids."

"How long has Jack been working at the Pioneer."

"Ten years, at least, but I don't mind. If he wasn't working there, he'd probably be drinking there anyway. This way we come out ahead and he comes home sober most of the time."

"Go on about the beepers and the phones."

"Okay. I was real mad at Jack for not telling me right away about seeing Mike and he tried giving me that old oath and secrecy nonsense again. I didn't buy it, but I know my Jack and I forgave him. He's like a little boy when it comes to the IRA and we're always giving money to NORAID. I'm sure he considers himself as some sort of IRA associate member, so he bought the beepers and the phone and Mike picked them up from him at the bar the next night. Then last Friday Jack went out for a couple of beers at the Pioneer and he came home with Mike."

"How did Mulrooney's eye look?"

"The shiner?"

"Yeah, the shiner and his nose."

"It didn't look that bad. His nose was a little swollen and his eye was a little black underneath, but it was all healing nicely. I figured that the person had to be quite a bruiser to do that to Mike. He's very strong and Jack says he's the toughest man alive."

"Didn't you ask him about it?"

"Sure I did. He told us that he had been out drinking in Montreal and that he had been jumped by some British merchant seamen. Said he took care of them good and I didn't want to know any more."

"It wasn't British merchant seamen who gave him that shiner," Cisco said. "It was Meaghan Maher and she did it while she was fighting for her life. The picture showing what he did to her was the one on top."

"Oh, I'm sorry," she said, but not to Cisco. Apparently, she didn't want to talk to him and remained focused on McKenna.

"What happened when Mulrooney got here?" McKenna asked.

"We all sat up late, having some laughs and a few more beers. Then Jack asked me if it would be all right if he went up to Hunter Mountain with Mike the next day. They were having some kind of Irish festival up there, so I said, 'Sure, go ahead.' They got up early on Saturday, took the kids to the park for a couple of hours, then dropped them off and drove up to Hunter."

"In whose car?"

"Jack's. I don't think Mike had a car then, which was one of the reasons he wanted Jack to go with him. Jack packed for a two-day trip."

"Did Mulrooney have any clothes with him?"

"I assume so. He had a knapsack with him."

"When did they get back?"

"Jack came back alone late Saturday night."

"Had he been drinking?"

"Nope, sober as a judge, which surprised me quite a bit. Jack likes his Irish festivals and sometimes forgets himself a bit."

"Did he tell you what they did up there?"

"Yes, but I'd rather you ask him about it."

"We will ask him, but now we're asking you," Cisco chimed in. "What did those two characters do up there?"

"I hope I'm not getting him into trouble," she said, speaking to McKenna. "Jack said that they went into the woods and fired some guns, target practice. Then Mike set off some explosives, tested a new kind of bomb he'd invented."

"What kind of bomb?"

"I don't know exactly, but they were little ones. Jack said Mike set them off after they left and had walked for five minutes. Said he used a cell phone to set them off. They didn't see the explosions, but they heard them."

"What else did Jack say?"

"That they stopped into a rest area on the thruway on the way home and Mike stole a car there."

"How did he steal it?"

"I don't know. According to Jack, he just opened it up and started it a minute later. Jack was real impressed with that."

"What kind of car was it?"

"I don't know."

"Do you know where Mulrooney's been staying?"

"No."

"Have you seen him again since last Friday?"

"No, haven't seen him again, but he called the night before last asking for Jack. All I told him was that Jack wasn't home."

That call was recorded on the wiretap, McKenna knew. He felt that Dorothy had answered all his questions truthfully, but he still had a few tough ones left for her. "What about this morning?" he asked, being as vague as he could.

"What about it?"

"What is Mulrooney planning to do to celebrate St. Patrick's Day?"

"I haven't the foggiest."

"Then what are Jack's plans?"

"I guess he'll take the kids to the parade, same as usual."

"How about Mulrooney's kids?"

"I don't know. Is Jack supposed to take them to the parade, too?" she asked suspiciously.

"Yes, he's supposed to pick them up in the Bronx, but we don't know if he's taking them to the parade. He's gonna drop them off with Mulrooney somewhere."

"Is that where that kidnap charge you were talking about came from?"

"That's it."

"Then Jack has less brains than I gave him credit for. He never mentioned a word about that to me."

"Do you know the Mullen boys?"

"Of course I know them, but that doesn't mean I like them. They're tough, tart little bastards, always giving their mother a real hard time. Jack's taken them to the parade a few times for her, but he knows that I don't want them near me."

"How about the suitcases?" McKenna asked suddenly.

Dorothy looked confused. "What suitcases?"

"I think it's time to talk to Jack," Cisco said.

"Good idea. I think it's time we all talk to Jack," Dorothy countered.

"No, Dorothy. You can have him when we're through with him," Cisco promised.

"Am I going back to the bathroom?"

"That's right," Cisco said, then stood up. Dorothy did as well and she followed Cisco out. McKenna heard the sound of a slap and then Cisco returned a minute later with a very meek-looking Jack. One side of his face was red, and the imprint of Dorothy's palm was clearly visible on it. At McKenna's direction, he took the seat vacated by his wife.

"Dorothy had quite an interesting tale to tell and we're looking for you to fill in some blanks," Cisco said.

"I swear, I'll tell you everything I know," Jack promised.

"So you will," McKenna said. "Let's start at the beginning, back in Belfast. Tell me about your cousin Michael."

"I grew up in The Lower Falls and we lived next door to the Mulrooneys. Michael and Patrick were older than me, so we didn't hang out together. But they were tough boys and they always looked after me. Nobody would dare harm a hair on my head when I was growing up."

"When did they join the IRA?"

"Long before they were born. They're from a good republican family, much stronger than mine. His father's a real hard man so he is. Fought with O'Connell in the old days and still hates the Brits good and proper."

"Did you ever join the IRA?"

"No. I would have and wanted to when I was sixteen, but Michael wouldn't hear of it. Told me to stay in school and study hard, said our family had already given enough men to the movement. He wouldn't even let me do the things that all the boys my age were doing, like running messages and throwing rocks at the Brits."

"Did you know when Mulrooney went to Canada?"

Again Jack looked surprised. "Not for years and nobody told me where he went."

"Didn't you ask around?"

"Of course not," Jack said, smiling at the idea. "Inquiring about wanted hard men isn't encouraged in Belfast, even if it's the Pope who's doing the asking. We just knew that he was all right because we would have heard if he wasn't."

"Then when did you find out he went to Canada and who told you?"

"Years after he left there and it was Mike himself who told me. I was here then, not exactly legal, and working as a bartender in Midtown where a lot of cops used to hang out. One day Mike walked in, big as life. He walked right up to me and hugged me hard. Said he'd heard I was working there and had been meaning to look me up and help me out."

"How did he help you out?"

"Lots of ways. Most important, he got me legal here. After that, he got me a job in the gas company."

"How?"

"Mike knew the chief of security, a retired police captain or something like that."

That would be Timmy Restivo's predecessor in the job at the Brooklyn Union Gas Company, McKenna knew, but he couldn't remember the man's name. "So Mulrooney told you about everything he'd been doing since he left Belfast?"

"Over the years, in dribs and drabs."

"Did he tell you he was still with the IRA while he was working as an NYPD Bomb Squad detective?"

"No, and he didn't have to. Everyone knows, once in, never out."

"Do you know where he went after he fled New York?"

"Not for sure, but I heard a few things at the Pioneer. Hard men stop in there from time to time when they're in town. I heard rumors that Mike was working for the movement all over the world."

"Did you know he was in Bermuda before you went there?"

"No. It was a perfect shock for us when we saw him."

"Did he tell you what he was doing there?"

"No, and I didn't ask. I just assumed that he was there on some business for the movement. When that Brit brigadier was blown up, I knew I was right."

"Tell me about when you first saw him on this visit to New York."

"Not much to tell. I was working at the Pioneer and he just walked in. Could have knocked me over with a feather, but I always figured I'd be running into him again sooner or later."

"Did he have anyone with him at the time?"

"No, but he told me that somebody had dropped him off there."

McKenna opened his briefcase, took out the two standing prison photos of Ambery and Crowley, and passed them to Jack. "Do you recognize these men?"

"Billy Ambery and Kiernan Crowley. Two hard men from The Lower Falls, but I haven't seen them since I was a boy. I had heard that they were in the Maze."

"Tell me about the trip to Hunter Mountain."

McKenna could see that his command had made Jack nervous and apprehensive, but he answered. "We drove up in my car, took about three hours. We went to a bar up there called the Yacht Club and Mike met a man there. Old-time hard man, but I didn't know him. Mike gave him an envelope and he gave Mike a suitcase full of blocks of C-4 and detonators. There was also a pistol and a silencer in the suitcase and two boxes of ammo."

"Was the pistol a 9mm Beretta Model 92?"

"I'm not sure. Is that the pistol the army uses now?"

"Yes, since 1985. The Beretta Model 92F."

"Then that's what it was. The hard man said it was the U.S. Army pistol."

"How many pounds of explosive were there?"

"I don't know exactly, but the suitcase was heavy. Maybe forty pounds."

"Did you ask Mulrooney what he planned to do with it?"

"No. I figured that if he wanted me to know, he would have told me. To tell you the truth, I was kind of happy that he didn't tell me."

"What happened next?"

"Mike wanted to make sure that everything worked, so we drove down a dirt road into the woods. First we did a bit of target practice with the pistol, then we tried a bit of the C-4 in some clever little bombs he'd invented. We left them there in the woods and walked a ways back toward the car. Then he let me set them off. Couldn't see the explosion, but we sure heard them. Worked fine."

"Describe these 'clever little bombs' for me."

"Maybe I can do better than that, but you'll both have to promise never to tell Dorothy."

"You've got one of these bombs?" McKenna asked.

"I'm not saying I do, but you have to promise. Not a word to Dorothy," Jack insisted.

"Okay, we promise," McKenna said impatiently. "What have you got?" but Jack wasn't satisfied. He looked to Cisco, waiting.

"Okay. You've got my promise, but this had better be good," Cisco said.

"I'll show you how good it is," Jack said confidently, getting up. "It's in the garage." McKenna and Cisco followed Jack through the kitchen and into the small, attached garage. It was used as a storage area and workshop. The walls were lined with stacked cardboard boxes and old furniture. "Dorothy never comes in here," Jack confided as he hefted a large box onto the floor from the stack. He took two new suitcases and an old toolbox from the box.

"You got the boys' clothes in there?" McKenna asked.

"Yeah, all new. Mike hadn't seen them for years and didn't know their sizes. I didn't either, but I was in a better position to estimate. He gave me five hundred dollars and asked me to buy the clothes and the suitcases."

Cisco opened up one of the suitcases. It was crammed with new boys' clothes. Jack had been clever enough to remove all the sales tags. "Nice job, Jack," Cisco said. "Now, where's the bombs?"

"Right here." Jack snapped open the toolbox. Two of Mulrooney's devices were in the tray on top, both with numbers painted on the tops. He gave number 39 to Cisco and number 91 to McKenna. "Dorothy would kill me if she knew I had these in the house," Jack said.

"How many of these does Mulrooney have?" McKenna asked.

"Lots, I guess. Enough to give me these."

"Why did he do that?"

"Because I wanted them."

"Why?"

"I don't know," Jack admitted. "Maybe having them here helps me think I'm part of the movement."

"How do they work?" Cisco asked.

It took Jack a few minutes to explain the simple detonation procedure.

Mulrooney had the separate receiving frequencies of each of his bombs programmed into his modified cell phone. He only had to turn his bomb on to activate the detonator, then dial the bomb number into Recall. Press Send and Mulrooney got his noise.

"Tell me about his new car," McKenna said.

"It's a pretty new maroon Chevy Lumina. On the way home from Hunter we stopped in a service area to get some coffee and use the men's room. When we came out we saw two guys leave the car and go into the McDonald's. Mike watched them to make sure they were sitting down to eat, and then he stole the car. Amazing, took him only moments. I waited in my car and he took his knapsack over. Next thing I knew, he had it started and waved as he passed me. Heard from him since, but that was the last I saw of him."

"Where were you supposed to meet him tomorrow with his kids?"

"At Bethesda Fountain in Central Park. Nine-fifteen. Told me he might be late, that I should wait until he got there."

"He beeped you to give you the instructions?"

"Uh-huh, but the beep wasn't to his usual number. Sounded like he was in a bar somewhere. Am I still picking up the kids?"

"Sure are, but you're leaving your kids home."

"What about the polygraph for me and Dorothy?"

"I don't think we'll have to do that. You're off the hook," McKenna said.

After leaving the O'Reilly's house, McKenna took 39 and 91 to Finan with a request. Finan briefly examined the devices, then took them into the Bomb Disposal truck and easily dismantled them for McKenna in minutes, removing from each the C-4, the detonator, and the AAA battery that powered the radio receiver once the small bomb was armed. He gave what was left of the inert devices back to McKenna.

THIRTY-SIX

The NYPD's radio shop in Queens occupied a modern, three-story facility bristling with antennas. The building was large enough to be police headquarters in any medium-sized American city. In New York, a city with forty thousand cops requiring constant communicative capacity while working between the skyscrapers and in the subways, it was simply the radio shop.

Before his assignment to TARU, Gaspar had worked as a technician and electronic jack-of-all-trades at the radio shop and Sheeran had given him the message. He was to meet McKenna there, but McKenna got to the shop first after the short drive from Jackson Heights. Although there was certainly an evildoer afoot in the land, Cisco was finally resting and snoring loudly in the seat next to him as McKenna called Rollins at Scotland Yard. It was ten o'clock in the morning there and Rollins was at his desk. "How are things progressing?" he asked McKenna.

"Things are certainly progressing, but it doesn't look good for us at this precise moment. We need some help, and I believe that you're in a position to give it to us."

"Naturally, I'll do whatever I can," Rollins said.

"There's a rumor floating around Belfast that you folks have developed a transmitter that detonates IRA bombs a trifle prematurely. According to this rumor, you've managed to blow some bombs while they were still in the bombers' hands."

"Yes, I've heard that rumor."

"Time's getting short here and I can't waste it on bullshit, Inspector. Do you have it or don't you?"

"I'm trusting you and violating the Official Secrets Act, but we have it. However, I must tell you that its uses are limited. It only works on a radio-detonated bomb, and then only once that bomb is armed."

"We're talking radio-detonated bombs here. I'll worry about the arming part later," McKenna said.

"Are you telling me that you want to borrow one of our Paddy Poofers?"

"Paddy Poofer? Is that what the thing's called?"

"Yes, colloquially. Rather derogatory and facetious term for such a thing, I know, but I don't come up with these names."

"The bad news for us is that I'd like to borrow one, but I don't think we have enough time for you to send it here. We have to make one."

"Really? If time is your major problem, I don't know if that's possible. I'm certain they must be rather sophisticated, complicated devices."

"We're gonna try. I've got a rather sophisticated guy meeting me shortly, so here's what I'd like you to do. Get ahold of the schematics and a technical person who knows how the thing works. When you've done that, call me back."

"That's a tall request, but I'll do what I can. Of course, I'll have to run it by my superiors first."

"Good. While you're doing that, try to keep in mind that we're fighting your miserable war over here."

According to Gaspar, Rollins had been wrong on both counts. After talking to the British technician and studying the schematics he had faxed to the radio shop, Gaspar concluded that the British secret weapon was neither sophisticated nor complicated. "No new technology involved," he told Mc-

Kenna. "Could build one in the basement of a Radio Shack in a day. With all the parts and tools we've got here, we're talking only hours. Of course, it won't be a small, mobile model like theirs, but we'll still be able to transmit all the frequencies from here."

After Gaspar had explained to McKenna in simple layman's terms how the Paddy Poofer functioned, McKenna thought that Gaspar was selling the British short. The key to the device was the computer program they had downloaded into the radio shop's communications computer. This program selected each ultrahigh frequency in the range known to be used in the IRA digital radio detonators and electronically instructed the transmitter in the Paddy Poofer to broadcast it for a microsecond before moving on to the next.

It took the Paddy Poofer just under fourteen seconds to cover all the frequencies in the range. That was too long for McKenna. Mulrooney could arm one of his bombs and be away before the Paddy Poofer found his frequency, so McKenna knew he had to take a chance and narrow the range. He gave the inert bombs to Gaspar. "How long will it take you to determine the frequencies these are set to?"

"Maybe fifteen minutes apiece."

"Then that's our new range for the Paddy Poofer. Just cover all the frequencies between the ones those are set to. Can you do that?"

"Sure, once I get it up and running."

It took McKenna only one phone call to establish that Mulrooney had stolen the car from the thruway service area merely for temporary transportation. The state police had taken the report from the owner at the thruway service area and the car was recovered two days later in Midtown. Mulrooney had left it parked at a fire hydrant.

McKenna wasn't surprised and hadn't expected Mulrooney to still be using the car. Mulrooney had grown up on the streets of Belfast, a place where some kids steal cars just to take their mothers to church. Since Mulrooney could so easily take one in under two minutes, McKenna figured that he used a different car every day and hadn't bought gas in years.

McKenna then hid out and took a nap in Brunette's office while Sheeran explained the plan of the day to the new teams arriving from home. In an effort to lull Mulrooney into a false sense of security, the teams set up near the Mullen home in Woodlawn and those surveilling Jack O'Reilly as he picked up Mulrooney's kids would remain on the old PD frequency, the one McKenna figured Mulrooney would be monitoring. The base would also maintain a sporadic chatter on the old frequency with nonexistent units spread throughout the city.

Meanwhile, the real manpower would be using the FBI radios Brunette had gotten from Shields and would be concentrated in Midtown. Those units assigned to surveil the British installations and Brenda McDermott's apartment building in Woodlawn would also be using the FBI radios.

It was D day and Sheeran wanted to field the maximum manpower possible, so he broke a few rules and further depleted his overtime budget. Most of the detectives who had been scheduled to go off duty at four that morning were permitted to remain working for more overtime dollars if they felt up to it. Sheeran had plenty of takers and was able to field an additional twenty-two teams. He also had every member of the Bomb Squad working and positioned throughout Midtown, as well as two helicopters from the Aviation Unit. It was Mulrooney's move.

McKenna awoke at seven-thirty, feeling refreshed. He washed up in Brunette's bathroom, then went downstairs to the Major Case Squad office. Eddie Morgan and three other men were there manning the radios, talking to one another over the air for Mulrooney's benefit. McKenna found Sheeran in his office, sitting back in his chair with his feet up on his desk as he read the morning edition of the *New York Post*. The headline on the tabloid was HAVE YOU SEEN THIS MAN? and McKenna could see that Mulrooney's old NYPD arrest photo filled the rest of the front page. The *Times* and the *Daily News* were stacked in front of Sheeran on his desk.

"How'd we do?" McKenna asked.

"The Jackson Heights stuff is there, along with everything Ray told them last night."

"How did they treat Ray?"

"Not too badly, considering. Matter of fact, better than I'd expected. See for yourself, but let me give you some good news first. I talked to Tavlin and you were right about Crowley."

"When he told Mulrooney he was on a pay phone, he was really sitting at Brenda's?" McKenna asked.

"Uh-huh. Mulrooney doesn't know we know about her. I've got a good team up there, just in case they show."

That's just an outside chance, McKenna thought. They're gonna all be in Midtown this morning. He grabbed a chair and picked up the *Daily News*.

The *News*'s front page also featured Mulrooney's old arrest photo under the banner and subscript:

HE'S MEAN, HE'S MAD, AND HE'S BACK
FORMER NYPD COP TERRORIZES CITY AND WORLD

The eight-page article described Mulrooney's history and heinous crimes, with special emphasis given to his most recent spree in Jackson Heights and at the Harbor Lights Motel. He had fulfilled every editor's dream: bombings, terror, murder, and mutilation, all wrapped in one large, nasty package.

Although Brunette took a few slaps in the article, there were no body punches thrown at him; it emphasized the positive role of the NYPD in the affair, crediting the department for identifying Mulrooney and associating him with his bombings and killings.

Brunette even fared fairly well in the editorials. While the fact that Mulrooney had worked for the department for seventeen years wasn't glossed over, his hiring was attributed to the looser screening policies of previous administrations. It noted that Brunette had tightened up the screening process considerably, leading McKenna to conclude that attacking a popular police commissioner like Brunette doesn't sell too many papers. However, McKenna realized that political popularity was a fleeting thing, easily eroded. Another bombing by Mulrooney involving major loss of life would leave Brunette with many tough questions to answer, and they wouldn't be asked with a friendly smile.

"Have we gotten any calls yet?" McKenna asked Sheeran.

"Three, so far. One came from a desk clerk at the Holiday Inn in Staten Island. He says Mulrooney stayed there one day last week. Paid cash, hasn't seen him since. One came from a guy with a brogue. Wouldn't leave his name, but he said he saw him in the Pioneer last week. Then, of course, we got one from a woman who said she was in psychic communication with Mulrooney and that she's pretty sure he was her father in her last life. She wants police protection before she'll tell us what he's thinking and planning, so she's not completely bonkers."

McKenna thought there was some good news in the calls. The fact that a man with a brogue who drinks in a radical, Irish bar like the Pioneer called with information indicated to him that Mulrooney had little support in the Irish community; the newspaper articles about the darker side of his activities had denied him one likely support base and a place to hide. The fact that Mulrooney stayed only one night in the Holiday Inn confirmed another of McKenna's suspicions: Like Martin McGuinn and Yasser Arafat, the man never slept twice in one place.

There would be more calls, so Mulrooney would be unwise to show his face around town with his picture plastered on the front page, McKenna thought. Matter of fact, he'd be crazy not to get out of town now.

Sheeran read McKenna's mind. "You think he's gonna stick around long enough to pull whatever he's planning?" he asked.

"Certain of it. We've still got big problems."

McKenna and Sheeran left the office in separate cars with different missions in mind, but both were headed for Midtown. They had each checked out both a PD radio and an FBI radio. Sheeran intended to get closer to the action and check up on his troops in Midtown while McKenna went to the Plaza to pick up Thor. He valued Thor's insight and wanted to tell him the plan of the day with one question in mind: What else could we be doing to get Mulrooney? In his present state of mind, Thor would have the answer.

THIRTY-SEVEN

The accounts in the newspapers about him and his history enraged Mulrooney, but he couldn't stop reading. Before that day, many people would have considered him a hero and a patriot, but he realized that he was now being portrayed as a monster to all. He would never be able to face his sons again under those conditions, but he had a plan that offered him a faint glimmer of hope. He thought he might succeed because he had already overcome the main obstacle. The body stretched out at his feet on the floor of the maintenance shed in the center of the park offered a silent testament to his success.

Mulrooney recognized that he had been lucky so far, but thought he might pull it off. With just a little more luck, those responsible for his misery would be made to pay.

Those responsible were Brunette and McKenna, but it wasn't Brunette who had brought him to Gramercy Park. As far as Mulrooney was concerned, Brunette's fate was already sealed. It was McKenna he was after. Feck with me and mine, I'll feck with you and yours, he thought as he threw the *Daily News* on top of the body. He had the doors cracked open on both sides of the shed, so he looked around outside once again to make sure everything was in place.

Through the spokes of the high wrought-iron fence surrounding the park, Mulrooney could see the Gramercy Park Hotel on the other side of East 21st Street. Parked across the street from the hotel was a news van, and a group of reporters were gathered in front. Mulrooney figured that they were all waiting there to solicit comments from either McKenna or his wife about the infidelity story hinted at in yesterday's *Post*, but they served another purpose as far as he was concerned. A show of activity by the reporters would tell him that either McKenna or, better yet, his wife was leaving the hotel.

Ambery and Crowley were also in place, dressed in blue maintenance workers uniform, armed with pistols under their jackets, and raking the grass outside the shed. Although Ambery still looked stiff and obviously in pain, Mulrooney knew that they were accepted in their disguises. None of the women with their children or the joggers strolling the inside track in the park that morning paid his men the slightest bit of attention.

Mulrooney crossed the shed to check out the other half of the park through the door on that side. As he looked around, he noticed a new family arriving in the park via the East 20th Street gate. While the husband held the gate open, his attractive young wife pushed their wide, ornate baby carriage into the park. He followed, holding the hand of his young daughter.

At first, it was the husband who held Mulrooney's interest. He was a big man and looked either Asian or Polynesian. He was wearing a suit and looking around as his daughter jabbered away to him. Everything about him screamed "Cop!" to Mulrooney, but there were a few other things about the family he noticed. Both parents had dark hair, yet their daughter's was sandy-colored. Then there were the noises coming from the wide carriage. To Mulrooney, it sounded like two babies crying loudly, and he knew that McKenna had a young wife and three children: a two-year-old daughter and a new set of twins. If it wasn't for two questions he had, Mulrooney would have acted on the assumption that he was looking at the McKenna family. Who is the big guy? was one question and, If that's the McKenna family, then where did they come from and why did they use the gate farthest from the hotel? was the other.

As the family walked across the park, they had Mulrooney's total attention. The woman was rocking the baby carriage as she pushed it slowly, and the man was engaged in conversation with the little girl. They passed from Mulrooney's view and he went across the shed to the other door to track them. "You see them?" he whispered to Crowley and Ambery. The two men said nothing, just nodded their heads as they continued raking the grass outside.

Then confirmation came from an unexpected quarter. One of the reporters outside the hotel had also seen them. He detached himself from the group, walked across the street to the park fence, and yelled to the woman. "Mrs. McKenna, can I have just a few minutes of your time?"

"No, you certainly may not. Leave us alone," Angelita yelled back.

"Listen to the lady, Tommy, or I'll come over there and give you a few minutes of my time. You wouldn't like that," Pao added loudly and with menace in his voice.

"C'mon, Pao. Have a heart. I've got a job to do," the reporter pleaded.

"To hell with you and your job. Get lost, leech," Pao yelled back. Then the family turned left and walked slowly on the path, away from the shed with their backs to Mulrooney and his men. The reporter didn't say another word, but he walked along the fence outside, keeping pace.

"The big one's a cop, so be careful. Kill him and get the woman and the little girl," Mulrooney whispered to Ambery and Crowley. "I'll cover you from here."

Once again, Ambery and Crowley merely nodded their understanding. They slowly walked on the grass toward the family, raking the ground as they went. Mulrooney stayed out of sight inside and took out his pistol. Bracing his arm on the door frame, he lined up on Pao's back as his men raked their way toward them. Angelita had stopped and was bending over the carriage. Pao stood beside her holding Janine's hand, still with his back toward Mulrooney, but he was looking all around with his other hand under his jacket.

"What the hell are you looking for?" Mulrooney said under his breath. "We're behind you and getting close enough. You big dummy, you don't have a clue."

But Pao did have a clue. When Ambery and Crowley were twenty feet from the carriage, they dropped their rakes and went for their guns. They weren't fast enough. Pao pushed Janine to the ground and whirled around with his gun in his hand in one motion. Crouching, he stepped to the side and fired six quick shots, three for each. Ambery and Crowley crumpled to the ground while Pao looked around with his gun at eye level, searching the park for another target.

"What the hell!" Mulrooney muttered. Pao's quick action had momentarily stunned him and his aim was off. His sights were centered on the place Pao had been one second before. As Mulrooney adjusted his aim to this new set of circumstances, Pao saw the edge of Mulrooney's head, his right arm protruding from the shed fifty feet from him, and the gun in Mulrooney's hand. He fired again.

Mulrooney felt the bullet pass through his right triceps, but that didn't bother him. He had been shot before and was no stranger to pain. Another man might have dropped the gun, but not Mulrooney. He knew that the best way to eliminate the pain was to eliminate the source. He fired twice, hitting his target both times, center mass.

Pao fell backward, dropping his gun as he clutched his chest. He thrashed on the ground, trying to get up, while Angelita hovered over him and Janine lay on the ground next to him, crying and frozen in shock.

Mulrooney considered giving Pao another bullet, but then he noticed a curious thing. Pao's legs weren't working for him—he was paralyzed, but still a source of some danger. Pao had abandoned the idea of trying to get up; instead, he was trying to reach his gun, just three feet from his outstretched hand. He couldn't, so he yelled, "Run, Angelita! Run!"

But Angelita didn't run. She couldn't leave her children and she wouldn't leave Pao, but she thought she had another option as she reached for Pao's gun on the ground.

She didn't. Mulrooney fired again and the bullet ricocheted off the ground, inches from Pao's pistol. Angelita froze, then calmly stood up and faced the shed.

At the first shot, every reporter across the street and every other person in the park had either dropped to the ground or scrambled for cover. The scene reminded Mulrooney of an air raid drill, with everybody hiding or stretched out on the ground with their hands over their heads. It's time to end this little drama, he thought. He shifted his pistol to his left hand, left the shed, and quickly walked toward his quarry with his gun extended in front of him. He kept aim on his target as he approached.

Angelita still made no move, although she saw that Mulrooney wasn't aiming at her. His pistol was centered on Janine, still lying on the ground and crying. "Keep quiet, Janine, and don't move," Angelita ordered. "Johnny's going to be all right, but don't move."

Janine obeyed, but Pao still moved. Lying on his back, he managed to prop himself up on his elbows so he could watch Mulrooney approach. There was a look of sheer hatred on Pao's face.

Mulrooney stopped at Ambery and Crowley and glanced down. He saw at once that Ambery was dead, hit in the chest with all three rounds, his unseeing eyes staring at the sky. Crowley's eyes were also open, but he wasn't dead. He was wounded, but he had been playing dead to avoid another shot from Pao. The bulletproof vest he was wearing under his shirt had saved him, but he had been knocked to the ground by the impact of Pao's rounds. All three rounds had hit Crowley in the chest, but one had passed through his right arm first as he had reached across for the gun in his shoulder holster under his jacket.

Mulrooney briefly considered shooting Crowley as the man looked up at him, but then he decided he still had use for him if he didn't bleed to death first. "Get up," he ordered, still keeping his aim on Janine. "That big bully can't hurt you no more."

Crowley did as he was told. He rose and amused Mulrooney as he tried to get his gun out of his holster with his wounded arm. Although shot himself, Mulrooney decided to help him. Still keeping his sights on Janine, he reached under Crowley's jacket with his wounded right arm, pulled out the pistol, and handed it to him. "C'mon, hard man," he said sarcastically, loud enough for Angelita to hear. "If any of them moves, shoot the girl first. Then shoot the lovely Mrs. McKenna."

Crowley followed Mulrooney to Pao and the McKenna family. The twins were screaming, but nobody else was moving. While Crowley covered Janine, as ordered, Mulrooney stood over Pao. "You paralyzed?" he asked, pointing his pistol at Pao's head.

"Yeah, you prick," Pao snarled up at him. "I hope your arm's killing you, but I don't feel a thing."

"My arm's fine, but let's see about you," Mulrooney said. He quickly shifted his pistol and shot Pao once in the left knee.

Both Crowley and Angelita jumped, but Pao didn't flinch. "I told you, scumbag. You can't hurt me," Pao said. "If you're such a good shot, why don't you see if you can put one between my eyes."

"Please don't shoot him again," Angelita pleaded. "He can't hurt you now."

"Shut up," Mulrooney said, then turned his attention back to Pao. "You'd like me to kill you, wouldn't you?" Mulrooney asked, but Pao didn't answer. He just glared up at him.

"No, big man. I'm not going to shoot you again," Mulrooney said. He reached down, picked up Pao's pistol, and tossed it near Ambery's body. "When we leave, you can crawl over and do it yourself. I know I would, if I were you. But I do still feel like showing off a wee bit, so let's see what else there is around here."

Mulrooney looked around, searching for a target, and then he found one. On the other side of the fence was the reporter who had started the whole thing. He was crouched behind a car, but his head was showing as he talked on his cell phone. Mulrooney shifted his aim from Pao for a second, fired once, and sent a bullet through the cell phone and through the reporter's head. "That's one you owe me. If you live long enough, tell McKenna that I'm in charge now," he said to Pao, then turned his attention to Angelita. "You and your tyke are coming with us," he said. "Pick her up and let's go."

"I'll do whatever you want, but please leave my baby here," Angelita pleaded.

"I'm leaving two of them here, but I'll shoot those screaming brats now if you don't mind me. Let's go."

Angelita picked up Janine and the four walked to the East 21st Street gate as Pao started crawling for his pistol.

McKenna picked Thor up in front of the hotel at nine-thirty. There was a constant stream of reports coming over the PD radio by then. O'Reilly had picked up the kids in Woodlawn and was at Bethesda Fountain with them, waiting for Mulrooney. The FBI radio was silent.

Thor had just gotten into the car when a transmission came over both radios. "Base to all Manhattan units. We're getting a report over the division radio of multiple shots fired in Gramercy Park. Thirteen Eddie is in pursuit of a black late-model Lincoln, eastbound on 20th Street from the park."

Could that have anything to do with us? McKenna wondered, but not for long. The next transmission convinced him that it did. "Base to all Manhattan units," came shouted over. "Thirteen George reports that Sector Eddie has blown up, East 20th Street and First Avenue."

McKenna reached for the radio, but wherever he was, Sheeran got to his first. "Squad CO to Base. Are any units still in pursuit of that black Lincoln?"

"Negative, Inspector. Thirteen George reports he was behind Eddie when the car blew up. The street's blocked."

"Injuries?" Sheeran asked.

"Yeah, Inspector. It sounds bad."

Fifth Avenue had been cleared of traffic for the parade and hundreds of cops lined the barriers, holding back the throngs of spectators that had already arrived, so McKenna used the avenue as his best way downtown, speeding with his red light on and his siren screaming. Along the way he monitored the radio closely and heard progress reports coming over the new frequency. Teams all over Midtown were pulling over black late-model Lincolns, but McKenna wasn't overly optimistic. Late-model black Lincolns were used by the many car services in Manhattan and next to yellow cabs, they were the most common cars cruising the streets of Midtown.

McKenna reached 20th Street and Second Avenue in minutes, but that was as close as they could get. The street was blocked with traffic, so McKenna and Thor left the car double-parked and ran down the block toward the many emergency vehicles already at the scene. An empty blue-and-white radio car was lying on its side, blocking 20th Street just before First Avenue. The left front fender was missing, its roof was crushed in, and every window was shattered. To the right of it was a badly damaged parked car, its left side pushed in, and behind it was another empty blue-and-white with its doors open and its roof lights still flashing. There were dozens of cops and firemen surrounding the destroyed blue-and-white.

McKenna surmised at once what had happened. Sector Eddie had seen or heard something at Gramercy Park and had chased the Lincoln with Mulrooney inside. They put the chase over the air and George had joined in. However, Mulrooney didn't like being chased, so he opened his door and dropped one of his little bombs from his car. When Eddie passed over it, he pressed his Send button and that was the end of the pursuit. The force of the explosion pushed the car onto its side and it hit the parked car, crushing its roof. The Sector George cops jumped out of their car and pulled the Eddie cops from the wreckage through the shattered windshield. Those cops were either at the hospital or on their way there.

Thor had reached the same conclusion as McKenna, but he was thinking clearer at the moment. "I think that maybe you should look for another bomb on this street," he suggested calmly.

He's right, McKenna thought. Who's to say that Mulrooney didn't drop other bombs during the pursuit. If he did, they're armed. McKenna was looking up and down 20th Street when his phone rang. "You better come over to Gramercy Park right away," Sheeran told him.

"Why? What's happening there."

"Just get here. Pao wants to talk to you."

McKenna was momentarily panic-stricken and felt his stomach churn. "I'll be right there."

"More trouble?" Thor asked.

"Yeah, big trouble," McKenna answered. "You're gonna have to take charge here. C'mon." McKenna ran to the destroyed radio car with Thor following. The highest-ranking cop there so far was a sergeant. McKenna grabbed him by the arm, startling him, and asked, "Sarge, do you know who I am?"

"Sure I do. You're McKenna."

"And this is Chief Thor Eríkson from Iceland. He knows more about what's going on here than anybody else here now. Do whatever he tells you," McKenna said. He turned and ran back up 20th Street toward Gramercy Park, three blocks away, leaving Thor and the confused sergeant standing there.

As McKenna ran across Third Avenue, he saw many radio cars and ambulances on the street at the south entrance to the park, one block away. Then he heard a shot and pushed his pace to the limit.

Sheeran was waiting for him at the gate, holding it open. He was trembling and looking grim. "Brian, I'm sorry," he said, putting his arm around McKenna's shoulder.

McKenna felt panic set in and he shook off Sheeran's arm. "What? Angelita?" he asked.

"He's got them, Brian. Angelita, and Janine, too."

McKenna felt dizzy and he grabbed onto the fence for support. For a second he imagined what Mulrooney would like to do to Angelita and his little girl, but the scene was too horrible for him to contemplate as pictures of Meaghan and Frieda flashed through his mind. He shook his head and focused on Sheeran.

"Snap out of it, Brian. We need you and there's not much time," Sheeran said. "Follow me!" He turned and ran toward a line of uniformed cops, detectives, and ambulance crews gathered in the middle of the park, but McKenna stood by the gate, stunned. Then he saw the twins' baby carriage at the edge of the line of cops and heard them bawling. A female cop was bent over the carriage, trying in vain to calm the boys down. McKenna found his legs and ran after Sheeran.

On the other side of the cops was Pao, lying on the ground with his back propped up against a tree. Blood covered his legs and the front of his suit from his chest to his stomach, but he was conscious and still armed. He held his pistol in his hand, pointed at the cops and waving it to keep everyone back. There were many spent shell casings and an empty magazine on the ground next to him. Pao had reloaded.

Lying facedown on the ground ten feet from Pao was the body of another man dressed in blue work clothes. There were two rakes lying next to him, one on each side, and he had been shot so many times in the head that his features were unrecognizable.

On the other side of the park, behind the fence and across the street from the Gramercy Park Hotel, many reporters and photographers were snapping pictures of the scene in the park and another scene outside the park: A covered body was being loaded on a stretcher into an ambulance. A uniformed cop guarded the park gate to keep the press from getting in.

McKenna looked down at the pitiful sight of his friend lying on the ground. "What are you doing, Johnny?" he asked.

"Dying, but first I wanted to apologize and explain," Pao said with labored breath, but his tone was conversational as he pointed his pistol at McKenna.

"You're not gonna shoot me, Johnny, are you?"

"Of course not. I'm gonna shoot this prick again." Pao turned his gun and quickly fired another round into the top of the dead man's head. McKenna jumped, startled, but all the other cops there had become used to the spectacle.

Pao returned his aim to McKenna, but he was smiling. "I do that every time they get too close. Sometimes just when I feel like it."

"Good for you. Nice shooting, Johnny."

"Thanks."

"Who was he?"

"Used to be Billy Ambery."

"Ambery? Good work, Johnny. Are you in pain?"

"I'm having a hard time breathing, but no pain. I'm paralyzed."

"Johnny, we have to get you to a hospital. You're bleeding to death right here."

"Good. Don't want to live in no wheelchair, don't think I'm gonna have to."

McKenna briefly considered just taking the gun from Pao and getting him to the hospital, but he decided to respect Pao's wishes. "Go ahead, Johnny. Tell me what happened."

"Not my idea. Angelita's. Boys were acting up. Mulrooney and his two punks were here. Sent them over to get her, he was hiding in the shed. Saw the two dopes, recognized this one right away," Pao said, firing another round into the top of Ambery's head. "He was too stiff, dropped them both. Didn't see Mulrooney till too late, but I winged him, too."

"Where's Crowley?"

"Prick must've had a vest on, but he's hurting, too. Got him in the arm. Bleeding bad."

"What was Angelita doing then?"

"Told her to run, but she didn't. Stayed with me. He said he'd shoot Janine if they didn't go with him. Gave me a message, said to tell you he's in charge now. Sorry."

"Nothing to be sorry for, Johnny. You did all you could," McKenna said.

"Not enough, but one more thing. May be important," Pao said, but McKenna could see that he was slipping fast. Pao's eyes were no longer focused on him and he dropped his hand holding the gun into his lap. McKenna ran to Pao and bent over him, and so did an ambulance crew with a stretcher. They started to lift Pao up, but McKenna stopped them. "What's important, Johnny?" he asked, holding on to Pao.

From somewhere, Pao found the strength to answer. "Parkie. Parkie uniform under his jacket."

McKenna knew at once what he meant. *Parkie* was what every kid who had grown up in New York called the Parks Department workers in their green uniforms, but McKenna didn't have time to think about it. Pao had closed his eyes and McKenna thought he was unconscious as the ambulance crew lifted him up and strapped him onto the stretcher. Then Pao opened his eyes again. "Brian?"

"I'm here, Johnny."

"Worried," Pao whispered, barely audible.

"What are you worried about, Johnny?" McKenna asked, putting his ear to Pao's lips.

"Don't see the light."

"What light, Johnny?"

"The light in the tunnel. Nobody waiting for me."

"Don't worry, Johnny. You'll see it, and the Big Guy's waiting for you," McKenna said. Through his tears, he stared down at his friend, then kissed him on the forehead. Then he noticed that Pao wasn't breathing, but he hoped that Pao had heard him before he had left to learn the big secret.

The ambulance crew tried to revive Pao as McKenna silently cried, but it was no use. Johnny Pao had waited around to offer his apology and give McKenna his message, but now he was dead.

Sheeran stood next to McKenna with his arm around him as the ambulance crew carried Pao's body away, but only until the park gate closed on them. "Pull yourself together, Brian," he ordered. "We'll all cry for Johnny later."

The command was unnecessary. McKenna had already pulled himself together and was thinking furiously, clearer than he had ever thought before. Why would Mulrooney be wearing a parkie's uniform? he wondered. Ambery's not wearing a parkie uniform, so Mulrooney must know that this park isn't serviced by the Parks Department. Something to do with picking up his kids in Central Park? Maybe, but maybe it has something to do with whatever else he's planning for today.

The twins were still crying, so McKenna turned to Sheeran. "Thanks, Inspector. I'm all right now. Just gonna attend to my boys, and then we're back to work."

"Good, but please make it fast," Sheeran said. Then he bent down, picked up Pao's gun from the ground, and put it in his belt.

McKenna walked over to the female cop rocking the baby carriage. Another cop was standing next to her. "Do you have any children?" Mc-Kenna asked her.

"Three."

"Perfect. What's your name?"

"Mary Anne Rutelege."

"And you?" McKenna asked her partner.

"Kenny Dulberg."

McKenna took his apartment keys off his key ring and gave them to Mary Anne, along with his address. Then he pointed out their new charges. "This is Shane and he gets the Similac. This one is Sean and he gets the Enfamil. The formula is in the cabinet over the sink. Don't mix it up or they'll make you really miserable. Both of you stay there until I get home and don't let anyone in but me."

"What time do you think that'll be?" she asked.

"Lord knows, but it won't be before I get their mother and sister back."

"You can count on us," Dulberg said.

"I know I can. Thank you," McKenna said, then watched Rutelege and Dulberg wheel his kids from the park.

"What now?" Sheeran asked.

"Mulrooney's gonna contact me and we have to be ready for that. But first I have an important call to make." He called the radio shop and got Gaspar on the line. "You got the Paddy Poofer together yet?"

"Just finished. I was just about to test it out."

"Don't do that!" McKenna said. "He's got my wife and daughter with him."

"Sorry to hear that. Complicates things a bit, doesn't it?"

"Yeah, quite a bit," McKenna said before cutting the connection. "Are any of the Brit places we're guarding near a park?" he asked Sheeran.

"None I can think of."

"Then it has to be something along the parade route, maybe alongside Central Park from 59th to 86th Streets."

"Yeah, but there's nothing to blow up there and I can't think of another park along the parade route."

McKenna took a mental ride up Fifth Avenue, searching the parade route for another park. He couldn't think of one, either. Then he noticed Joe Walsh and his Crime Scene Unit team standing outside the shed, taking photos of the interior. "What's going on in there?"

"Another body," Sheeran answered. "The guy who usually works this park."

"Sam?" McKenna asked.

"Yeah. Sam Goldman. You know him?"

"Sure I know him. Nice old guy, worked here for years. Ambery is wearing his clothes." McKenna walked over to Walsh with Sheeran following. Stretched out on the floor of the shed was Sam, dressed in jeans and a sweatshirt. He had been killed by a single bullet to the head and there was no exit wound, so McKenna knew Mulrooney had used his silencer when he had shot him. The shed was sparsely furnished with two wall lockers, a work bench with drawers underneath, a small table with two chairs, a cooler, and a large wire trash container. Garden tools hung from pegs on the wall and a single lightbulb hanging from the ceiling illuminated the shed.

"Has this place been searched yet?" McKenna asked Walsh.

"Not yet. We've only begun processing the crime scene, but it has to be photographed first."

"Forget the pictures, Joe. We don't have time."

"What are we looking for?"

"Two parkie uniforms," McKenna answered, gratified that, for once, he knew more about a crime scene than Walsh did. Both of the wall lockers were locked, so McKenna searched Sam's body for the keys. They weren't there. "They took Sam's keys, the uniforms are in lockers," he said, then searched for tools to break the locks. Sheeran found a hammer and a chisel in one of the drawers under the workbench and did the honors, breaking both padlocks.

The first locker was a bust, containing only one of Sam's clean and pressed blue work uniforms and a blue jacket. The two green Parks Department uniforms were rolled up at the bottom of the other locker.

"How did you know they'd be here?" Sheeran asked.

"Easy. When Pao told me Mulrooney was wearing a green parkie uniform and I saw Ambery in Sam's blue uniform, I figured the other two stashed their parkie uniforms in here after they changed into Sam's clothes."

"He was killed for his clothes?" Walsh asked.

"More than that," McKenna said. "Mulrooney can't show his face, so he killed Sam for the clothes and so he'd have a place to hide and watch while Ambery and Crowley were doing their raking act outside. Sam usually starts work around six, so that's when they ambushed him here, probably just as he was opening the shed."

"How'd they get in the park? Climb the fence?"

"I guess so. I bet Crowley climbed over and let the other two in."

"Bastards," Walsh said. "Mulrooney could've just tied the old guy up. He didn't have to kill him."

"Not his style," McKenna said. He took the parkie uniforms from the locker and unrolled them on the ground, front up. Both uniforms had a smeared line of dirt across the top of the jacket and the upper leg part of the pants.

"Looks like they were doing some kind of heavy work in a park somewhere," Sheeran observed.

"Maybe digging to plant a bomb?" McKenna asked no one in particular.

Walsh ran his finger across the dirt smear on one of the pants legs until he had gathered a small sample. He rubbed the dirt between his fingers, then brought the sample to his nose and sniffed it. He had that wondrous, good-thing-I'm-here look on his face, so McKenna and Sheeran knew he was on to something. But Walsh wasn't ready to divulge his secret, yet. He took his magnifying glass from his coat pocket and searched the dirt smear on the pants legs until he found what he was looking for. He smiled again, took a tweezer from his pants pocket, and picked a small, light-colored thread from the pants leg. He held it to his eyes for a second, then nodded knowingly.

"For Christ's sake, Joe! What?" Sheeran implored.

"The men who wore these uniforms have recently been working hard planting trees."

"That's a burlap fiber and some topsoil you've got there?" McKenna guessed.

"Not entirely correct, but please don't take all the fun out of this for me. The fiber *is* burlap, a piece of the burlap bags the roots were wrapped in. However, the dirt is a mixture of topsoil and peat moss that seeped out of the burlap bags as these men carried the trees to wherever they were planting them."

"Now just tell me what kind of trees they were," McKenna said, not really expecting an answer.

"Certainly." Walsh turned the pants pockets inside out and picked up a few green needles clinging to the pocket fabric.

"Pine trees?" McKenna asked.

Walsh examined the needles with his magnifying glass. "Hemlock needles, to be more precise," then he rolled the needles between his fingers. "Still full of moisture," he observed. "They planted their trees sometime last night."

But where, McKenna wondered again. Once again, he retraced the parade route in his mind. Then it came to him. "The library," he shouted.

"Bryant Park is right behind it and I think the library might even be on Parks Department property. That's what he was doing on 41st Street, scoping out the location."

"You're right. It's gotta be the library," Sheeran shouted back. "Do you know what's going on there today?"

"No."

"We've got ILGO there, demonstrating on the steps."

McKenna was sure that was the target. Mulrooney hated gays, and ILGO, the Irish Lesbian and Gay Organization, had been the center of controversy for years. The Loyal Order of Hibernians ran the parade, and every year ILGO applied for permission to march in the parade under their own banner. Every year the Hibernians denied the request and the issue had run its course through the courts, going first one way and then the other as it progressed through the system.

The majority of New Yorkers saw no harm in letting ILGO march as they liked, but not the Hibernians. One year when it looked like ILGO was going to prevail in the courts, the Hibernians had threatened to cancel the parade. Finally, the court of appeals had decided the issue in the Hibernians' favor.

ILGO and many politicians, including the mayor, had publicly disagreed with the court's decision, but there was nothing they could do about it. So every year ILGO was allowed a place along the parade route for an organized demonstration, and this year it was on the steps of the library. "Is the mayor gonna speak with them to show his support?" McKenna asked.

"I guess so. He does every year."

And Brunette's with him, McKenna thought. With one action Mulrooney wipes out ILGO, the mayor who supports them, and the police commissioner of the department that fired and arrested him. "Do we still have the surveillance going on 41st Street?"

"No. With so many places to surveil, it seemed pointless," Sheeran said, shaking his head and smiling wryly. "I cut it last night. It's a shame, because that's where Mulrooney's going."

"I don't think so, not with Angelita and Janine with him and not with everyone knowing his face. He's gonna be watching the parade on TV somewhere or listening to it on one of the Irish radio stations. He'll set his bomb when the mayor and Ray get there." McKenna looked at his watch. Tenfifteen, they were out of time. The parade started at ten o'clock at 28th Street and Fifth Avenue. Only twelve blocks to the library, so the parade should be just about there. It had to be stopped.

Sheeran was way ahead of him, already on his phone to the office. He ordered the parade halted, the library steps cleared of demonstrators, and Fifth Avenue evacuated from East 40th to East 42nd Street. He also wanted the Bomb Squad at the library in force.

"Has O'Reilly still got the kids at the fountain?" McKenna asked Sheeran after he had finished his call.

"Yep, they're all there. I've got six men watching them."

I wish we would've had six cops watching my kids, McKenna thought. Or, better yet, two Johnny Paos.

THIRTY-EIGHT

Thor was standing next to the car on Second Avenue when McKenna got there. "There was only one bomb, the one that went off," he said.

"How are the cops?"

"One dead, one critical. Serious head injuries."

"Damn!" McKenna said. He got behind the wheel and unlocked Thor's door. Before starting the car, he told Thor what had happened in Gramercy Park and his suspicions about the library.

"He's got the two best hostages he could possibly have right now," Thor commented.

"But what's he gonna do with them in the end?" McKenna asked, dreading the thought.

"You're luckier than me, because right now they're valuable to him. I think he will keep them safe until he's clear."

"And then?"

"Then he'll make a deal. He'll exchange them for his two kids."

How can he do that? McKenna wondered. He'd have to know we'd grab him after the exchange. Unless . . . "He's got to have another big bomb planted somewhere else. He'll threaten to blow it unless we let him get away."

"No, he just has to say he's got another bomb planted. He figures that after he blows up the library, you'd be ready to believe him."

Would that work for him? McKenna wondered. Then the same transmission came over both radios. "Base to all Manhattan units. Subject just called 911 from the area of the South Street Seaport. Sixteen-second call. Manhattan units to respond?"

McKenna listened as two ventriloquists in the office answered up on the PD radio for Mulrooney's benefit. One reported his team's location as Broadway and Houston Street and the other said they were at East 19th Street and Third Avenue. Both were about a mile away from the South Street Seaport and McKenna thought that their reported locations should give Mulrooney some comfort.

Meanwhile, Sheeran was out there somewhere busy, directing units to the Seaport over the FBI radio. Six were close and one was actually there, but McKenna was sure that Mulrooney had already moved on.

"What would he be doing at the Seaport?" Thor asked.

"There's loads of open parking lots there under the East River Drive. He just stole another car," McKenna answered. He took an earpiece from his pocket, attached it to the FBI radio, and waited for his phone to ring.

It did, seconds later. "His call to 911 was for you," Eddie Morgan said. "He wants you to call him, says you have his number."

"I do. Get everyone out here ready," McKenna said.

"Okay. Keep him talking, give our teams a chance to get close," Morgan said, then hung up.

"Base to all Manhattan units. Stand by. The subject will be on the phone soon," came over on both frequencies.

McKenna put the earpiece in his left ear so that he could monitor the teams' progress as he talked. Vernon had been right on the money so far, so McKenna quickly reviewed the points he had made: Mulrooney will sound friendly, but don't believe anything he says; he won't keep any promises he makes, but will make good on every threat. McKenna resolved that if Mulrooney sounded friendly, he would reciprocate to keep him on the line. Reading Winthrop's phone number from his notebook, he dialed.

Mulrooney answered at once. "Hello, Brian. How you feeling this fine morning?"

"Very poorly, considering."

"You know who I have here with me, don't you?"

"Yeah, I know. Please don't hurt them and I'll do whatever I can for you."

"Base to all Manhattan units. He's on the East River Drive, heading north. He just crossed 14th Street," McKenna heard on both radios, but it also came over his phone. He had been right—Mulrooney was monitoring their radio.

Mulrooney didn't answer at once, but McKenna heard one of the base ventriloquists report on the PD radio that he was leaving the Seaport and getting on the drive. He was happy to also hear that transmission come through his phone. It was only the PD radio that Mulrooney was listening to, and according to the other transmissions coming over from nonexistent units, nobody was close to him.

But that was very wrong. The transmissions from units coming over McKenna's earpiece told him that many units were close and getting closer. Team Thirty-one was eight blocks behind him on the East River Drive.

"Now that you mention it, there is something you can do for me," Mulrooney said at last. "Are my kids still at the fountain?"

"Yes, they're there."

"Good. Get over there right now and tell them that all that stuff about me killing those girls was a lie the Brits put you up to. Would you do that for me and make it convincing?"

"I'll get right over there. I promise that I'll make them believe me," McKenna said.

"Base to all Manhattan units. Subject's still on the drive, just crossed 25th Street."

"Thank you, Brian," Mulrooney said. "Give me your number so we can chat whenever I want to."

McKenna gave him the number for the cell phone and Mulrooney cut the connection.

"Base to all Manhattan units. Subject's off the phone. Last location was the drive and 30th Street."

"Squad CO to Base," Sheeran transmitted on the FBI radio. "We got any units available to cut off the drive at 42nd Street or 63rd Street?"

There were three units who could possibly make it in time, but then help came from another quarter. "Aviation Two to Squad CO. We can land on the drive at 60th Street in thirty seconds. If he sees us coming down, he'll think we're landing at the 60th Street Heliport."

"Ten four, Aviation Two. Do it," Sheeran ordered.

"On the way down."

McKenna wasn't sure if he liked the plan, but any plan was better than no plan. He waited and listened. The helicopter was down and northbound traffic on the drive was stopped. Then his phone rang. "Traffic's slowing down a bit and I think you're responsible," Mulrooney said. "If it doesn't clear up in thirty seconds, I'm gonna shoot this little girl in the arm."

McKenna's heart dropped to his stomach. "Please, don't do that," he pleaded, but Mulrooney had already cut the connection. He grabbed the PD radio and screamed, "Aviation Two, this is McKenna. Get back in the air now or he's gonna shoot my daughter."

"Ten-four, McKenna. We're taking off now."

"Base, where was he for that last phone call?" McKenna asked on the FBI radio.

"The drive and 43rd Street."

"Team Thirty-one, what's your location?"

"Stopped in traffic on the drive and 39th Street."

Oh God! Please don't let him shoot my little girl, McKenna thought. "McKenna to Team Thirty-one. Let me know the instant traffic starts to move."

"Team Thirty-one. Looks like it's starting to move up ahead."

Thank you, God, McKenna thought as he started the car.

"Where are we going?" Thor asked.

"To tell some lies to some kids. Gonna have to convince them that their father is still a wonderful man."

"What about the library?"

"We'll stop there on the way."

"Team Thirty-one to Base. We're involved in a collision on the drive at 42nd Street. He dropped some bombs on the pavement and set them off after he left. It's about a block ahead of us, three separate explosions. Get as many ambulances as you can to the drive and 43rd Street, there's cars laying all over the place up there."

Wrecking cars and killing people to keep the cops far behind him, McKenna thought. How are we ever going to get this guy? He turned on the siren and headed for the library.

The Bomb Squad was there and so were many television crews, all set up, when McKenna and Thor arrived at the library at ten-thirty. The head of the parade was halted one block away at Fifth Avenue and 40th Street. They had stopped marching, but they hadn't stopped playing; the sound of bagpipes filled the air. The Bomb Squad was on the scene at Fifth Avenue and 40th Street, but nothing else had been done. The sidewalk across the street from the library was still thronged with spectators standing behind the barriers and facing a line of uniformed cops and at least two hundred ILGO members were still demonstrating on its steps.

McKenna had feared that Mulrooney would detonate his bomb as soon as he learned from his radio or TV that the steps of the library were being evacuated. If he did, he wouldn't get Brunette and the mayor, but he would certainly thin ILGO's ranks. Brunette was at the head of the parade and he had feared the same thing, so he had orchestrated the evacuation operation.

McKenna saw it in action seconds after he arrived and knew that Brunette had gotten to the ILGO leadership and informed them of the threat. All at once, the ILGO members ran from the library steps and the cops cleared away the spectators across the street. In under a minute, the library steps and the area around the building were deserted. The TV crews filmed the entire evacuation, live.

Taking a look at the library, McKenna guessed at once where the bomb was. Standing on either side of the library's steps were two massive, ancient Greek–style, concrete urns. There was a stately six-foot hemlock tree planted in each one. McKenna was certain that those trees hadn't been there when he had spoken to Mendez on the steps two days before. He also thought that it was a Parks Department van that Crowley had stolen to transport the trees to the library.

Finan was there and he shared McKenna's suspicions about the trees. As soon as the steps were cleared, he ran toward them from the bomb disposal truck, leading four detectives carrying ladders and shovels. One of them was Dennis Hunt. He was the first one up the ladder placed against the urn on the left side of the steps while another detective climbed up to the urn on the other side. Both were digging when McKenna's phone rang again. "I see you intend to spoil my surprise," Mulrooney said.

So it's a TV he's got in his car, McKenna thought. "We're trying to stay ahead of you."

"Base to all units. He's on the Major Deegan Expressway at 160th Street, heading north," McKenna heard over Mulrooney's phone. He's in the Bronx and I know where he's going, McKenna thought. Got to keep him on the phone.

"Is that my old pal Dennis digging up my stuff?"

"Yes, it's your old pal Dennis. You probably know quite a few of the guys on those steps."

"Probably, but I could kill them all right now. Maybe I should."

He could, McKenna knew. Must have a powerful transmitter with him, so how do I stop them?

McKenna could come up with only one possible way, but it was an option fraught with risk. Leaving Thor on the sidewalk, he ran across the street and up the library steps. He waved his arms to make sure the TV crews would focus on him. "Can you see me?" he asked Mulrooney.

"Yeah, I see you and you're taking a big chance. You know, I wouldn't mind taking you out as well."

"I know you wouldn't, but your two hostages lose a lot of their value to you if you blow me up."

"You and I both know I'd still get some value out of them. You've got a lovely wife and a very pretty little girl here. They look like a lot of fun to me."

"Please don't even talk like that. I'll do whatever you want," McKenna pleaded.

"Then how come you're not doing what I want? How come you're not on the way to the fountain?"

"I'm on my way now. No more stops, I swear."

"Good. Call me after you talk to my boys. I want to talk to them."

"I will. You'll be hearing from me shortly, I promise."

"That's a good lad. One more thing. Tell Dennis he owes me a big one. I've decided to let them all live."

"Thank you. I'll tell him," McKenna said, but Mulrooney had already cut the connection.

Hunt had finished excavating the loose soil around the tree in his planter. "The roots are still wrapped in burlap, Lou," he called down to Finan.

"It's gotta be in there, Dennis, so be careful," McKenna shouted up to him. "He says to tell you that you owe him one for not blowing us all up."

"Yeah, I owe him one all right."

Hunt was passing the tree down to Finan and another detective when

McKenna took off again, running for the car. Thor was right behind him. "He's in the Bronx. They're both wounded, so he's going to Brenda's to get patched up," McKenna said as he started the car and took off.

"I know, and so does your Squad CO. I was listening to the radio while you were on the steps. He's got all your teams headed there and the team watching the place is waiting for him. Your squad CO told them to take no action if he shows up, just report and wait."

"That's good. I don't want any shoot-outs with my family in the middle, but Mulrooney's gonna get there before the reinforcements arrive," McKenna said. He drove up the cleared Fifth Avenue and into Central Park at the 72nd Street transverse road. Bethesda Fountain was located in the middle of the park, so he pulled off the road onto a grassy spot near the entrance to the long, wide steps that led down to the fountain. He and Thor were just about to get out of the car when a shout over the FBI radio stopped them.

"Team Fourteen to Base, emergency message."

McKenna recognized Cisco's voice but didn't know his assignment.

"Go ahead, Team Fourteen."

"We've got him in front of Brenda's house. Crowley, Angelita, and Janine just got out of a dark blue Chevy Caprice, New York registration G239TX. Mulrooney's the driver. He's wearing a long brown wig and it looks like Crowley's hurting. Bleeding bad from his right arm, but he's got his hand under his jacket. I'd say he's got a gun on them."

Thank God it's Cisco up there, McKenna thought.

"Team Fourteen to Base. Crowley's into the building with Angelita and Janine. Mulrooney's taking off, maybe looking for a parking spot. Who do you want us to go for?"

McKenna brought the radio to his mouth, set to scream, "Crowley! Go for Crowley!" but once again Sheeran had beat him to the radio. "Squad CO to Team Fourteen. Get Mulrooney, Cisco."

"You got it, boss. We'll get him."

Right decision, McKenna realized. We know where Crowley is, so why risk a hostage situation right now that would further endanger Angelita and Janine? Get Mulrooney.

Then Sheeran made a mistake. "Units close to Brenda's to assist Team Fourteen?" he transmitted. None were, but they were getting there. So many teams answered with their locations that the airways were jammed for fifteen seconds before Cisco could get through.

"Goddamn it, everybody stay off the air," Cisco shouted. "He saw us and he's running. We're two blocks behind him, headed down Kotonah Avenue toward the Bronx River Parkway and moving fast. No, change that. He's making a right. Must be about 235th Street."

Mulrooney's right in his old neighborhood and knows every turn, Mc-Kenna thought. Since Cisco's doing the talking, Bobby Garbus must be doing the driving. Too bad.

"We just turned on 235th Street. He's about a block ahead of us," Cisco transmitted. "Looks like he's slowing down. Goddamn, Bobby! Watch that thing!"

The sound of the explosion filled the airways, but Mulrooney didn't get Cisco and Garbus. "He's dropping some nasty things in our way, but it exploded behind us. We're gonna get him," Cisco transmitted. "Still east-bound on 235th, picking up some real steam. Permission to shoot?"

Cisco didn't bother waiting for permission. The sound of his shots came loudly over the air, but nobody was complaining. "That's got him thinking," Cisco transmitted. "He's slowing down. No, he's turning on, on . . . God, I don't know where the hell we are, but he's turning and headed south. Slow down on the turn, Bobby. Make sure he didn't drop another nasty on us after he made the turn. Ah, there he is. Wait! Stop, Bobby! There's another one. Stop!"

McKenna waited for Cisco's next transmission, but there was none. Sheeran used the downtime to direct teams to Brenda's apartment building, but told them to take no action until Emergency Service, the Bomb Squad, and the Hostage Negotiating Team arrived there. He also told them that he would be on the scene in five minutes.

While Sheeran was talking, McKenna took out his phone and called the radio shop. Gaspar answered.

"Turn on that Paddy Poofer," McKenna said.

"I just did, thirty seconds ago."

"You been listening to the radio?"

"What else do you think there is to do in the radio shop? We listen to all the radios; makes you crazy. Hold on." Gaspar was off the line for a moment before he returned. "A Five-two Precinct unit is reporting that they've got Cisco and Bobby at Epler Avenue near 235th Street. The bomb blew up in front of their car."

"Are they all right?"

"Wrecked the car and Bobby's unconscious, but Cisco's out of the car and screaming. He dropped his radio when the bomb went off and he can't find it."

But Gaspar didn't have the up-to-date news. Cisco had found his radio. "Team Fourteen to Squad CO," he transmitted.

"Squad CO. Go ahead, Cisco."

"Will somebody else please get that guy, or do we have to do everything around here? I blew out his back windshield, so I might have winged him again. Anybody who sees that car will know that hombre came across Cisco."

"Don't worry, Cisco. We'll get him for you. How's Bobby?"

"He's coming to, but he wrecked my car. I'm gonna knock him out again as soon as he's feeling better. Brian, you on the air?"

McKenna picked up the radio. "I'm here, Cisco."

"Janine was crying, but she looked fine. I don't know if I should tell you this just now, but Angelita took a punch. Her mouth was bleeding and she spit some blood in front of Brenda's house on her way into the building. I think she tried to hit Crowley with it, but she missed."

That would be Angelita, McKenna thought. One of them clocked her, but she can't be intimidated.

"Team Thirty-three to Squad CO."

"Squad CO. Go ahead, Thirty-three."

"We're in front of the McDermott building now. There's a lot of blood on the sidewalk and it can't all be Mrs. McKenna's. Looks like Crowley's losing a lot."

Then McKenna's phone rang again. He turned his radios down low before answering. "How did you know about Brenda?" Mulrooney asked.

"Crowley. You thought he was at a pay phone, but he beeped you to that number three times."

"That dopey bastard's caused me a lot of trouble, but that's all right. Who were those clowns chasing me?" Mulrooney asked.

"Cisco Sanchez and Bobby Garbus. You know them?"

"Not personally, but Sanchez has always had a good rep. How are they?"

"I understand they'll be fine."

"Then understand this. I'm not looking to kill any cops here, I just want you all staying out of my way."

"I'm staying out of your way, but I'm not the one in charge."

"I think you're bullshitting me, McKenna," Mulrooney said, his voice rising. "Did you talk to my kids yet?"

"Sorry. Not yet, but I'm about to."

"Where are you?"

"Just parking. We're near the fountain."

"I know what you're thinking, McKenna. I know you've got Crowley surrounded at Brenda's place, so you're thinking that you're gonna get your wife and your brat back. You're thinking there's no reason to mind Old Mike."

"I wasn't thinking that at all. Nobody's making a move to take Crowley. Believe me, I know you're still in charge."

"That's smart of you, because Crowley won't be taken alive. If he doesn't hear from me soon, he's gonna shoot those two. Then you can lose some people getting him if you like and I'll show you another surprise I've got in store for you. I want to be talking to my kids."

Mulrooney cut the connection and McKenna felt the panic rising within him again. He picked up the FBI radio. "McKenna to Squad CO."

"Go ahead, Brian."

"Where was he for that last call?"

"Didn't know he called you. He wasn't using Winthrop's phone. Must've been at a pay phone."

Then he's stopped, but what's he doing? McKenna wondered.

"He's stealing another car," Thor said, and McKenna agreed. He couldn't drive the Chevy around any longer with the back window shot out and everybody looking for it.

"He said that Crowley was going to shoot Angelita and Janine if he didn't call him soon," McKenna transmitted.

"He's lying, Brian. We're talking to Crowley on Brenda's phone. He's scared and confused, doesn't know what to do. He says he'll kill them if we try anything, but he sounds weak."

All that makes sense, McKenna thought. Crowley's losing blood and he has to be confused. Sheeran's right, Mulrooney was lying to me. He didn't know that Cisco and Bobby were gonna jump him, so why would he have told Crowley to kill them if he didn't hear from him? But there's still a danger. "Inspector, can you make sure Mulrooney doesn't get through to give him a plan?"

"Will do. If Crowley hangs up on us, we'll cut Brenda's line until we want to call him again."

"Thanks, Inspector." McKenna opened his car door.

"Where are you going?" Thor asked.

"To talk to Mulrooney's kids for him."

"Don't do that."

"Why not? Can't hurt right now, one way or the other," McKenna said.

"Yes it can hurt. It would make him happy, make him think he's still in control."

"So what am I supposed to do? Piss him off?"

"That's what I'd do. Piss him off and get him angry with you. He's going to make some more threats, but laugh at him. Let him know that it's over for him."

"And then?"

"He'll realize that you're right, if he hasn't already. Then he'll come for you."

Could Thor be right? McKenna wondered. Vernon said Mulrooney would be fatalistic and we know he's fearless. But come here for me?

McKenna ran over all the possibilities while Thor watched him in silence. Then came the distant sound of bagpipes; the parade was again on the march and getting closer. They were playing "Amazing Grace," one of McKenna's favorites. He considered it a good sign. "You're right, Thor, and that's what I'm gonna do. Piss him off real good, but first I have to make sure any threats he makes are idle chatter." He called the office and Eddie Morgan answered.

"Do you know how many pounds of explosives were recovered from the library bomb?" McKenna asked.

"Bombs. There were two of them, one in each tree. Eighteen pounds in each, packed it in the roots behind bags of nails. He really planned to do some damage."

"Thanks, Eddie. You just made things simpler for me and took a load off my mind." He called Sheeran next and told him what he had in mind.

"Okay, Brian, it's your call. I just hope you know what you're doing."

"I hope so, too. Could you have the units at the fountain grab O'Reilly and the kids? Keep them all there, but have them make sure those kids don't have that cell phone with them."

"Will do. I'll also send some teams back to Manhattan to help you out."

"Thanks." McKenna and Thor listened to the radio as Sheeran complied with McKenna's wishes. O'Reilly and the kids were grabbed and they had the cell phone. Six teams were on their way back from the Bronx. Then another transmission came across on the FBI radio. "Team Thirty-five to Squad CO."

"Go ahead Team Thirty-five."

"We've got the Chevy Caprice he was using. Hundred and sixty-first Street near Yankee Stadium. He must've stolen another car here."

"Team Fourteen to Team Thirty-five. What kind of shape is that car in?" Cisco asked.

"You're gonna love this, Cisco. The back window's shot out and so is the windshield. You also got his TV and there's lots of blood in the backseat, so I guess that's where Crowley was sitting with Angelita and Janine. That right?"

"Sure is. How about the front seat? Any blood up there?" Cisco asked.

"A little, not much. Maybe you hit him."

"Of course I did," Cisco transmitted. "Thought he could throw bombs at Cisco and get away scot-free, did he? Well, I guess Cisco changed his mind."

McKenna wasn't so sure; he attributed the blood in the front seat to Pao's bullet. Nothing happened for five minutes and not a word passed between McKenna and Thor. Each was lost in his own thoughts until McKenna's phone rang again. Again, he turned his radios down low before he answered. "This is the last time I'm asking," Mulrooney said. "Have you talked to my kids, yet?"

"Just did. Told them what a perverted, murdering coward you are. Told them that they're lucky to be here because you can't get it up anymore."

Mulrooney didn't answer at first, and McKenna could imagine his reaction. "Let me talk to them," Mulrooney ordered.

"I would, but they don't want to talk to you."

"McKenna, you just killed your wife and kid."

"Think again, Mulrooney. Crowley surrendered. Angelita and Janine are on their way here right now to meet me. You see, my wife and kids like me. Might be because I'm not a coward like you."

"Coward, am I?" Mulrooney shouted.

"That's right, and a pervert besides. If your boys have the stomach for it, we're gonna have a real picnic here. I'm gonna buy them some lunch and show them some pictures of what you did to those helpless women you like torturing. That should be fun, don't you think?"

There was another silence before Mulrooney answered. "I've got a proposition for you," he said calmly.

"I bet. You gonna tell me that you're going to blow something else up?" McKenna asked sarcastically.

If Mulrooney was surprised at McKenna's guess, it didn't come through in his voice. "That's right. I always thought it a shame that those Arabs who blew the World Trade Center ignored the Empire State Building. There's a noon flight for Bangkok leaving from JFK. United Airlines. If my boys aren't on it believing I'm a saint, good-bye Empire State Building."

"Really?" McKenna asked, then laughed. "Tell me, how much explosives do you have planted in the building?"

"Enough to blow out a floor and the elevator shaft. Without elevators, that building wouldn't be much good."

"Gee! That would take at least a couple of hundred pounds of C-4, wouldn't it?"

"That's what I figured."

"Then explain this to me," McKenna said. "If you had all that C-4, how come you took your dopey cousin all the way to Hunter Mountain just to get another forty pounds of it? Besides everything else, you're a liar, Mulrooney."

"Do you really want to take a chance on that?"

"Sure do. Blow it up, big shot."

McKenna waited for Mulrooney to answer, but the line was dead. McKenna picked up the FBI radio and turned up the volume. "Squad CO on the air?"

"I'm here, Brian. He used his phone, was headed east on the Cross Bronx Expressway. Maybe going Upstate or to Connecticut."

"Not anymore he's not."

"Did you rile him up good?"

"Sure did. He's coming back."

THIRTY-NINE

McKenna and Thor were parked in the trees near the vehicular entrance to Central Park at 106th Street. Since Fifth Avenue was closed because of the parade, McKenna had figured that Mulrooney would take Park Drive South as the quickest way to Bethesda Fountain and his kids. Then he would abandon his car and sneak through the woods to the fountain, hoping to see his kids and get a shot at him.

"How you holding up?" McKenna asked Thor.

"Hard to believe, but fine. I haven't been able to sleep, of course, but that hasn't bothered me. The only thing I can focus on is getting Mulrooney."

"And killing him?"

"I hope not. Too quick. I want him in jail in Iceland so I can torment him every day for the rest of his life."

"How would you go about doing that?"

"Don't know yet, but I like to think that I'd find ways to keep him miserable. I owe that man a lot of misery."

McKenna took Thor's line of thought as a good sign. It made Thor seem more human, less perfect, and easier to work with. Then Sheeran called with great news and another good sign. "We've got them out. Angelita and Janine are fine."

"Thank God! How?"

"Crowley was talking to us on the phone and he just passed out, loss of blood. Angelita and Brenda jumped him at the same time, but Angelita came up with the gun."

"Was Brenda in on it?"

"Maybe, but it doesn't look that way. In the end, she might've been as much of a hostage as Angelita and Janine. Crowley was out of his mind with pain and Brenda kept trying to talk him into surrendering."

"Where's Angelita now?"

"Sitting here in my car with me and Janine. Where are you?"

"Park Drive South and 106th Street."

"Angelita wants to talk to you."

"Put her on."

Angelita wasn't exactly fine. McKenna knew her well enough to tell that she was in a controlled rage. "He hit me, Brian. Knocked out two of my teeth, and everything is loose on top."

"Who? Mulrooney or Crowley?"

"Mulrooney. He also threatened to kill Janine. For a long time I thought he was going to do it. I thought that animal was going to kill our little girl."

McKenna felt his own rage mounting and tried to keep it under control. "I know, baby. Don't worry, I'll take care of him," he said soothingly.

Angelita wasn't to be calmed. "See that you do. Hurt him bad, make him suffer as much as you can."

How has he changed my Angelita to make her talk like that? McKenna wondered, worrying. That sure doesn't sound like her.

There was only one thing McKenna could think of to say. "I will, baby. Don't worry. I'll see you home soon." He hung up and was still worrying when another transmission came over the radio.

"Team Nine to Base. We think we're a block behind him. Amsterdam Avenue and 118th Street. If it's Mulrooney, he's in a black Corvette and moving fast. Wait, it's got to be him. He just blew a red light without even slowing down. Eastbound on 116th Street."

"He's getting close," McKenna said to Thor. "If he comes into the park here, we're gonna see him in a minute." He put on his seat belt and Thor did the same. Then they heard the sound of sirens in the distance, but getting closer. "You sure you're up for this?" McKenna asked.

"Wouldn't miss it," Thor said grimly.

"You got a gun with you?"

"No."

"Then take mine." McKenna gave Thor his pistol and two loaded magazines. "Use it all if you get a chance."

"Team Nine to Base. He's at 108th and Central Park West, headed south and moving fast."

Then McKenna and Thor saw him. Mulrooney took the turn into the park at high speed, but the Corvette handled it well. Mulrooney was past them and headed south as McKenna floored the gas pedal and skidded onto the roadway, then barely avoided tragedy. Joe Mendez and Joe Sophia in Team Nine turned into the park at high speed, but they weren't in a Corvette. Mendez swerved all over the road and McKenna just missed hitting them. The two cars accelerated side by side on the winding road, but they weren't a match for the Corvette. Mulrooney was way ahead and out of sight.

I've got to get him to arm one of those bombs, McKenna thought as he managed to pull ahead of Mendez and Sophia. He grabbed the PD radio, hoping Mulrooney was still listening. "Mulrooney! It's me, McKenna. I'm right behind you, you filthy coward. I'm gonna get you for smacking my wife."

It worked. As they rounded a curve, they saw Mulrooney ahead, going slow. Then they saw his brake lights go on. "He must've stopped to drop one in the road," Thor yelled.

Mulrooney had, but the Paddy Poofer broadcasting the detonation signals from Queens found the frequency before the two cars got to the bomb in the road. It went off before Mulrooney pushed his Send button, before McKenna and Thor passed over it. But it was close. The force of the explosion rocked the car and, for a moment, McKenna thought he was going to lose control as he veered from side to side on the two-lane roadway. As he drove through the smoke, he saw the Corvette ahead, widening the distance.

"That must have got him thinking," Thor yelled as he took aim and fired three shots out the window at the Corvette. One of the shots broke the back window, but it didn't slow Mulrooney down.

"We don't want him thinking," McKenna shouted. "We want him angry and arming another bomb." He picked up the PD radio again. "You missed me, Mulrooney. I'm still coming and I'm gonna ram this car up your ass," he yelled into it.

Mulrooney was ahead and out of sight again as McKenna passed the 86th Street entrance to the park. There was another curve ahead, so he hoped that Mulrooney would arm another bomb and drop it while he was out of sight.

That was Mulrooney's plan. As McKenna rounded the curve, he saw the Corvette ahead. Mulrooney had stopped and had his door open.

Thor resumed firing. His shots hit the rear of the Corvette, breaking a tail light and blowing the left rear tire. Mulrooney got out of the car and McKenna experienced the kind of tunnel vision common in shoot-outs. Hurtling down Park Drive South, his world went into slow motion and he could see only two things. One was the hole in the barrel at the business end of the pistol in Mulrooney's right hand and the other was the small, bright, green light on the bomb he held in his left. The pistol was aimed at McKenna's head and Mulrooney had armed his bomb.

McKenna slammed on his brakes and ducked down as Mulrooney fired. The bullet crashed through the windshield and hit his headrest. The car was in a skid and McKenna's brakes were better than Mendez's. He and Thor were jarred by the impact when Mendez's car hit their rear, and they were being pushed toward an explosive end. He knew the bomb was going to blow, but if it wasn't soon, it was going to kill them all.

Thor continued firing as McKenna counted the seconds and had reached three when another two bullets came through the windshield on the passenger's side. One of them grazed Thor's ear, but he kept firing.

McKenna raised his head at the count of four, just in time to see Mulrooney stagger. Thor had hit him and then the Paddy Poofer found him. The bomb still in Mulrooney's hand went off in a brief flash of white light followed by fire and black smoke. Then the Corvette blew in a larger explosion.

McKenna's car was slowed by the force of the blast and hit by pieces of the Corvette, but that was good. He regained control and searched ahead through the smoke for Mulrooney and the Corvette. He couldn't see them. Mulrooney was no longer there and neither was the Corvette. He managed to finally stop the car, but not soon enough. His left front tire came to rest on a piece of Mulrooney, his mangled right arm.

Both McKenna and Thor got out of the car, looking for other signs of the Corvette and Mulrooney. The Corvette was easier—burning pieces of it were ahead on Park Drive South and in the woods on both sides of the road. As for Mulrooney, he was harder to find. He was hiding all over the landscape.

EPILOGUE

There were fire engines, many ambulances, hundreds of cops, and thousands of people. It seemed to McKenna that everyone who had come to see the parade was now on Park Drive South. The roadway was closed and thousands of people lined the barriers placed two hundred feet from the scene of the explosion. Everyone wanted to see the end of Mulrooney, and some of them were horrified when they stumbled across small bits of him. The cops were hard-pressed keeping them back.

The press was there in force, snapping pictures and interviewing any detective who felt like talking. At the moment, that didn't include McKenna. He had brusquely put off the first reporter who had tried to interview him and word got around quick among the press corps. They left him alone, for the moment, and turned their attention to Thor.

The Icelander was wearing a bandage around his head, but his wound didn't seem to bother him. For the first couple of questions he was as congenial as ever and the press remained fascinated with him. That ended when a young reporter asked him about Frieda. Thor just stared at the man for a moment, then turned and walked to McKenna. A few brash reporters tried to follow him, but were stopped and pushed back by a couple of alert uniformed cops.

"I'm no longer fine, Brian. I have to get out of here," Thor said.

McKenna could see that Thor was finally losing his composure, and that worried him. "Where do you want to go?" he asked.

"Back to the hotel for a while, I guess. Then I've got to start making arrangements to take Frieda home."

"I can't leave just yet," McKenna said. "Can't you stick around a bit longer?"

"Only if I want to make a fool out of myself. I'm losing my focus."

"I understand. Want me to get you a ride?"

"No thanks. I'd rather walk. See you later." He patted McKenna on the arm and started walking slowly down Park Drive South. To McKenna, he looked like a lost soul, a man suddenly without purpose.

Unfortunately for the reporters, Brunette wasn't ready to talk to them, either. He found McKenna hiding out in the back of an ambulance and looking very dejected.

"You okay?" Brunette asked, concerned.

"Kind of drained, but I guess I'm gonna be okay," McKenna answered. "Yourself?"

"The same. Never got a chance to thank you for saving my life."

"I wish I could've done more."

"You thinking about Johnny?"

"And Frieda. Those two are all I'm gonna be thinking about for a long time. I can't look into Thor's face without feeling the tears back up, and I'm dreading the thought of facing Patti and trying to explain why her husband's dead. His family will never see him again so mine can see me every day."

"How's Thor holding up?"

"I don't know. If I had to guess, I'd say he'll be fine in a couple of years. Never the same again, but still better than most," McKenna said. "To tell you the truth, I'm worried more about Patti."

"Don't. She's a strong girl and I'm sure she won't blame you," Brunette said. "It'll take a while for her, but life goes on."

"I should be there with her at a time like this."

"Don't worry about that right now. You'll pull yourself together and do all the right things."

"Have you spoken to her yet?" McKenna asked.

"Not yet, but I'm going to Bellevue as soon as I can get out of here. She's there with Johnny now, but she's a good trooper. I hear she's trying to console the wife of that 13th Precinct cop Mulrooney killed."

"How's his partner?"

"Not good, I hear. They're still operating on him, but Mulrooney's filled up operating rooms all over the city."

"The East River Drive?"

"Yeah, that was bad. Four dead and thirteen injured, last I heard."

A uniformed sergeant interrupted them. "Excuse me, Commissioner. We have a lady who wants to see Detective McKenna. Says her name is Kathleen Mullen, also says that he'd probably want to talk to her."

"Do you?" Brunette asked McKenna.

"I guess I do."

"Bring her over," Brunette ordered.

The sergeant left and returned with her. Kathleen Mullen looked like she had experienced a tough time dealing with her life over the years, and McKenna was sure she had suffered. Yet, she appeared to be radiantly happy at the moment.

McKenna offered her his hand, but she just brushed past it and hugged him. "Thank you for giving me my life back, Detective McKenna."

"I'm glad that at least some good has come out of this," McKenna said after she released him. "How did you get here so fast?"

"I work on Madison Avenue, only blocks from here. I ran over as soon as I heard about it on the news. Can I see him?"

"I guess so, if you want. But I have to warn you, he's not pretty. He's still being reassembled."

"I don't care. I just have to make sure for myself that he's dead before I'll be able to go on."

"What are your plans, if you don't mind my asking?"

"Change. Everything's going to change. I'm going to quit my job, sell my house, and get myself into shape. Along the way, I'm gonna get my kids into shape."

"We have your kids, you know," McKenna said.

"I know. Have you met the snotty little bastards?"

"No, and I don't think I want to."

"You will by the time I get them raised. They're monsters right now and they treat me like dirt, but that's gonna change, too. They're gonna learn to respect me, I promise you that."

"Good for you," McKenna said.

"How will you live if you quit your job?" Brunette asked.

Kathleen's smile grew even wider. "The insurance money. We'll be just fine."

"You kept an insurance policy up on him?" McKenna asked, amazed.

"Wouldn't you if you were me? I always knew he'd end up like this. Prayed for it, actually. Prayed every day."

"Then take a look at him and go start your life, Kathleen," McKenna said. "At least your prayers have been answered."

Kathleen insisted on shaking both McKenna's and Brunette's hands before the sergeant escorted her to her grisly wish.

"Can you believe that?" McKenna asked Brunette.

"Sure I do. She's out of the shell Mulrooney put her in and she's got something to look forward to for the first time in a long time. I'd bet those kids are going to turn out just fine."

Then McKenna received another surprise. Sheeran had also found him and was approaching with Janine and Angelita. Janine looked fine, holding Sheeran's hand and waving to the crowd like a movie star as photographers snapped her picture.

Angelita looked terrible. Her jaw was swollen, her lips were caked with blood, and McKenna thought she would have difficulty speaking until she told him why she had come. "I have to see that filthy, perverted pig," she said clearly through clenched teeth before he could even kiss her and hold her as he longed to do.

"I'm sorry, Brian, but she insisted on coming here," Sheeran explained.

"Daddy, I want to see him, too," Janine said.

God, what did that man do to my family? McKenna wondered. Everyone wants to see his body just to make sure he's dead. "Angelita, you shouldn't do this," he told her. "He's not very pretty right now."

"Good," she said, obviously satisfied with that news and managing a painful smile. "He deserved to die if anyone ever did, but this was too fast for him. He should've suffered for what he did to Johnny."

McKenna had no answer for that.

"And look what he did to me," Angelita said, pointing to her jaw.

"Don't worry, we'll get everything fixed for you right away." He tried to hug her, but she pushed him away.

"I always knew you'd get him and now you have," she said. "Show him to me."

"I'm not gonna let Janine see this," McKenna said.

"Of course not. Just me."

If Angelita doesn't snap out of this soon, she's going to wind up lying on some psychiatrist's couch and Janine is certainly gonna need some counseling, McKenna thought. I guess I have to get this over with. "Okay, I'll show you all the pieces. Wanna start with his arm?"

"Which arm?"

"His left."

"Okay, let's start with that. That's the arm he hit me with."

Angelita left Janine with Sheeran and she followed McKenna to the middle of the roadway. Mulrooney's arm was still there under a blanket. He lifted the blanket and she stared hard at the mangled arm for a minute, wearing an evil smile McKenna had never seen before and hoped never to see again. Then she muttered a curse and kicked the arm before McKenna could stop her. The crowd cheered as the press photographers snapped away.

"Angelita, this doesn't look good," McKenna said.

"I don't care. What part of him is next?" she asked calmly.

McKenna thought he could speak Spanish fairly well, but during the next ten minutes he learned some new words from Angelita as she stared at the bits and pieces of Mulrooney. He had never seen her so enraged. Mendez was standing next to them and McKenna thought of asking him what she was saying, but Mendez just shook his head when McKenna caught his eye.

Then Angelita surprised him when she turned suddenly and hugged him. She began sobbing like a little girl while McKenna patted her back and stroked her hair. It went on for five minutes before she stopped.

"I'm okay now and I'm always gonna be okay," she said as she dried her eyes. "Just promise me that after today you'll never mention that man's name again to either me or Janine."

"That's a promise. What do you want to do now?"

"You can take me to Bellevue."

The hospital? She certainly needs some medical attention soon for that jaw, but why Bellevue? McKenna wondered. "Wouldn't you rather go to Beth Israel?"

"No, Bellevue. We should be with Patti and Johnny. We owe those two everything, and we're going to be paying back Patti Pao for the rest of our lives."

Amen! That's a debt we're certainly going to pay, McKenna promised himself.

Sheeran offered to drive them and McKenna was happy to accept. He sat in the back next to Angelita with Janine on his lap.

"Daddy, there's something important I forgot to tell you," Janine said.

What now? McKenna wondered. "What is it, baby?"

"Happy St. Paddy's Day."